The Children of Chorazin

The Children of Chorazin
and Other Strange Denizens

Darrell Schweitzer

Hippocampus Press
New York

Copyright © 2023 by Darrell Schweitzer

Published by Hippocampus Press
P.O. Box 641, New York, NY 10156.
www.hippocampuspress.com

Cover art and design © 2023 by Jason Van Hollander.
Hippocampus Press logo designed by Anastasia Damianakos.

All rights reserved.
No part of this work may be reproduced in any form or
by any means without the written permission of the publisher.

First Edition
1 3 5 7 9 8 6 4 2

ISBN 978-1-61498-400-9 (paperback)
ISBN 978-1-61498-406-1 (ebook)

Contents

Uncle's in the Treetops 9
The Red Witch of Chorazin 23
The Girl in the Attic 35
The Hutchison Boy 45
Not in the Card Catalog 57
Down to a Sunless Sea 71
A Prism of Darkness 85
No Signal 93
Come, Follow Me 99
Odd Man Out 111
Madness on the Black Planet 123
Going to Ground 131
The Martian Bell 135
Were—? 145
Boxes of Dead Children 149
The Return of the Night-Gaunts 159
All Kings and Princes Bow Down unto Me 167
The Festival of the Pallid Mask 175
A Dark Miracle 183
A Predicament 191
The Thief of Dreams 197
Killing the Pale Man 211
Appeasing the Darkness 223

The Bear Went Over the Mountain 239
The Interrogator 251
The White Face 263
Acknowledgments 273

*For Jason Van Hollander,
who has splendidly adorned so many covers of my books.*

Uncle's in the Treetops

Yes, I can tell you about it.

It was in the Leaf Falling Time, when Uncle Alazar was in the treetops. He could come close to the Earth then, out of the midnight sky. You could hear him among the upper branches in the forest, sometimes skittering like a squirrel, sometimes hovering there, his wings buzzing and fluttering like those of some enormous insect. Whose uncle was he, precisely? There were stories about that, often contradictory. I'd been hearing them all my life. He was one of us, one of the Burton family, though whose brother and how many generations back was not at all clear. He dwelt among Those of the Air. He spoke to the dark gods. He had gone to them, out into the night, and had never come back, not really, only able to return halfway like that, and was utterly transformed, beyond humanity altogether. Sometimes we Burtons heard him whispering to us. He reached into our dreams. My father had heard him, in his time, and my father's father, and *his* father; though not my mother, because she was only a Burton by marriage and there was something about the true blood that went back for years and years . . . but I digress.

Now, mind you, the village of Chorazin may be isolated, and it may be different in its customs, but it's still in Pennsylvania, not on Mars, so we do have some things in common with the rest of the world. We have Halloween here, and Leaf-Falling Time (old Indian name) is pretty much the same as Halloween, so we indeed have kids in costumes shuffling noisily through the leaves from house to house, collecting candy. They travel in groups only, and make all that noise to scare away Zenas, who was one of us once, so the story goes, but he too went into the darkness on such a night and became part of it—whether he was still alive or not was a matter of some debate—and he supposedly had long, sharp fingers like twigs, and you really didn't want to meet him.

It was on such a night, after the candy and costumes were put away. I'd gone as Darth Vader that year, my brother Joram as a vampire. We sat on our porch in the dark with our parents, my brother and I—he was ten, three years younger than me—and two very distinguished visitors, Elder Abraham, who is our leader, and his assistant Brother Azrael. They questioned Joram and me closely, and spoke to us both in a very old-fashioned way that I knew was part of the ritual.

My father sat wordlessly, while my mother let out a little sob.

This was a serious business. People who went out into the dark sometimes did not come back.

"Joram," said the elder. "Tell me in truth, hast thou heard thine uncle's voice clearly and comprehended his words? Wilt thou act as his messenger?"

"Yes, I will," my brother said.

The Elder turned to me. "And thou?"

"Yeah. Me too."

He reached out, and took both of us by the hand, and joined our hands together, and he said, "Then you have to go. Go now."

I knew the rest, and we didn't have to rehearse it. The signs had manifested themselves. The stars had turned in their courses, as if tumblers had fallen into place in a lock, and gateways in the sky were open, and Uncle Alazar could come racing back out of the dark depths to speak to us on this night.

It was a very special time. To our people, though not to other Pennsylvanians, I am sure, a holy time.

My father spoke only briefly, to me, "Thomas, take care of your brother."

"I will, Dad."

So, hand-in-hand, my brother and I went. You could conjure up an almost bucolic scene, despite the spooky undertones, two boys holding hands for comfort, or so they wouldn't lose one another, two brothers making their way (noisily at first, kicking up leaves, then less noisily) into the wooded hills beyond the town, to fulfill some ancient rite, like a confirmation or a walkabout, some passage into manhood perhaps.

So we followed the unpaved road for a little bit, then cut across the fields, into the woods, beneath the brilliant stars, and what, I ask you, is wrong with this picture?

There are things I've left out.

The first is that I hated my brother intensely. I didn't show it, but I'd nursed my hatred in secret almost since when he was born. I didn't even know why at first. He was smarter than me, cleverer. My parents liked him best. When we were very young, he broke my toys because he could. He did better in school. (Ours was perhaps the last one-room school in the country, so I saw when he won all the prizes. That meant I'd lost them.) But more than that, *he* was the one Uncle Alazar had showed a special interest in. It was Joram's dreams that Uncle had entered into, so that Joram would sit up in his bed sometimes and scream out words in strange languages, and then wake up in a sweat and (absurd as it seems) sometimes come to me for comfort. And I pretended to comfort him, but I was false, always false, and I held my hatred in my heart.

This was all very distinct from sounds you heard overhead at night, that might have been squirrels or just the wind rattling branches, or a voice you heard from far off, like somebody shouting from a distant hilltop and you couldn't make out what they said, only the wailing, trailing cry. That was all my father had ever heard, or my grandfather, or my great-grandfather, because the gods, or Those of the Air, or even centuries-lost-departed-uncles did not communicate with us all that often, and it was very special when they did. Which of course made my brother very special.

And I was not. That was the next thing.

I had lied to Elder Abraham. I had heard nothing, myself. Once again I was false, and to lie to the Elder like that is a blasphemy, but I did it, and I had no regrets.

I had also promised my father that I would take care of my brother. That promise I would keep. Oh, yes. I would take care of him.

We walked through the woods in the dark, for miles perhaps. My brother was in some kind of trance, I think. He was humming softly to himself. His eyes were wide, but I don't think he was seeing in the usual way. I had to reach out and push branches out of the way so he wouldn't get smacked in the face. Not that I'd mind him being smacked in the face, but that didn't fit with what I intended, not yet. He seemed to know where he was going.

Uncle was in the treetops. I heard him too now, chittering, scrambling from branch to branch, his wings and those of his companions flapping, buzzing, heavy upon the air.

Joram began to make chittering noises, not bird sounds, more like the sound of some enormous insect, and he was answered from above.

I looked up. There was only darkness, and I could see the stars through the branches, and once, only once, did I see what looked like a black plastic bag detach itself from an upper branch and flutter off into the night; or that might have been a shadow.

I let Joram guide me, even though he couldn't see. I had to reach out and clear the way for him, but he was the one who led me on, even as we descended into a hollow, then climbed a ridge on the other side. The trees seemed larger than I had ever seen them, towering, the trunks as thick as houses; but that may have been a trick of the dark, or the night, or the dream which was pouring into my brother as he chittered and stared blindly ahead, and maybe I wasn't entirely lying after all, and maybe I really did feel a little bit of it.

We came to a particularly enormous tree, a beech it felt like from the smooth bark, with a lot of low branches all the way down the trunk to the ground. My brother began to climb. I climbed after him. By daylight, in the course of normal kid activities, I actually was a pretty good tree climber, but this wasn't like that at all. We went up and up, and sometimes the angles of the branches and the trunk itself seemed to twist strangely. Several times my brother slipped and almost fell, but I caught hold of him, and he clung to me, whimpering slightly, as if he were half awake and scared in his dream.

Did he know what I intended? He had every right to be scared. Hah!

Still we climbed, and now there were things in the branches with us, only way out on the swaying ends, and the branches rose and fell and rose and fell as half-seen shapes alighted on them. The air was filled with buzzing and flapping sounds. Joram made sounds I hadn't known a human throat could ever make, and he was answered by multitudes.

Then the branches cleared away, and we were beneath the open, star-filled, moonless sky, and Those of the Air circled around us now. Joram and I sat where the trunk forked, my arm around him, while with my other hand I held onto a branch. I could see them clearly, black creatures, a little like enormous bats, a little like wasps, but not really like either, and one of them came toward us, chittering, its face aglow like a paper lantern, its features human or almost human; and I recognized our legendary relative, the fabled Uncle Alazar whose special affinity to our family brought him back to this planet on such occasions as this, when the signs were as they needed to be and the dark, holy rites were to be fulfilled.

Now that Uncle was here, and I had used my gibbering brother to guide me to him, I had no further use for Joram, whom I had always hated; so I flung him from me, out among the swaying branches, and down he fell: screaming, thump, thump, thump, crash, thump, and silence.

I was almost surprised that none of the winged ones tried to retrieve him, but they didn't.

Uncle Alazar hovered before me, his eyes dark, his face inscrutable.

"I am afraid my brother isn't available," I said. "You will have to take me instead."

And they did take me. Hard, sharp fingers or claws seized hold of me from every side. Some grabbed me by the hair and lifted me up.

I was hanging in the air, with wings whirring and flapping and buzzing all around me, and yes, I was terribly afraid, but also I was filled with a fierce, grasping, greedy joy, because I had *done it* and now Uncle Alazar would have to reveal the secrets of the darkness and of the black worlds to *me,* and I would become very great among our people, a prophet, very special indeed, a great one, perhaps able to live for centuries like Elder Abraham or Brother Azrael.

Uncle's face floated in front of mine, filled with pale light. He spoke. He made that chittering sound. It was just noise to me. He paused. He spoke again, as if expecting a reply. I tried to reply, imitating his squeaks and chirps or whatever, and then, suddenly, he drew away, and made a very human "Hah!" sound, and they *dropped* me.

Down *I* went, through the branches: screaming, crash, thump, thump, thump, crash, thud. There was so much pain. I couldn't move. I don't know if what followed was a dream, because the next thing I knew Zenas had found me, he of the stiletto-sharp stick-like fingers, remember? He was naked, and very thin, his body elongated, almost like a snake, with way too many ribs, and his face was partly a man's face, with a wild mass of hair, but his eyes were multifaceted and there was something very strange about his mouth. His jaws moved sideways like those of a praying mantis or a hornet, and he leaned down, out of my field of view, and came up again with a mouthful of bloody flesh. Zenas was *eating* me. I felt the bones of my legs crunching. I screamed and screamed and he went down and came up again with his mouth full, and gulped it down the way an animal would, and went back for more. I knew this couldn't be happening. It was impossible. I should have been dead by now. I should have bled to death, my guts gushing out like water from a balloon that's been slashed open. I went on screaming and the pain just wouldn't end. It went on and on. I pounded my fists on the ground to try to make it stop, but it did not stop.

At one point he stared into my eyes, and I was terribly afraid that he would take them. But he just remained there, making clicking sounds as if he were speaking a language I did not know. He was there long afterwards in my dreams, with his bloody saliva dripping down onto my face, burning.

And when I awoke, in my own room, in my own bed, I was swathed in bandages. My face was covered by something thick and heavy, but I could see out, and I could see that both of my arms were in casts and my legs were gone.

They tell me I screamed non-stop for another six months. I had to be put in an attic. There are, in Chorazin, lots of embarrassments hidden away in attics.

More than once, after I stopped screaming, Elder Abraham and

Brother Azrael would come to see me, always late at night. They stood silently over my bed, regarding me, saying nothing. I could read nothing in their expressions. Once the Elder had a glowing stone with him, which he touched to my forehead. I didn't dare ask what that was about. I didn't dare say anything.

When my reason returned, more or less, and I had healed as much as I could, I was brought down from the attic, and began my new life as a cripple. My father had built a low, wooden cart for me. I could sit in it and reach over the sides to push myself along. No one mentioned Joram.

Almost a year had passed. That year, at Leaf-Falling Time, or Halloween as you'd call it, I sat with my parents on the porch as costumed children came up, fearfully, to receive a handful of candy, then scamper off. I just sat there in the dark, a lump of disfigured flesh. I don't think they knew I was awake, or could hear them when they whispered, "What is it?" and "That can't be him."

It was that year, too, on the evening after Halloween, which would be All Souls' Night (Halloween being the Eve of All Hallows—get it?) and that's what we called it too, that Elder Abraham led us all out into the woods, into the Bone Forest, where generations of bone offerings, our dead, animals, others, dangled from the trees and rattled in the wind. By torchlight he delivered a memorable sermon. I heard it all. The way was too rough for me to get there in a cart, so my father carried me in a satchel on his back, and I crawled up out of the satchel and clung to him, my arms around his neck, and looked over his shoulder and saw the Elder in his ceremonial robe and holding his staff with the glowing stone on the end of it.

He spoke about change, transformation and transfiguration, about how, in time, the Old Gods would return and clear off the Earth of all human things, and only those of us who were changed in some way would have any place in the new world. And he emphasized something that I thought was aimed just at me, that this change comes as inevitably as leaves falling in the autumn, or a tide on the seashore, rushing in. There is *no morality* to it, for such things mean nothing to the darkness and to those who dwell there. What happens merely happens because it has happened, because the stars have turned and the gateways between the worlds have configured themselves *just so*.

If I'd been better read, better educated, I might have called it fate. That year I became better read and educated. I got out more, wheeling my way here and there around the village, sometimes scaring the younger children and making other people turn away. For months I had been desperately afraid of mirrors. I could feel that my face was thick and stiff and my cheeks didn't move properly. I was afraid of how disfigured I might be. But in time was I angry. I had become a monster. I should damn well look like a monster. Finally I dared, and snatched up one of my mother's mirrors and saw that I was indeed hideous, as if my face had been half dissolved and partially reshaped, until I looked a little bit like an insect, a little bit like Zenas, though I did not have multifaceted eyes and my jaws and teeth worked normally.

Fate, education, yes. There I went, scurrying and scooting around town, the object of horror and fascination. I went to the general store, where Brother Azrael kept his collection of ancient books and scrolls locked away in a back room. Those weren't for just anybody to read, but he unlocked the door to that room, and let me read them. He patiently tutored me in the languages required. He spoke to me of things we had known since the most ancient days, since before even Elder Abraham was alive, and Elder Abraham was over a thousand. ("He remembers when Charlemagne was king," the Brother told me, and later, from a more conventional set of encyclopedias, I learned who Charlemagne was.) That was the essence of our faith, what other people would call a religion, or the beliefs of a cult, that we had no faith, that we knew with certain knowledge that Elder Abraham was indeed that old, and that there are things in the sky and the earth that you can talk to, and that the elder powers will one day rule again where mankind rules now. These things are merely true, we know, from what we have seen and what we have done.

Yes, I even read part of the *Necronomicon*. It should not be surprising that someone as eminent as Elder Abraham or Brother Azrael should have a copy. I read it in Latin, which wasn't hard. For all my brother Joram had excelled me in school, I proved to have gift for languages, once I applied myself.

What comforted me most was that nowhere in all of this was there any discussion of *right and wrong* or of *morality*. It was just as the Elder had said. Things happen because they happen. In the larger scheme of things, by the standards of the Abyss and of the Black Worlds beyond the sky, such human concerns are irrelevant. Therefore I felt no guilt over what I had done. I had suffered much, but I was not sorry. It was like the leaves falling, or like a tide rushing in at the seashore.

I was also still a kid. I was, by my count, more than fifteen, and I should have been getting a bit old for Halloween, but I told my parents that I wanted to go out one last time, and either they felt sorry for me, or maybe they were even afraid, so they didn't stop me as I worked for hours on my "costume." If I was going to have to move around on wheels, I decided, I would go as a tank. I built a shell out of plywood and cardboard, complete with a swiveling turret, and I fit it over my cart, so I could indeed go out disguised as a goddamn Panzer tank from World War II, complete with an iron cross and swastikas painted on it. As a finishing touch, it was a flame-throwing tank. I rigged up a cigarette lighter and an aerosol can in the turret.

This did not work out well. When I trundled up to the first house and shouted "Seig Heil! Fuck you! Trick or treat!" the aerosol can exploded and the tank went up in a fireball and I set somebody's porch on fire, and then everybody was trying to beat the flames out with rugs and such before I burned down the whole village. I was screaming once more, and I was hurt, but my screams gave way to screeching and chittering the likes of which no human throat should be able to utter, and I was *answered*, right there in town, from some point above the rooftops, and I began to understand what was said.

Like I said, I had a gift for languages.

Once again I was in the attic for a while, gibbering. The Elder came and touched me with his glowing stone one more time.

I should mention that I had only one friend during this period. My parents were my parents, and Brother Azrael was my teacher, but the closest thing I had to a friend was the muddy kid, Jerry, or more formally Jeroboam. He was odd like me, not that he was misshapen or missing any limbs, but that his special talent was that he could swim through the earth as if through water, so that any time day or night when he felt the call, but especially on certain festivals, he would sink down into the ground without smothering and converse with our dead ancestors, or with others that lay there. Sometimes he would raise up the dead, or bone-creatures, like skeletal beasts, for us to ride on as we went to places of worship and sacrifice. The result of this was that he was always dirty; even when he tried to wash himself, he never got it all; and he could feel the dead beneath the ground whenever he could touch it with his skin, so he went barefoot much of the year, except when it was very cold. It was hell on his clothes too, so he would turn up at school that way sometimes, barefoot and smeared with mud and nearly naked, but that was just Jerry.

He was the one who told me what had happened in the village during the year I was in the attic. Something about a teacher who'd come from outside, and tried to change things, and who died. I thought it was funny. Jerry thought it was sad. Well, he was younger than me. I think that despite everything, he didn't get it. *There is no morality. Nothing is right or wrong.*

Nevertheless, he was my friend, even if he did betray me at the end, if that's what he did.

It was at the Leaf-Falling Time, yet again. Such things happen at particular times, because the cycles turn and the gates open.

I was in the attic. I wasn't confined there anymore, but I had grown to like it. It was only because my senses had begun to change, to become more acute, that I heard a very soft footstep on the stairs. Jerry, when he's barefoot like that can be almost totally silent, but I knew it was him, and it was. He had been swimming in the earth. Despite the cold of the season he only wore a pair of filthy denim cut-offs. He was covered with mud, but his face was streaked with tears.

He stood at the top of the attic stairs, looked at me, and said softly, "I know what you did."

And before I could make any argument about leaves and tides and there being no morality, something clumped and scraped and grabbed

Jerry by the hair from behind and threw him, yelping and banging, down the stairs.

Joram. I suppose while Jerry was swimming around among the graves, he'd met my late brother, and Joram demanded to be taken to visit dear older brother Tommy, and now that this was accomplished he'd tossed Jerry aside like an empty candy wrapper. I only had to contend with Joram. You don't grow older when you're dead, so he was still ten years old, but he'd changed. He wore only shreds of the sheet he'd been buried in, and he moved strangely because his bones were still broken, and his face was terribly pale, his eyes very strange, his fingers long and thin like sharpened sticks.

He screamed at me, not in words, but chittering, and I understood how much he hated me, how much he resented that I had stolen his role in the future among the stars.

There's no morality. No right and wrong. We do what we do.

He lunged for me, shrieking. His mouth was distorted, almost like an insect's. I could see that his teeth were sharp points. His fingernails were like knives.

But I skittered aside. Since I had very strong arms, and there was only half of me left, my body was light, and I'd learned to move like the half-man, Johnny Eck, in that movie *Freaks*. (Brother Azrael had a secret TV and VCR hidden in the back room of his store. He'd showed it to me.) There were hoops of rope strung all over the attic rafters, and I grabbed hold of them, and swung out of reach, then moved like a monkey in treetops while Joram hissed and shrieked and crashed into furniture and shelves and storage boxes. I made it past him and down the stairs. I skittered right over Jerry, who was still lying there, stunned. Joram came after me.

That was when I heard real screaming, human screaming, from downstairs in the parlor. Two voices, a grown man and a woman, in utmost agony. My parents. But by the time I got to them it was too late. Zenas was there, all awash in blood, looming over them, gobbling. He had killed and partially eaten both of them. There was blood all over the walls and ceiling.

Joram was there. He shouted something to Zenas, who looked up, then began to follow me.

I scrambled out the front door and across the lawn, with Joram and Zenas both in close pursuit.

And came face to face with Elder Abraham and Brother Azrael in their ceremonial robes, both of them holding burning staves. Behind them the people of the village were gathered, costumed, not for Halloween festivities, though it was Halloween, but for something a lot more serious. They all wore masks, some like skulls, some like beasts, some like nothing that had ever walked the earth.

Zenas caught hold of me and lifted me up, and began to strip away the flesh from my back and shoulders, but Elder Abraham struck him with his staff, and he exploded into a cloud of blood and bones and flesh. Then Brother Azrael struck Joram, and he was gone too.

The Elder explained that some who go into the darkness and are changed and come back are failures, or of limited use.

But it would not be so for me.

Though I was hurt and bleeding, someone bore me up, and I was carried at the head of a procession, alongside the Elder and the Brother, with all the people behind us, singing. We filed through the Bone Forest. We went past the standing stones beyond it, into the woods again, on for miles, our way lit by the burning staves. The light reflected off eyes in the forest. I don't think it was wolves, but we were followed. I was even aware that Jerry was with us for a while, his arms crossed across his bare chest against the cold, limping from where he'd banged his knees on the stairs, trying to keep up.

When we came to the great tree, and the Elder bade me climb, Jerry didn't try to follow me. He was of the earth. He was never a very good climber anyway. Besides, he wasn't supposed to. This climb was for me alone. It was my fate or my destiny, if you want to call it that.

Elder Abraham spoke to me, in my mind, in the chittering, clicking language of Those of the Air, not using human words at all any longer. He didn't need to.

All these changes, he said, *all these sufferings and sacrifices, are stages in your transformation, for only those who are transformed, one way or another, have any place in the world that is to come. You have climbed, step by step, up a ladder, never faltering in your course, and that is good. You are the one who will climb on our behalf into the realm of the gods, and learn their secrets, and come back to us when it is the season, as their messenger. For this you must leave your humanity behind. All of it. Shed hate and fear and hope and love like old clothes.*

So I climbed, easily seizing one branch after another, swinging like a monkey.

The air began to fill with presences, with buzzing, flapping wings. Uncle Alazar was there. He bade me come to him, and I let go of the last branch, and allowed myself to fall.

But this time he and his companions bore me up, out of the tree. For an instant I could see the dark hills, and the fields, and the few lights of Chorazin in the distance, but then I was surrounded by the stars of space, and I lost all sense of time in that cold, dark voyage. The black planets loomed before me, Yuggoth, and more distant Shaggai, and others without names, beyond the Rim. We swooped low through an endless valley lined with frozen gods, those that slept and waited and dreamed while the cycles turned. Their immense shapes were like nothing that ever walked the earth, or ever will until the end. They spoke to me, inside my head, in muted thunder, and I learned their ways.

Again space opened up, and we were falling, swirling around and around into a great whirlpool of the void, for a thousand years, I think, or a million, or for all of time, while in the far distance and faintly I heard the throbbing, pulsating drumming that is the voice of ultimate chaos, which is called Azathoth.

There was no morality in all this, no good or evil, right or wrong. These things *were*. They *are* and *shall be*.

Other such notions I had left behind, discarded with my humanity.

That's the story. Uncle's in the treetops. So am I. He and his fellows worship me now, because I went so much farther than even they ever did. I am like a god to them.

Joram is not here. Zenas is not here. Neither are Elder Abraham or Brother Azrael, though they can sense my presence, and we converse.

I returned to Earth, to Chorazin in the Pennsylvania hills, because the time and the seasons and the motions of the stars decreed. I fell backwards through millions of years. But I did not arrive precisely back at the point from which I'd departed.

I manifested myself to my old friend Jerry, who was a grown man now, though he looked pretty much the same, long-limbed and smooth-skinned and always covered with mud. I don't know if he was exactly glad to see me, but I don't think he was afraid.

The Elder and the Brother had not changed at all. They do not.

I can't actually touch the earth. I can't come down. You will have to come to me if you want to know more. Climb.

The Red Witch of Chorazin

My father grew up in Chorazin, Pennsylvania, and he told me a lot of stories about it when I was young, but to me they were mostly just that, stories. It's in the flyover part of the state, where nobody goes, where the roads wind between dark hills and you notice, mostly at night, that civilization is only in the valleys, and just barely, so that *anything* could be crawling for miles along those ridgelines and go unnoticed. Some of the stories were scary and some were wonderful. The town (if it was big enough to be called a town) was run by Elder Abraham, who must have brought his people there from somewhere else originally, because he was said to be a thousand years old. With him came Brother Azrael, who could make his eyes glow in the dark when he wanted to. He kept a room full of ancient scrolls and books that only he and Elder Abraham were ever allowed to look at. There was a kid in school with my dad—a little one-room schoolhouse, if you can believe it—who always went barefoot except in the very coldest weather because he could feel the dead beneath the ground that way. Of course he could do it with the palms of his hands, but going around on all fours all the time would be awkward, and in any case most of the kids went barefoot in warmer weather. It was that kind of place. So no one would have noticed even if there had been a need to hide what that kid, Jerry, did. But there wasn't. Everybody knew. His real talent was that he could sink down into the earth and "swim" underground without suffocating, the way some witches do in old stories, and he would meet the dead ancestors down there, and talk with them. Sometimes he even brought them up on special occasions. Sometimes he would return with strange bones, or treasure.

Jerry was always muddy, like Pigpen in the Peanuts comic strip, but no one cared, because that was who he was and what he was. He had a sister who was a lizard girl. There was an uncle who was always found impossibly high up in trees late at night, out on the end of delicate branches where you'd think even a squirrel couldn't go; he would hoot like an owl or call out to the sky in a language nobody except Elder Abraham and Brother Azrael could understand.

And there was a walking skeleton that you *didn't* want to meet late at night; and sometimes in the dark, winged things came down out of the sky and snatched someone away. Maybe that happened. Maybe it was just something made up to keep children indoors when they needed to stay indoors.

A lot more my father wouldn't tell me. When I asked him, "Was it like belonging to a cult?" he just changed the subject.

Other things he didn't tell me included why he left or whether or not he had any particular talent of his own, like Jerry or the tree-dwelling uncle.

But he did tell me about the Red Witch, who was, I gathered, something of a legend even among the Chorazinites. She was a daughter of the people, but she became strange, even to them. She had a "discontent" that made her depart from the town and haunt the hills around it. The saying was "Look where the sun sets and the shadows begin" because if you saw the sun setting behind the hills, particularly in winter, with all the trees outlined black against the sky and the shapes of the bare branches and spaces between them outlined *so* clearly and *so* far away—if you saw the sun setting like that and it was in the *wrong place* then it wasn't the setting sun at all. It was the Red Witch, who was clothed in fire some people said, a fire that didn't burn her but which could be deadly to anything else. If you looked at her, as you watched her moving along the ridges among the trees, you would be drawn to her. You'd want to go to her. You'd have to go. And people who went to her did not come back, so the story was.

Only, I met the Red Witch myself when I was twelve. Dad suddenly insisted that the family go on a "picnic," and off we went. He would take no argument. *Now.* We were going on a picnic right now, in the middle of the week, when he should have been at work, and I could tell that even my mother looked at him like he was crazy, and my baby sister Alice, who was six, just went along hoping it would be fun, and I was hoping that a really good story would come out of this.

We drove and drove, up from Philadelphia, through the Poconos and then turned left, keeping below the New York state line, where there is a great deal of nothing, just long, dark hills and dark valleys. Dad said that the Grand Canyon of Pennsylvania is in that area, and maybe we'd get to see it. We just kept on going. Mom clearly had no idea why or where and was beginning to look a little alarmed. I was almost getting bored and hungry. In the back seat with me, Alice had gone to sleep in my lap. It was almost four in the afternoon, in the late autumn, mind you, when the leaves were off the trees and it was starting to get cold and dark early.

Then suddenly, Dad pulled over onto the side, where the road curved between the hollow of two hills, a very dark and remote spot indeed. We hadn't seen another car for, like, two hours.

"Let's have a picnic!" he said, and out we all piled, rustling in the dead leaves, climbing part of the way up the hillside until we came to a large stone that made a kind of table. I remember looking up in the empty branches and thinking this would be a great place to go hunting for cocoons, which I could bring back to the science class in school, but first we got out the food and ate. We didn't say much other than things like "Please pass the pickles." There was a certain weird intensity to all this, as if it were a job that had to be done. I could tell that Mom was upset about something she wasn't saying, and Alice noticed it, and I could tell, with the result that this picnic was no fun at all, and I really just wanted to get out of there and go home.

But then Dad said he had to go off and "do something," and he walked up to the top of the hill and over it, and disappeared among the trees. I thought he'd just gone to pee, but when he didn't come back after maybe an hour, as Alice and I sat there silently, Mom said something about "business," which made no sense at all.

By now the sun was starting to go down and the woods were dark, and Alice was starting to whimper. I insisted that I should go look for Dad, and much to my surprise, as I'd expected an argument, Mom merely said softly, "Yes, go ahead."

So I went up the hill toward the ridgeline, and the sky was a lurid red in front of me, and I could see the leafless trees outlined like bare bones, and, you know, I don't think I was facing southwest at all. I think this was all in the *wrong place,* because as soon as I got over the top of the hill, there was the Red Witch, waiting for me, floating in the air a few feet off the ground, wearing a long, flowing scarlet gown that was so bright it might have been made of fire. It was too bright to look upon directly, so I could only shield my eyes, and see her a little better as she moved among the trees and the intervening trunks eclipsed some of the light. I saw her face clearly. Her hair floated in the air as if she were underwater. She was smiling, and it was almost a friendly smile; but there was something about her eyes that was too strange to quantify friendly or unfriendly, good or evil. I didn't like it at all.

And my father continued along the ridgeline, following her. I know this because I *remember* it, as if in an incredibly vivid dream, but no, more than that, as if they were my own memories, as if I myself had trudged up through the tangles of sticks and briers, up as the land rose and the light before him was blinding. He groped his way forward, his face streaming with tears. But he knew what he was doing and why he had to follow and why he could not turn aside. It was all inevitable to him, like something out of a story he'd heard as a boy.

They must have gone for miles along those ridges, against the darkening sky, and the people of the valleys must have looked up and crossed themselves, or made whatever signs they make, because the sun was not setting where it was supposed to, but moving the way that no setting sun ever should.

They came to a cabin. She went in first and beckoned him to follow, and when he did follow and she shut the door behind them, at first the light was brighter than the heart of any furnace, but then it dimmed and the room grew almost dark, though there was a faint layer of fire over everything, the rough log walls, the crudely cut floor, the furniture—a table and a couple stools—made of stumps and logs and branches. He noticed a few dishes on the shelves, a pot in the fireplace, as if in some other time, under some other conditions, someone had actually lived here. The Red Witch now was merely clothed in scarlet, with that same layer of pale fire flickering over her that was flickering over himself. He held out his hands to marvel at it. He felt no pain, no heat. He thought of the fantasy that every child has, when lying sleepily on the floor staring at burning logs in a fireplace, that the logs are hills and valleys and somewhere *beyond the fire* there is a strange country of bright, glowing air, an unreachable country that recedes to infinity, like the world on the other side of a mirror. He wondered, then, if he had somehow passed into the land of fire.

"It is hard to understand at first," she said, as if she knew what he was thinking.

And it did not seem at all strange to him, now, at last, that she should know what he was thinking. Were they not, he thought, both part of the same dream?

"Not like that," she said.

And she showed him some books she had stolen from Brother Azrael's hoard. They too were covered in gentle flames. Fire danced across the pages, but did not consume. The writing glowed. Somehow it shifted before his eyes until the scripts in no language ever written on Earth became clear to him, as if his brain were rearranging itself to a new setting.

I don't know how long he stayed there or what they did, or how long she had studied those books becoming what she was. I do not know what they came to understand in the end, what incredible wisdom they gained, what arcane and torturous rites they went through to reach a new state of being, or whatever it was.

I only know that she explained to him that if you're going to leave Chorazin at last, you have to go all the way.

And he said that it was so.

And when the time was come at last, the two of them went hand in hand to the door of the cabin, and opened it, and outside there was no forest anymore, only the vastness of space, swirling stars reaching off to infinity like the country beyond a mirror.

Even this parted before them like a curtain, and there was only fire and light.

He felt both the resignation of surrender and an adventurous expectancy.

They stepped through.

And I also remember, at the age of twelve, coming down that hillside in the gathering dark and telling my mother that I couldn't find my father.

I told her he wasn't anywhere. She just said, "Then we'll have to wait, I guess," and she tried to keep me and Alice occupied by pointing out flights of birds. It was getting too dark to identify trees. For a while we watched the half dozen deer that came out of the woods down in the hollow, at the other side of the road. But they ran off when Alice made a noise. My sister wasn't having any of this. She was tired and cold and scared.

So we drove back to Philadelphia and my sister and I grew up without having a father.

No, I don't mean *not having a father* in the sense of his being dead, or him having deserted us, but in the sense of him never having existed at all. No explanation. I couldn't even claim to be a bastard. It is indeed very hard to understand at first, something that won't become comprehensible until you've stared for years at burning, alien lettering in strange books made out of fire, and you've probably gone mad in the process. My sister did go mad. They said it was schizophrenia. By the time she was in her teens she had to be institutionalized, and I never saw her again, because I could not bear to, because I had a great deal of difficulty dealing with the way all those memories from the first twelve years of my life had been torn out like unwanted pages, maybe burned to ashes, in any case no longer connected by any sort of chronological coherence to the rest of my life, even as my mother sank into inexplicable, unreachable depression and despair and receded from me. I, in my adolescent rage, learned a lot of new words like "slut" and "parthenogenesis" until I got slapped up the side of the head in therapy and made to understand that if I didn't want to go the way of my sister (or my mother: what did she know, what was she hiding, what was consuming her like a crumpled up newspaper tossed into a fire?) I would have to learn to shut up and accept the fact that there were just a few *blanks* and contradictions in the way I constructed my life within my own head.

When I was eighteen I ran away from home. I tried to join the army first, but they threw me out, and there followed my "living in a cardboard box in the streets of New York" period, wherein I eventually found ways to put my particular grasp of unreality into street performances, which brought me a small amount of attention in the press; whereupon I graduated from psycho-bum to wannabe poet to working in an avant-garde bookstore to street theater to, incredibly, real theater and beyond, where I could actually make a living. My back-story was *so* amazing and heart-warming when improved upon in endless magazines: homeless, fatherless boy from a family of lunatics becomes star of stage, screen, and the occasional TV commercial, instantly recognizable to thousands and "That guy, what's his name? The weird one."

"That guy," a.k.a. William Henry Stanton (named after his imaginary father), actually did manage to steal a few moments of happiness from the jealous gods, to use an expression which doesn't describe the situation very well. Suffice it to say that in *this* fictitious memory of my life, which is laid in upon the rest like bright pages torn from another book that do not match the surrounding text at all, I did in fact manage to settle down, marry, buy a house in the suburbs and have the statistically requisite 2.5 children.

Point Five was because my wife, Alyson, whom I loved very much, was pregnant.

Then there was Billy-Boy, who had the same string of names as me, only we didn't want to call him "Junior." (Even he agreed that was lame.)

And my beautiful daughter, who, even when she was born had a beautiful smile, so we named her after that girl in the French movie, Amelie. She was six. By all indications she was going to grow up to be as irresistibly charming as her namesake.

Suffice it to say that my life was actually going rather well when, by a commodius vicus of recirculation, to borrow some gibberish from my street-poet days, on a certain autumn day I was hurrying madly about the house to make sure I was ready and presentable for an important audition, when I went into the bathroom one last time, and there, in the mirror, drifting from side to side like a computer screensaver against a dark background, was my father's face.

In the rush of things I did what I'd learned to do in my profession, ad-libbed: "Look, I'm in a hurry. Can my mental breakdown please wait?"

"Billy-boy, this will be hard for you to understand at first," he said.

I hadn't been called that since I was twelve, in another life.

"I'll bet," I said.

I was searching my mind for another smartass reply when suddenly *she* was there, the Red Witch herself, in the mirror, coming through the mirror, filling the bathroom, then the whole house with fire.

"Hello, Billy," she said.

I heard screaming. I saw my wife crumple up like a burning newspaper. I saw my beautiful daughter go off like a firework. My son was calling out to me something like *Daddy, Daddy, it hurts, make it stop*, only there was something wrong with his face; it was hollow, like a paper mask, filled with fire from the inside, disintegrating as I watched.

Then I was on the floor, on my knees, screaming, and my Alyson was shaking me by the shoulders, hard, and shouting at me, "What's wrong? What's wrong?"

And I stopped, and looked around me, stunned, at the interior of the house which was very much as it always had been, save that I'd knocked over the laundry hamper when coming out of the bathroom. No fire anywhere.

I gave her a goofy smile. "Christ, do I need a vacation—"

"Are you sure that's all it is?"

"Yeah. Yeah. Working too hard." And suddenly I was manic, "Let's go on a *picnic!!!*" And I herded and cajoled and damn near bullied the lot of them into getting ready all of the sudden, packing a few things, hustling out into the car. It was mid-day. We were going to have to make good time if we were going to get where we were going in time for a picnic.

"What about your audition?" Alyson said, astonished, alarmed.

"Fuck the audition. Let's go."

And we went, eastward across Connecticut, down the Hudson Valley, over the Tappen Zee Bridge, through the Delaware Water Gap and past any part of northern Pennsylvania anyone has ever heard of. All the while Alyson stared at me as if she were sure I'd lost my mind but didn't have any better idea than to play along. Billy-boy (Junior) in the back seat was messaging steadily on his phone, no doubt telling Facebook and the world that he was being kidnapped and his father's brain had been taken over by monsters from outer space.

You don't know the half of it, kiddo, because I distinctly remembered stepping through that cabin door, hand-in-hand with the Red Witch of Chorazin, into infinity.
I remember passing from starry darkness into brilliant light into darkness again.

I remember dwelling for ten thousand years on a sunless planet, amid colossal stone memnons that slowly groaned out an almost infinite text which, if it were ever completed, I somehow understood, would mean the end of all existence.

I beheld and spoke with intelligences in the darkness, as vast and inexorable as tides, existing on such an impossible time scale that any human experience, all of human history, would have been, to them, less than the infinitesimal flicker of an electron.

There was so much more, beyond my reach even then.

In a dark place, where the road curved in the hollow between two hills, I pulled the car off the road.

It was early winter. The leaves were off the trees. The air was cold. Not a really good day for a picnic, particularly considering how late it was.

Yet we shuffled up the hillside, found a table-like stone, ate our sandwiches.

Then I said I had to go off and do something.

My son looked at me very strangely. I think he was crying.

But I made my way up over the ridge line, into the apparent sunset, where the Red Witch was waiting, and I followed her for miles through the darkening forest, until we came to her cabin. We went in. She closed the door after us.

Inside, she opened a burning book and pointed to a passage which explained everything.

Then she said, "We have to go now."

She opened the door again. Stars. Infinity.

I closed the door, and, before she could react, drew a pistol out of my pocket and emptied the magazine into her face.

"No! This is not what I want! Fuck this! I want my life back. I want Alyson and the kids and my acting career and my happiness! Not this! Not this!"

But the Red Witch only smiled at me sadly and said, "You didn't think you could break away that easily, did you? It's not like that."

Her face was like a burning paper mask, beginning to disintegrate inward from the edges.

"I'd better go look for Dad," Billy-boy said.

"Yes, go ahead," his mother said.

If you'd rather believe my mind has been taken over by monsters from outer space, please do so now. The rest doesn't get any better.

Having emptied the pistol's magazine, still screaming, I threw the gun at her and ran out of the cabin, into the forest, right into the arms of the Skeleton Thing That You Really Don't Want to Meet in the Dark.

It had me by the hair. It yanked my head back, as if to break my neck. Its claws tore into my throat and chest. I could see its face hovering above mine like a screen-saver, drifting from side to side, mouth wide, teeth like nails, eyes burning.

It didn't say anything. Before it could, someone grabbed me by the ankles and yanked me down *into the earth* and I was being dragged through mud and stone and darkness like a drowning victim hauled by a lifeguard. Someone had his arm under my chin, and I hung limp. I felt him swimming, down, down through the dark hills beneath the roots of the forest. Somehow I could breathe or had no need of breathing. I saw, far below us, bone assemblages as huge as whales, swimming there. There were dead faces all around us, of the ancestors, who spoke in whispers I could not make out, in some language I did not understand.

Then we rose up again, out of the ground, and crawled onto a wooden porch, spitting out mud, trying to wipe the mud out of our eyes while someone poured hot water over us. I looked up then and saw a woman in an old-fashioned dress with her hair in a bun. She put down another bucket of water, dropped some towels beside them, nudged me with her foot and said, "So the prodigal returns," then added, "Clean yourself up, you two. Supper's ready."

I knew who my rescuer was: Jerry, short for Jeroboam, whose special talent was swimming beneath the ground. He was older than he'd been in the stories, when I had gone to school with him, but not nearly as old as he should have been if you tried to figure it out by adding up the years. But I didn't try to add them up. What year was it anyway? What meaning could that possibly have?

Jerry was wearing only a pair of very brief, cut-off denim shorts, the easier to wash the mud off, presumably. My own clothing was a complete wreck, so when the two of us went inside, I had to borrow a pair of way-too-large overalls and a t-shirt. That was when Jerry's mom noticed that I really did have some nasty cuts all down my front. So she took me in the bathroom and cleaned my wounds and touched them up with iodine and alcohol. As I sat there on the edge of the bathtub, being worked on, I looked down at the damage and at my own completely hairless chest and belly. I glanced up at the mirror, afraid of what I'd see, but I saw only my own face looking back, my twelve-year-old face.

Once upon a time there was a boy who left Chorazin. He walked over the mountain, into the sunset. But he came back.

"When you leave Chorazin," the Red Witch said, "you have to leave everything behind. That truly means everything."

Her face crumpled like burning newspaper and was gone.

"No one can leave Chorazin who is *of* Chorazin," Elder Abraham said. "You can only create superfluous patterns, in which you have left, but they are like extra pages in a book. We are all temporary patterns in the black seas of nothingness, even our gods, swirls and eddies of the current. Chorazin itself is a pattern, of which we are a part, more distinct perhaps, which may even survive for a time when the Old Gods return from the blackness in which they sleep. But nothing lasts forever. The black sea is forever."

The Elder spoke such wisdom as is seldom shared with anyone other than Brother Azrael. He'd come to dinner. We were deeply honored, all of us. Jerry had changed into something a little more presentable, though he never did manage to get all the mud out of his hair or from between his toes.

"Even that only masks the Gate," I said. "I think we got as far as the Gate. But we could not see beyond it."

"Yog-Sothoth is the Gate," said Brother Azrael.

"There are many gates," I said.

"But all are one in Yog-Sothoth."

In Chorazin there is a girl they have to keep chained in an attic. Her mind has completely gone. They say that she has flaming red hair but she is horribly disfigured, as if she's been shot in the face several times.

"William," the Elder said to me. "One day, I think, you may become the greatest of us all."

The Girl in the Attic

Chorazin, Pennsylvania was (and is) a small town, if you could even call it that: a few farms, a cluster of houses around a single street, a church with the steeple blasted off and its white wooden sides still charred, a one-room schoolhouse by a stream, a general store with gas pumps out front that usually don't work, and a surprisingly overlarge graveyard near a circle of standing stones where the people gather on certain occasions, at the times preordained by the turning of the stars and seasons, to perform certain rites. The town itself is a secret, hidden away in the upper, central part of the state near the New York line that is mostly blank on a map, amid long, dark valleys where there are only occasional specks of light at night to be seen from the winding roads.

It has its own secrets, too, some of them hidden even from itself.

In one of those houses, a house where no one lives, and which has been boarded up for years, there is a girl chained in the attic. She was once strikingly beautiful, almost fully grown. But her face is gone, blown away by gunshots in the course of some adventure. Her mind is gone, so the common report has it, and she sits perpetually on the floor, her head resting on her drawn up knees, her arms limply at her sides. She makes no sound and never stirs, requiring neither food nor water nor cleansing, for her body has turned hard, like wax or even soft stone; neither dead nor alive and she has been thus for years or centuries or just a few days. It is hard to tell on this last point, because time itself in Chorazin can slip, as if trying to climb a muddy slope and sliding back down again.

Despite which, the girl is still kept chained by her ankles to a vertical beam in the center of the room which holds up the roof, just in case.

The elders check on her from time to time, as the stars tell them, and repeat a certain word over her. Then they go away and she remains just a story, though at one time she was none other than the Red Witch of Chorazin, the girl covered in fire, whose wandering along the dark ridgelines beyond the town could be mistaken for a sunset.

But her fire had gone out, her face gone from misadventure, her mind gone, her body a stiff shell.

A secret, without a name. No one spoke her name, though the elders still knew it.

The secret was that her mind was gone because it had departed elsewhere, traveling in something like dreams, first into the houses nearby, then beyond. People sensed her passage like an unsettling breath of wind, only there for a second, then gone. She drifted over the hills once more, down into adjoining valleys, alone and incorporeal in the night.

Once she met a man in the woods, who had parked his car and come up from the highway for some reason. She embraced him and before he could even scream he burst into flame and was consumed almost to ashes. She herself was not burnt, though she was clothed in flame again, as the Red Witch had been, for a little while at least. If the charred corpse was ever found, it did not matter. The man was a stranger. Possibly the incident found its way into a supermarket tabloid like *Weekly World News* as a "mystery of spontaneous human combustion," but if so that did not matter either, because there were no supermarkets in Chorazin and nobody read tabloids. It had rained that night. The forest was wet and the fire did not spread.

Once, too, in her dreams, after she had drifted among the stars, perhaps for an eternity folded back on itself so that the ending of the dream took place at the same instant as the beginning, she dwelt on a black, sunless world in a jagged valley where bestial stone gods sat in two infinite rows, whispering; and one of those gods leaned down, with the thundering voice of an avalanche, and said to her, "Now awaken."

That was how it began, a secret in the attic.

She raised her head from off her knees, in the attic. The red flame burned within the ruin of her face.

She tried to speak, but made only a little sound.

At first the chains baffled her, but then she stepped out of them, perhaps incorporeally, or else like a snake shedding its skin. She herself did not know how it was done, but the sensation was very physical. She was standing naked in the cold attic. She listened, and heard the wind whistling softly over the roof, and, somewhere far away, what might be a cowbell ringing. She walked barefoot down the attic stairs, feeling the smooth, gritty steps one by one.

The door at the bottom was closed. She fumbled with the doorknob clumsily, as if her hands had forgotten what to do next. Then she squeezed the knob, without turning it, and the door was covered with pale fire, which did not consume, and gave off no heat. But that was enough, and the door opened.

She found herself in a familiar hallway. There was a wash stand outside one of the rooms, with a big bowl in it, filled with dust. This struck her as an odd place for a wash stand. She attempted a smile and continued on.

She came to another room that she knew very well. The door was open. She went in. She wanted light, but there were no candles, and the oil lamp on the stand by the side of the bed was empty. With a concentration of her mind, she made light. It was as natural as breathing. Soon the walls and furniture were all aglow with pale fire, as she'd used to open the attic door, tiny flickering white flames that did not burn or give off heat, like St. Elmo's Fire perhaps, something she'd read about in books, in sea stories. For all she had traveled widely now, she had never seen St. Elmo's Fire, so she could only guess it was like that.

Still naked, oblivious to that fact, she lovingly explored the room, reaching out to touch the things that were hers: a whole shelf of porcelain-faced dolls in fine dresses, now, like everything else, faded and covered with dust. When she'd grown too old to play with dolls anymore, she had placed them on that shelf in a neat row, as a memorial to her former self, and there they had remained.

There was another shelf of her books, and a stack of *St. Nicholas Magazine for Boys and Girls,* something else left behind but not discarded. She got down a particularly treasured volume, opened it, and saw written on the endpaper in pencil, in a very childish hand, "This book belongs to: MARIE." Yes, that was her name, she recalled now, but it was her everyday name, the name she used all the time, not her *other* name, the one for secrets, which only the elders knew.

Still holding the book, she sat down on the dusty comforter that covered the bed. She read through the book for a few minutes, then put it aside and lay down, stretching languorously, carefully noting and savoring each sensation. She stared up at the ceiling, remembering when she had lain in this bed and stared at that ceiling for so long that she imagined rivers and mountains and whole, strange countries in the ripples and cracks of the plaster; but she had done that when she was very small, and now that she had journeyed much more widely, the ceiling was only plaster.

A tear ran down her ruined face.

After a while she felt cold, and sat up. She went through the closet, and was distressed to find that most of her clothing was chewed to shreds by moths, but at last she found some things that she could wear, however dusty: underthings, a blouse, a skirt that went down to her ankles, stockings and high shoes.

Then she sat down at her dressing table, to comb her hair, which was indeed a mess. In the mirror, her eyes and nostrils and slightly open mouth and the holes in her cheeks were filled with fire, so she looked a bit like a badly-carved jack-o'-lantern.

Now the gentle fire spread through the whole house, consuming nothing but filling the house with light. She listened where she sat, in increasing anticipation, to the house coming alive with sounds and smells. Someone stirring in the kitchen. Pots clanking. A small dog barking. And finally a voice calling out, "Marie! Time for dinner! Come down!"

So she went down, still relishing, exploring every sensation, running her hand gently along the railing, stopping to gaze at each of the framed prints on the wall, which showed either her ancestors, or strange beasts, or both.

"Marie!"

At the base of the stairs she stood for a long time gazing into the parlor to her left. Her sheet music was still on the piano. She noticed her younger brother John's toy Noah's Ark on the table there, with the pairs of wooden animals carefully arranged two by two.

"Marie! It's Thanksgiving!"

Indeed it was. To her right was the dining room. There, indeed she found her family seated around the table, her father in his three-piece suit with watch-chain, smiling, the ends of his moustache pointing upward as he did; her brother Johnny in his sailor suit, sitting still for once; her mother in her lace-collared dress. The family spaniel, Mister Ears, had settled down in the corner with a bone.

The whole room, and the family glowed with the same magical, pale fire that filled the house with light.

It was Thanksgiving, but this was Chorazin after all, so Thanksgiving was not quite the same as elsewhere, any more than her brother's toy Noah's Ark in the other room had been quite the standard model. (Two of the creatures were shapeless, flowing things; something half like a man, half like a cuttlefish crouched on the roof of the Ark to welcome the passengers aboard.) Papa gave thanks to the Whispering Voices of the Air, and to the Winged Ones That Come, and to the Earth Shaker, and to the Gods We Await. The thanks was not so much for the repast before them (turkey and sweet potatoes and beans with almonds, bread, puddings, and candied fruit) but for the expectation that when the Earth is cleared off, they who were faithful would find some place in the new, strange, and transformed world. Amen.

Nevertheless, Marie was happy to be here, in this one perfect moment. She wanted nothing more than to remain suspended in it forever like an insect in amber.

If this was a dream, she didn't want to wake up.

But, to her horror, she heard again the voice of the colossal stone god, the one that bent forward as an avalanche, telling her to wake up, and wake up fully.

No, she said, under her breath.

And aloud she said, "I love you, Mama. I love you, Papa. I even love you, Johnny, and Mister Ears."

"We love you too," said her mother.

But her mother was burning. There was a fire behind her face, as if she were a paper doll and a smoldering candle had been shoved inside her. Now the flames burst out, not the gentle flames that illuminated everything, but the kind that devoured.

"Mama!"

Marie tried to concentrate, to *will* the fire away, and gradually it receded, but her mother's whole face was gone, and her head began to crumple inward, even though her hands were going through the normal motion of buttering a piece of bread.

Her father began to say something, but he too was burning. Marie rushed from her seat over to him, put her hands on his shoulder, and whispered, *"Don't, don't, don't,"* and the flames died down, but then her brother screamed. She threw a glass of apple juice in his face. Behind her the dog exploded like a firework and flames raced up a curtain. She raced from one place to another, trying to put the flames out one way or another, but soon the whole house was genuinely on fire and she heard parts of it crashing down upstairs.

It was only by the utmost effort, drawing on all the power of her many dreams, of her prior adventures, what had been called her witchcrafts, on all the secrets and spells and powers she had learned or gained on other worlds among eternal stone gods, that she *almost* got things under control, and once more the walls and all else were covered only with the faint, unburning, tiny flames that she had spread with her touch. She actually managed to eat some of her dinner. The turkey was especially good, and the sweet potatoes, but she didn't have much appetite, because her parents and her brother sat there like smoldering corpses and the curtain was still burning slowly. She felt her hold slipping, and the flames raced up the curtain again, blackening the ceiling.

She began to sob softly.

That was when someone placed a hand on her shoulder and said, "Come away. You know you can't stay here." She heard her *secret* name spoken, the name from her dreams. By that name was she addressed by the two chief men of Chorazin, by Elder Abraham and his assistant, Brother Azrael. She turned in her chair and beheld them. Of course she knew them both. She had known them all her life and had been told that Elder Abraham, the founder of Chorazin and father of the people, was a thousand years old. She believed it. She had no reason to doubt. She knew how time in Chorazin could slip like someone trying to climb a muddy slope. Now the two of them stood before her. The Elder wore a black robe and carried a staff with a glowing stone on the end of it. The Brother wore a suit of an unfamiliar cut.

"I don't want to leave," she said. "I want to stay home."

"You can't," said the Elder gently. "You know how this has to end."

"Yes, I do," she said at last.

The whole house shook as part of the roof must have collapsed into the second story.

"That being the case," said Brother Azrael, "we'd better go."

She let them lead them out of the house. They let her stand for a while, weeping, as it burned and collapsed into rubble.

Then, part way down the path to the main road, they met a boy who looked to be in his middle teens—starting to get tall, no beard yet. She could see him clearly by the glare of the fire. He was naked but for a very brief pair of cut-off shorts, as if he were planning to go swimming, and she could tell that he was also very dirty, streaked with mud. He looked cold. He was hugging his shoulders. She did not know him. She had never seen this particular boy before, but she knew exactly what he was. Always in Chorazin there is one called the Muddy Man or the One Who Goes Below or by various other names, who swims through the earth as if through water, as witches do, who can go deep down into the darkness to converse with buried ancestors or with gods, and bring up treasures. But the Muddy Man she was used to was a long-limbed, gnarled fellow named Enoch, in his sixties or seventies, with wild hair and matted beard, who favored a leather loincloth.

This had to be the latest of his successors. Of his many successors.

She understood that in the actual life she had lived, in her girlhood, this boy and she had never been contemporaries. Of course she didn't know him. Time was tricky like that, in Chorazin.

They all walked a ways in silence, through the graveyard, past where bones dangled from trees and rattled in the wind, to that place of standing stones and a stone altar. There the Elder removed his robe and placed it on the altar, and stood naked but for a leather loincloth. Marie remained as she was. Her clothes would be ruined, no doubt, but it didn't matter. She wasn't coming back. She understood that much.

His staff in his left hand, Elder Abraham took the boy by the hand with his right. The boy in turn took Marie-*who-had-another-name* by the hand, and as Brother Azrael chanted slowly, invoking the Hidden Gods Below, the three of them, the Elder, the boy, and Marie, sank down into the ground, the mud closing over them like quicksand. The Brother's voice followed them for a long time. She was not afraid. She had known too many miracles to be surprised that they could somehow breathe, or that they didn't have to breathe, even as the boy led them, as all three of them swam, hand-in-hand, down and down into the darkness, until the dead of many generations surrounded them like curious fishes, and she met her mother and father again, and even her brother John, who, she learned, had lived to be seventy-four, until a mule kicked him in the face and he died, in 1940. It was an intense, sweet reunion, as they tried to share all their lives, all their dreams, and there was even laughter, then sadness and she knew she had to go on.

Down they went, again, until things like skeletal whales rose up out of the earth and swarmed around them. Down, until the solidity of matter itself became as tenuous as smoke, and she saw stars, and a blackness before them, opening up. Shapes loomed before them, speaking with voices deeper than thunder, in words no human tongue had ever formed, and they called out her secret name.

The Elder and the boy—whose name was Jerry, Jeroboam actually—could proceed no farther. The rest of the journey was for her alone. She took her leave of them. At the very end the Elder said to her, in the wisdom of his thousand years, "All these things have been only a gestation. It is nearly complete. Go."

All these necessary things. Everything she had lost.

Then her eyes were fully opened and her mind cleared, and she remembered, not as if awakening from a dream, but as if she were living it again *right now*, how when she was thirteen years old her parents had taken her out into the night and held her naked on the stone altar like a sheep to be slaughtered. Elder Abraham and the Brother were there, and many others, chanting until their voices were drowned out by thunder and a band of light stretched down from the sky, all the way to this infinite abyss which she now confronted, where even Elder Abraham had not been able to follow. It touched her, inside, filling her, burning. She screamed. She wept. She struggled to get away. But they held her fast.

"Take it," her father and mother had shouted to her. "Take the flame inside you."

She felt none of their love now. At that last thanksgiving, they had loved her. Now their faces and their hearts were hard, as if she had been reduced to the status of a thing, indeed, like a sheep to be slaughtered and as routine as that.

Burning, raging, she broke away, fleeing, to haunt the hills around Chorazin for a century and more.

But even that was only part of the process. The Gestation. Now she entered into the completion of her great task, into her kingdom, to reign as queen.

These things are true. They are written in the prophetic books Brother Azrael keeps in the locked room in the back of the Chorazin general store. Marie's *other name* is written there by no human hand, in no human tongue. The Gestation is described. Therefore we worship her, as Queen of the Sky, and as Mother of Those Who Are to Come.

The Hutchison Boy

Caleb Hutchison was over at our house, playing video games with my son Jackie the night the world ended.

It was cold that evening. Late October at the New Jersey shore is not exactly beach blanket weather, but there was Caleb at the front door of our cottage as he always was, dressed in rags that must have been adult cast-offs, a checkered flannel shirt that fit him like a tent, with the elbows out, and baggy jeans torn off just below the knees; he was barefoot as always, which wouldn't have been unexpected for a beachfront in July, but in thirty-something weather with the wind howling and spray and maybe even sleet ratting against the windowpanes, and him sopping wet with his pale, wispy hair plastered to his head, and himself so appallingly skinny that his limbs looked like pale, bluish sticks, the result was that before he could say more than a faint "Hello" my wife Margaret had screamed, "Oh my God!" and hauled him off to the bathroom, where after a minute or so I could hear the shower running and steam poured out from under the bathroom door. Then the hair dryer was going, and by the time she produced him again Caleb wore a pair of borrowed jogging pants and a sweatshirt that drooped down to his knees and a bathrobe over that and fluffy slippers, and only *then* did he manage to blurt out, "Can I play with Jackie now?"

A minute later you could hear the two of them laughing over the assorted beeps, whistles, and explosions from the game console in the TV room.

The borrowed clothes were actually mine, because, for all he was about the same age as Jackie, twelve or so, Caleb was a full head taller and his build was so different from that of our rather short, chubby offspring that nothing of Jackie's would have fit.

It occurred to me that Caleb hadn't been shivering. Margaret had described him as "cold as ice" but he hadn't seemed the least bit uncomfortable.

"*Where* are that boy's parents? That's what I want to know," Margaret whispered to me angrily.

It was a good question. I didn't have an answer.

"That kid's got some kind of weird skin condition," she added. "I've never seen anything like it."

I just remained silent.

It was later that night that the power went off and never came back on again. I don't think it ever will.

As for the question of where Caleb Hutchison's parents were, the answer was they lived somewhere north of us along this remarkably undeveloped stretch of southern Jersey ocean front, past what the kids called Dead Man's Cove for its alleged piratical associations, a swerve of shore and bend of bay that was actually *rocky* along its edge—unusual in these parts—so that it was more practical, especially at low tide, to wade across than make your way around by land, particularly if you were barefoot, which helped explain why Caleb usually showed up at our place wet; which explained nothing at all, really, such as why Caleb showed up at all, but I confess I was not paying attention.

Caleb had become Jackie's new best friend that summer. I was glad for that, because Jackie was picked on at school and it was good for him to have a friend at all, even a weird one, even if they made a Mutt-and-Jeff or Laurel-and-Hardy–type pair. (Caleb, oddly, knew those references. Jackie, of course, did not.)

Could I *meet* Caleb's parents sometime, like maybe when I drove him home some night?

No, there wasn't any road to their place. Caleb always left on his own, wading along the water's edge, even if it was very late.

Besides, they were busy with their "church."

We were different, I knew. I and my family were summer people. They were all-year-round people, though I gathered, not native New Jerseans, but originally from somewhere much farther north, some place in New England I'd never heard of, whence the family had fled years and years ago after the Great Persecution of 1927, whatever that was.

(I tried to look it up on Wikipedia. Nothing. Another of Caleb's stories. He was full of stories.)

Okay, so my son's best and only friend and constant companion was this weird urchin whose parents probably belonged to some even weirder cult and probably chanted gibberish while sacrificing nude virgins; girls, I hoped, which would leave Jackie safe, and Caleb too; and this is where I admit that I'm selfish and a bad parent and neglectful—though never abusive toward my own kid—because, you see, our presence at the Shore that year was not entirely a vacation. I was trying to work. Here I was the alleged Highly Artistic Novelist, the hottest thing since Thomas Pynchon, and, for all I lied non-stop to agents and publicists and editors about How Well The Book Was Coming, the truth of the matter was I was tearing my hair out and completely empty of ideas and writing shit that I couldn't show anyone. Margaret was a teacher of languages nobody cared about, who was about to be laid off from the Philadelphia school system, and, oh by the way, an up-and-coming part-time professional photographer who suddenly seemed to be a no-timer because she couldn't get any assignments. So you will appreciate that the two of us were . . . under a considerable amount of stress for our own vain and petty (not to mention financial) reasons, and when we were not on the phone, begging or cajoling or telling outright lies, we were all too often screaming at each other, enough so that she said we needed counseling and I said she needed a shrink or maybe just a lobotomy. And for all, in some deep, inner drawer of my brain I still loved her and Jackie and wanted everything to be happy the way it once was (in our imagination at least), there were surely times when I concluded that my whole life up to this point had been a mistake and I should have remained unmarried and become a shoe salesman.

A sure thing. I mean, everybody needs shoes, right?

Except maybe Caleb.

The deep dark secret, I think, is that Margaret likewise was glad Jackie had a friend, for all the right, maternal reasons, but for all the wrong ones too. Translation: it got him out of the way so we could fight with each other and not have him see it.

May and June, I heard a lot about Caleb at the dinner table, but I hadn't met him. Margaret seemed to be in on the secret well before me; maybe she had; maybe, I sometimes suspected, this Caleb was a collective hallucination between the two of them, the kind of imaginary playmate who told Jackie the most remarkable things. I mean, why else would a twelve-year-old who liked video games, comics, and Japanese animation be asking me if there really was a golden city under the ocean near here, a place with shining pillars, where fish-men lived forever and worshipped a god that looked like a giant frog?

No, I had to admit, I didn't know anything about that.

Maybe it was something he got out of the comic books, which, I understand, have become a lot more challenging than they were when I was Jackie's age, or maybe it was the anime, which never made sense to me anyway.

But Caleb knew all about that kind of thing.

And there was that night when neither Margaret nor I had noticed that Jackie was gone until it was almost dawn, and we caught him sneaking back into the house, and he admitted that he'd been out on the beach with Caleb, looking at the stars where they "opened" (which was apparently Caleb's phrase) and making marks in the sand with sticks that somehow glowed (whether the sticks, the marks, or both, I am not sure) while talking to voices from out of the air.

That we didn't do anything, that we just let things proceed without any intervention, I feel guilty about now. Yes, it was bad parenting.

It must have been about the first of July that I came home from what I was pretending was a research trip, and there was supper on the table, and an extra place set because we had been joined by the elusive Caleb, who smelled of seawater and was barefoot and wore cut-offs and a ripped tank-top that fit him so badly he looked damned near naked in the thing. My first thought is that this is the kid who is so skinny that when he comes into the schoolroom sideways the teacher marks him absent, and my second was that I wondered if he ever went to school. The next thing I did was give him an old Philadelphia Phillies T-shirt of mine, which fit him like a nightgown, but he put it on and gravely said, "Thank you, sir."

Oddly, for a kid who knew how to say "Thank you, sir," he also gave me the initial impression at dinner that he didn't know what a fork was for, but he was a good mimic, and sly about it, and I could tell he was watching us before he did anything, and after a minute or so he definitely had the hang of it. He ate ravenously too, everything Margaret could feed him, but it was like all the food went into hyperspace, not into his stomach, because it never seemed to make him even an ounce heavier.

But when he started to talk, I forgot all that, even as I forgot I was talking with a twelve-year-old at all. I began to wonder if Jackie's new friend wasn't the next budding Einstein, because he did mention hyperspace, and something about "angles in space-time" and the stars being "right" and a lot of stuff I just couldn't follow at all. I glanced over at Margaret, and she looked blankly back and shook her head; but, incredibly, Jackie, who had never been very good at school, seemed to have some idea what Caleb was talking about, as if it were a private language between them. And they *did* use some gibberish words between them, a little furtively, which definitely were *not* English, maybe something from that weirdo church that Caleb's parents belonged to.

But then dinner was over and the two of them ran off into the TV room and they were just kids again.

That summer, you will recall, was the Summer of Strangeness, or the Time of Signs, or whatever you want to call it. There were lights in the sky at night, which nobody could explain, sometimes great swirling spirals of color that would last until dawn. Sometimes the stars themselves seemed to ripple. The pundits and the papers and the Internet were full of talk of UFOs and the Second Coming and gravitational disturbances, solar storms, and whatnot. It was also a time of storms on Earth, and after Superstorm Obed wiped out Miami and New Orleans pretty much for good this time, and the sea level rose even faster than the Global Warming alarmists said it would, people began to get the idea that this was, maybe, serious. As a result, several new wars broke out in the Middle East, and a couple in Europe, and the End of Days Militia made its famous stand outside of Tucson and died to the last man.

There were things seen in the ocean, sometimes photographed and shown on Facebook (before they were mysteriously taken down) that didn't make much sense either. And I can tell you that not too far from us, down in Port Norris, something washed up on the beach, the size of a railroad car, with flippers but with an almost human face. I saw it myself. I stood there in the mid-day sun watching the thing melt away like wax. The newspapers said it was a whale. Then they didn't say anything.

With phone service intermittent and a national emergency declared, our failing careers seemed to have less and less to do with reality, but still Margaret and I soldiered on. By about the middle of August Margaret got a call telling her that she definitely would not be returning to her job in the fall, and on the 20th my literary agent shot himself, so, yeah, it was a great summer.

Jackie and Caleb did what boys do, off by themselves much of the time. They seemed to be having fun.

Caleb came over a lot more often. He was around most days, at least until he and Jackie went traipsing off on their latest adventure.

One day Jackie asked me if the two of them could borrow a shovel.

"Are you going to dig up pirate treasure?" I asked him.

"Yeah, Caleb knows where there is some. Over by the Cove."

I looked over at Caleb for confirmation, but he just glanced down at his feet and wiggled his toes in the sand. He was wearing the ill-fitting tank top again that day, and it struck me that for all the tank top didn't cover much of anything, he was still almost impossibly pale, but he didn't have sunburn either. There was something odd about his eyes. They seemed about to pop out of his face.

But I didn't say anything and just gave them the shovel. Off they went, and very much to my surprise, they *found* something. I won't say they unearthed an old-fashioned sea chest, but when they came back they'd converted Jackie's T-shirt into a sack by tying the sleeves together; and when they dumped the haul out onto our kitchen table, it thumped heavily, and, God damn it, really looked like gold. Margaret protested as sand and pebbles rattled onto her clean floor, but she was as quiet as was I when she stared at the gleaming heap of strange jewelry and a misshapen crown of some sort and dozens of what might have been coins, though they were irregular in shape and the size of large cookies, and stamped with what might have been swirling tentacles.

Caleb rummaged among the pile and selected a pedant that looked a bit like a fish and partially like a man. It was on a thin chain. He put it around his neck.

"This is all I need," he said. "You can have the rest."

Jackie found another such pendant and put it on. Margaret only gaped at the two of them, speechless. Then they went outside like nothing had happened, and were just boys again, and I think they spent much of the night on the porch swing, reading manga comics by the porch light.

I swept the rest of the gold into a cardboard box. Judging by its weight, I did not doubt that it really was gold. I couldn't imagine where it had actually come from.

"Well, this ought to alleviate our financial worries for a while," I said, and the look Margaret gave me indicated that she knew as well as I did just how stupid that sounded.

But even stupidity may contain its own nuggets of wisdom or turn out to be prophetic, because only a few days later there was a "completely unprecedented" earthquake in eastern Pennsylvania, and the earth swallowed up a good deal of Philadelphia, even the high parts in the northeast, which were definitely above the fall line. When a neighbor finally got through to my cell phone he said our house was gone. There was nothing worth salvaging. "Just a smoking hole in the ground," is what he said.

So we were going to have to stay down at the Shore beyond Labor Day. We registered Jackie in the local school, and he started to attend. Caleb was not in his class, or there at all.

Then there came the cold night in October when the power went out for good.

Jackie let out a yell. "Dad! Can you fix it?"

I went and checked the circuit-breakers, but no, I could not fix it. The phone was dead too. I tried my cell. No signal.

I couldn't fix it. Nobody could.

So there were the two of them, sitting alone in the dark in the TV room, and I tried to tell myself it was only my imagination that Caleb's eyes seemed unnaturally wide and faintly luminous.

Then the sounds came. That was also the first night of the Boomers or the Voices from the Sea or the Heralds of the Apocalypse, or whatever you want to call them.

At first I thought it was a ship's horn, then a foghorn, then several foghorns. Caleb got up. He led Jackie by the hand. Margaret and I could only follow the two of them out into the darkness, down to the beach. It was still raining, and there was sleet in it. Caleb led us all. He'd kicked off the fluffy slippers and discarded the bathrobe, but, still wearing my sweatshirt and running pants, he stood in the surf, gazing out to sea, where, in the otherwise impenetrable gloom, lights began to appear; like spheres rising out of the black water, like moons, I thought, no, like eyes opening. From out of that darkness and distance, from those glowing whatever-they-were came the sounds, a deep and thunderous booming at first, but then the notes began to modulate and they became a kind of song, which Caleb *answered,* making whistling and howling and screeching sounds that I swear no human throat has ever made.

Jackie tried to imitate him, but his own was a little boy's voice, and the result was a series of yelps, barks, and squeals.

And Caleb said to him, "It's the Call. I told you it would come." He still held Jackie by the hand and started to lead him deeper into the water.

It was Margaret who actually had the nerve to do something. You might say she had the balls in the family. She was the one who rushed forward, yanked Jackie away, and said, "No, you don't! You're coming home right now!"

"But it's the Call, Mom!"

"I don't care if it's fucking Santa Claus," she said under her breath, and hauled him, squalling and protesting, up the beach and back toward our house.

Caleb turned to face me, waste deep in the water. His eyes were definitely luminous now, like those things far out to sea.

I wanted to demand of him the truth, who he was and why he had come into our lives, and, more to the point, *what* he was.

But I didn't. I don't give myself any credit, but I think it did take a certain amount of courage to confront him at all.

All I said was, "Go away, Caleb. Leave us alone. Don't come to our house anymore. Don't play with Jackie."

He said nothing. He sank down into the water. He must have been swimming.

That of course solved nothing. It wasn't hard to predict what happened next. One night Margaret caught Jackie at the window, leaning out into the dark, trying to make those sounds, and, in the distance, something answered him.

She was really afraid now. I could tell that. This brought us together. You know that little drawer deep inside my brain, in which I kept what was left of my love for my family? It creaked open, just a bit. I didn't argue when Margaret insisted that Jackie start sleeping in the same bed with us again. None of this "he's a big boy" crap. I knew what she meant and what she felt. I was afraid too.

During the days we just sat around the house. There was no use going out. Such neighbors as we had didn't know anything. If the government was making any rescue efforts, it wasn't doing it here. Power did not come back on. The phones didn't work. The sky was filled with strange auroral effects, even in the daytime. Margaret tried to read. Believe it or not, I actually wrote a good scene in my much-delayed novel-in-progress. Jackie pretended to do schoolwork.

But there inevitably came a night when Jackie slipped out of bed as if he had to go to the bathroom, and it was maybe as much as an hour later before I was suddenly wide awake, my heart racing, and I realized that he was gone. I got up. I took the flashlight we kept by the bed and searched the house. The back door was unlocked. No further explanation necessary.

Margaret was up by then too, weeping.

I tried to play the hero. I told her I would find our boy and bring him back.

Now a hero has to have a weapon, so I rummaged around until I found a small hatchet we sometimes used for firewood. That would have to do. It was cold that night, almost winter. I put on a winter coat and fisherman's boots in case I had to do any wading, and, hatchet and flashlight in hand, I sallied forth.

The night was moonless, but brilliant with starlight and the auroras. The stars *did* ripple, like painted dots on a black cloth caught in a wild wind. The surf pounded. The Boomers, far out at sea, sang.

I made my way northward along the shoreline, the way Caleb had always gone. I knew where I was going. At Dead Man's Cove the tide was high, and the waves breaking in towers of spray. I had to make my way around the landward side, which must have taken nearly an hour. Then I trudged on and on until I came to an ancient ruin of a house, sagging to one side, as if the wind had nearly blown it over.

I didn't have any doubt where I was, whose house this was. I pushed the front door open without bothering to knock, and probed inside with the flashlight. If anybody was home, well, that was what the hatchet was for. No one seemed to be.

The first thing I noticed, inside, was the smell. For all the wind whistled through gaps in the walls, the air inside was close and stank of death and decay. When I found my way into what must have been the kitchen, I understood why. There, spread out on the floor, was the remains of a large dog, just skin and scattered bones, like what's left over when you've eaten a bony fish and scraped all the meat out.

And in the living room I found the very similar remains of what was clearly a human being.

Beyond that was a small room off to the side. Here a bare, broken-up mattress lay on the muddy, sand-tracked floor. But next to that, nearly folded in a cardboard box, were a couple pairs of cut-off jeans that I certainly recognized, and a tank top, and my old Philadelphia Phillies T-shirt. This had been Caleb's room. He had definitely lived here. Next to the clothes was another box filled with manga and comic books that Jackie had no doubt given him.

There was no sense searching further. In the living room, near to the flayed man, a dozen or so books, some of them quite old-looking and quite thick, lay piled on a broken table. There were also a few flyers and leaflets. I could make out the words ESOTERIC ORDER with the flashlight. It was only some while later that I returned to the house and took some of those books and read the ones I could. Some were in languages I could not even begin to identify.

I found Caleb waiting for me back at the Cove. He stood waist-deep in the frigid water, naked. Behind him, a fog was coming in. The Boomers or Heralds or whatever they were still sounded, but their light was little more than a soft blur. The surf was quiet. The tide was going out.

I could see that Caleb had begun to change. I can't really say how he looked. He was still as skinny and pale as ever, but most of his hair, which had never been very thick to start with, was gone. He looked a bit like an old man with bulging eyes, or maybe like some long-limbed, aquatic insect.

He was sobbing. A very human sound. He held my son's limp body in his arms.

I did not have to ask to realize that Jackie was dead, drowned. He was not naked. He was wearing, absurdly, swimming trunks.

"I'm sorry," Caleb said. His voice was that polite, little boy's voice again. "I thought I could take him with me. Only those who change and answer the Call can live. That's what our deacon says. I thought Jackie could come too."

He waded slowly forward, as if to hand Jackie's body over to me. I could see then that Caleb's fingers had mutated into claws, and there was webbing between them, and the sides of his neck expanded and contracted rhythmically. He had rudimentary gills.

Well I didn't care if he was sorry or what his deacon had said, and if I'd had a gun I would have shot him right there. Instead I hurled the hatchet into his face with all my strength. Hit him too. I think the blade only glanced off, but it left a big gash on his forehead. There was blood all over his face, rather shockingly (to me at least) bright red. Then he was gone, and there was nothing left to do but haul my son's body out of the water and take him home and bury him.

* * *

Not much more to tell. We are living, I have concluded from reading what I could of the books from the old Hutchison place, at the end of days. Other people seem to agree. Once it occurred to me that even if our power was out, it still should be possible for me to turn on the car's ignition and then use the radio. I searched the dial. I found only one station, on which a certain crazed preacher and wannabe presidential candidate was saying that God had visited his wrath upon us because we had tolerated gay marriage, and Jesus wanted us to kill all the homos. I flicked it off. I certainly didn't want to spend my last days listening to that asshole. I'd rather come to my own conclusions.

It's mostly dark now. A darkness has fallen upon the world. I am not sure the sun still rises. My wife Margaret disappeared into the darkness. I heard her screaming, and something like a black trash bag with wings had fastened itself over her face, and after a while she wasn't screaming anymore, and several more of those things attached themselves to her and carried her off into the air.

I still haven't entirely figured Caleb out. Was he really my son's best friend? Was he as much caught up in the inexorable current of events as the rest of us? I gather from my reading, particularly from a celebrated account of the Great Persecution of 1927, that his kind tend toward a heavy, squat build. So was he some kind of hormonally deficient freak, a throwback to the more human part of his ancestry, or was he just too young, the Call forcing him through changes he wasn't ready for?

There are no answers. It doesn't matter. I cannot hear the Call now myself, but I have dreams of vast cities under the sea, and of an island emerging into gray daylight amid heaving seas, and of vast potency stirring in the darkness of a tomb.

Not in the Card Catalog

Nick Blackburn had actually seen an apparition in the library as a young man. He told me about it. He told me everything before the end. He was twenty back then, and a student working as a library assistant as part of his studies, and one night he happened to be in the farthest reaches of the periodical stacks on the fourth floor just a few minutes before closing, when he glimpsed a sudden motion out of the corner of his eye. He glanced down an aisle, and saw someone, or *something*. It was very odd. A human figure, yes, a person, but there must have been something wrong with his vision, or the air, because the figure seemed out of focus somehow, and strangely garbed, and there was something about the face which wasn't right, although he couldn't say precisely how it wasn't right.

When those eyes met his he froze. He could have sworn his heart stopped, but of course it did not. Nevertheless, he hesitated, like a deer caught in headlights, and in an instant the other was gone. Only several seconds later did he come back to himself sufficiently to make his way down that aisle, which opened into a little study section—some chairs around the table—and he called out, "Hello? Anyone here? We're closing in two minutes. You'd better get downstairs right away or you will be locked in."

There was no sound. He searched around, then shrugged, assuming the person had gone downstairs. It was only when he returned to the open section that he noticed on the table a book that didn't belong there, or in this section at all. This was a large, thick codex, lying open: very old, it looked at a glance, possibly even handwritten, not printed; a manuscript book, on vellum. The pages were very thick and a faded gray in color. It certainly wasn't a bound volume of *Harper's Magazine* or even the *Arkham Advertiser,* which would have belonged in periodicals. It looked like a stray from the rare and restricted collection, but there were very strict rules about such things, and his first thought was that he could get in quite a lot of trouble for allowing something like that to be left lying about.

Then he heard distinct footsteps among the stacks, and went off in pursuit of the late lingerer. It was always a concern at Miskatonic that people would attempt to conceal themselves after closing and make off with some treasure.

This was decidedly odd. He was certain that he was led away from the book, halfway around the floor, then back. When he saw the book again it was closed, and there was something even odder about the binding. It almost looked as if a pair of disembodied, skeletal hands had been set into the leather somehow and were holding the book shut with intertwining fingers.

When he went to pick it up, to check its number to see where it belonged, he somehow couldn't. That was hard to explain too. It was almost as if he was in a dream, the way you can be running in place, unable to move or escape a pursuer no matter how hard you try. He reached, and his hand could not get there, and then the book was simply gone, as if he had dreamt the whole thing and now awakened.

This was a long time ago, as I've said. 1972, to be precise. The times being what they were, Nick actually said aloud to himself, "Wow, what have I been smoking?"

And again he heard something moving, though now it sounded more like a rat scurrying along a shelf. He looked around, found nothing, and went downstairs.

Of course he hadn't been smoking anything. Smoking was strictly forbidden in the library.

It was only much later that he actually asked the formidable head librarian, Mrs. Hoag, "Is this place haunted?"

She was sitting at her desk as he spoke, and she put down a folder she'd been going through and glared at him over her glasses. "Mr. Blackburn," she said, "this library is famous for its restricted collections. Half the world knows we have the *Necronomicon* here under lock and key. There have been, it will be admitted, strange things that have happened here, notably a ghastly incident back in the 1920s. There are of course legends. This is precisely the sort of place one expects to be haunted. If we let in tourists, they'd demand it. But we are serious workers here and we do not have time for hauntings."

You will note that she had not explicitly denied the possibility of hauntings, only stated her—and ideally his—lack of interest in them.

I should say a word or two about Mrs. Hoag. Nick Blackburn certainly did. She was old even then. No one knew how old. She was apparently a widow, and rumored to be either the daughter or the granddaughter of that Professor Armitage who had been involved in the "ghastly incident" back in the 1920s, in which someone had died horribly, right inside the library, or so the story went.

Mrs. Hoag was an iron-gray woman who kept strictly to herself, never spoke of her background or inquired of anyone else's, and ran the library like an empress, very much *her* way, allowing no deviation. In fact, she had resisted such modernities as computers or an electronic catalog until very late, into the twenty-first century; as a result the old card catalog is still there—but I am getting ahead of myself. Despite her rigidity and her aspect, Nick told me, people who worked there respected her. She was far more than a tyrant or an administrator or someone who shelved books. She was an accomplished scholar in several esoteric fields, and once in a great while, if you were around her often enough, she could discourse brilliantly on precisely the kind of forbidden lore you would expect someone who had control of the Miskatonic collection to have mastery of. Cosmic, mind-blowing stuff. You see, *some* of the place's reputation was and always had been fully justified. There's even a celebrated account, if you know where to look for it, of what precisely happened in the library back in 1928 and why the carpet in that spot always seems inexplicably stained and moldy, no matter how many times it is replaced—but I digress. Mrs. Hoag could be fascinating. She could proffer just enough hints to open vast vistas—Nick never knew if that was her intent, though he said she was always careful not to do any *harm*, not to tell anyone, particularly impressionable undergraduate students, how to actually *do* anything.

Suffice it to say that Mrs. Hoag could be open to the idea of strangeness, and she took seriously her assigned task of keeping the lid on much of it.

But this evening, she had no time for ghosts, it seemed. There was nothing more to be said. Nick went home.

That was his first encounter, he told me later, with *The Book of Undying Hands*. The reason he had been unable to lay his own hands on it, much less read any of it, was, as he curiously phrased it, that the book wasn't "ready" for him yet.

Now fast-forward thirty years. In that much time, one moves on through life. I had become a professor—English literature; there's far more to study at Miskatonic than medieval metaphysics—and by the age of fifty-something had become fat and balding, divorced, childless, and, I suppose, rather staid. After working at several other colleges around the country and an exchange sojourn at Oxford, I found myself on the faculty of my old alma mater, with little more to look forward to than several more years of half-interested students (and the occasional bright one), the publication of a few more books that nobody would read, and retirement.

Nick Blackburn, on the other hand, had led a colorful life, as much as I had been able to gather the details. His family was mysteriously wealthy—and just plain mysterious—and so after getting his degree he had managed a several-years-long "tour" around the world, in the course of which—we had been friends, though not especially close—I lost touch with him entirely. He apparently wandered off the tourist routes several times and joined some sort of lodge or secret society that had branches in Bucharest and Prague and other far more distant places, including, so I am told, Borneo. (In the course of this he'd picked up half a dozen languages with enviable ease.) He'd once nearly gotten himself into considerable trouble in Tibet, when he made friends with certain black magicians of the Bonpo sect, something his Communist minders *really* didn't want him meddling in. Police had tried to grab him in a cave, but he'd fled under a mountain with the other magicians, and there were some difficult-to-follow descriptions of "angles" and "planes" and a "gate" through which he not only evaded arrest but turned up, inexplicably, a month later, in Nepal, where a combination of family influence and his credit card "burning white hot" got him home in one piece.

We renewed our acquaintance when he returned to Miskatonic. That was the irony, wasn't it? Here he'd done this Indiana Jones act all around the world, in genuinely remote and exotic locales, and developed an involvement in the occult such as the popular stereotype would expect from a Miskatonic grad—I did not slip when I wrote "the other magicians" above, for by now he surely counted himself as one of them—and when it was all over, here he was back in Arkham, *working in that same library*, middle-aged, largely friendless, with most of his family fortune gone.

We used to go out for drinks together.

I felt like a character in a story. Settle down in an exclusive gentleman's club or some weird tavern, get a few drinks into my well-traveled colleague, and he would start telling one of his incredible yarns, which you didn't know whether to believe or not.

"It was in Tibet, in the month under the mountain, that I found the book again," he said.

"What book?"

"What book do you think? *The* book. *The Book of Undying Hands.* Oh, it wasn't the same, but I recognized it all right. The first time I saw it, when I was a kid, it looked like a medieval codex, with covers as massive as a castle door, pages of stiff vellum, exactly what I would have expected at the time. But in Tibet it was like a road map that folded out in a zigzag pattern. But it still had the hands. Not the same hands, but hands, these were withered and yellow, probably those of some late member of the fellowship, who were called Black Monks of Tsa-Neng. I touched those hands, and they yielded to me, meaning that the book was ready for me at last. The script was not the Tibetan one, or anything I recognized. The characters seemed to wriggle across the page like tiny snakes, but after a while they did something to me. My vision changed, and I was able to understand them, almost as if a voice were whispering inside my head. After a few days I could converse freely with the Black Monks in their own secret tongue. I could even understand what they were doing, when they wrote strange things onto the book's blank pages."

"Now wait a minute," I said. "Do you mean that this is a *contemporary* work, that it is still being compiled?"

He took a long sip on his drink, ran out, and ordered another. Only after some interval, as if he were carefully trying to arrange his thoughts, and, as Mrs. Hoag used to do, tantalize without giving away too much.

"It is still being compiled, but it is by no means contemporary. It is older than time, older than mankind or this planet, I am sure, but it has the curious property that it attracts, then absorbs its authors, first fascinating them, filling their minds with incredible knowledge, granting them awesome powers so that they may gain *more* knowledge, but in the end compelling them, as its servants, to yield up into the book everything they have learned, until each one becomes *part* of the book."

"You mean it's an anthology, then? The Cosmic Omnibus of Madness and Sin, that sort of thing?"

"More like a Black Hole that's going to suck up the entire intellectual universe. No, perhaps I exaggerate a little bit. It is an entity in itself, not alive in any sense we could understand, but a *force,* certainly, something with a will of its own, which appears where it pleases and cultivates its contributors—not authors—who contribute the way a fly contributes to a Venus fly-trap, but willingly for the most part, because by then they are so much a part of it already that they want nothing more than to yield themselves up to its greater consciousness."

"That is," I said, "seriously insane."

"You may be wondering whose hands those are that hold the book shut, or open it when the time is right."

"I hadn't. But you're going to tell me."

"They are the hands of the most recent 'contributor.' The withered, yellow hands I had seen in Tibet were those of an ancient Black Lama. By the time I left, they were those of one of his younger colleagues."

"Eew. You mean the book bit the guy's hands off?"

"Don't be childish. He became physically, and metaphysically, part of the book and of the collective entity that manifests itself as the book. He therefore no longer existed in human form, nor had any need to."

"Seriously insane."

"From your limited perspective, certainly."

Outside on the street afterwards we encountered three men—I guess they were men—in odd, shapeless clothing, with what looked like flour sacks over their heads and eye-holes crudely cut out, as if they were on their way to a cut-rate Ku Klux Klan rally. They came within half a block of us, then turned down an alley. When we passed the alley, there was no sign of them.

"Now *that's* peculiar," I said.

"Not the word I would choose," said Nick.

I had the sense that he was not surprised at what he saw, and perhaps alarmed, but not yet ready to explain.

If you want to talk about peculiar, or strange, or believe-it-or-not, how about this?

Mrs. Hoag was still the head librarian. The students said behind her back that she was older than God, but she was still there, and the subject of her retirement simply never came up. Now she and Nick Blackburn were "thick as peas in a pod," which is no excuse to go all Freudian. No, she wasn't his mother figure. But he was not her naïve young assistant anymore either. They were colleagues. They understood and shared quite a lot.

It might well have been through his influence that she had yielded to modernity somewhat, although certain rigid rules still applied. No one ever took anything from the restricted section to a copy machine, and portable scanners or cameras were not allowed. There had been another unpleasant incident in the 1980s, involving *The Book of Eibon* (in this case the ineradicable stain was on one of the walls). The library had computers now, though, as I've mentioned, the old card catalog still remained, more a museum piece for most students than anything to use. I used it, though. I looked up *The Book of Undying Hands* shortly after Nick told me about it, and sure enough, it was not there. You could look up *Necronomicon* and there was a card for it, stamped "SPECIAL PERMISSION REQUIRED." For this other, nothing. I tried the computer catalog too. Zilch, as expected. That could have meant, simply, that the university didn't have a copy, I mean *the* copy, which was apparently well-traveled in its own right. It would have fit right in, but it hadn't found its way home yet.

Until it did.

This is where I enter the story, I am afraid, as an actor, rather than a mere observer.

I was the one who found *The Book of Undying Hands* in the Miskatonic University Library. I found it near to where Nick had, back when he was twenty, in the periodical section on the fourth floor, although not open on a desk as he had. It was stuffed into a shelf of *Shakespeare Quarterly,* spine inward, so I could see that the pages were indeed held shut by a pair of human hands that looked to be still alive. They must have been fresh. The book must have taken on newer contributors on its way here, because these were not the hands of some Tibetan lama, but of a large, strong black man. For a moment my mind raced, as I tried to think of any prominent African-American scholars who had gone missing recently, but I couldn't remember any, and maybe it hadn't been an American at all. This was crazy. I was accepting this all too easily, but of course I was *looking* at something completely crazy, and when I reached for it, there was something wrong with space or the angles or my senses, and I couldn't touch it.

I heard a shuffling step behind me, and turned around suddenly and there were two of those guys with the sacks over their heads practically leaning over my shoulders. There was something about their eyes. I couldn't see their eyes, just black holes. There was something misshapen about them. Their faces *wriggled* under the cloth as human faces shouldn't or *can't.*

As soon as I confronted them, they backed off, running away in opposite directions.

I ran after one of them and called out, feeling stupid as I did so, "If this is some kind of goddamn fraternity prank . . ." But in a minute I was out of breath and there was no one around.

When I went back to the *Shakespeare Quarterly* shelf, the book was gone. Unsurprisingly. Not that they took it. It wasn't ready for me, so it had moved itself, of course.

How easy it is to say that, once you understand.

On my way out of the building I encountered Mrs. Hoag. She must have read much from the look on my face.

"Is everything all right, Professor Gregson?"

I didn't know her nearly as well as Nick did, and I didn't know how much she knew I knew, or whether I'd be getting Nick in any sort of trouble, so I merely said, "Yes, yes. I am fine. Is Nick Blackburn around?"

"No, he had the early shift today and has gone home."

"Well, good evening, then."

"Good evening."

I tried calling Nick's cell phone and left several messages. I finally got him about nine o'clock that night. I suggested we go out for a drink. He said it was too late for that.

I told him what I had seen, and he just said, "Uh-huh, uh-huh," as if he were waiting for me to get finished so he or I could get to the interesting parts.

Then he told me what had happened to *him* early today, about noon.

He'd been working at the information desk when suddenly this *apparition* heaved up over the counter and damn near smothered him.

"One of those guys in the sacks?"

No, it wasn't like that at all. This sort of apparition was more the kind you get in big-city libraries, a massive, shapeless person, clearly a stranger to soap and to shaving—so the near-smothering was mostly from the smell—ragged and overdressed for any weather, and moving in such a way that he almost seemed to have something else, an animal perhaps, tucked under all that filthy cloth. This creature's—or person's—stained fingers held out an equally smudged index card in which was written the title *The Book of Undying Hands* in surprisingly neat and ornate script, with the authorship attributed to "Legion."

"I need this book," the person said. "I know it is here. I must have it. It is calling to me." Much to Nick's surprise, his "customer" was also able to pronounce the book's title in perfect Latin, *Aeternarum Manum Liber,* then in Greek, *Athanaton Cheiron Biblos,* explaining it had many names and titles over the ages.

It was not as if this was the sort of thing Nick was going to have right under the counter and be able to hand to him—unless the book chose to manifest itself that way—so the best he could try to do was stall and ask, "Have you tried the catalog?" and then say, "I am going to have to see some ID. Are you a student here?" though he knew perfectly well . . . and it was unthinkable that such a person would be a member of the faculty, this being a respectable college despite its reputation.

"It is *here,*" the stranger said. "I have *dreamed* of it. I will find it myself."

With that he lurched past Nick's desk, but was stopped in his tracks by none other than Mrs. Hoag, who actually held up some sort of talisman, from which the stranger recoiled.

It was obvious that there was long-standing enmity between them, as if they were ancient tribal enemies who loathed one another in their very being, and whose ancestors had done the same.

"Get *out,*" she said. She began to chant something. The intruder made grunting noises that almost formed into words, but became a kind of howling.

This being the middle of the day, there *were* other people in the library at the time, and they were staring.

She moved toward him, almost touching him with the talisman or whatever it was, and he all but melted away and practically *slithered* out the front door, or so Nick described it to me with only minimal hysteria and exaggeration.

He was so shaken by this that he fumbled everything he tried to do afterwards, so Mrs. Hoag sent him home early, which is why, when I was in the library later that evening, I had missed him. How imperceptive of me, when I met her on the way out, that I had not been able to tell that anything of the sort had happened. She had seemed her usual unflappable self, and certainly there was no ineradicable stain on the carpet.

When Nick had finished telling me this, we talked for a while, and then we hung up. I couldn't sleep that night. I couldn't think. I couldn't concentrate on anything.

An hour after he got off the phone must have been when he was murdered.

Horribly, the police told me when they talked to me about it. He had been beaten to an almost unrecognizable pulp, and then the bastards had *cut off his hands* and taken them away. I thought I knew why. I was *certain* I knew why. But it was not something I could tell the police.

It was quite late, almost 3 A.M. by the time the police were done with me, and by then I was certain of what I must do. I was certain the crisis was at hand, that things were happening *right now* or had *already happened*. What I was most afraid of was that it would be too late, and I had wasted too much time with police questioning, during which I had provided very little useful information.

Instinct told me to call the head librarian's office at the Miskatonic Library, despite the hour. I did. Mrs. Hoag picked up. I said I had something I needed to tell her at length. She told me to come over, despite the hour. There was no one around on the campus, not even security guards. If the surveillance cameras picked me up, so what? I doubt they got anything important.

As I got out of my car, I saw some of the guys with the sacks over their heads, standing up out of the bushes. I ran for the service entrance Mrs. Hoag had told me to come to, and she let me in, locking the door behind her.

By then there were figures wearing sacks all around the building, groping at doors and windows.

She took me into her office. The bright lights were on, and there, on her desk, open, lay *The Book of Undying Hands*.

There was much to explain and little time to do it. I told her what had happened to Nick, and as I did, I began to blubber, realizing now that he was dead that he really had been a good friend, one of the few I had, and I had lost a great deal. Mrs. Hoag let this pass, but said we must be strong. Nick would want us to be strong. The reason he'd been killed, she told me, was to *prevent* him from becoming part of the book.

"That's why they took his hands," I said.

"Yes."

She explained further that there were two factions or sects throughout the world obsessed with the book. One served unrestrained chaos. Their creed was sheer nihilism, their purpose the destruction of mankind and the world, either for the perverse fun of it or because they served some vaster, cosmic powers that desired this end. The other faction sought to understand and control the powers of the book. Its purpose was unclear, its morality ambiguous, its ultimate goals a mystery that, supposedly, one could only understand by full mastery of the book. *Only those who are of the book understand the book,* the saying went. The choice was between black and gray, between the howling abyss and shadows. The latter were humanity's best bet. The competition, then, was between *our* faction and the others, a matter of who could insert as much of their self-gathered knowledge, their very souls, into the book the fastest. The book itself was supremely indifferent, gorging itself on anything and everything whenever an adept of either faction was sufficiently prepared and worth assimilating.

"It's a matter of maintaining balance," Mrs. Hoag said. "That was Nick's mission originally. I sent him out on his quest around the world. You didn't know that, did you? He worked with me from the very beginning, from when he was a student. He never stopped. His was a brave man, Professor, and I am sure he was a true friend to you. Now your task is to hold off his enemies until I, as best as I am able, can take his intended place."

At that point I heard the glass in the front door to the library breaking, as if someone had gone at it with a battering ram.

Quickly she gave me the same metal talisman she had used that afternoon. She had written out several chants or spells on index cards, carefully marking access and stresses, because I had to pronounce them correctly if they were to do any good.

I heard things crashing, computers knocked over, furniture overturned.

"This is very dangerous," she said.

"You don't have to tell me that now. I've figured that much out."

"I mean we actually don't know which side the Black Monks of Tsa-Neng were on." She shrugged. "Well, I've got to try."

She sat down at her desk, turned the pages of the book until she came to a blank one, and began to write.

My job was to go out and hold the fort as long as possible. I found the main lobby of the library filled with shambling figures with shapeless sacks over their heads. They all had eyes like black pits. Leading them was a hulking thing, scarcely human at all, which could only have been Nick's "customer" from earlier in the day. He or it, I had come to understand, was a foul descendant of someone or something else, which had tried something like this once before, back in the 1920s in Dr. Armitage's day.

But there was no one as strong or as wise as Dr. Armitage to defend humanity now. There was only me. I held up the talisman, and the horde drew back for a time, but they recovered their courage and advanced. I shouted the incantations I had been given, trying to read them from the index cards. I dropped one of the cards. I retreated into the head library's office and moved a desk against the door, all the while chanting what I could, holding the talisman.

This worked for a while, but eventually they forced the door open and heaved the desk aside. I struck out with the talisman, pressing it into the face of their leader, who howled as his flesh sizzled and smoked. But it was not enough. The others caught hold of me. They flung me around like a rag doll, slamming me against walls and filing cabinets, and then the inner door which led to Mrs. Hoag's office. I think they intended to use me as their battering ram to get in.

The rest is pretty confusing. But before I blacked out I saw the book, on Mrs. Hoag's desk. She was not there. The book was closed. I distinctly saw the big guy, the leader, reach for the book, but it *vanished*, leaving him angrily groping at thin air.

He howled. The others lost all interest in me and let me drop to the floor.

Of course, when I woke up in the hospital some days later I had a lot of explaining to do. The police thought it very suspicious that I had been the last person to speak with Nicholas Blackburn, who was dead by extreme violence, and then I somehow got myself mixed up in this. Mrs. Hoag was missing, I gathered. There was no body. What was I doing in the library at 3 A.M. anyway? One of the detectives, speaking fluent cliché, said, "It just doesn't add up."

But there is at Miskatonic an *inner committee* unbeknownst even to most faculty members, which investigates certain matters. Dr. Armitage had founded it back in the 1920s. Once I explained myself to them, there were no further inquiries. The library was closed for a while. The damage was repaired. When I was sufficiently recovered, I returned to my teaching.

It was many months later that I found *The Book of Undying Hands* in the periodicals section again. It was open on the table this time. I was able to read a page, in English, in Mrs. Hoag's neat handwriting. I didn't understand very much of what I read, and I did not try to touch the book, much less turn the page, though certainly I felt the impulse to do so. I looked away, but not quickly enough to avoid noticing that the hands on the covers were pale and withered.

I forced myself to go about my business. A half an hour later, when I came back to that part of the room, the book was gone.

Down to a Sunless Sea

At the weary conclusion of a long and sometimes frightening drive I arrived, on a mid-autumn night when the world was ending, at the beginning of a causeway jutting out from the Maine coast. Winding roads and bridges connected a series of tiny islands to this point, where I beheld, stark against the sea and the mad, rolling auroras, the crumbling, almost Gormenghastine pile of Starkweather Manor, a.k.a. the Castle, below the towers of which, on the rocky beach, some Starkweather ancestor was alleged to have sold his soul to the Devil.

You may conclude that the family was not popular with the neighbors, in addition to being both insane and insanely rich.

Yes, *those* Starkweathers, no relation to Charles Starkweather, the spree killer of the 1950s, but the somewhat more respectable, tragic clan after whom the Starkweather-Moore expedition of the 1930s was partially named. You may remember that, or not. It was the *second* Miskatonic expedition to the Antarctic, the one that disappeared without a trace—although there are contradictory reports on even that—but before there could be much follow-up the Depression, gangsters, and the rise of Hitler crowded it out of the headlines. Nathaniel Starkweather, the current heir, lost his grandfather (Matthias Starkweather) in that expedition. His father, Joseph Starkweather, a noted scholar, sometime professor, eccentric, and lunatic, became so convinced that voices from the sky were calling him to another planet that he tried to fly from a parapet and died with a splat on the very beach where his remote forebear had met the Devil.

What is missing from this picture is that I had been perhaps Nathaniel Starkweather's only boyhood friend, back in the days when my own father (Ph.D., Harvard; Dept. of Ancient Languages, Miskatonic), who was also nuts but not nearly as wealthy, was working with Joseph

Starkweather on some translation project which, the only time I ever saw any of their papers, looked like gibberish but got me severely punished for even glancing at it. That aside, my father's extended "sabbaticals" and our summer-long visits to the Starkweather abode hold mostly pleasant memories for me. Nathaniel and I were both eleven when it started, and fortunately we got along famously. He showed me the secrets of the house and island (yes, there really was a mummy case and an iron maiden in the basement, but the latter had no spikes), and I thought it was really neat to be best friends with a real-life Pugsley Addams. He actually had the kind of chemistry set that enabled him to blow things up on the beach. If his house was filled with trapdoors and mysterious voices and very likely haunted, that was fine with me too.

My mother was dead by then. His mother was dead by then. We became very close.

Later, when we went to different colleges, we stayed in touch, mostly by email, swapping elaborate fantasies and imaginary adventures back and forth, signing ourselves with nonsense names like "Zebo Von Starkraving" and "Le Comte de Droolebuckette." He also signed himself, with increasing frequency, "Roderick Usher."

Yes, we both saw the parallels.

That was why, like the protagonist in the Poe story, I could not refuse when I received a message from him that contained not a hint of "fantastic progress made, revelations at hand, madness to follow" but a simple, "Come at once. I need you."

After college, life happened. We did not see each other often. In keeping with the scholarly traditions of both our families, Nathaniel deigned to teach at Miskatonic, where his career was, so I gathered, short, dramatic, and highly controversial, after which he retired back home and became a wealthy eccentric.

Maybe now, at the end of things, there is something to be said for eccentric, reclusive, bachelor New England scholars after all.

I, on the other hand, had gone the more conventional route. After some youthful attempts at decadent aestheticism and two books of poetry that sold at least a dozen copies each, I settled down to the life of a professor of nineteenth-century literature at Columbia. Married and divorced. Two grown sons.

Nevertheless, when I was summoned, I came, and so I made my way very carefully in the dark along that causeway, well aware that there was no guardrail, that a slip might not drown me right away because the tide was out and the sea bottom was rocky (do they have quicksand in Maine?), but I could end up with the car hopelessly stuck. What with the world ending, I didn't think I could call Triple-A and a tow-truck.

I had driven up from New York, first calling my sons in Seattle and Austin to make sure they were all right. I wasn't sure where my ex was.

New Haven was burning when I went through it, and somewhere in Rhode Island a band of crazy people in streaming, yellow, tattered costumes swarmed out of the woods onto the highway and scratched up the sides of my car with knives, but I swerved to avoid most of them, and if I knocked over a couple, I did not stop to find out.

The world was ending, yes. That was the night that Buenos Aires went off the air, for good and forever, as the black wave or cloud or singularity or whatever it was that was spreading out from the rapidly warming South Pole got that far, moving inexorably toward the Equator.

My friend Nathaniel had his own theories about that, which he explained to me at length, but I am getting ahead of myself.

I drove carefully until I reached the house, which loomed over me, a riot of towers and walls and strangely shaped windows, mixing everything from Moorish to Gothic architectural styles as imagined by that same Devil-dealing ancestor. But for one flickering light in a high window, which could have been a kerosene lamp, the place was dark. I wondered if the electricity was out.

But no, as soon as I pulled up to the gravel circle around the front door, the light above the door went on. I got out of the car and went inside. Given the sort of place it was, you would have expected a cadaverous servant or at least a vaguely sinister robot to greet me, yet I found myself alone in a foyer, an umbrella stand to my right, a large, broken wall mirror to my left.

More lights came on, and I was led up the front stairway. I had not actually been here in at least twenty years, but I caught glimpses of rooms I remembered: the "armory," which really was crammed with suits of armor, pikes, swords, shields, old guns, shields on the wall; and the "public library," the room Nathaniel and I were allowed into as kids, where the ceiling-high shelves offered everything from crumbling, leather-bound tomes to comic books. (Did the Starkweather family own a copy of *Action Comics* #1, containing the first appearance of Superman? Yes, they did. It was kept in a folder in a drawer. We both appreciated it for what it was and read it as boys, gingerly and with awe. Never mind the forbidden gibberish his dad and my dad were working on. *This* was impressive.) I was also amused to pass, on the stairs, a series of ledges along which ran a very elaborate model train line, which wound all through the house and had been used in our kid days to deliver books and or snacks or whatever between floors. There was a bundle of rubber-banded index cards and a pair of socks in a gondola car, but I didn't see any engine.

More lights flicked on, and I was directed up to the third floor, into a spacious room which had been at various times a dining room and a studio, and there, on a couch, silhouetted in the dark against a starry sky seen through an enormous circular window (which I knew could be seen for miles when lit up at night, and was known locally as the Devil's Eyeball), sat my old friend, whom I had not actually seen in the flesh in a good twenty years.

A small desk lamp on a broad table in front of him switched itself on. He rose, and took my hand, shaking it vigorously. He actually embraced me, and spoke a little bit tearfully, I think. "I'm so glad you came. I'm so glad."

A little startled, I sat down at the table. As best I could see my friend in the uncertain light he hadn't changed much. He was his familiar pale, thin, wiry, nervously energetic self with a lock of still dark hair that kept falling over his face and bug eyes. I, on the other hand, had started to grow fat and bald. I now seemed many years his senior. I suppose time abuses us all differently.

Another light flicked on and I saw that a meal had been laid out.

Nothing special. Just some kind of pre-packaged, microwaved dinner and a glass of wine. There was only one place set. Nothing for him.

"Let me guess," I said, speaking in my best Bela Lugosi voice, "You never drink . . . wine."

Given that a third of the globe had already been devoured by an impenetrable, spreading void that showed no sign of slowing down, despite what government scientists claimed, despite what the thousands of hysterical radio preachers shrieked about the judgment of God, maybe a little macabre levity was in order.

But Nathaniel merely said, "No, really, I already ate, and I figured after your long drive . . ."

"The rest stops were all closed. Fortunately I had a full tank of gas. You're right, though. There were no restaurants open."

"Actually, I do drink wine. Probably too much." He reached into the darkness and produced an open bottle and a glass.

I ate in silence for a while. I listened to the house. I knew he wanted me to do that. He listened too. I heard creakings and groanings. The wind seemed to be picking up outside, though I could see through the Eyeball that the sky was clear and moonless. The auroras still waved and flickered, sometimes in colors that were almost impossible to define.

From somewhere came a sound a little like a cat yowling, but there almost seemed to be words.

"So tell me, my dear Droolebuckette," he said suddenly. "What do you think is going on?"

"We're sitting here. I'm having dinner."

"Very funny. With the world. You know what I mean."

"No idea, really. Martians? Sinners in the hands of an angry God? Space-time warp?"

"Bullshit," he said. He reached for a TV remote and suddenly a flatscreen came alive at the far end of the table. We were not watching live reports, but something he must have compiled. First, footage of that impossibly ancient black stone city in Antarctica, as it had appeared perhaps eighteen months ago, in searingly undeniable plain view as the snow and ice had melted away. News reports of the new expeditions, flyovers, even attempts at exploration. This should have been enough to change human history forever, to totally alter our perspective of our role on this planet and in the universe. (More clips of scientific pundits, the Pope, and the Dalai Lama; the Chinese president claiming it was all an imperialist hoax.) The implications never had a chance to sink in. Soon thereafter, silence from the Antarctic continent. A spreading darkness originating in the mountains somewhere beyond that city. Attempted flyovers, which all disappeared. It couldn't even be photographed overhead from space. Satellites in polar orbits just vanished. They did not crash, burn up in the atmosphere. They were not shot down. They just *weren't*, as if they had entered another universe, which had no connection with ours. From higher latitude orbits, there were angled shots of the Southern Hemisphere that seemed to show some kind of eclipse. The entire continent of Antarctica was no longer visible. Speculation followed that the Earth was being swallowed by a black hole, which had somehow *awakened.* (That was what one of the more befuddled pundits said. The more confused he seemed, the more he seemed to make sense.)

Then there was footage of an Argentine warship firing missiles one by one into the great Nothing that rose out of the sea like an infinitely high wall blocking out the sky. The missiles streaked in. There were no explosions.

The screen went dark.

Nathaniel poured us both some more wine. We both drank in silence.

"Well?" he said, almost demanding an answer from me.

"I have no idea. I honestly have no idea." Of course, right under the surface of everything I said, everything he said, I was afraid, he was afraid, and I thought he was teetering toward hysterics.

The end of the world. As simple as that. No qualifications.

"Yes, you do. Your last idea wasn't too bad. Space-time warp. My theory, which is sort of like yours, but which is mine, which is my theory"—he was imitating John Cleese, Monty Python, the theory of the Brontosaurus—"goes something like this: Einstein or somebody said the universe is expanding like a balloon that is being inflated. Whether we live on the inside of the balloon or the outside, I forget. It does not matter. But what if somebody stops inflating the balloon and *turns it inside out?* Huh? What then?"

"We all get flushed down the cosmic toilet? What?"

"Maybe we just go out of existence. Or maybe there is something on the other side, some other form of existence, maybe even something wonderful."

"And how do you know this?"

"My grandfather told me."

Mind you, Nathaniel Starkweather's grandfather disappeared a good twenty-five years before he was born.

You might think the two of us insane, considering what followed. It makes about as much sense as the universe being turned inside out like a plastic bag.

That night my friend refused to say anything more about conversations with his grandfather. He cleared away the dishes. He shooed me upstairs to a bedroom I had never seen before, which had a huge bay window with a spectacular view of the auroras and a four-poster bed with curtains.

Somehow my luggage had been brought up, perhaps by a cadaverous servant or sinister robot or maybe loaded bit by bit on the electric trains.

"You must be tired," he said. "We'll talk in the morning."

I tried to protest. I couldn't get a word in edgewise. He had excuses. He promised revelations. I followed him to the door, but as he slipped out, just before he closed it in my face, he indulged in one more bit of macabre whimsy.

"Tell me, if you were whistling past a graveyard, what tune would you whistle?" he said.

"I think *Peter and the Wolf* is traditional."

"Try *Dies Irae*. Now get a good night's rest."

Then he closed the door, and *locked* it, which of course was only for dramatic effect, because there was another door at the other end of the room. I tried that one, found it open, and saw that a stairway led down into the labyrinth of the house.

A good night's rest? He had to be, to use a technical term, fucking kidding.

I would like to think that everything that followed thereafter was a dream. Or maybe I died in an accident on the road somewhere around New Haven after an encounter with cultists and all this was a posthumous fantasy.

Let me try to sort that out.

The first thing I did when I was alone, as any minimally sane person would, was try to get on the Internet with my phone. Unsurprisingly, there was no signal.

More surprisingly, there was a radio on the nightstand, and it actually worked. I turned the dial and picked up yet another crazy preacher screaming that God did this us because we failed to kill the fags, as it says in the Bible. There was a lot of static. I caught snatches of emergency bulletins. Someone somewhere had set off an atomic bomb or two or a dozen in an attempt to slow down the Phenomenon, as it was being called. No word on the result.

Maybe I fell asleep. Maybe I dreamed that I woke up and tried to call my son Roger in Austin, but there was no signal. I could only hope that he and his family had piled into their car and were making their way north.

Madman! It is without the door!

I paraphrase Roderick Usher again, loosely.

The Poe story comes to its climax when the supposedly dead sister has clawed her way out of the crypt and now stands, swaying, staggering, dying, right outside the door, the inescapable nemesis resulting from her brother's over-hasty burial or blunder or whatever it was.

He actually said, *she now stands without the door*. I say, *it*. There was no *person* waiting outside the door, just the entire Earth dissolving like an Alka-Seltzer tablet in a sea of nothingness.

But what happens in the *middle* of "The Fall of the House of Usher"? I had gone over this with my students many times. Roderick and his pal sit around in denial, having aesthetic experiences, futzing around with music, leafing through old books. I suppose that is what you might do if you know you are doomed, that your own death is without the door, and there is nowhere to go.

So for several days (or maybe I dreamed it, dying) we lived as if this was just a friendly visit between dear old friends. I suppose our minds were numbed. We were in denial, or else we were just past the stage of screaming and running around, because there was no place to go. That is the only reason this narrative has such traces of coherence as it does. As someone remarked, the certainty that you are about to die shortly focuses the mind wonderfully.

Yes, the skies were strange and the winds howled—the Phenomenon was doing something to the Earth's atmosphere, possibly sucking it all away—but we didn't go out. When I pressed Nathaniel to explain to me why I was actually here, why he had summoned me, the best answer I could get was, "Because I knew you would come. To comfort me."

Either that was incredibly selfish or very touching. If the world was doomed, if the Whatever from the Antarctic wastes was to overwhelm us at the last, he wanted to die alongside his best friend. Was that what he had in mind?

What could we do in the meantime except wallow in nostalgia? And wallow we did. We even reread that copy of the first Superman comic. We explored the house again. We got the electric trains going, clearing books and debris off the tracks in various rooms. More seriously, we entered the Secret Library, where we had been forbidden to go as boys, and rummaged through the filing cabinets, the bookshelves, and the desk. I am sure Nathaniel had done this before, or could have done this at any time since he lived there. So it was for my benefit, but most of what we found was indeed gibberish. I did open a thick folder of photocopied pages from the *Necronomicon*, the Latin version at Miskatonic. I could tell they were old, on clay-coated paper, the kind of copying that darkens and fades with time, 1970s technology. Our respective fathers must have broken a lot of rules and expended a lot of nickels to make that. Did it do them any good? *His* father ended his life with a splat on the rocks outside. Mine . . . I could not say what precisely had become of my own father, which is very curious, when you think about it.

The one interesting thing we found was a slightly browned notebook giving an account of all that happened, this story, even the parts I haven't gotten to yet, in my own handwriting.

Okay, here comes the really crazy stuff. What has gone before was realism, strict realism. The rest, I cannot vouch for.

    I am writing to tell the world, my readers, if there ever shall be any readers to come after—I am writing this by hand in a notebook because nothing electronic is likely to be working for much longer—one last pretentious literary effusion—I am writing to say that Nathaniel Starkweather was made of sterner stuff, that he was not some self-obsessed wimp like Roderick Usher who just lounged around languorously, awaiting his doom, but that he was actually had a plan. He was onto something.

    What I can't work out is whether or not we wasted precious time with all that languorous comic-book-reading, putzing about with electric trains, or rifling filing cabinets for useless photocopies of the *Necronomicon*. Maybe these things have their own time. Maybe we had to wait for a gate or a door—*Madman! The door!*—to open of its own accord. The cosmic cycles turn. The stars and worlds are aligned. Maybe we had to wait for that.

Meanwhile, the radio worked again for a little while, just long enough for us to learn that the Blackness or Void or Phenomenon was well above the equator now. Mexico had disappeared, as had Florida and much of Texas and Louisiana. It would not be long now. I could only hope that my son and his wife and kids had gotten out of Austin. There was nothing I could do for them.

Let us say that the end of it all began, it all started, when I awoke from a dream—or was it from a dream within a dream within a dream?—and I saw, in the dim dawn twilight, a man standing by the side of my bed. It wasn't Nathaniel. It was a stranger dressed in a heavy, hooded parka and other such clothing as would be appropriate for an Antarctic expedition. He held out in his gloved hands a stone, a five-pointed thing like soapstone with strange markings on it. He expected me to take it, and I did take it, and I looked down at it for a moment, and when I looked up again he was gone, though he had left a puddle of half-melted snow on the carpet.

I brought the stone down to breakfast and laid it on the table in front of Nathaniel. Over hot chocolate and cereal he explained to me what it was.

"You recognize it, don't you?" he said.

"They brought something like that back from the first Miskatonic expedition, the 1930 one. I saw it in the University Museum."

"This one is from the second expedition."

"The second? But nobody came back—"

"My grandfather did. He gave me one long ago. None of the previous explorers or professors had any real idea what it was for or what it could do."

So my friend told me a story that went back many years into family history. His father, who had failed to understand, who tried to force matters in a way they could not be forced, had indeed died of an ill-advised plunge. But Grandpa Matthias Starkweather, the one after whom the expedition was named, was *not* dead, although he was not, strictly speaking, alive either, in any conventional sense. He had uncovered secrets vaster than the human mind can conceive. He had been translated into another form of existence altogether, into another universe, and he had done this *with the full cooperation* of the Elder Things, those ancient alien beings who had built the fearsome black stone city on the slopes of the Mountains of Madness well before mankind ever appeared on this planet. Their initial contact with our species during the 1930 expedition was unfortunate, and ended tragically for all concerned. But later there had been an understanding. The Elder Ones could no longer reclaim the planet. They were too few. Their powers were waning. They had been themselves overthrown and pushed aside by later evolutions. What they sought, what the last awakened survivors of the disastrous 1930 encounter had been seeking, was the entrance to the *sunless sea,* far down below their enormous city—not merely in some watery, underground cavern like something out of Jules Verne, nor at the Earth's actual, physical core, which is of course molten and crushing, but . . . how can I express this? Imagine that plastic bag of reality that has been turned inside out, filmy, insubstantial thing that it is, floating on some vaster sea of darkness, and imagine that you can sink below it, through a tear or gap, into that greater darkness. Not the chaotic nothingness that is dissolving the Earth like an Alka-Seltzer tablet and utterly transforming the physical universe. No, not like that. You sink below material things, as into a sea, into a realm of pure dream, which only the most powerful dreamers either human or Elder have ever glimpsed: a place of gods, described in elusively ancient writings as Kadath in the Cold Waste or Ulthar, beyond the River Skai.

There, to be safe.

There, you sink down.

All this, as Nathaniel led me up a flight of stairs, and another, and another, into an attic or a tower and something beyond that. As we donned heavy fur garb, such as you might wear for a jaunt to Antarctica. He bade me carry the five-pointed stone in my hands. He had another one, just like it.

Sometimes I wasn't sure we were still in the house. Sometimes we seemed to be on a bare stone mountaintop, a plateau high above a wasteland of ice and snow.

But that couldn't be possible, could it? Two places at the same time?

"Maybe we are both insane, and dying," Nathaniel said. "Or maybe not."

There seemed to be a third person with us.

We were in a room again, but it was cold, and the walls were made of stone, and there stood all around us great, winged creatures. You know the description: radiates, half-vegetable, with a bizarre tangle of sensory organs, and starfish heads.

I think we *were* in two places at once, as, somehow, planes of space intersected, both in the attic and elsewhere, far away, in a stone chamber inside that black city in Antarctica.

The things around us were alive. Or some of them were. Others were just husks, empty skins, incredibly indestructible remnants.

Oh, by the way, New York just disappeared. Then Boston. I don't know how I know this.

"Grandfather brought me here many times over the years," Nathaniel explained.

The main reason Nathaniel had quit his career at Miskatonic and become a recluse was that his grandfather had managed to contact him in his dreams and appear to him as he had appeared to me, but for much longer periods of time. They had taken journeys together. They had had their own adventures. They had already ranged through time and space.

That is the part of the story that has been left out, even in this version.

The very last survivors of the Elder Race had given Matthias Starkweather the chance to come back and save his grandson, as the last representatives of the human race, and that grandson, Nathaniel, out of true and exquisite friendship, out of a love that surpasses understanding, had contrived to bring me along too.

Reconsider Roderick Usher. What if his heightened senses revealed to him far more than the terrors of the grave? What if he heard the angels?

But it wasn't like that. We were in Nathaniel Starkweather's tower, at the pinnacle of Starkweather Manor. Because of its particular shape, because of the way it seemed to reach up on some nights and thrust at the moon, the locals had their own name for this structure too, another part of the Devil, a somewhat different organ, let us say. But the term is rude and vulgar. I will not repeat it. Far below us, surf washed over a rocky beach.

Away to the south, the stars were going out one by one. There wasn't much time left.

But time had become confused. I was able to write all this out, even the parts that hadn't happened yet, and leave the notebook in the library, where the pages slowly turned yellow with age.

I am not entirely myself. Another mind touches my own.

It is not a human mind, but I am not afraid of it anymore.

Why this blackness, this devouring void? Grandpa Starkweather explained that to me. Remember that guy Danforth, the survivor of the 1930 expedition who looked back when he shouldn't have? Unlike Lot's wife, he did not turn to a pillar of salt, but he did go mad. He could never put into words what he saw.

What he saw was a manifestation of the Shoggoth Brain. Those amorphous beings that had overthrown the radiate Elder Ones continued to evolve. They merged together, their entire race, into one vast and godlike intelligence, but an intelligence utterly hostile to anything we could ever call life. And *even that* was only a manifestation of something greater. An animate, devouring Void. Danforth saw this rising up out of a sea of living chaos beyond the ultimate mountains. Mockingly, it wore *his own face*. He saw it open its mouth impossibly wide to vomit forth that darkness which would obliterate the Earth and the entire starry universe; that darkness of which Yog-Sothoth is the Gate, that which is Azathoth, the primal chaos.

Reconsider Roderick Usher.
Madman! It is without the door!
The Void has *come*. It is *here*.

Here's what we have to do. We have to strip naked despite the cold and *put on* those skins of the Elder Things, the husks, and merge into them, until they come alive again and we are they and they are we and we are altogether.

We have to run. We have to leap. We have to spread our wings, and swoop into the safety of dreams, down to the sunless sea, which lies beyond all physical things.

Maybe Nathaniel's father tried this once, but somehow did it wrong, and that was how he ended with a splat on the beach.

But I don't think we're going to have a second chance.

We have to get it right this time.

A Prism of Darkness

The last night on Earth of Dr. John Dee, Mortlake, England, March 1609:

He knew what was coming for him on the stairs. What he found fearsome about the dark was not the unknown terrors it might hold, or the fathomless abyss which he had come to contemplate more and more in these past weeks and months, but that he knew precisely what was there.

He heard the footsteps.

The room filled with a black mist. The candle on the desk where he worked assumed a strange halo.

Still as if this were no more than an ordinary visitation, he puzzled over a difficult passage in the Greek text he was translating, and jotted down some notes without looking up until he was done.

Before him, like a paper lantern floating in swirling black smoke, hovered a yellow mask, strangely fashioned, the shape behind it not quite possessing the familiar contours of humanity.

The eyes opened, and they were very dark, but somehow intense at the same time, like obsidian fire.

Remembering a play he had once seen, back when he'd had time for such things, he spoke aloud, *"Ah, Mephistophilis. . . ."*

The other quoted back at him, *"Stand still, you ever-moving spheres of Heaven."*

Dee laughed. "I hardly think so. I hardly think you have come to offer me that, my old friend."

"Am I your friend," said the other, "or your patron?"

He looked at the growing piles of pages before him, the fragile, half-charred copy of the Greek text, and the newly scribbled, growing pile of the English version he had worked so long to render. Yes, this other had commissioned it of him, when all his human colleagues turned away from him and laughed, or just forgot about him, as the king and the emperor had forgotten about him in his old age and poverty.

Only his new patron cared.

Or his master.

He looked at the pages. Even as he sat there, his palsied hands trembling, his fingers barely able to hold his pen, the pages seemed to increase in number *all by themselves,* covered with his own handwriting or something like it, as if the dark and forbidden work on which he had embarked now had continued from its own inertia, as if the book were *translating itself,* without any further effort on his part.

What was the purpose of the translation anyway? He could only wonder. Surely learned men could already read the Greek, or, easier still, a Latin version that was purported to exist, and this was hardly the sort of thing to be popular with the half-literate, rowdy crowds that finger-stained their way through broadsides and quarto copies of frivolous plays.

Surely the only purpose for such a translation was so that the content of the book, the thoughts and vistas and terrors that it contained, could be filtered through a single mind, even a mind as drifting, as failing as his own. If that was what was really going on. If the book really was, now, *translating itself.* He was no more than a focal instrument now, like a prism through which light passes. Or in this case, darkness.

"A prism of darkness," he said aloud.

Indeed, the darkness seemed to close around him. The candle's light lost its color, until it was almost gray.

The mask floated before him, and before him too, as if revealed from out of the folds of some infinitely dark, indistinguishable cloak, was a single pale hand, not quite skeletal, but thin, delicate, and somehow shifting before his uncertain eyesight like mercury made flesh.

"Are you ready to go with me then?" said the other.

"I am. I would see these wonders about which I have thus far only read."

He reached out to take the hand that reached for his. He slid down from his high stool, but his legs buckled under him, and he stumbled, and fell, and hit his head on something.

"Father!" someone cried. "Father! Oh, help him up!"

Strong hands took hold of him. He reached up to where his head hurt. A more gentle hand pulled his own away.

"I think it's only a bruise."

"Shall we send for a doctor of physic?"

"Sister, I am a doctor of physic."

They were helping him to his feet, and the deeper of the two voices said, "Can you stand, sir?"

"Will he be well?"

"I think we should get some wine in him. Then put him to bed."

"He's worked so hard at his labors."

"He needs rest."

Now they were gently easing him down the stairs. They sat him in a large, comfortable chair before a table. There was a cup pressed into his hands.

For a time it seemed that the voices around him were that almost bird-like babble-babble of the Enochian tongue, the language of the hosts of angels, which he had once tried so hard to learn. But, no, they were only speaking English, and he knew them.

He opened his eyes fully and saw that he was seated before the table in his own dining room, on the first floor of the house. There was no swirling black mist. The candles had no strange halo, nor had the color been leached out of their light. A fire burned merrily in the fireplace.

"Father, look," said his daughter, Katherine, who cared for him in these last years, "it's Arthur, come to visit."

"Back from school?"

"No, Father. From court. I spoke to the king some days ago."

"Ah yes, God save His Majesty . . ."

"Here, drink this." Someone pressed the wine cup to his lips. He drank, and it did seem to relax him. Once brother Arthur and Katherine were convinced that he had not injured himself in his fall, that he was as sound as he might be at such an age, they all sat together. An hour or so passed. They dined. He ate little. Arthur, who was a grown man now, not the boy who had gone away to school, chattered on about his attempts to find royal favor, and how, if he did, the king might send him to Russia in a few years.

"I'm not sure when I'll be back. It might be a while."

He understood what that meant, that he would never see his eldest son again. But then, he would never see his first wife again, whom he could hardly remember, because she was dead, or his second wife, Jane, who was dead, or several of his children, who were dead, so it made very little difference to add one more to that list, and after tonight, he knew, nothing much mattered. He wouldn't be seeing Katherine again either. Something about ever-moving spheres of Heaven, and voices that were not the voices of angels.

"This has been a very pleasant dream, and I am grateful for it," he said, as he got up from the table.

Suddenly the room was dark again, and he felt that darkness somehow draw away from him, as if from a small room in a wood and plaster house he had now stepped into a vast cavern without seeing that he did so.

Then the lights came up and he was in a place he knew, in the palace at Whitehall, and Her Majesty the Queen (whom he knew to be dead) sat before him in all her glory, and she said to him, "Doctor Dee, will you scrye for me?"

Indeed, all his instruments had been placed on a table before the throne, and there was a chair provided, and he sat, and he began to work his art, peering into his black Aztec mirror until he saw there the faces of his dead wives and children, and he saw many others he had known, who were dead, including that rogue and scoundrel, Edward Kelley, who had so cruelly used him and robbed him of gold, honor, reputation, and even for a time his Jane's favors . . . but that was all fading now, and he spoke to the queen of what he saw with the aid of his magic stones and mirror and crystal ball . . . and it must not have pleased her when he described monsters lying deep within the Earth, made of the very stone, yet still alive and dreaming. He told, too, of black worlds rolling in the infinite darkness inhabited by winged demons made of living fungus (but no angels), and of depths deeper still, wherein lurk such powers as have no concern for mankind or mankind's doings or mankind's imaginings.

"And what of God, then?" demanded the queen.

"I do not see him here, Majesty. With regret . . ."

There was a sharp tone in her voice, a rising displeasure, and he imagined that she frowned, but he could not see it because her face was like the mask of a porcelain doll. He knew she painted makeup onto makeup as she assumed her seemingly timeless, regal state, and wore at least an inch of it, so that indeed the pale mask through which her angry eyes blazed seemed to float in a room otherwise filled with black, swirling mist.

In time he rose, and bowed as gracefully as the infirmities of his age allowed, and, without permission, he left the queen's presence, saying only, "This has been a pleasant dream and I am grateful for it."

He only dared do that because as he turned from her he took the hand of the figure in the yellow mask, which led him into the darkness once more. Slowly, painfully, he climbed a cramped, twisting stair, and found himself again in his own study, in the upper story of his house, where the candles had burned low and the light had lost all color, fading into a dull gray, like the color of a foggy evening, as the night closed in.

He saw that the stack of Englished pages was substantially higher than it had been, and he watched the delicate pages of the Greek text of the *Necronomicon* turn themselves slowly. It seemed that in some remote dream, or other existence, he still sat at that desk and did the work, but his eyes only beheld the pages increasing themselves, and the Greek text turning, and the handwriting appearing on pages of blank paper, like some secret message in invisible ink, revealed by the heat of candle-flame (however colorless).

Said the other, quoting the old play again, *"That time may cease, and midnight never come."*

"But midnight has already come, and is past," said John Dee.

"Are you afraid?"

Dee looked around the room one last time, noting what remained of his beloved accumulation of books, and his instruments, after pillage and poverty had thinned the collection considerably.

"My life has been a pleasant dream, and I am grateful for it."

"Then come."

The last thing he saw was that the stack of translated pages had ceased growing. The Greek text had closed itself. The work was done. It would go on now, of its own volition, through the years, finding its own readership, transforming (or corrupting) souls.

Somehow he had the memory of *having done* although not of *doing,* as if some other self, in another dream had wrought and labored, and read the matter that was accumulated there, writing all of this into his own memory like a postscript.

He stepped forward, hand in hand with the one in the yellow mask, the one whose name and legend he knew, that Crawling Chaos which came down from the stars in ancient times and took the form of a man, and moved among men in secret, to subvert and to mock.

All this streamed and focused through his mind, like light through a prism, thought it was more an *anti-light,* not any mere absence of light, but something more active than mere darkness. In this darkness then he tumbled, as the other held him firmly by the hand. He fell among the stars of heaven, splashing among them as among glowing foam. Then there was more darkness again, and he saw shapes rising up around him, and he beheld their faces, serene and primal and utterly indifferent to him and his life and to his queen and his country and to all the strivings of mankind; beings that were both alive and dead, to whom humanity was not even a comedy to be laughed at, but *nothing* at all, and he knew the truth of what the book told him, that *these* were the masters of the Earth and of the Heavens, not Jehovah, not Jesus, not angels, that there wasn't even a Satan in that dark abyss to work his damnation.

He thought one last time of that old play, and how the sorcerer screamed "Ugly Hell, gape not!" and prayed that his soul be changed into droplets of water and hidden in the ocean; but here, in the sequel, after he had been carried off, there was no Inferno to torment him. No devils waiting. Yes, he saw the fires that burned at the core of creation. Yes, he saw how the Earth and the moon and the sun were all but infinitesimal specks in the chaos of the universe. He saw how spheres undreamed of by philosophers turned in spaces no words or mathematics could describe, and how when those spheres were aligned just so, the Great Ones would one day return and the Earth, its trivialities, empires and kingdoms, lords and philosophers, learned treatises and absurd plays by some drunk who got killed in a brawl, theology, geography, mathematics, poetry, would all be reduced to the same measureless, unaccountable dust.

And in the end, after he had sojourned for a time upon some black planet beyond the reach of light and there absorbed vast wisdom from the whispers of beings that were like living stones, whose voices were like slow winds whispering over mountaintops, the one in the yellow mask, whose name, among others, was *Nyarlathotep,* came to him at last and bade him take the final step, to complete their journey to the dark chamber in the center of the universe where Azathoth howls blindly.

So they traveled, descending through a tunnel made of swirling worlds and stars and dust, and they heard the demon drumming, and the pipers, and the howling, and before the sound became deafening, the other spoke to him again.

"Have you any regrets?"

"All these dreams have been a pleasing diversion. I do not regret them."

And they two bowed down before the dark throne and made their obeisance.

And even after that there was a kind of survival, a kind of duration, and he understood that the ultimate message of the *Necronomicon* had travelled through the prism of his own mind, through space to the end of space, and through time to the end of time, and now he could discern it at least dimly, in the very fabric of the cosmos (if that too were not also a dream).

And to his companion he said, "Everything to this point has been a lie, but I would have the truth."

"The truth?"

"Yes, that."

And before even those quicksilver hands could respond to stop him, he reached out and snatched away the yellow mask.

He felt an intense cold. Perhaps he heard a scream, or a whisper in the language of angels.

Perhaps he knew everything now. Perhaps he knew nothing. Perhaps there was nothing *to* know.

No Signal

When the time came at last, Edmund Marshall, poet, eminent author of books on natural history, professor at a prestigious university, loving husband and father, knew that, however reluctantly, he must leave his satisfactory life forever. It was an instinct in the blood, like what birds feel when, after flying north for so long, inexorably, they turn south.

Therefore he put down his fountain pen, gathered the pages and notes of his latest work in progress into a folder, then scribbled a note on the folder to his chief graduate assistant, "I guess you'll have to finish this," and placed folder and pen in the middle of his office desk. Handwriting manuscripts for someone else to keyboard was a privilege still allowed to tenured senior professors. Perhaps he would be the last ever to exercise it.

He paused for a moment, trying to organize his thoughts as neatly as that file, to focus on what he should do next. He glanced at the photo of his smiling wife and exquisite sixteen-year-old daughter, and thought that he should call his wife, not to explain, because no explanation was possible, but just to hear her voice one last time, to make small talk.

He felt real pain now, and something bordering on panic. His heart was racing. He was beginning to sweat.

He realized he couldn't quite bring to mind his daughter's name.

He snatched up the phone on the desk and dialed. The line was dead. Then, as he got his coat, he took his cell phone out of the pocket and tried that. No signal. Ridiculous, of course. Here, in the middle of the city, in the middle of the campus, there had always been signal, but now there was none.

All he could do was put the cell phone back into his coat pocket.

Outside, he noticed at once that something was gone from the world. A lot of his work, his field work, took him outside, and although his teaching position kept him firmly shackled to an urban office and classroom much of the time, he loved the outdoors and had a sharp eye for living things; but now it seemed as if the world itself were an image badly printed on a magazine cover, with one of the color filters missing. As he walked across the campus, he saw no birds, no squirrels. The spring flowers seemed to lack vitality, as if they were made of paper. If anyone greeted him as he walked, as students often did, he did not hear them. The sounds of the people around him faded into a dull static.

He continued on his way, like a salmon leaving the ocean forever, to swim upriver one last time to spawn and meet its fate. Only he didn't think this had anything to do with spawning.

He left the campus and made for the subway, as he would when commuting home, though he wasn't going home, not now. The token he dropped into the slot was, he noted with only minimal interest, featureless.

It seemed that there were no other people on the platform. Maybe there were, but they vanished in the periphery of his vision every time he turned his head. Any background noise, much less any human voices, faded into a murmur like the sound of waves that you hear when you're falling asleep on the beach.

He wished he could have fallen asleep, then awakened from a bad dream back into his real life, but that was not to be.

The train came for him alone. He stood in the middle of the empty car, surrounded by graffiti and faded, ragged posters for old movies and old products he vaguely remembered from childhood. If there were more stops, he was not sure. If people got on and off around him, if they talked and lived their lives, they were on another wavelength and he could not quite perceive them.

He tried to weep. He searched around inside himself for that emotion and could not find it.

The train roared and rocked in the black tunnel, but after a while even that faded into a susurrus of soft background noise.

No Signal

He could not tell when the train stopped. He had no memory of actually getting off, and was only aware that he was walking up a flight of stairs, past a broken escalator, out of total darkness into the gray, half-light of an utterly empty, cavernous station in which there was *no sound at all,* not even the echoes of his own footsteps.

He passed a newsstand covered with ragged, yellowing newspapers and magazines with curling covers.

Outside, it did not seem that hours had passed, that he had somehow made the transition from a spring morning into an unnatural twilight; more a matter that light, too, and color had been leached away. The cityscape before him had an oddly two-dimensional look to it, like some vast construct of cardboard cutouts on an amateurish movie set, feebly backlit.

The only thing real to him was the cold. It was very cold, and the air had a dusty, acrid taste. His eyes watered. His throat was raw. He put his hand over his mouth and tried to breathe through his fingers, as if that would somehow help.

Then there were people around him, rushing in the opposite direction from the one in which he was going. He pressed through the stream of them. They buffeted against him, like puffs of wind. Close up, he could see them clearly enough, but in the distance they seemed to flicker and fade, like shadows on an ill-lit wall. They were all, he realized, in flight from something. He felt their muted fear, their exhaustion and despair. One woman, very young, but dirty, haggard, gaunt, with a limp, motionless child over one shoulder clung to his hand briefly and said, "You will help us, sir, won't you? You will stop him from getting out? You will do it?"

He made no answer, but kept on, one foot ahead of the other. Ahead, the darkness roiled, like smoke.

Then he was alone again. The darkness closed behind him, featureless, with only the cutout buildings looming before him. He found a door. It didn't have a doorknob, but a crude circle painted where the doorknob should be; yet it opened at his touch. Inside, he passed through many featureless, empty rooms, rendered very slightly less than utterly dark by curtainless, rectangular windows, until he came to a stairway and began to climb, passing a door of the disabled elevator on each landing. He never paused, but continued his ascent because he could do nothing else, go in no other direction, as helpless as the salmon working its way upstream.

That woman had asked him for help, begged him to do what had to be done. He couldn't think what that might be, but he resolved to try. He *had already* resolved to try. That thought he had already formed, before any of this began. That much he could still cling to. He wished he'd been able to find the words to reassure her. Too late for that.

At the very last he came to a room which, quite shockingly, was lavishly furnished, like a throne room, actually cluttered with faded, dusty hangings and furniture and with vast crystal chandeliers hanging unlighted from the ceiling, and what looked for all the world like gold-covered mummy-cases lining the walls, only the faces on them were not of stately Egyptian kings at all, but hideous parodies, diseased, deformed, and lascivious.

And before him, in the center of the room was a great mirror, set in an elaborate fixture of black ivory, as if held up by two gigantic hands so finely and intricately carven that they could well have been alive.

He stood before that mirror, and he saw, reflected in it, himself, but *not* himself; a figure that had all the same features and even wore the same coat, but which somehow possessed that wrongness you can see in photographs of Hitler or Charles Manson, an evil that is not expressed in fangs or horns, but in something far more subtle, instantly recognizable but impossible to describe.

The figure was laughing at him.

"You must have figured it out," it said. "You must already know that he who overcame me once, who bound me into this mirror *for the good of all*, has been dead for some time, and the spell which holds me here has worn off, after a year, a century, a thousand years. Who knows? It does not matter. My reflection lived where I did not, lived a lie, dreamed a dream that might have fathered whole generations of *nothingnesses*, each suffering from the delusion it is real and solid and human, and that its offspring were real and solid and human. *That* might have been you. Or it might have been your great-great grandfather. But that's over with now. *Pfft!* All done. Sorry! Nothing you can do about it."

"Someone asked me to try," he managed to say.

With almost theatrically convenient coincidence, there was a large hammer on a table by the mirror. He snatched it up. He struck at the figure before him, which still laughed as the hammer seemed to pass through something even less resisting than the surface of a still, clear pool of water. There was no splash, no ripple, as he realized that he was *already on the inside* and that the reflection of a hammer striking the inside of a mirror isn't going to break anything. The other was already walking away from him, into featureless darkness, fading from view like the dot in the middle of the screen when an old-fashioned TV set is turned off.

At the very end, he rediscovered his power to weep, to rage, to pound his fists uselessly against the smooth glass. He even remembered his wife's name, and his daughter's, and for an instant, before he forgot it all forever, every last moment of their lives together flashed through his mind.

He even thought to get his cell phone out of his pocket once more, and try to call them, to say goodbye, and to *warn* them.

But there was no signal.

Come, Follow Me

"I long for Christ!" the man cried. "I long to see my Savior!"

He was delirious and near to death, but at least we could save his soul. Some patrolling knights had found him on the road from Damascus and brought him to our hospice, which was a station for travelers and pilgrims bound for Jerusalem. And at times it was truly a hospital, a place to bring the dying.

"Brother Physician, you'd better see this one at once," one of my fellows said, and I came. At the sight of the small wooden cross I wore the patient sat up on the stretcher and waved his arms so wildly he had to be restrained as he cried, "My only hope is in Jesus! My only hope!"

It was all we could do to get him into a bed. Then all the strength seemed to go out of him, and for a moment I feared that the life had departed from him, but then he opened his eyes again—that mad, terrified stare I shall never be able to forget.

"I *must* see Jesus," he said.

"Jesus is with us all," I replied, "but only saints see him in this life. Be patient, my friend."

From his sobs, from the pained look on his face, I knew I had said the wrong thing. I was being condescending, as if explaining something to a simpleton or a child.

Then he said something that troubled me deeply.

"If only I *could* still believe that Jesus is anything more than a tiny speck in the blackness of the abyss! You can't possibly understand. You have not seen what I have seen."

"Just pray," I said under my breath. "Pray for the gift of faith."

All the while my hands were working. The brothers and I got the man's clothes off—filthy, shapeless things he had probably worn for years. He raved. He blasphemed. We whispered prayers and tended to him as best we could. Comfort his body first. Then we could try to heal his soul, for it was evident that he had suffered not only physical injury but some grave spiritual hurt.

He wouldn't give me his name. I couldn't tell how old he was, so old and haggard he seemed, so ravaged. Worse yet, he was covered with hideous, stinking wounds of a sort I couldn't account for, as if some monstrous creature, like an enormous spider perhaps, had pierced him with a dozen poisonous limbs. His hair was clotted with foulness. We had to cut away most of it, and then washed him, and this only revealed bizarre, putrescent wounds all around the sides of his head, as if the top had somehow been sliced all the way off and put back again.

I and the other brothers crossed ourselves, knowing that we were in the presence of something demonic.

But still we worked, applying such ointments as we had, even if we knew that his physical body was very likely beyond healing.

By the time darkness had fallen, I was alone with him. The other brothers had gone to tend to other duties. I sat beside the newcomer, by the light of a single candle, praying softly. It was all I could do.

Therefore I alone heard his story. His lips had been moving for a while before I was even sure that he was speaking, and it took a while for his voice to rise, like the subtle susurration of a tide, only slowly forming actual words. It was as if he had been telling the tale for some time and I had only come in on it.

". . . can you *imagine* how it was for us, then, surrounded by the pagans like that, Turks as far as the eye could see, their campfires as numerous as the stars in the heavens? Oh, yes, on that hill we fought them for days, and every evening when the fighting stopped and we fell down exhausted, there were fewer of us, and fewer still who had any hope. Great were the feats of arms, I am sure, but no one is going to make any songs about them . . . only blood and shit and the screams of the dying . . . terrible thirst, such that some of us lowered rags into the sewer in the ancient, ruined fortress and tried to drink the foulness that dripped. . . .

"Near the end, when all had given over to despair, a select company sat apart in the darkness, gazing down from the defended height over the plain, knowing that they might live to see another sunrise, soon, but it would be their last. There was Jehan, a knight, and Ulrich, a knight, and Godric, who was Ulrich's squire, and a boy called Jon. No one knew who he was or where he'd come from. Even he didn't know. All they knew was that if they did not die cleanly in the upcoming battle, very likely they'd be eaten alive, their guts hauled out of their bellies and roasted as they lay screaming—for every man had heard such stories flowing freely from maddened tongues—or worse yet made into eunuch catamite slaves to the demon Mahound, which had also been whispered from rank to rank. Maybe some of the company still prayed, but it brought little comfort, knowing that the holy hermit who had spoken so forcefully of his visions from God and led them to this place had also conveniently managed to be elsewhere when the end came. The Greek emperor Alexius had also betrayed them, only too happy to send this unruly horde into Asia to die.

"Maybe somebody prayed. Maybe those four did. Maybe they abandoned all their hopes and all their ideals and prayed to Satan, and if they did, and if Satan had raised them up to this height and said, *I will give you kingdoms of this world if only you will fall down and worship me*, I think he would have had many who would have accepted his offer. When death is devouring you like that, you *see things*. There are *revelations*. When Jesus hung dying on his cross, what great, dark gateway opened before *him*?"

I forgot myself. I felt a combination of wrath that was no doubt sinful, and righteousness that maybe wasn't but was still medically inadvisable, and I shook him hard and said to him, "When the Lord suffered on his cross for the redemption of us all, I am sure he saw the heavens open up, and he heard the voices of the angels."

But the man on the bed only looked at me and said plaintively, "Are you sure?" Then he turned away, and sighed, "Shit . . ." and was still for a long time. I realized that, once more, I had erred. The one hope was to let all his blasphemies pour out of him like the foulness of a flux, and then, when he was empty of them, try to direct his thoughts toward the hope of Heaven. I prayed to God for the wisdom and strength to do this.

Meanwhile, I would have to listen to it all, to his despair talking, and try to forgive everything I heard.

Just then I thought there was something at the window, like the flapping of a large bird, and then there was a scratching, almost as if something had gone skittering down the wall outside. I got up and went to the window and looked out. I saw only the desert night. I closed the shutter.

When I sat down by the bed again, the man's eyes were opened, and he seemed entirely lucid, as if a fever had passed from him. With one side of his mouth upturned slightly, almost a snicker, he said, "You'd like to hear the rest, wouldn't you?"

"If you want to tell it, yes."

"All right then, Brother. Imagine that those four sat on the peak of that hill, their backs to the ruined fortress, the campfires of the enemy spread out before them, and then, out of the darkness, out of the air itself, came a voice that said, *"Come, follow me."*

I caught my breath and said nothing. Was he, devilishly, trying to bait me?

He laughed, softly, bitterly. "Don't be so shocked, Brother. I know it wasn't the first time that line was ever used, but it's still effective, don't you think?"

I didn't know what to think. I had the fancy that the man before me somehow *wasn't the same* as he had been a moment before, as if he were possessed by many souls, and now an entirely different one was speaking. I began to be afraid. I fortified myself with prayer.

He went on speaking.

"Now, imagine further that the *air itself* opens before you like a door, and flickering into sight is one clad all in streaming black tatters, who is definitely not an *angel* sent from any Heaven you've read about in your scriptures, but a power nonetheless, an awesome Potency, who holds out his hands and says, 'Come, follow me.' He reaches out to those who are lost, who are despairing, to think themselves already damned, and they *take* his hands, all four of them do, clasping desperately, and somehow they are wafted away. But I am getting ahead of myself. First, consider that company: Jehan, the pious and heroic soul, who really did give up his wealth and lands to come and fight for Christ and free the holy places. I think his was the blackest despair of them all, knowing that he would never do any of those things. Then there was Ulrich, the bastard son of a petty lord who barely managed to inherit the armor he wore and the sword he carried, and knew that if he wanted anything more in the world he was going to have to seize it for himself, *even this*. Godric, his squire, was even more likely to cut your throat for a handful of coppers than was his master. Jon, the boy, cannot be accounted for. A holy idiot, like the Hermit who had begun the whole farce. Perhaps he too saw visions. Perhaps he still believed everything he had been told. You will have to admit, anyway, that this was not a very likely lot for an apparition to single out, but who knows the ways of ghosts and presences that float in the air? It was to those four that the thing came, and those four who were borne up, walking in the air like drifting smoke. For a time they soared over the plain, looking down on the campfires of the Turks. Then they were among the clouds, and, later still, on solid earth again, making their way across deserts and rocky plains, over mountains, through windswept and ragged and sometimes frozen landscapes like nothing any of them had ever seen before. Sometimes their mysterious guide was with them. Sometimes he walked right beside them, and even broke bread with them, for somehow, like Elijah supplied by ravens in the wilderness, they were never without food. Sometimes he hovered in the air, in the darkness, unseen, but present all the same, filling their minds with terrible, waking dreams in which they saw before them, across a realm of impenetrable darkness, a black tower that rose into the stars, and there was *one* light in the window there, high above the world, and somehow they knew that within that lofty chamber atop the tower above the world there sat one who was not a man but far greater, who wore a yellow, silken mask that moved strangely as he spoke, one who would answer all their questions and reveal to them all secrets and every purpose.

"It was the boy Jon who wept for Jerusalem, who tried to run away and turn back, but could not, for the others, or perhaps even the dark companion seized hold of him and would not let him go.

"It was Jehan, the true believer, who swore that he would learn all the secrets of this demon in the silken mask, but not bow down to it, or to anything of darkness, instead turning from there, armed with all the magic and power of that place, to conquer all of further Asia for Christ.

"To him the dark one said only, *'If this notion comforts you, dream it a little longer.'*

"Ulrich and Godric were probably only looking for something to steal, and concerned more than anything else with the fact that they were still alive, while their fellows with whom they had journeyed and suffered and prayed and fought for so long were being disemboweled and devoured or gelded and buggered by the Turks. Men like that live only for the instant. They let causes and purposes come as they will. They did not worry about the fate of their souls. Are they not perhaps the wiser?

"Don't answer. You cannot answer. You were not there. You did not cross thousands of leagues, to those places where the map says 'Here there be monsters' or shows the Paradise Terrestrial—beyond them, even, into unknowable darkness and distance. What perils did they face? What savage peoples did they encounter? How were they preserved against all odds, if not by an angel with a flaming sword? No, not an angel. A flaming sword, maybe. Four distinct Elijahs in the wilderness. The black ravens came to them, and spoke to them in ancient tongues, which somehow, gradually in their dreams, they came to understand.

"In the end they came, yes, for unimaginable purpose, to that black tower they had seen in their dreams, which stands above the Plateau of Leng near to the world's edge. Words are not adequate to describe what they experienced. Perhaps winged presences from out of the darkness, things in nothing resembling human shape, raised them up, piercing them obscenely with manifold, misshapen limbs, so that their fates were ultimately even worse than those of their abandoned comrades, who were merely savaged by the Turks. I say to you that in a swimming red vision of pain, each of them was indeed raised up, like Christ nailed to his cross, and they screamed out to Christ or Satan or

Mahound or to things that have no names that human tongues can speak. The four of them, Jehan, Ulrich, Godric, and Jon, saw the darkness open before them, and their eyes were dazzled by the light from that lone window, and they were all deposited on a black stone floor and caused to make obeisance to the godlike thing upon the black throne. Jon indeed did cry out to Jesus at this point, but no matter, *no matter,* ever again, for him or any of the others.

"And the thing behind the silken mask spoke to them, the mask itself moving strangely, the words forming in their minds like something rising out of the dark depths of dream, and it said to them, jokingly, '*Welcome, friends, who have come of your own will to serve and to be made greater than you ever could be otherwise.*' Was it *laughing?* Is there even a word that can encompass such a thing?

"All I can say is that at this point Jehan thought to reach for his sword, but found he could not move his limbs, for something like a huge crab or spider had pierced him obscenely and was *inside* him, and wore him like a cloak. Ulrich wet himself. Godric, who was actually far more treacherous than his master, babbled some absurdity about *making a deal.* The boy Jon went mad, if he had not been mad already, although his sanity or lack of it had no particular relevance. Certainly he screamed the loudest, squealing like a stuck pig as the thing on the throne *removed* its silken mask and revealed itself fully, flowing down onto them, like a centipede, like a serpent, like nothing anyone has ever seen outside of Hell, as it *touched* them and wriggled its way inside all four of them at once, and all was made clear.

"Were they borne up again, or was it some kind of vision, a memory the thing brought to them? For an aeon, it seemed, they hung suspended in space, knowing only pain, there in absolute darkness, until suddenly the lights of a million stars burst out of the darkness and dazzled them. They were borne, they and the winged presences that accompanied them, like specks of dust on some vast current, far beyond any heavenly spheres described by the philosophers, swallowed by a whirlpool of stars that spewed them out into that realm of chaos at the very center of the universe, where they heard the piping that cannot be described, and saw the dancing shapes that the eye could not follow. They and even their unmasked master bowed down before *that* which is called—words fail me here, only gibberish syllables—*Azathoth*, the *Supreme Discord,* which is beyond all light and darkness, all gods and souls and angels and demons, all worlds. There, there, they bowed down and were newly baptized into an obscene brotherhood from which there could be no defections and no faltering.

"And when all this faded, and they seemed to awaken from one dream into another, they went forth renewed from that hideous Citadel of Leng on a new crusade, to sow darkness and terror into the world, to prepare for the ending of days, when your Christ and your Satan alike shall be as motes in the vast, devouring whirlpool of stars that leads to the throne of damnation beyond all possible hells.

"That is why I *long for Christ,* Brother. Because I have passed beyond all hope of him."

At that, the speaker ceased his tale, and made a sound that was half like sobbing and half like laughter, and then there was a liquid rattling deep in the back of his throat that made me think that his death was upon him as he lay unconfessed and unredeemed. His whole body shook. He streamed with sweat and a black slime that oozed from his ears and nose, and from his very pores. I took hold of his hands and folded them together and, weeping myself, pleaded with him to think of Jesus.

"Oh yes, I remember Jesus," he said, "and still I yearn for him—"

"Good, good. Think on that."

I held up my crucifix for him to kiss, but he swatted it away.

"The servitors of the Yellow Mask walk among us, Brother. Not even your Christ can stop them."

"No! You are suffering from a disease of the brain. God will forgive you that, if you cling to hope. It's not your fault."

Now he became calm again, and once more, indeed, it seemed as if an entirely different intelligence inhabited his ruined body, and now I was trying to outwit—what? a demon? a madman?—for the salvation of this man's soul, and I knew somehow that my enemy was vastly older and *wiser* than me. Nevertheless, I did not despair. I disputed, with logic.

"Consider," I said, "that your story is fantastical. Impossible. It cannot be true."

"It is beyond anything you could understand as truth."

"No, wait, wait. Think for a moment. *When* did all this supposedly happen? When did you come to the East? You mentioned the Greek emperor Alexius, who has been dead for *fifty years*. His grandson Manuel rules in Constantinople now. And your leader, the one who absconded, that was Peter the Hermit, was it not?"

"Yes," said the other with a low sigh in which, I could tell, there was no forgiveness. "It was."

"Can't you see? It's been too long. No one could still be alive after so many years, not even the boy Jon."

"Jon is dead. There may be no deserters from our crusade, but still he did not serve us long. He proved too weak a vessel. He didn't make it back."

"Then which one are you?"

"Which?"

"Of that company. The four. Who had this adventure."

And again he laughed. "Not the pious Jehan, I assure you, nor either of the two scoundrels. Which then? Which? Ah, a pretty problem. It has a pretty solution—"

Then before I could respond he sat up with tremendous vigor, swung himself around, his feet on the floor, and he leaned over and seized hold of me around the throat with a grip like living iron. He could have broken me like a twig then, or snapped my head off, but that was not his purpose, no, only to squeeze slowly until I could not cry out as his burning eyes gazed into mine and I was dazzled.

I barely managed to say, *"Are you . . . Satan?"*

How he laughed wildly, howling, and he shook me and said, "Brother Simpleton, have you understood *nothing?* Well allow me, then, to explain all things in a way that will be clear, *even to you.*"

The impossible happened before my eyes then. His face began to flow like melting wax, and to assume a strange, elongated shape, with protrusions or bulges where no human face has anything of the sort, and he *flowed* out of his ruined body, sloughing it off as a snake sheds its skin, and with his manifold and malformed poisonous limbs he pierced me and *entered in* to me, sliding like a thousand knife-blades beneath my flesh as if to cut me open and gut me and wear the shell of me like a cloak. The pain was beyond imagining and the smell intensely foul, like excrement, blood, and decay.

Somehow I managed to scream. Somehow I managed to burst from the room, shouting that Satan was among us.

But it wasn't Satan, and my shouting did no good. All around me, my brother monks, and the hospitaler knights, and such pilgrims as were among us lay as if sleeping or dead. I didn't know which. I only know that as I staggered outside, into the courtyard, the air was filled with presences I could barely make out in the darkness, vile, ancient things hovering like enormous bees, their rapidly vibrating wings thundering softly.

I fell to my knees then. I tried to pray, to Christ and to his Holy Mother, but the Other within me, inside my own body, now spoke with my own lips, almost as if he were trying to comfort me, saying, *"Do not be afraid. There is no point. You are beyond that now."*

I have learned a great, great deal, though I am abysmally ignorant. Everything and nothing has come unto my understanding now. I have learned that Those from Outside, one of which now wears my body like a cloak, are mightier than gods, but they have their limitations too. In certain turnings of the stars they are all-powerful, and in others they *cannot live,* and in these times, moments, hours, intervals of lucidity like awakening briefly from a nightmare that never truly ends, I am once again myself, able to conclude this tale, to write it down, to hide what I have written before That which I have become discovers what I have done and my very thoughts betray me.

Quickly, then.

When the human envelope wears out, when it dies, as ultimately it must, however the influence of the Outside may prolong its existence, then That which wears it discards the shell and takes on another. Some trace of the former soul, the memory of the one who was before, remains. Such a preparer-of-the-way, walking unseen among men like the advance scout of an invading army, may have worn many bodies, and thus possess the memories of a great number of dead men. *My name is Legion, for we are many.* There was no problem with the chronology of the story, you see, because the one who told it to me was *none* of the four adventurers who made their way to the dark plateau. Fifty years ago? A hundred? It does not matter, for he was the one who *brought them there,* and *long* before that, *centuries* before, one of his names had been Judas Iscariot. His fate was far more terrible than what has been written about him anywhere. For a thousand years and more he yearned piteously for Christ because he *knew* what voice spoke out of the darkness when the sky over Golgotha opened up. He witnessed it all, and he understood, because that darkness touched him too.

Not that it matters. Not that anything matters. I yearn, but in vain. We are all swallowed up. We all bow down before the throne of Azathoth in the end, not of Jehovah.

That is all.

Come, follow me.

Odd Man Out

Later, Simon Harding did not remember whether it was dark out yet, or even if the sky was clear or it was pouring rain, but he was aware of precisely when the doorbell rang, because it caused him to get up at 7:39 P.M. (according to the clock on the VCR), clear his lap of his present project, and go to the door in the middle of a mildly interesting History Channel special about survivals of Hellenistic art in central Asia.

There was a woman standing at the door, breathing hard. She looked bedraggled to his inexpert eye, but maybe it was some new hairstyle. He had an impression of a pale face, long, extremely dark hair, and usually pale eyes—a light green perhaps. Possibly she'd been crying.

But he didn't have time to note many details because she immediately thrust a parcel into his hands and said, "Please. It would really, really mean a lot to me if you kept this. Just keep it. That's all I ask. I have to go now."

Before he could say anything she ran down the walk and was out of sight, blocked from view by the neighbor's hedge, and Simon was left just standing there, while the television babbled on behind him. He remained in the doorway for a full minute before going back inside, trying to make all this compute, because he wasn't the sort of person to whom things *happened*. Of course the thought crossed his mind that maybe it was a bomb he held, but he wasn't the sort of person who was worth blowing up either.

The only word that came to his mind, which he subvocalized, was *odd*.

He knew that he was an odd man. Nobody had to tell him that, though his associates and very few friends sometimes did. He was a slightly built, stoop-shouldered man of thirty-nine, with a round, smooth face that had always made him look much younger than he really was until he started to go gray. Until then even his appearance had provided him with one more excuse for not "growing up," not engaging in life; so much so that his mother had to scream at him when he turned thirty, "For Christ's sake, I think I gave birth to a *robot*. Don't you *feel* anything? Go get drunk, chase ladies, do *something* to prove that you're *alive!*"

But his mother was dead now and she'd left him this matchbox of a house that served his needs well enough, so his life continued on its undeflected course. He'd majored in classical languages in college and had given some thought to being an archeologist, but the opportunity never came, and so he'd drifted—by way of one of his very few passions, coin collecting—into a job at the Berwyn Numismatic Company in a suburb of Philadelphia, where he became the in-house specialist in ancients, designed and wrote most of their catalogues, and also developed a considerable reputation for the uncanny, painstaking way he could clean off dirty or encrusted coins, sometimes restoring into pristine (and valuable) condition what would otherwise be worthless lumps of metal.

It was typical of him—and odd, he would have acknowledged—that he put the package aside on the mail table without opening it (having concluded it wasn't going to explode) and went back to his work and his TV show, sitting down, spreading a towel on his lap, and placing his tools and materials—a combination of box-cutting razors, X-Acto knives, and dental picks, a wire brush, a can of a metal-polisher called NEVR DULL, and a little bottle of Deller's Darkener ("To cover up a multitude of sins," he would joke to his colleagues when, rarely, he joked)—and went right back to work scraping carefully away at a mass of metal and dirt the size and shape of a smashed plum, which did indeed contain what he hoped would be a very fine specimen of Sear #3293, a large coin of the Roman emperor Severus Alexander (A.D. 222–35), provincial, from Cyzicus in Asia Minor, with a profile of the rather baby-faced (passive, mediocre) emperor on one side, and on the other, Zeus seated in the center, with a complete array of the signs of the zodiac around the rim. It was the astrological interest that made this coin valuable. A nice one could be worth four or five thousand dollars.

That the coin didn't even belong to him, but was something he'd pulled out of a junk lot at the shop and taken home to work on, didn't concern him very much. Such restoration was what he *did*. Inasmuch as he had any trace of fancy or romance in his otherwise prosaic self, he liked to imagine that as he scraped and picked and cleaned, as ancient faces emerged sharply detailed from the dirt of centuries (Bulgarian mud, usually), he was reaching out and somehow touching people who had been dead for millennia, and was, in a small way, bringing them back to life.

It was an odd notion, yes, but he was an odd man and he knew it, so he kept on working well into the evening. Severus Alexander emerged from the dirt slowly, his chin visible first, then his mouth and a hint of the eye and hair, until Simon looked up and realized that it was past midnight and the History Channel was showing something about the Pacific Theater during World War II (a historical period that did not interest him). He *did* have to get up early tomorrow to go to work. An important customer was coming in. Therefore he switched off the TV and left the towel, his tools, and the coin on the coffee table in front of him (with piles of papers pushed to either side) so he could return to them with a minimum of effort, then went off to bed, slept without any dreams that he could remember, and went on about his business.

Later still, surprising himself with such an imaginative turn of mind, he remembered the *Krazy Kat* cartoons of George Herriman, in which Ignatz Mouse, madly in love with Krazy Kat, used to draw the attention of the object of his hopeless affection by hurling bricks.

And sometimes, if one brick to the head doesn't do the trick, a second is necessary.

The second (metaphorical) brick was waiting for him when he got home from work. In his mail, in addition to the usual bills, magazines, and coin catalogues, was an envelope addressed from himself to himself. He remembered that you can't just send an anonymous letter anymore, that for "security reasons" the Post Office insists on a return address, even if it says Al-Qaeda-in-America, Secret Headquarters,

New York (though he suspected that marking it SPECIAL RATE: ANTHRAX ENCLOSED would get you into trouble); so this was as close to anonymous as anyone could manage. He knew he hadn't mailed anything to himself recently.

He opened the envelope. There was no note, just a clipping from today's newspaper telling how Stephanie Ann Collins, aged twenty-eight, had leapt to her death off an overpass above the Pennsylvania Turnpike near Valley Forge yesterday evening at 5:30, splattering herself across the hood of a tractor trailer going about 70 miles per hour.

That was when the second brick hit. He could only let the rest of the mail slide to the floor, then sit down and say aloud, "But that's *wrong!*"

Of course it was the same woman who had come to his door *two hours later,* who had pressed the mysterious and still unopened parcel into his hands. He tried to remember a quote from somewhere, something to the effect that if you chance to attend a catastrophe, you will never recognize it in the morning papers. *Wrong.* The paper had it *wrong.*

Inevitably he turned to the package, and, with one of his X-Acto knives, opened it carefully. Inside, wrapped in bubble plastic, was a sculpture of some kind, very abstract or unfinished, done in some kind of soft stone. It reminded him of some of the very archaic, pre-classical Greek work that, as one art critic had put it, is "so primitive it looks modern."

He turned the thing in his hand. It was (perhaps) a female figure, rising from waves or out of the earth, a great mass of material waiting to be carved away.

Unfinished, he decided.

Now he actually *felt* something. His mother would have been proud, he supposed, but he was more annoyed than anything else, that his routine was interrupted by . . . what? Intimations of supernatural dread? No, the paper had merely gotten the time wrong. Some sense of empathy or even pity for this wretched woman who for some reason had come to him before ending her life? What was she to him?

He admitted that the envelope, no matter what, presented chronological difficulties. He couldn't deal with that right now. He made himself a quick supper, turned on the TV, and resumed his work on the Severus Alexander coin. The going was slow. The encrustation was hard as concrete. It was giving him prematurely arthritic fingers. About nine o'clock the X-Acto knife slipped and he cut himself rather badly. Cursing, he tried to stanch the blood with the dirty towel, but then, realizing what he was doing, put tools and coin carefully on the table again and went upstairs to the bathroom to take care of himself properly.

He couldn't concentrate much after that. He stared at the carving. He tried to read an article in a specialist journal, *The Celator*. He drifted back to looking at the carving. He thought of the clipping, which, he insisted, meant nothing to him, so little that in an act of defiance he set it on fire in the kitchen sink and washed the ashes down the drain.

He stared at the carving, or half-finished statue, or whatever it was. He was tempted to smash it, to throw it out in the trash, but he did not.

Realizing his evening was wasted, and that the television had been on for hours without him noticing, he turned the TV off and went to bed.

And dreamed, not the usual anxiety dreams, or dreams that break off their scenario as the dreamer tries to find a place to urinate. This was different. It was as if he were reliving experiences with incredible vividness, but they were not from his life.

He was younger. The girl with him was younger still, almost a child. They were laughing, holding hands, and running through grass and across a muddy path, barefoot—he'd never do that. He might be a sloppy housekeeper but he was personally fastidious. In his dream, she broke from his grip and ran on ahead. "Hey, Stephanie, wait up!" he called out, and he awoke with her name on his lips, sat up in his darkened bedroom, and listened to the silence of the house. Near at hand there was only the whirring of his electric clock. No creaking timbers. No mysterious footsteps. No howling in the far distance, not even the single, forlorn barking dog that is expected at this point.

When he couldn't sleep anymore, he got up, went downstairs, turned on the light, and spent a long time gazing at the crude statuette or whatever it was before setting down to work on Severus Alexander.

He made some real progress, though the work went slowly with the bandage on his hand. There was a heart-stopping moment when a huge, semi-circular piece of corroded metal flew off all at once and landed on the coffee table with a clatter. He'd closed his eyes out of reflex, but when he opened them and faced the moment of truth, he saw he had not destroyed the coin but revealed, in stunningly sharp detail, the whole back of the emperor's head, every textured hair visible. Part of the Greek inscription at the coin's rim was now legible. Yes, this was a very fine specimen indeed, or it would be if the reverse proved to be in similar condition, without pitting, just enclosed in its encrustation and not devoured by it. With a little careful work—now it was time to get out the *dull* blades, which could clean and smooth without scratching—this coin could be worth thousands.

He kept on working until it was time to go to the shop.

It wasn't *that* morning but the one after when he discovered the bare, muddy footprint on the kitchen floor. It wasn't his print, of course. Much too small, too slender. A *state of denial,* he knew, is what you are in when you irritatedly wipe out such a thing with the heel of your slipper.

He turned to the statuette, expecting it to be changed, as if someone else had been working on it, but no, there were no chips lying around it.

Too obvious. He knew, after another night of dreams that he was being haunted, or more precisely, meta-haunted, haunted by the idea of being haunted, resentful of the *intrusion* into the routine of his life. The absurdity of it all upset him the most. He was hardly the sort of shining, heroic sort that such a girl would turn to before (or after) hurling herself off a bridge into traffic. *Why me?* was all he could ask.

The dreams that night had not all been pleasant. Some involved being locked in closets or basements in a huge house, or beatings administered with rulers by hideous Catholic nuns screaming that the body is a vessel of sin. In these dreams he wasn't in his own body, not even a younger version of himself, but in *hers.* That was weird enough, suddenly being a (teenage?) girl, but weirder still, in the dream, he (she?) seemed to drift off into sleep-within-sleep (meta-sleep?) and dream a dream (meta-dream?) in which she (Stephanie) was crouching at the bedside of thirty-nine-year-old Simon Harding (the skinny guy with black hair going gray), reaching out to touch his hand.

Then he was himself, lying in that bed, and he distinctly felt someone touch his hand.

He sat up, alarmed, listening to the clock and the silence of the house, and that was when he snapped on the light, got into his slippers, hurried downstairs, and found the footprint on the kitchen floor.

It being Saturday, he didn't have to go to work, and there weren't any coin fairs this weekend (though he checked his calendar, just in case), so he sat through much of the day in his pajamas, whittling away at Severus Alexander. It was unusual for a single coin to require this much time and effort. The average dirty coin he could clean—or discard—within an hour. But *this* was special, not only because the coin itself was valuable, or even because things were going so well, but because he felt a secret, inner sense of release, even *triumph*—things he could never describe to anyone, even to Stephanie—and he caught himself with alarm when he had *that* thought. Who was she that he could confide anything to her?

Yet it *was* liberating, when the rock-hard dirt fell away, when the NEVR DULL, an oil soaked in cotton, darkened the impacted soil, loosened it, and clean metal appeared underneath. Something trapped was being set free. He had now pretty well cleaned the obverse, the portrait side, and done it well, without any of the bright scratches he would have to smooth out with one of his dull blades, then touch up with Deller's Darkener. Severus Alexander, aged about twenty (a mama's-boy ruler murdered by his disaffected troops at twenty-eight), was depicted in profile, gazing up at Simon sideways. Now it would be only relatively easy, patient work to clean out the spaces between the letters and get the dirt out of the emperor's (left) ear.

Obsession, Simon knew, for his vocabulary and his grasp of such concepts were quite broad, quite sophisticated, is when you focus entirely, completely on one thing, and go on and on and on—as when you work all day on cleaning a coin, sitting at the sofa in your increasingly smelly pajamas, forgetting to eat or bathe, shutting out any other possibilities but what you're doing. An odd fellow, yes, but very skilled in his special way. The vague outline of the reverse of the coin became clearer and he could see Zeus seated, and the zodiac spinning around him, and as the various lumps and bits came off and fell clattering onto the glass surface of the coffee table, there did not seem to be any actual diseased metal, any pits in the exposed coin surface; *yes,* this was turning out very well indeed.

No, there was not someone (much younger, with bare, muddy feet?) sitting next to him as he worked. *No,* when he finally got up to go to the bathroom—thank God he still had enough sense to do that—there were not muddy footprints on the tiled floor. (But to be sure, he wetted a paper towel and got down on his hands and knees and wiped the floor thoroughly.)

Downstairs the History Channel blathered.

It almost came to him that, yes, this is really crazy. He took a shower, changed into his usual around-the-house wear (running pants and a sweatshirt), and went downstairs to prepare himself a microwaved TV dinner, for breakfast or supper he was not sure. It was twilight out. The clock said 6:15. He was not sure if this was still Saturday evening or if he'd somehow slipped into Sunday morning, but being an odd person, someone who stood apart from the rest of the human race almost as much as his mother had berated him for doing, he was allowed his eccentricities.

Later, he fell asleep on the sofa and dreamed of Stephanie again—not that he *was* her, more that he was hovering in the air nearby; even in the dream he felt some relief at that. He saw her huddled in her darkened room, afraid, reading some trashy romance novel by flashlight. Somehow in the dream he knew what she was thinking, trying to imagine how some tall, strong, handsome hero was going to come and sweep her away.

When Simon awoke it was still twilight, whether morning or evening he was not sure, and there were muddy footprints on the bathroom floor. Somewhere in the back of his head he heard or remembered someone who sounded like his mother but *wasn't* scolding him (her?)

for getting *dirty* and being a vessel of sin.

Having a nervous breakdown was a phrase Simon knew, just like *been living alone too long* and *needs to have a life,* and numerous other clichés in which he was fluent, and to which he had equally rehearsed answers about being himself, living his life as he wanted, being an individual, etc. etc. But he did not progress all the way to *went completely bonkers,* because he clung to rationality, to a detail his *reason* supplied, which was that none of this actually made any sense, and therefore could not actually be happening as it seemed to be happening. (See *state of denial,* above.)

What he found himself doing, almost before he'd realized it, as if he were awakening from a dream, was having a phone conversation with a certain Sergeant Schwartz at the local police station, pretending to be Stephanie Ann's uncle Simon.

"I particularly need to know if the newspaper report is accurate."

"As far as we know it is," said Sergeant Schwartz.

"I mean about, specifically, the time. Five-thirty. Did she really . . . die at five-thirty?"

"Yes, she did. The trucker pulled over immediately and called us on his cell-phone. If I may ask, why does this particularly matter?"

"Because it's impossible, damn it! Because two hours later she—"

And Simon knew he had blurted out way too much, or, to use another fluent cliché, spilled the beans, which was more metaphorically appropriate than *really put his foot in it.*

"I think we need to continue this conversation at the station, Mr., ah—"

"Uncle—"

"Just in case you remember something more."

Suddenly terrified, Simon hung up.

Much, much later he had fallen asleep again, uncertain of the time or what day it was, he lay in bed in the half-light (or dreamed he did) and Stephanie was there beside him, very warm to the touch, and she reached down into his pajama bottoms and touched him in a way he had never been touched before *by anyone* and he awoke shouting in the throes of an orgasm.

When he realized what had happened, disgusted, he got up, took a shower, changed into a fresh running-pants and sweatshirt combination, and stood trembling in front of his mirror, trying to turn this way, that way, to go away, to stay, like a robot in conflict with its own programming.

Then, slowly, deliberately (and this time, barefoot, something he never did), he made his way downstairs and sat down on the sofa in front of the coffee table. He worked on the coin. He *finished* the coin, giving it a final smoothing with the wire brush. It was indeed a magnificent specimen. Not that he was a thief, but he had no thought of returning it to his employer, at least not yet. First, he went into the dining room, set Stephanie's uncompleted self-portrait sculpture (for he did not doubt that was what it was) on the table, and then laid the coin down in front of the statue, like an offering to a household deity.

But there was no response to that, so he spread out his tools once more and, selecting the appropriate razor-knife, began to carve the soft stone. He was *not* afraid that he would wreck it. His hands seemed to know what they were doing. *He* had never shown any particular artistic talent—cleaning coins was as close as he got—but now, as he watched, almost detachedly, he shaped the stone into a likeness of Stephanie, whom he had seen in life only once, briefly, whose photograph in the paper he had burned and washed down the sink, but whom he felt, from his dreams, he knew more intimately than he knew any other person.

The phone rang. He reached for it. It was Stephanie.

"Do you love me?" she asked.

He couldn't answer.

"Don't say anything. Just think it."

She was emerging, like a living thing wriggling out of mud, out of the shapeless mass of stone that was not Stephanie. He remembered the old joke—or maybe it was something a famous sculptor actually said—about how you chip away everything that isn't the statue.

There was a pile of stone chips on the table now, some on the floor, some in his lap. The work was going beautifully.

For a moment, an impossible, terrifying moment, it almost seemed that the thing moved in his hands, was warm, almost hot to the touch, and the face turned toward him and *opened its eyes.*

He ran more definitions through his mind, starting with *losing touch with reality.*

The phone rang again. He picked up. It was his boss, asking where the hell he was, as this was not Saturday or Sunday but the following *Thursday* and he was undecided whether to fire Simon or put in a missing person report.

"I'm terribly busy right now," Simon said, and hung up.

He worked at a steady, obsessive pace. Memories of things he had never lived, never experienced flooded through his mind, some good, some terrible.

She was coming alive in his hands. He heard her now, upstairs in the bathroom. He heard the soft patter of her bare feet as she came down the stairs. He felt her leaning over him from behind, touching him, breathing on him.

Yet when he turned, she was not there.

The phone rang.

"Mister Harding—"

"What?"

It was Sergeant Schwartz.

"We traced your call. It turns out Stephanie Ann Collins doesn't have an uncle. We need to talk to you, Mr. Harding, about your involvement with her. Would you be willing to come down to the station?"

"No I would not. I am terribly *busy.*"

"We're sending a car for you, Mr. Collins. We really need to talk to you, in light of recent developments."

"I don't know anything about that," Simon said. "I don't know anything."

"Stephanie's grave has been disturbed. The body is missing."

It occurred to him, in a detachedly rational manner, that police didn't act this way. By tipping him off, they'd give him a chance to flee. Better to just show up on his doorstep unannounced and catch him unawares. Then again, they might do it for a bit of sadistic fun if they were already right outside, about to break his door down.

He could imagine the headlines: POLICE SMASH NECROPHILIA RING! STOLEN CORPSE FOUND!

See *out of touch with reality,* above. Cross-reference *obsession* and *bonkers.*

No, it wasn't like that. It wasn't like that at all, Stephanie reassured him, when she called again. She was coming for him. They would be happy. They would be together forever.

"Where?" he asked.

She didn't say where. But they would be happy.

"Why me? Why a total stranger?"

Because he was special, she told him. Because he had the skill to bring her back. Because she'd had, maybe, second thoughts right after she'd let go of that bridge railing over the Turnpike.

"Your life was so empty, Simon," she said, "that there was room for me to move in."

He thought he heard police sirens. Maybe that was a dream. There was a knock at the door. He remembered a story he'd read once in school, called "The Lady, or the Tiger?"

Only in this case, which was which?

Madness on the Black Planet

In the end, as the two of them descended to the surface of the Black Planet, Astronaut Adam Robinson had only his rage. It boiled up inside him inchoate and incoherent, beneath the level of verbalization or even thought, as he understood at some primordial level, at the base of his brain stem perhaps, that he, and all humanity for that matter from the beginning of time, had been royally shafted, made ridiculous before a cosmos incapable of responding with even laughter.

It might have been something close to precognition.

The only words he managed 10 utter were, "Oh, fuck."

Ten minutes after the lander had separated from the orbiter, something like a shadow had passed over them, touched them, penetrated them in a way human senses couldn't follow, filling his mind with strange visions.

The first objective result of this was that all communications were cut off. The instrument panels in front of him all blinked out, then came back on again, but now nothing responded to his touch or command.

Secondly, his colleague in the seat beside him, Pasternak, had chosen this rather inconvenient moment to go mad. So much for the tight-lipped brilliance that had gotten crews out of sticky situations as far back as Apollo XIII. It wasn't happening this time.

The Black Planet was swallowing them. He saw it outside his window, swelling to blot out the stars. It was not what anyone expected, no frozen landscape of ice and craters like most Kuiper Belt objects, but *pure blackness*, like a negation of the universe where the planet was supposed to be: a planet that truly had no name except for one or two fabulous ones found in ancient and decidedly unscientific texts written by persons of infinite unreliability.

Robinson thought of it as the mouth of Hell, which was equally unscientific.

Indeed, scientific considerations included the fact that, in all probability, their third teammate, Zhou, left behind in the orbiter, was history by this point.

Pasternak maintained a thin veneer of sanity as he repeated over and over again into his microphone, "Lander to Orbiter, we do not read you. Come in, please." But he went on and on at it, like a broken record, until at last Robinson nudged him on the shoulder and said, "Hey, I don't think that's going to do any good."

That was when Robinson could tell that the other man just wasn't there anymore, by the vacant look in his eyes, by the drool that was running down his chin inside his space helmet.

Now the broken record switched to, "Houston, we have a problem. Houston, we have a problem. Houston, we have a problem." That merely confirmed the diagnosis and added to the absurdity, not merely because Houston was so far away that any sort of radio message—in the unlikely event they were still transmitting—would take months to get there, which made any sort of conversation impractical. Besides which, Houston might still be the capital of one of the larger surviving chunks of the former United States, but they hadn't come from Houston, or from any official space agency, not that there *were* any official space agencies anymore, now that cities were burning, oceans washed over continents, and the mad auroras rolled. No, this had been strictly a *private* mission, the brainchild of the last of the surviving grandsons of the infamous Delaroche brothers, oligarchs who could buy or break governments, and who survived and flourished in what newspaper reporters used to call their Fortress of Solitude: in fact, an immense compound and artificial island located in the Florida Archipelago near the ruins of Miami, invulnerable to nuclear strikes or large meteorite impacts, so the story went, not to mention mere political revolutions and natural disasters. It had been tried and tested sorely of late, and it was still there, gleaming.

Of course there was a spaceport and if Compton Delaroche, last of the line, desired it to it be used, it was used.

Robinson, Pasternak, and Zhou had only met the old man once, when they were jointly interviewed for this mission. Even then, they'd sat opposite him at the end of an enormously long mahogany table in a darkened room, where they could not see his face clearly. Robinson thought it had rippled, like a flag in a breeze, and his every instinct made him want to rush to the other end of the table and break the bastard's scrawny neck, or else just get the hell out of there, regardless of what was offered, regardless of the state of the world he was fleeing back to. Better to perish among the millions than sell your soul to the Devil, no, something worse than the Devil, something out of the visions that were filling his head now, something he raged against and wanted to destroy for the sheer obscenity of what it was doing to his mind and his world and his universe.

But he had done none of these things, because Compton Delaroche willed that three astronaut candidates be recruited and trained and sent off. There was something in his voice, or in what his mind broadcasted, or in how reality rippled and shifted and changed in his presence so that there was only *one* will and *one* voice and all other living things were but detached limbs animated by his ever-reaching mind.

Now the force that held the lander like a toy in hand set the vessel down gently on the surface of the Black Planet. There was hardly a bump, just the subtle sensation that they were no longer moving.

Robinson turned to Pasternak, who was still babbling into the microphone, checked the seals on his suit and the gauge on his oxygen tank, and then gently led him out of the lander.

"Hey, buddy, you'd better come with me."

"Houston, we have a problem."

"Yeah, I think we do."

He took his crewmate by the arm and directed him down the ladder to the surface.

Now they could both look up and behold the features of the Black Planet. There were stars in the sky, but if it were visible, Robinson could not even make out the sun, much less the Earth or even Jupiter. All too distant. Specks lost in a star field that looked like gleaming smoke. But they did not search the sky for more than a few seconds anyway, because now the Black Planet did indeed seem to have mountains of gleaming ice, higher than known in the solar system, an impassible barrier toward which the two men instinctively walked. The rational part of Robinson's mind told him that those mountains must be hundreds of miles away, and, given the lack of atmosphere and the enormous size of the Black Planet (twice the size of Earth but somehow less dense, so his steps felt impossibly light), very likely hundreds of miles high as well. There was nothing to do but die, as their oxygen ran out in the middle of the featureless plain.

But that was what the rational side of his mind told him, and he was not entirely sure he was in control of himself now. He saw things in memory that his eyes did not see—winged, white, many-limbed creatures rising into space, cities of featureless stone, gardens of frigid fungus in starlight—and sometimes he felt that he was someone else, a disembodied intelligence watching Astronaut Robinson making his way uselessly across the plain, dragging Astronaut Pasternak by the arm.

The rational part of him knew that as soon as the shadow or whatever it had been had taken control of the lander, something had entered his mind, and Pasternak's mind. Pasternak had not stood up under the strain. But he, Robinson, could still think for himself. He was still aware. He felt that rage for freedom that comes to an animal in a trap. It was enough to keep him going.

Much of what followed thereafter didn't make any rational sense. Possibly they covered impossible distances walking, without their bodies growing over-tired or their oxygen running out, or the distances themselves were illusions, or somehow space and distance were not the same here as they were on Earth. It seemed like no more than an hour before they actually reached the foot of those mountains, and he reached out and touched the hard, smooth surface, and all the mountains, as far as he could see, rippled like shapes made of rain, and vanished, to be replaced for a time by the apparition of an almost endless cityscape of black, featureless pyramids and structures that tilted at strange angles the eye could not follow, and of shapes like walking hills moving in and out and between and through these structures to a rhythm he could not follow but which seemed to indicate a kind of dance, increasing in frequency into a kind of frenzy.

Then this too was gone, and he and his companion made their way over trackless miles of wasteland, knee deep in snow so darkly gray it was almost black, toward an ever-distant tower with a burning light in the window, like a beacon, like an eye, irresistible.

By now Pasternak was screaming words Robinson could not make out, words in no human language at all, but sounds that almost meant something in his dreams, in his visions, in whatever pollution was filling his head.

"Houston, I think we have a problem," Robinson said. "No kidding. We really do."

He did not know exactly how he and his companion finally made it to their destination. Perhaps they were lifted up by winged, multi-limbed monstrosities and delivered there. Perhaps the tower was made of bones, but alive, writhing, and many-limbed, and it lifted them up through the lighted window as if shoveling two morsels into its mouth. Pasternak screamed all the way, but then grew silent as they—or at least he, Robinson—suddenly *knew where they were:* inside that meeting room in the Delaroche Complex/Fortress off the remains of Florida.

Something sat at the far end of the mahogany table, clad in a misshapen business suit, wearing a silken mask that rippled like a flag in a gentle wind.

"You can open your helmets. The air in here is perfectly good."

Reluctantly, Robinson unsealed his helmet. No, the air was not perfectly good, but he could breathe it. There was a sharp, acrid smell, like burning, and also a faint but indescribable foulness.

Pasternak fumbled with the catches on his helmet. Robinson helped him.

"Here, refresh yourselves," said the other.

Two plastic water bottles came rolling down the length of the table.

"No, thank you," said Robinson.

Pasternak seemingly couldn't figure out what to do with his.

By this point, like tumblers inside his mind falling at last into place, Robinson found the solution and perfect focus to his own rage. He understood. He recognized that voice, which he had heard at their initial briefing, and in his head and his dreams so many times since. It was the voice of Compton Delaroche, or whatever Compton Delaroche had become or whatever being had impersonated Compton Delaroche all along.

"Fuck you, bastard!"

The yellow mask rippled. The other said, "You have not disappointed me until now. I had hoped that the climax of all human history would finish on a better line than that."

The lock within his mind sprang open. He was momentarily free. Now he did what his instincts had screamed for him to do at their first meeting. For all the clumsiness of his spacesuit he lunged along the length of that table and caught hold of the thing in the yellow mask. He felt its brittle neck bones crumbling into nothingness in his hands. It felt so, so good. He pounded with his fists as the rest of the body disintegrated and a cloud of thick, choking dust filled the air. He staggered back. He tried to close his space helmet again, but he was too late, because now, after a transition he could not remember or perhaps could not perceive, it was he who was sitting at one end of the table in that darkened room and addressing Astronaut Pasternak, who stood at the other.

The thing, the *otherness,* was inside of him now, awake in his own body, as if he were mad, fractured into a multiple personality, and the prevailing opinion was that the others, the countless monstrous *others,* were real and Adam Robinson was the delusion. His mind was filled with hideous memories that were not his own, of a time on Earth when he—that which had never been Adam Robinson—had appeared in Egypt and beasts licked his hands.

He—Adam—could follow the remaining conversation within the room only as if eavesdropping.

The thing spoke out of his own mouth, first with the voice of Compton Delaroche, then, as it became accustomed, with the voice of Astronaut Robertson.

It was Pasternak who mentioned Kadath in the Cold Waste, the Gardens of Ynath, and "more distant Shaggai." It was he who realized that all through the universe vast forces were awakening and, by means Robinson could not begin to comprehend, listening intently to this conversation as it somehow rippled through the very fabric of being.

It was the voice of Adam Robertson that explained that the entire purpose of human existence, the very reason such an evolutionary train of development had ever been allowed to begin, was so that mankind would, at the very end, destroy the Earth, or at least render it sufficiently chaotic that it more suited the desires of the *others* rather than humanity. He, through many guises and many millennia, had shaped events toward the intended outcome. He—that which was *not* Adam—was merely a watchman. Now that humans had, of their own resources, reached the Black Planet, an alarm went off, for if human beings had gained such powers and capacity, they probably had or would very soon carry the plan to its ultimate conclusion.

The stars were right. The time was right. It was not like tumblers in a lock. Wrong metaphor. More like the completion of a circuit.

That which wore Adam Robinson's body turned in its chair and raised a hand. A curtain drew back, revealing an immense circular glass window that looked out, not on the surface of the Black Planet, but into the depths of space. The star field, like smoke in a wind, rippled. Gaps were appearing in it. Gates were opening.

It was Pasternak, who was mad, who now ran down the length of the length of the table, not to assault anyone, but to leap headlong through that window. The glass shattered. The air roared out of the room, taking with it stray bits of paper, the water bottles, and even a portrait of the original Delaroche Brothers off the wall.

Robinson tried to speak, but his lungs ruptured. A cloud of half-frozen blood spewed out of his mouth. Somehow he was still conscious. That which possessed his body now didn't need lungs. He couldn't think clearly. His mind was not his own. Other thoughts, other memories, other visions overwhelmed him. He wondered if it meant anything that the first and last human beings in existence were named Adam. Probably not. He tried to form something with the lips, what had been his lips but were now only borrowed as the dominant entity within the body was momentarily startled by the breaking glass. He tried, maybe he succeeded in forming the words FUCK YOU one last time, one last shout of nihilistic defiance addressed to the whole universe. Maybe no one heard it, but, he was certain, that was the best epitaph mankind was going to get.

Going to Ground

So in the end he simply yielded to what had previously balanced somewhere between a wry observation and a morbid obsession. In the course of the many road trips he'd taken for his work, as he made his way up through northeastern Pennsylvania, through Scranton, Mt. Pocono, Jim Thorpe, and Chorazin, and into New York State by way of Binghamton and on to Rochester or Albany, he had begun to notice, particularly while driving alone late at night, how remarkably *empty* the landscape was of any trace of mankind at all, and how civilization, in the form of villages, farms, or rest stops, was only in the valleys. The ridges of the forested hills that stretched on for endless miles seemed absolutely primordial. He'd joked once to his wife that if an invading army of orcs ever followed those ridge lines and refrained from shooting off fireworks or playing their boom boxes too loud, they could make it nearly to the state capital in Harrisburg without being detected. Sometimes, at sunset, in the winter, when he could see the bare trees silhouetted the glare of the sky, he fancied that he could glimpse mysterious shapes darting between the black trunks; and he imagined, too, that the light from beyond those hills was not entirely of this world.

Therefore, on this last night, in his great pain, he drove without knowing where he was going, like an animal mindlessly going to ground, and he pulled over in the middle of a particularly dark stretch of nowhere, without even the distant glimmer of a farmhouse in sight. He let the car roll into what might have been a natural clearing or the remains of some abandoned field, then, because his nature must have been methodical somewhere else in his life, he put the gearshift in park, shut off the engine, pulled the parking brake, turned off the headlights, carefully removed the keys from the ignition, then got out and locked the car, placing the keys in his pocket.

His memory wasn't working. If he tried to think back more than a few minutes there was nothing. There was only the distress of inexplicable grief, which was giving way to a curious mental numbness. He did not know what he was fleeing from, only that he must *go*. It was like *letting go*, as if he had dangled from a railing over an abyss and released his grip, falling down forever. The impression was reinforced all the more by the fact that the ground dipped slightly as he began walking, and he stumbled into a ditch and lost his glasses before regaining his feet. But then he instinctively began to climb the rocky hillside, into the trees. Before long the darkness had closed around him entirely. He caught hold of the trees—thin, leafless—and hauled himself up.

It was like swimming in a dream, up, up, away from a black void that threatened to swallow him, as if he were ascending into the sky.

Like a dream, it was silent. He heard only his own gasping breath, his heartbeat throbbing in his ears. Like a dream of drowning perhaps. The forest lacked all the usual night noises: crickets, birds, even the sound of branches creaking in the wind.

Instinctively, he struggled ever upward, perhaps for hours. Perhaps, as in a dream, there was no time, and this night would never end and he would go on climbing forever.

He wept softly, not entirely sure why. Something floated out of the darkness of his lost memory, like a painted white sign drifting up from the bottom of a murky pool, and it came to him that in the morning, if there was to be a morning, the sensational headline in the papers would say considerably more than MAN WALKS IN THE WOODS.

But what it would say, he somehow didn't want to find out. He refused to formulate that thought. He knew he mustn't. It was like when your mother tells you: *Don't pick at it.*

Don't.

Don't.

Don't.

Only after a very long time did he realize that he was not alone.

It wasn't so much that he heard anything, and he did not see anything but the darkness. Without his glasses, in any case, everything less than a few feet away would be a blur. When he looked up he saw nothing at all, either because the sky was overcast or because he could not make out the stars. (On a clear night, he knew, the stars out here could be brilliant, wonderful. This was not a clear night. Either that or, somehow, there no longer *were* any stars.)

No, he just *felt* a certain closeness, a proximity as when you are groping in a lightless tunnel and you reach out your hand, you are almost certain of the nearness of the wall, even if you can't quite touch it.

He continued for an endless time, certain that a great number of others were all around him, like a rising tide, sweeping him along; but that was when, catastrophically, either by malign accident or the perverse doings of Poe's Imp, which he often explicated in his professional lectures, he did not do the easy thing and just go with the tide, but *stopped.*

Something crashed into him, nearly knocking him over. He stumbled, staggering about noisily in the fallen leaves and underbrush, and he even called out, from stupid reflex, "Hey, watch where you're—"

Then he *did* hear motion all around him, like the rising susurrus of a tide and—as the protective armor that encased his memory began to break—he recalled that he had a cigarette lighter in his coat pocket. His fingers, more than his mind, knew to how get that lighter out and flick it on.

The glare of the flame might have been a suddenly rising sun.

The faces revealed around him were all dead. He was sure of that. They were dead. No, their eyes did not glow. Some of them did not even have eyes, only dark pits. They were pale, so very pale, and he knew they were all corpses or ghosts, dead, walking up this hillside in the forest with him, yes, like a tide in their inevitability.

"Have you lost your way?" one of them said.

That was when he was certain, very certain, more fantastically certain than anything else in his life that this was wrong, so very, very wrong—and *why WOULD they say that he was mad?*—to paraphrase the line he used to use to punctuate his very popular Poe lecture up at the universities in Rochester or Albany.

"I don't belong here," he said. "I'm not one of you."

He tried to make his way back down the way he had come. He

pushed his way through the crowd of the dead, shoving them aside, smelling the foulness of them, their butcher-shop odors of blood and spoiled flesh. Sometimes a hard, cold hand would grab hold of him, but he always managed to break free, and he was running now, running, almost flying, hurtling back down the hill, back toward—what?

And that was when he remembered everything. Maybe it was his perverse imp after all, or just malign something or other, picking, picking; and the armor that had shielded him thus far suddenly turned into glass and shattered into a million pieces. He sat down, weeping once more, as it all came back to him, everything he had forgotten, everything that had blasted his brain out into merciful, dark amnesia, now coming back, like a fire rekindled from smoldering ashes as he helplessly relived it all, the screaming argument, the obscenities, the struggle, the thunderclap moment in which his life, his existence, all his future *snapped* and was destroyed.

The gunshot.

The morning's headline which would read something like COLLEGE PROFESSOR MURDERS FAMILY, FLEES.

Something like that.

He could only sit on the hillside now, with the dead passing all around him, drifting up that slope. He could only wait until the last of them approached him, and he perversely flicked the cigarette lighter one last time; the last of them walking up to him, his wife, Margaret, with the whole front of her blouse soaked in blood, and then his twelve-year-old daughter Ann, who wasn't supposed to have been there, who had come home too early from band practice and blundered in on something she wasn't supposed to see.

Half of her face was blown away, but she was the one who said, "Why, Daddy? Why?"

He had no answer. He could only protest that this was all wrong, that he didn't belong here, as cold hands took hold of him and led him up the wooded hillside after the others, up, up toward that mysterious ridge line where the black, naked trees stood silhouetted by pale fires burning beyond them, fires which, he was certain, no passing motorist, however observant or imaginative, ever saw from the highway.

The Martian Bell

It was at the age of seventy-three that Gabriel Watson, a widower, suddenly awoke in the early hours of the morning with the answer.

Maybe it was a miracle. Maybe it was just cosmic sloppiness, like someone carelessly leaving a door ajar.

Either way, he turned on the light, sat up, and reached over to the other side of the bed, where his wife used to sleep, as if to awaken her too. She was gone now, of course. He knew that. But it was force of habit.

No, this was for him alone.

He swung around, sitting on the edge of the bed, and sat there for a moment, listening to the sound he'd heard all his life as if he'd heard it now for the first time.

It was the sound of a bell, ringing softly at the very edge of his perception, like something half-remembered from a dream, a steady ding-ding like the bell of a buoy rising and falling in a gentle tide.

It had always been his secret.

From his earliest childhood he'd heard that sound, and it had taken him a while to figure out that not everyone else heard it. Sometimes, when he was young, he'd found it comforting or even beautiful, as if someone or something, maybe his guardian angel, had wanted to remind him he wasn't alone.

Later in life, he'd come to seriously doubt that.

He'd been almost five the first time he'd tried to find its source. He'd gotten up, as he was doing now, dressed, as he was doing now, and sneaked out of the house early one Saturday morning to wander for what seemed like hours through the deserted, darkened neighborhood in the fog and damp, the passage of time distorted and distended as if the sun were refusing or unable to come up; and he followed that sound. If he glimpsed monsters looming over him behind the houses, or if he had indeed followed that ringing bell to its source and found it, that might have been a dream. Maybe he found the bell set in a little stand in the middle of something like a card table, ringing of its own accord, and if the things seated around the table—hunched, shrouded, hideous things with triangular faces and gleaming multifaceted eyes like enormous insects—looked up at him in surprise as he interrupted their game—for they were indeed playing some kind of game, with cards held in their very human-like hands, and round disks like checkers pieces moved along a board of some kind—that might have really happened, or maybe it was a dream too. Perhaps one of them rolled dice and moved a piece or drew a card to make him *think* it was a dream. He ran from them. He tripped and fell several times. The vision faded out, indeed, like something from a dream that fades away quickly when you wake up, only it didn't fade all the way, because he still heard the bell, which he probably wasn't supposed to. That was the slip-up, the sloppiness, the door left ajar.

Was it possible those things didn't even know it? He didn't ask himself that at the time, but the question came up later. After that first time, when he showed up for breakfast that morning and his mother demanded to know how he'd gotten his knees muddy already, he had no explanation.

Now, aged seventy-three, fully dressed, he stuffed a flashlight and his keys into his pockets and made his way downstairs through the house that had become much too large for him, and let himself out through the front door, locking it gently behind him, as if he were sneaking out and didn't want anyone to catch him.

On the doorstep, he listened to that distant ringing.

He had learned to keep things to himself as a boy, never confiding in his parents or teachers or even friends, especially after he'd made a few attempts to describe what he thought he knew and heard and the other kids said things like "What bell?" and "You really are a ding-a-ling, aren't you?" and they laughed at him. After that, nothing. If teachers complained that he was "withdrawn" and even "devious," that was fine, because it was precisely by being withdrawn and devious that he made his way through childhood and adolescence without too many bumps. There had been an incident in the fifth grade when a teacher caught him with a whole copybook full of obsessive drawings of those creatures, faces like praying mantises, hunched shoulders, too long and perhaps excessively jointed hands holding cards while they huddled around their gaming table and pushed little checkers pieces around the board.

When the teacher had asked "What are these?" he'd lamely said, "Martians."

Much to his surprise, she wasn't angry. She even said something about how imaginative he was and how he had artistic talent, while the rest of the class snickered. She was one of these new teachers who had a lot of funny ideas about letting kids find their own way and didn't seem to believe very much in discipline.

But as things worked out, he never became an artist.

Throughout all these years he still heard that bell, all the time. It was never obtrusive, but it was always there.

When he spent his twenty-first birthday lying on his back in a rice paddy in Vietnam, cursing as bullets whizzed right above his nose and he struggled with his M-1 rifle, which was jammed the one time he actually needed it, he heard the ringing bell constantly through the whole experience, between the bursts of machine-gun fire and the cries of his buddies as his entire platoon was wiped out.

The bell meant *game in progress.* It was not over. It was still going on. He saw the Martians then, seated above him. He was lying at their feet as if they'd calmly set up their little card table and gone on with their amusements right in the middle of the firefight. Their eyes flickered and sputtered in the darkness like failing floodlights.

One of them held up a single round piece, a polished disk, which he somehow *knew* represented himself, his life, his destiny, his role.

He almost forgot himself and started to sit up, to see what they were doing, when a bullet winged the side of his helmet, and he went down again with a splash, as if he'd been hit on the head with a hammer.

The Martian looked at the piece and looked at Gabriel, as if it were contemplating throwing this piece away, just tossing it off into the night and the farther reaches of the rice paddy, from which, of course, it could never be retrieved.

He looked into the creature's face as if to plead, *Please don't. Just don't. Please—*

It flipped the piece into the air the way you'd flip a coin.

This much could be dismissed as a battlefield hallucination, the medics told him, when he was rescued and found to be, indeed, the only survivor of his luckless platoon. (How many other gaming pieces were tossed away that night?) When he mentioned he had a "ringing in the ears" they checked him out for the usual things and gave him a few pills and made noises about "combat fatigue," but he had no demonstrable hearing loss, and he knew better than to draw too much attention to himself while in the army, the better to get out quickly; so he said nothing more about it, although he still heard that gently ringing bell, ding-ding, ding-ding, like a heartbeat, one-two, one-two, like the metronome of his life.

He had his ups and downs after that.

The first thing he did upon returning to civilian life was to go back to his parents' house in that same neighborhood where he'd lived when he was five years old, but after a night or two of lying in his old bed listening to that distant ringing, he got up, dressed, and sneaked out of the house in the early hours of the morning and disappeared from the lives of everyone he had ever known.

Maybe he really was mad then. He vanished into the wilderness of some remote state, and lived alone in the woods for five years, a mountain man, a hermit, haunted by the ghosts of the dead men of his lost platoon, talking and talking and talking to himself about Martians.

When he came out of the woods again, it was, coincidentally, 1976, the year the Viking lander made it clear that there were no insectoid card-sharps on Mars, but they were still Martians as far as he was concerned.

That year he cleaned himself up just enough and got a job as a busboy in a run-down restaurant outside of Seattle. He was twenty-six.

By the time he was thirty, he owned the restaurant.

By the time he was thirty-five, he owned a whole chain of restaurants and was rich and even slightly famous. That was the year he got married, to a wonderful woman named Patricia, by whom he had two beautiful daughters, and he was sufficiently happy that he was almost willing to *thank* the Martians, or at least whatever Martian that was playing the piece that held his soul or represented his life or whatever it did for how well things were turning out.

Then his wife and kids were killed when, implausibly, a tank truck filled with gasoline flipped over the divider in the middle of a freeway, landed right on top of the car Patricia was driving, exploded, and so completely incinerated the lot that there wasn't enough left to bury in anything other than a small urn.

A major food-poisoning scandal put an end to the restaurant. He avoided going to jail, but by the time he was forty he was living in a cardboard box.

And he emerged from the cardboard box, and, although he'd never shown any sort of literary inclinations before, he suddenly became a street poet, then a coffee-house performer in San Francisco, and he made his way up through the literary world to achieve a certain celebrity, and he was offered a professorship at a small college, and from there he branched out into theater and became a playwright with an existential piece called *The Martian Gamesters,* which, he explained again and again to the press, wasn't actually science fiction because all the recent probes and robots had shown that there are no bug-eyed card players on Mars.

Things might have gone well for him again, except for the child-molestation charges, which were entirely false, as he managed to convince the judge but not the public. Now a pariah, his career over, the university let him go, and cardboard-box real estate loomed, but this time he'd managed to hoard enough resources that he was able to move to Chicago, change his name, and set up shop as a rare coin dealer. Not that he'd ever shown any interest in numismatics before, but somehow the expertise and talent just poured into his brain. He was good. He was very good. He was also incredibly lucky. He went down in coin-collecting history as the guy who found a golden "Ides of March" aureus in a junk box in a flea market. It was covered with ancient mud, but when he took it home and cleaned it, that's what it turned out to be, the coin put out by Brutus, the assassin of Caesar, showing a freedman's cap and two daggers and the letters "Eid Mar" on either side because the Latin phrase for "So we finally got the bastard" was a little too wordy to fit on a coin.

It was only the second specimen known, but exhaustive testing and expert examination determined that it was not a fake.

Almost sixty, Gabriel married Martina, who had already raised a family and gone through a divorce and was looking for someone quiet to spend the rest of her life with. Gabriel fit the bill, because he never talked to Martina about Martians or ringing bells and he often sat up all evening studying coins or catalogues while she knitted and watched TV.

All well and good until in her middle sixties she began to die painfully, hideously, of cancer and there was nothing he could do but watch.

And, the day after the funeral, the coin shop was destroyed because, by an incredible coincidence that almost defied description, a twenty-ton safe was being carried via helicopter right overhead that morning just as he was unlocking the front door. The cable broke and the safe fell, crashing through the roof, all the way down into the basement where it ruptured the oil-burner and sent the whole place up in one enormous fireball. The force of the explosion heaved him sprawling backwards across the sidewalk, where he came within inches of being run over by a bus; but fortunately he was hauled out of the gutter by a paperboy, who said, after the two of them had gotten clear of the flames and falling debris, "Jeepers, was that your shop? I hope it was insured."

It occurred to him that he had never before in his life actually heard someone say "Jeepers," that that was absurdly contrived, but in reply all he said was, "I feel like I'm in a fucking Road-Runner cartoon."

Truth to tell, the twenty-ton safe *had* borne the letters ACME on its side, though by now they had burned off in the resultant inferno. Somebody had a sense of humor. But he wasn't laughing.

It was shortly after that that Gabriel Watson awoke in the night, at the age of seventy three, and realized that he knew the answer.

But the game wasn't over. Not quite yet.

As he walked, silent and alone in the misty dawn through his suburban neighborhood, listening to that eternal, infernal ding-ding, ding-ding, a teenage girl who looked quite a bit like what either of his daughters might have if they'd lived that long came running out of nowhere and slammed right into him. She did not knock him over, but he staggered back, and she clung to him, and they found themselves embracing each other while she sobbed and said, in a thick, foreign accent, "Will you help me? Please, will you help me?"

She was obviously in distress. She had been running a long way and she was dressed only in a torn nightgown, barefoot and splattered, and he saw too that her tear-streaked face was bruised and swollen and her lip bloodied.

And he said, "Yes, I can help you. I know what to do."

He did, because he had figured it all out, finally.

She followed him, dubiously. He led her by the hand for several blocks. They came to an open field and crossed it. She looked at him, puzzled, as if to ask where they were going and why. She seemed almost ready to bolt. Slander to the contrary, he had never harmed a young person and never would, but, because he had the answer so clearly in his mind now, he would have been quite capable of hauling her over his shoulder if that was what it took to get her where they had to go.

Fortunately, that did not prove necessary.

Where they had to go was more or less where they were, in the middle of that muddy field.

He called out, "All right, you bastards, show yourselves."

He heard the bell ringing. Ding-ding, ding-ding.

And they were there, right in front of him, five or six Martian players (the number always seemed indeterminate, no matter how many times he saw them) seated around a table. The bell was right there, ringing, ringing of its own accord.

The Martians stared at him, their wide eyes like streetlamps.

The girl let out a little cry, a moan. Maybe she could see them too. Maybe not. He didn't have time to find out.

The Martians gestured. This time, there was something very different.

An empty chair, pulled back. They were inviting him to sit down and join in the game; and he understood what the game was and how it worked. He'd figured out most of it already, but the rest of the rules and strategies came flooding into his brain as if someone had flipped open the top of his skull and poured it in from a glass.

He realized that he *could* take his place among them, that he *could*, oh so easily, learn to enjoy their obscene pleasures; but this repulsed him and only strengthened his resolve.

Therefore he reached out and removed one piece off the board. It felt like smooth metal in his hand, like a coin, thick and heavy like an Eisenhower dollar or a Roman sestertius, and a little warm; and as he held it he suddenly knew that the girl standing next to him was named Marta. She was seventeen years old and had been born in a Romany camp in Bulgaria. She was half-Gypsy and even her mother didn't know who her father was, and out of desperate poverty, to avoid literal starvation to death, she had been sold, and then trafficked, and forced into prostitution in Italy, then used as a drug mule, then sold again as a mail-order bride to a man in America who wasn't American and couldn't speak any language she knew and treated her halfway between a slave and a dog.

Gabriel Watson knew all this, holding that gaming piece in his hand, and because he had figured things out he gave her that piece. He had removed it from the board and now he pressed it into her hand, and he said to her, "Your life will be better now. Keep this safe. Don't let anybody have it! Go! Go!"

Her unborn child's life would be better too; she was, he knew, a month pregnant by the monster of a man she would hopefully never see again.

"Go!" he shouted after her, as she began to run, clutching her soul or her fate or whatever it was precisely, clutched in her fist.

Then he sat down at the table. He looked at each of the players, straight into their utterly expressionless eyes. He surveyed the table, the game board with its twisting paths, the cards that were being dealt out to him from the deck, cards that said things like HIT BY 20-TON SAFE,

RAPED BY A GORILLA, WINS PULITZER PRIZE, FINDS IMPOSSIBLY RARE AND VALUABLE COIN IN A JUNK BOX AT A FLEA MARKET, LEGS BITTEN OFF BY GIANT JUNGLE SPIDERS, and so on.

There were, placed in front of him, also, a pair of dice, several stacks of what were very clearly poker chips, and what might have been a bowl of blood.

He took his cards. He held them close, looking at them. He gazed over the top of them at his follow players, and smirked, almost laughing, but bitterly, and he said to them, "Fuck you."

Just that. He did not care if they were Fates or Norns or gods or actually depraved extraterrestrials who got their jollies screwing with human lives. Was that *human pain* which had been distilled into the bowls in front of each of them, from which they pleasantly and casually sipped?

Still the bell rang, ding-ding, ding-ding, a sound that transcended and suspended all time and space, which reached to the very ends of the universe to signify *game on*. The sound was definitely not beautiful or comforting now that he knew what it meant.

"Fuck you," he said again, and he reached out and grabbed hold of the bell. He slid his fingers inside it, caught hold of the clapper, and it *stopped ringing*. For the first time in his life he did not hear it. Of course he had never figured out why he'd heard it in the first place, why he had been able to, when millions upon millions of human beings up and down the centuries had struggled and suffered through their twisted, arbitrarily jerked-about lives *without* being able to hear it, with no idea at all of what was happening to them, much less that anything could be done about it. Yes, they could invent myths of Norns, Fates, gods, or even Martians, but as far as he knew no one else had ever before sat face to face, around the gaming table, with these creatures that *did* thus derive their sadistic pleasure or genteel amusement, or sate their ennui, or whatever it was they did—certainly nothing that produced wisdom, nothing that was worthwhile, worth all the suffering, the helplessness, the raised and crushed hopes. Why him? Was he a freak with some kind of brain defect that let him see what he shouldn't? A mistake? A miracle? A bit of cosmic sloppiness like a door left ajar?

"Fuck you," he said yet again, because magically, anything you say three times is true and has special power. He stood up suddenly and hurled the bell off into the darkness as far as he could throw it.

The gamer-things, which he had called Martians, but which clearly were not from Mars, actually *spoke* to him for the first and only time, all chittering and squeaks and croaks, just gibberish. Before they could react he flipped up the table and scattered the game and ended it.

He picked up his chair and started to swing it into their hideous faces, to pulverize them all . . . but he found he was swinging at nothing, just spinning around, and then he didn't even have a chair in his hands.

Spinning. Gasping for breath from the exertion.

Everything was gone. The world was gone. All around him was only a darkness, which slowly lightened into a white fog, like the mist in the morning when there is no wind to blow it away.

"Fuck you," he whispered, uselessly repeating himself at this point, remembering his wives, his daughters, his buddies from Vietnam.

He remembered, too, the old joke, that profanity is the last recourse of the fucking inarticulate. Because he was inarticulate now. He had nothing to say. He couldn't form a thought. He couldn't describe anything.

But rather than wait passively for whatever was to come, he decided to walk into the fog, to see what might be on the other side of it.

Were—?

So you begin in the traditional manner, by selling your soul to the Devil, only the traditional accoutrements have been dispensed with in this day and age: no midnight conjuring of a demon raised in a swirl of smoke from within a pentagram, no parchment produced out of an infernal sleeve to be signed in your blood. None of that. If you truly have the intent, if your mind has been consumed with hatred and desire to the point that you are ready, then the Dark One is already there. Something moves in the periphery of your vision. Some shadow shifts. A pile of papers topples over in your dingy abode. There's a glimpse of something small and black, for just an instant. It could be a cat, but you don't have a cat, do you?

And you are not even certain that you have bargained away your soul, only that you have changed and there will be a price. No trickery over the fine print.

Maybe you do end up with a magic salve or a belt made of animal skin, or else it's just a way of touching yourself, a feeling, that lets you stand out in rowhouse front yard late one night, *naked*, and if the neighbors get an eyeful, well, fuck 'em. The almost frigid autumn air is wonderful on your skin, but after a moment you're burning up, not in pain, but raging with newfound power and the sensation is like, is like ... to be honest with yourself, you have to admit it's like jerking off only a million times more intense. Nothing about the full moon, because the moon is down when you begin to change. Your body ripples like mercury, your flesh melts into smoke, and you shrink down, the earth rushing up to embrace you. You have many forms now. You are the master of all the world's secrets, and with a repertoire like that turning into a mere *wolf* would be oh so clichéd, not to mention impractical, because a gigantic lupine trotting about in an urban neighborhood is likely to attract unwanted attention. So your first choice is a snake, an enormous, black python-like thing of no precise species, which wriggles its way in the darkness at surprising speed. Yes, yes, the sensation is still intense; you touch and feel everything in a way you never have before, like a super-orgasm indeed, like a thousand explosions propelling you along—and the image comes to you for just a second, something from your reading years ago, of an old-time proposal for a spaceship called Project Orion that involved a thousand atomic bombs set off one by one to drive mankind's ultimate phallic symbol into the shadowy depths of the cosmos—and forget the Freudianisms, which are ridiculous. Your mind cannot hold such thoughts, for it is no longer a human mind.

As a serpent, then, you come upon a dog, and strangle it for the sheer joy of killing. You become, after that, a dog, in the image of the one you just killed, but of course did not bother to consume. No one notices stray dogs. But to make your way all the way across town to where you intend to go—that much the human mind, or the superhuman mind you have become, can stay focused on—involves crossing railroad tracks and a highway, so it is better to fly. You change again and again, each sensation more ecstatic than the last. You become a bat, a pigeon, even an eagle. In the dark, no one is going to notice a black eagle swooping among the skyscrapers, settling down into the far, southern end of the city, which is almost another city set apart. Some still-human part of you asks, in the name of scientific curiosity, where the extra mass goes and comes back from, when you change into something small, something large again, something small. Snake, dog, bat, eagle, even a moth.

But it does not matter. This is not a problem in physics.

You glide down among the old, residential streets, the nineteenth-century houses. Then you're on four legs again, then two, then four, running, and with eyes sharper than any human eyes, an acuity of night-vision you would never have believed possible, you can make out a house number from blocks away, in the dark. Yes, that one. Here.

Now you do have to focus, with more than human intensity, if you are to bring this off. You must think about the one you hate. You just stoke your rage like a fire, into something more than human anger. Yes, your actual motivations are base, and even hackneyed. Revenge, vanity, jealousy, wounded pride, maybe even a broken heart. All this you focus on that son-of-a-bitch Fletcher, who had been your friend before he betrayed you with contempt, the arch-manipulator who took over the enterprise, business, whatever it was—stay focused; the precise details do not matter—even though he didn't give a damn about what had been your dream, what you had poured your heart and soul into. He, the bastard, just enjoyed taking it away from you. He has no vision, no soul, no human capacity for compassion or sympathy, much less for goodness. He just enjoys jerking people around. He was the one who got you marginalized, then fired from the company you had helped found.

Yeah, him. What you propose to do is ring his doorbell at four o'clock in the morning in the middle of a work-week and appear to him in human form, *naked*—and you do, and he comes to the door about the time you manage to mouth the syllables "Hi there, Fletch!" The look on his face is beyond human in the degree of his astonishment, and he can only exclaim, "What the *fuck*—?"

Then you actually do follow expectations for a situation like this. The form of an enormous wolf is indeed appropriate, and still in the process of assuming such a shape you lunge at him, pushing him inward from the doorway and onto the floor, and he's screaming in pain and terror louder and more shrilly than you ever thought a human being could as you're ripping his guts out, literally, splattering them every which way with violent shakes of your head, and you have the joy of actually tasting the fucker's still-beating heart between your teeth and on your tongue.

After he is dead, there is more screaming. You look up and there on the stairs is a woman that the remote, fading, human part of your consciousness recognizes as Anne, the woman you once loved or thought you loved, before Fletcher the Prick took her away from you, not because he loved her, but for the sheer malicious fun of doing so.

Well, you don't love her any more.

The feelings are so intense, orgasm after orgasm after orgasm of blood and killing, that you can't stop yourself; you don't even think about it anymore, and before long a good deal of Anne and the child she happened to have with her are splashed over the floor and walls and ceiling, and you've devoured a good deal more.

At the very last, upstairs, you loom panting and dripping blood over the last two children, infants asleep in their cribs.

But only for a moment.

Of course by now the commotion has aroused the neighborhood, and when cornered you howl and slash your way through the crowd, killing more for the incredible joy of it, but before long they're shooting guns and some remnant of your rational mind wonders if the immunity to all but silver bullets might not be one more traditional accoutrement dispensed with in this modern age; so it seems expedient to change before their unbelieving eyes—and some of them are even trying to capture the festivities on cellphone cameras. You can just imagine how this is going to look on Facebook.

And then you can't, because you are something that crawls and wriggles, something that flies, something with dripping jaws and huge leathery wings entirely unknown to scientific zoology, some personification of all human nightmare.

Several more times, blocks away, then miles away, you kill again, for the joy and hunger of killing.

Then, when the sky begins to lighten and the frenzy leaves you, you are lying on the ground . . . in a woodland. Maybe a park. You don't know. No more thoughts of place, much less street addresses. There are only sensations.

Your flesh melts yet again, like smoke, into . . . what? That which crawls, that which wriggles, four legs, two. Large, small. You cannot remember. You have no mind left to remember. You have become an essence of bestial nature, a thing, predation incarnate, but that is all.

You will not be returning to your former life, not even to gloat, much less to recover your standing in the world.

That's all gone.

Maybe you made a bargain and maybe you bartered something away, but in doing so, in its absence, you have entirely forgotten what it was you have lost.

Boxes of Dead Children

When the last of the workmen were done installing his "effects" into his new abode and the last of their trucks disappeared down the rough, gravel road, he really wished he could just blow up the little bridge that connected him with the rest of the world and become the most spectacular recluse since Howard Hughes. He pressed down, hard, on the imaginary plunger. *Boom!* The place was called Eagle's Head for some obscure reason, a little knob of land off the Maine coast at the end of a peninsula, amid tiny, rocky islands. High tides had washed away just enough that where he stood was an island now, too, but for that bridge, and if he could blow it up, well, all the better, because a gazillionaire minus his gazillions still has some resources left and he was sure he could continue to pay the private security firm he employed to float baskets of groceries over to him once a week and otherwise restrict access and leave him alone.

His was a name anyone would know, once a celebrity, the Boy Inventor (aged twenty-something), creator of ———, essential element in the daily lives of millions (who have to pay for it), the new Thomas Edison, who used to be in all the papers as an inspiration or perspiration of the American Dream, but was now, at sixty-something, if you believed hostile sources, the pirate entrepreneur who'd cheated his buddies out of ———, and was pursued by the slings and arrows of congressional investigations, not to mention a mysterious Woman in Red, several distraught ex-wives and former offspring—a.k.a. money-grubbing leeches—plus any number of lawyers, lawyers, lawyers, until he had made his way in abject retreat by swerve of shore and bend of bay to Eagle's Head, Maine, and a curiously long-vacant but "fully furnished" property which a Martha's Vineyard realtor who owed him a debt of discreet gratitude had managed to procure for him.

Boom.

He turned to regard his new acquisition, and the odd thought came to him that if aliens had beamed up bits and pieces of famous edifices from all over the world and glued them together at random, that would only begin to explain the architecture of this place, which had everything from Gothic towers to Romanesque windows to twirly Italianate pillars to a classic, wooden, late Victorian wooden porch on which one could enjoy the sea breeze.

It occurred to him a little later, as he sat on that porch in the evening, that he had so much privacy here that if he wanted to lounge about in a lion-skin loincloth while reading old Tarzan novels, he bloody well could, because amid his vast personal library he actually owned an expensive set of Edgar Rice Burroughs first editions he'd once picked up on a whim, and he did not doubt that the wardrobes inside contained a lion-skin or two; and besides, he was, despite his considerable falling-down in the world, still rich enough to be "eccentric" rather than merely mad, like that crazy du Pont before he'd finally shot somebody.

But a mosquito bit him, and then another, and another, something no amount of isolation or money could do anything about at this time of year, so he went inside. It was not loincloth weather.

Inside, the hallway, which the realtor had described to him as an "atrium," was filled with *stuff*. He was very much into *stuff*, things, objects of art or curiosity, which became a kind of expression of his mind, like graffiti written on the fabric of reality, to an extent more than one of his ex-wives had described as pathological: *stuff*, his own and that of his rather mysterious "fully furnished" predecessor who had built this little hideaway back in the days of Newport mansions, when anything smaller than the palace of Versailles was accounted a "cottage." He himself, the product of a simpler age, had grown up watching *The Addams Family* on TV and had always wanted to live in a house like that, and now, as nearly as possible, he did, complete with a stuffed bear, a samurai statue, and a two-headed concrete tortoise in the living room.

But there was something else here, too, something he couldn't quite define, some sense of an Other, no doubt caused by the presence of a good deal of antique *stuff* that was not his—i.e., that had not accumulated through the remembrances and associations of *his* life. The theory of *stuff* held that whoever lived in a bare, pristine apartment with no stuff in it was probably not worth getting to know. His predecessor must have been interesting, at least.

So what he was doing here was intruding into the lingering mind of *someone else,* hoping to fuse his own with it. The bronze and lacquer dragon clock in the atrium, or the life-sized, age-darkened, papier mâché bobblehead figure of a Chinese attendant had not been his, but they intrigued.

Concerning the former owner, who had left the place boarded up while his estate was left in suspended animation for decades, the realtor had said very little.

Boom. If only he could blow up every connection to the outside world and merely disappear into this place, into the woodwork and accumulations of the house itself. He had to admit to himself, when he had such thoughts, that he was tired, not young anymore, and there were so many things in the world he no longer cared about, most of which had lawyers attached.

But it wasn't as simple as that of course. No isolation can be perfect, particularly if you want modern conveniences. The electricity worked. It worked well enough when he found the electric train layout and followed an antique steam engine as it rattled across tabletops and over the lintel of a door, then through a hole cut in the wall, along a ceiling on a high ledge, up a spiraling staircase, one, two, three stories, until it came to an attic room that had been laid out with an immense tabletop display of a rolling prairie, a station in the middle of it where the train came to a stop, and, stretching in all directions, hundreds of tiny gravestones, most of them with names written on them, but some still blank.

Then the power went out, and he was drawn naturally to the fading light of a window. He could see, across Penobscot Bay, a lighthouse in the distance, two or three sailboats beneath a darkening sky, and, below him, on what must be the back lawn, a single grave, a real one, in the back yard, surrounded by a fence.

He spared himself such clichés as *Well, that's weird,* and he didn't feel particularly afraid. He wasn't quite sure what he felt.

The oddest thing that came to him just then was the temptation, not to blow up his last bridge to the outside world, but to reconnect. So he pulled up a chair and sat down by the window, in the fading light, and got out his cellphone and turned it on. Yes, there was a signal here. He was online, before long fingering his way up and down the screen, reading news, wandering over the Facebook, and then he found a mention of himself in the form of a crudely Photoshopped image of his face on a devil's body with a wriggling boy and girl spitted on his pitchfork and a caption: IS IT TRUE THAT THE RICH EAT BABIES?

Before he could even turn the phone off a voice behind him in the room distinctly said, "That is not a good idea," and somehow the phone was snatched out of his hand.

He turned around in alarm and said, "Who's there?" but of course there was no one there, just the shadow-filled room with the strange train layout and the tiny graveyard.

That the place should be haunted only seemed appropriate. If it were not, he should call the realtor and ask for a discount.

Call him with what? His phone was gone.

He must have dropped it. He could come up here in daylight, with a flashlight if necessary, and search for it.

Then he'd have a long talk with the ghost. Maybe the two of them could become friends, and commiserate without fear of wiretaps and lawsuits.

He realized this was not a normal reaction, but then, he was not here to be normal.

This was well beyond the level of lion-skin loincloths, something deeper than mere eccentricity.

He tried to open himself to the influence of the house, as he explored room after room, some filled with old furniture, shelves crammed with newspapers, another crammed with plaster, life-sized figures of clowns, yet another with every inch of wall space covered with very old, dusty, mounted heads of birds and animals, including what might have been a pterodactyl. Often it was hard to see, because the power was off. Sometimes he just groped. Once he thought he was running his hands over a mummy case. It smelled of wood and exotic spices. Splinters came off on his fingertips. But he could see nothing until he finally found yet another winding staircase which took him down to the kitchen.

Just then the lights came on.

It was quite a modern kitchen, refurnished and stocked as he had instructed. He opened the freezer, got out a frozen entrée and popped it in the microwave, which cheerfully chirped at him as he pressed the bottoms.

He resisted the temptation to actually turn the television on.

As he ate his meager dinner in silence, his hand drifted over to a large book that lay on the table, an album of some kind. He opened it, and saw that it was indeed a late nineteenth-century photo album, each of the pictures in a stiff cardboard setting hinged with cloth, all black-and-whites of course, some of them badly faded, a couple of them tintypes and one on glass.

They were all pictures of children, the boys in stiff suits or even sailor suits, and short pants, their socks neatly drawn up to their knees, the girls in frilly dresses and bonnets. It took him a while as he turned the pages, from photo to photo, to figure out what was wrong with their faces, their blank expressions. A couple of them seemed to be wearing round, smoked glasses, or else they had pennies on their eyes.

They were dead, one and all. He knew that it had once been the custom to photograph the dearly departed one last time, and so such pictures did exist, and a whole album of them like this was a fascinating, if decidedly morbid—and no doubt very valuable—collector's item; but, still, as he came to this conclusion, he snapped the book shut. He laid his fork down gently. He reached for the TV remote.

And then the power went out again.

"You have your little hobbies. I have mine."

Now he actually was alarmed, but at something more mundane than a ghost.

"Who the hell's there? Who's there?"

He groped around in a drawer. He found a steak knife. Armed with this, he turned to face the darkness threateningly.

"I *said*, who the hell's there?"

There was no answer. He heard only faint creaking and snapping. Old houses "settled," he knew. Maybe it was windy out. Maybe there were branches scraping against windows.

Knife in hand, he made his way around the kitchen, tapping things with the tip of the knife the way a blind man would with a cane.

There actually was a small flashlight in one of the drawers.

"I *said*, who—"

He flicked on the flashlight then jumped back as the beam revealed a face, right in front of him, but then he realized it wasn't a face at all, but a framed oval-shaped photo on the wall, of a man in a stiff collar and a suit, but whose face was somehow indistinct, and becoming even more indistinct by the moment, fading away as he watched.

He turned off the light. He briefly considered that maybe flashlights were bad for old photographs.

And while he stood there in the dark, he considered his options, some of which were, he knew, very traditional in a situation like this. They included:

Running screaming into the night.

Or making his way to the master library upstairs by candlelight and spending the evening poring over ancient, blasphemous, eldritch, forbidden, and crumbling tomes in arcane languages (which he would somehow be able to read), until he had ventured into truly forbidden territory that sufficiently altered his mind that he was no longer even remotely sane and all the more willing to invite in tentacular spooks from outer space, while incidentally discovering in a climax of mind-blasting horror what precisely the former owner of this house (of sinister repute, both the owner and the house) had been up to.

Calling in a team of professional ghost busters with their instruments and their technobabble, which would ultimately lead them to yadda-yadda—see previous paragraph.

Going out into the back yard and digging up that grave with his *bare hands*.

Or just lying out there and listening to the voices from out of the ground.

Or waiting for the power to come back on and then watching TV. Something he could relate to, like *Big Bang Theory,* because he too was an awkward genius whom nobody understood. This option included calling out for pizza, even if it was quite a ways for a delivery. First he'd have to find his phone.

Or none of the above.

What actually did happen after that was a little hard to follow. For one thing, he lost track of time. It was dark. It stayed dark. He wondered if the sun would ever rise. He thought he remembered distinct instances of sleeping, on a couch, or in a huge, canopied bed, and of getting up several times to go to the bathroom—fortunately the plumbing worked, even if the electricity didn't, and he laughed and repeated to himself the old joke in a comic-geezer's voice about, *I have an old man's bladder. Imagine how upset he was to discover it missing.* But it was still dark, and more than once he made his way down to the kitchen by candlelight and ate whatever he could find that didn't require cooking. And always, he avoided looking at the photo on the wall, or any of the ones in the album.

Now what was interesting was that he had the distinct sense that it was *his* album, and he began to remember how he had taken those photographs, one by one, and under what circumstances, which was very odd indeed, because he hadn't taken them. He, the inventor and entrepreneur and the subject of rude Photoshopped pictures on Facebook, had done nothing of the sort, and those weren't digital photographs anyway. He had no idea how to use the sort of antique equipment that must have been employed in the creation of those pictures, even if, during his ruminations, he had found a whole room full of cameras and metal basins and bottles of chemicals.

Once he actually heard someone knocking loudly at the front door. He saw the gleam of headlights in the driveway. But he didn't answer it. That was for someone else, in another time.

He hadn't come here to be normal, he kept telling himself.

Time to break out the old loincloth and go swinging through the vines.

But that was not what he did—this not being loincloth weather—

as he made his way slowly upstairs, through rooms filled with his own *stuff*, glimpsing by candlelight his comic-book collection, his movie posters, the glass case containing the Aurora model kits of the Frankenstein Monster and Dracula he'd built as a kid—as he was the sort of person who went through life *accumulating*, never letting go of anything—then into another room filled with his trophies, for innovation, for excellence, for making lots and lots of money and keeping most of it from anybody else—and after that the room full of stuffed, mounted heads, which brought back to his consciousness like bright bubbles of memory rising from a dark pool the vivid recollections of how exactly he had killed each one of these creatures. And yes, the pterodactyl was a joke, a clever fabrication given to him by a friend one Christmas after he'd returned from an expedition to Mato Grosso in 1922 and they'd both sat up reading aloud passages from *The Lost World* and getting a jolly good laugh over it. He found a closet filled with old suits and put one on, because a gentleman, even at home, had to maintain a certain standard. His fingers seemed to know what to do with the stiff, detached collar, even if his mind didn't.

He was a gentleman, despite some of the things that went on in that room filled with cameras and metal basins and sinks, and even though they didn't involve, exclusively, photography.

There was a room of knives. The walls were covered with them, each in little sheaths. Thousands of them.

And then it seemed that he was riding in the passenger car of a train, the steam engine whistling and roaring, as he gazed out the window past a landscape that seemed to twist over tabletops and along the lintel of a door and through tunnels and up spiraling flights of stairs until he found himself disembarking at the final stop, which was an old-fashioned wooden train station in the middle of an impossibly flat landscape covered with perfectly regular gravestones as far as he could see.

At the same time he was in the room where the toy train's track came to its terminus, where moonlight streamed in through a window, and he heard the sound of a foghorn from across the bay. Why would they blow a foghorn on a moonlit night? He wasn't sure, but they did.

"Choo! Choo! End of the line!" someone said.

"Who the *hell* is there?"

"We have our little hobbies. Wanna see?"

He followed, by candlelight, as the Other led him to a higher loft, the true attic of this part of the house, a long, low room under the eaves, and for just a moment what he saw looked, impossibly and absurdly, like something he'd seen in the dark once in that scenic metropolis of Shell Pile, New Jersey, a soft-shell crab farm out in the middle of a field, consisting of row upon row of rectangular tanks stacked on top of one another in a metal framework. But these were not tanks. They were boxes, white cardboard boxes, like gift boxes, the kind you'd get a doll or new suit in, carefully stacked row upon row on metal shelves.

"Look."

None of the boxes had lids. Inside each, surrounding by crumpled wrapping paper the way a new doll might be wrapped, lay the corpse of a child. He knew each of them. He remembered them. He knew their names. He had gently placed pictures of every one of them into his album.

Now some of them were starting to shrivel up or blacken, which made him sad, because he remembered how beautiful they had been.

But no, he argued, *he* hadn't done any of this. That was someone else. It was as if his memories and that of some *Other* were getting all mixed up now, but he was sure, no, that he had never been in this room before the *Other* had tricked him into it; and that was *not* his own picture on the wall in the kitchen with a face that faded away; and the children in the boxes did *not* call out to him and demand to know why? Why? Why did you hurt me? He hadn't hurt anyone. They were having such fun. Like the joke with the pterodactyl was such fun. No one asked him, *Well, what about that guy you buried in the Pine Barrens near Shell Pile?* And he did not have to explain, as one might to a child, that to get where he had gotten, much less to hold onto what he had obtained, whether it be a perfect Aurora model kit of Dracula or a million dollars in hoarded rare gold coins that nobody else knew about, much less his legendary gazillions in the stock of ——————, well, sometimes you have to do things that just have to be done, however unpleasant; so no one asked him about the fire in the sweatshop in Bangladesh either, and no one even said, *Who do you think you are kidding? Do you really think you can just hide away from the world and from the past forty years of your life with your head in the fucking sand? That doesn't work very well for ostriches either.*

That's not a good idea.

Good? Bad? He knew that he was not a bad man, and who was to judge anyway? Some things were beyond judgment.

He ran out of the loft, back down into the lower part of the attic, where the toy train was, where he could see through a window a distant lighthouse across the bay, and somehow, miraculously, his phone was right there, by the chair, where he'd dropped it, still on and glowing.

The last good idea he had involved scooping up that phone off the floor and pressing in a number he knew. His youngest daughter. He hadn't spoken to her in a very long time. He sensed, he hoped, that she didn't hate him quite as much as everybody else. If only he could just speak to her—

"That's not a good idea," the Other said.

"Yes, it's a very good idea!" he said, "a very good idea."

The phone was ringing.

"A very good idea!"

"Daddy? Is that you? What's a good idea?"

"I don't know," he said, and then he couldn't think of anything more to say.

Someone took the phone out of his hand and threw it across the dark room.

But of course there was no one in the room with him. He was standing there, alone, wearing an old-fashioned suit, and in the upper loft were boxes and boxes of dead children, whose names he knew.

Later, there was a loud knocking at the door and he looked out another window and he saw the policemen down there in the driveway, and he laughed at the ridiculous jalopies they'd come in and the absurd uniforms they wore, like something out of an old, silent movie, but he knew they'd never find him, because he was here now and he was part of the house and he could just fade into the darkness until they'd gone away.

"Boom," he said.

The Return of the Night-Gaunts

They bore him up, soaring, into the darkness, far beyond the lights of the city, over black mountains with pinnacles as sharp as teeth, their touch chilling, their claws hard as iron, and yet he was not afraid. The whimsical thought came to him that he was like Scrooge carried off by the spirits in Mr. Dickens's famous if mawkish tale. But no, it wasn't like that. Such as he had any volition left, he shook off that ridiculous thought and merely observed, objectively and passively, what was below him.

The Cold Waste.

He was not afraid because he knew his companions. He knew what they were. They were familiar. They had come to him again, as he had always known they would.

He felt only a quiet sense of awe.

"Funny how early interests crop up again toward the end of one's life."

If all this had started a few months before, on what might have been the last perfect evening he would ever know, he had certainly not realized it at the time. The weather was uncommonly warm for late October, so he was not yet imprisoned within his meager dwelling. He could still go out, and did, and in the course of his wanderings discovered, much to his delight, a woodland not more than three miles from his home that he had never explored before. The city was his native place. Its streets and towers were as familiar to him, as much a part of him as his own body; but here was a remaining pocket of the unknown, affording him one last glimpse of "adventurous expectancy" as he gazed through the trees at the remote urban skyline, its domes and pinnacles aglow in the fading sunset, floating in the air, like something out of a dream.

He stood there, deeply moved, as the Hunter's Moon rose, two days short of full, and if something passed across that moon briefly, it must have been a bird or a bat or a wisp of cloud, and he did not notice.

He recalled that ecstasy he had felt as a child, when, in his pagan phase, in woods similar to these, he genuinely believed he had glimpsed the god Pan with his retinue of nymphs cavorting between the tree trunks. As a grown man given to reason he was beyond such things, of course. He regretted that. The best he could do was try to cling to the memory of the sensation, to hold onto it as long as he could.

If, from overhead, there came a sound like a tent flap blowing in the wind, it must have been, indeed, something blowing in the wind, a mere distraction.

Only in full darkness, after the night had begun to get uncomfortably chilly, did he make his way home, into the city, onto the ancient hill.

He let himself in quietly. His aunt had gone to bed. He was quite used to preparing late meals for himself—something out of a can, cold, a couple slices of bread, and coffee with extra sugar.

When he settled down to work that night, mostly catching up on letter-writing, he found it hard to concentrate. It was like dreaming while awake, he had the momentary impression that he had become weightless, like a thing of smoke, and had fallen *through* his window into the clutches of those dark things that waited for him outside, that bore him up and away.

He closed his eyes and rubbed his eyelids and shook his head to get back into focus. Out his window the city lights twinkled. He laughed softly at the irony: less than a year ago he'd written a tale for a friend about a much younger writer who'd sat in paralyzed horror at this very desk, gazing out over the darkened cityscape he saw now, while a hideous thing from a distant, haunted steeple merged its mind with his own as it came racing to devour him.

He held his pen above the page. Such impressions were not coherent enough, not entertaining enough, to be worth relating to his correspondents.

A gentleman, of course, knew better than to be tedious. One only shared what would be of interest to the other.

He was forty-six, but he felt like a tired old man. It wasn't a pose. No amusing self-caricature as "Grandpa." He merely felt as if all the energy had gone out of him, and such brief, imaginative flashes as he still had were like the twinges an amputee allegedly feels from a missing limb.

The cold set in. He was imprisoned now, inside his rooms. Weariness or discouragement precluded any new tales, no matter how much hordes of mostly young, naïve, and endlessly energetic fans demanded them of him. They did not understand. Perhaps one day they would, it being the fate of all random biochemical, molecular phenomena such as himself and they to pass from non-being into being and back into non-being again, gaining at best an ironic glimpse of their precarious position in an uncaring and meaningless cosmos.

Yet one must live as if it were not so. There were a few bright moments. He sent two unpublished tales to the editor who had rejected so many others, merely as a formality so that no possible source of badly needed income might be said to have been neglected, and both were purchased. That brought in enough money to keep the grim carnival going on a bit longer.

That year they had a Christmas tree. It wasn't that he had ever believed in Christ, or in Santa Claus for that matter, but the tradition soothed him, and he and his aunt amused themselves decorating it until their tiny quarters glowed with resplendent light. He hadn't been able to go to New York as he so often did to be with friends—poverty, his heath, and the cold all precluded it—so he spent the holiday with his lone aunt, surrounded by such remnants he had been able to retain from better days, the familiar furniture, pictures, and books. For the moment, again, he was content, or at least without suffering.

When he opened a package from one of his young correspondents and dust and soil trickled out onto the floor, and then the shattered remains of a human skull was revealed, his aunt exclaimed, "Disgusting!"

But he said, "No, it is an entirely appropriate gift from a young ghoul to a venerable elder of the clan."

Later, he carried the dead thing into his study and set it down on his desk, idly fitting some of the pieces together, thinking that another of his young friends, who was so clever, could probably repair it, coat it with lacquer, and mount it on a stand as a suitable *memento mori* of the sort that sorcerers always seemed to keep on their shelves amid crumbling tomes and dusty vessels.

Only after he had been sitting there for some time did he glance up and see the shape at the window.

It held his rapt attention. He knew exactly what it was, black-horned, slender, with membranous wings that flapped slowly as it floated in the air. Its bifurcated tail twitched from side to side. *It had no face,* as he had known it would not.

And yet, for the first time ever it spoke to him, not with sound, but with a kind of merging of the mind, like what had happened to the young writer in that story of his when confronted by the horror from the steeple. He was it and it was he. He rose from his desk and went around to the window. He placed his hand on the glass and *it did the same,* the taloned claw much larger than his own hand, the nails clicking against the pane. The glass was intensely cold, and then it shattered, crumbling into powder, and he felt only numbness in his arm all the way up to the shoulder, and an undeniable dread as the thing was in the room with him now, crouching low, its folded wings scraping against the ceiling.

He stepped back, around the side of his desk, and the creature followed him. It *touched* him, its claw passing into him as if it or else his own body were made of smoke. It reached *inside* him, then withdrew, holding up its index finger—for it had, indeed, five fingers, and its claw, despite the huge talons, was surprisingly human-like—to where its mouth should have been, as if it were *tasting* something.

You will be with us soon, it seemed to say, inside his mind. But he rejected that. He tried to rub his eyes and shake his head and force himself awake, even if this at no point had seemed to be a dream.

Later, after an indeterminate interval, perhaps after a genuine lapse of memory, he was at his desk again, shivering from cold, and he realized that one of the panes in his window was gone, and snow was blowing into the room. It was late. There was no sense awakening and alarming his aunt over this, so he made do as best he could, tearing a side panel off a cardboard box and affixing this over the gap with adhesive tape. They would have to get a repairman in to replace the pane. He couldn't account for how it had become broken. There were shards underfoot. He swept them up with a broom and dustpan. He could only explain it—to anyone else—as the wind. Merely the wind.

He sat down again at his desk, gazing gloomily at his ever-increasing pile of unanswered correspondence. There was a blank sheet of paper on the desk, and his pen lay there, its cap off, ready for him to write. But, again, he could hardly find the energy. Back in his prime, such a vision as he had just experienced might have proved the basis for a story. He had once attempted an entire short novel filled with dream-quests, and winged apparitions, and strange vistas beyond our world. The failure resided in a file drawer now, even as a corpse in a morgue resides in a drawer.

Or he might, at least, have given a vivid account in a letter, for the appreciation of those few sensitive souls intrigued by such things.

Now, nothing. He wrote of other things. He argued politics and economics with his friends. But he did not soar.

His health grew steadily worse. Some days he could only lie about wrapped in blankets, writing or reading for a few minutes at a time. His "grippe," which had bothered him before, now returned with real pain. It was hard to eat or sleep.

If he could not sleep, he would have no more fantastic dreams. No more visitations in the night.

They paid for the broken window pane out of the sadly depleted exchequer.

The Philosopher, he told himself, must accept what comes, and merely observe in a detached way, the follies and sufferings of mankind. If one could derive some momentary pleasure from an aesthetic association, immersed in one's culture-stream, that was all well and good, but even that only had meaning in the moment it was experienced.

Sometimes his feet swelled up and he could not even wear normal shoes, but had to make do with an old pair with the sides cut out, like sandals.

Then, for a while, he felt a bit better, and some of his energy returned. Miraculously, the winter had proven, overall, a mild one, so that walks in the town proved occasionally possible even as late as January. For brief moments it seemed as if somehow his life could go on as before, but each time the weakness and pain would catch up with him again. He thought of a story he'd read once, called "The Torture of Hope."

He revisited old, familiar places, the Athenaeum where Poe used to meet Sarah Helen Whitman, the house in Benefit Street that had been the subject of one of his own failed and never quite published stories. The graveyard below Benefit Street, which held so many associations.

To his friends he put up a brave front. He complained of piled-up work, correspondence, a massive revision job on a textbook.

But no new tales. No new visions.

Often, when he could sleep, or at least drowse, he heard wings flapping outside his windows.

He began typing his letters when his hand grew too unsteady to hold a pen reliably.

When he finally saw a doctor, the man's manner was grave.

He reported to correspondents that he was taking three "nostrums."

But they did little good.

When his condition had proven undeniable, the doctor told him and his aunt the truth. He had already known it. *As before August 20, 1890.* He looked forward only to oblivion, thinking of the old Stoic epitaph, *I was not. I was. I am not. I don't care.*

Indeed, after he had been taken to the hospital in an ambulance and had received a few visitors, one of them said to him, "Remember the ancient philosophers." He smiled at that.

But otherwise there was only pain. He had tried to keep a diary of his symptoms, to focus his own mind, and with a vague idea that the doctors might find it useful, but some days he could write little more than the word "pain."

The rational man, the philosopher, the would-be artist understood that fancy, fantastic visions, and otherworldly things are created artificially for the amusement of one's friends. They are appealing precisely because one *cannot* believe in them, any more than we believe in Christ or Santa Claus or other such emanations of the human mind. Mere electro-chemical sparks in the darkening universe.

Therefore, what happened next must have been a dream.

The creatures were in the room with him again, several of them, their faceless faces hovering over the bed, their great wings hunched beneath the ceiling. They reached with their talons into his body and drew them out again, placing their fingers to where their mouths would be, if they had mouths, as if they were feeding around a trough. But he wasn't afraid of them. They were not hostile. They were merely impossible things from his dreams, the subject of one of his sonnets, and now here they were, speaking to him again, without words, as his consciousness merged with theirs, and he saw himself lying in the bed, from their perspective a mere fragile shell, and he seemed to share some of their memories of black planets rolling in the void, and the swirling whirlpool of stars before the ultimate throne of chaos.

He was not afraid, because he did not believe. The philosopher understood that it was not a matter of belief. The philosopher accepts merely what *is*.

This wasn't a Faustian bargain when they offered to take him away with them, into their dark and strange and wonderful worlds. He wasn't at long last compromising his rationality and caving in to superstition. If, in his dying mind, he had merely created one last pleasing illusion to ease his passing, let it be so. It did not matter. There was no right and wrong of it. No true and false, not anymore.

The philosopher merely observes, dispassionately.

"Yes, I will go with you," he said aloud. "I shall look forward to the journey with adventurous expectancy."

He raised both his arms and held out his hands.

* * *

Howard died this morning. Nothing to do.

Maybe it was a little bit like *A Christmas Carol,* Scrooge carried off by the spirits, but without the moralistic ending.

They were soaring. They bore him up, a great flock of winged shapes. They carried him over the impossibly tall, dark mountains. He saw black worlds rolling in the void. He saw, too, lands he knew only in fancy, Ulthar beyond the River Skai, the Dreamlands, and Kadath in the Cold Waste.

They raced toward that distant tower with the single light in the window, where One sat waiting.

He felt that perfect balance of dread and dark wonder that he had never quite managed to capture in one of his stories.

Soon he would know the secret of the silken mask.

All Kings and Princes Bow Down unto Me

There was a girl by the name of Anna, twelve or thereabouts, of an age to be noticing boys though not yet with any serious interest, but old enough for her head to be filled with extravagant notions of romance, which she had acquired from reading and from movies. She was also certain that she was or should become an old-fashioned girl, though she wasn't entirely sure what that entailed. But it did seem fitting that a romantic, old-fashioned girl should on occasion slip out at night and dance in the moonlight.

So, having entertained *this* notion for some time, she finally put it into practice one spring night, and, well after the rest of the household was asleep, she slipped out of her bedroom window and dropped to the lawn by the side of the house. In her nightgown. Barefoot. The night was only moderately cold, and the ground beneath her feet was a little colder still, but not enough to be uncomfortable.

The full moon was up, and bright, shining through a thin haze of cloud, so that it seemed a white night, such as are more often experienced in winter, when the combination of diffused moonlight and snow on the ground makes things visible in stark, silhouetted detail at astonishing distances. Tonight, moonlight on pavement and suburban rooftops gave the same effect.

These were ideal moonlight-dancing conditions, and she swirled, with her arms out, her nightgown flapping gently in the slight breeze like a flag, or maybe like a sheet of laundry hung out on a line. She danced to the front lawn, and then to the street, humming softly, and she admired the way her shadow was cast, huge and wide, flickering over bushes and lawn and the front of the house as she moved.

But there also seemed to be another shadow, dark and still, beside her.

Taken by surprise, a little alarmed, she fell silent, and turned once more, toward that shadow, and saw nothing.

She danced, and the shadow was beside her. She twirled in the middle of the street, down the block, half running, and she saw nothing but moonlight and her own shadow, and again she began to hum, even sing softly. It was like a dream. She was alone in a dream. Dreaming thus, she came to the end of the block, and crossed an empty lot, beyond which a winding, unpaved lane gleamed like a white ribbon in the moonlight. Here the suburbs suddenly ended, and on the other side of the lane was a farmer's field, stretching to the horizon. Since it was early spring the crop, whatever it was, was newly planted, so most of the earth in that field was still bare, giving the same effect that snowy ground would on a white night in winter.

It was as she stood amid the pebbles and dirt of that unpaved lane that she noticed, far away across that field, the same black shadow she had seen before, now definitely coming toward her with long strides. It too seemed to flap around the edges, like a black cloth, a mourning cloth, a shroud, it occurred to her, somehow hung out on a laundry line. But it was clearly moving.

At this point the dream, which wasn't actually a dream, turned a bit unpleasant, and she felt a chill, not so much from the cold of the night air as from that unpleasantness, and she stopped dancing. She turned about once more, toward home, and found herself face-to-face with a tall figure draped in ragged black. Only the face was visible. It seemed to be a man's face, but there was more than a little strange about it: as remote as the moon on a winter's night but less brilliant, just icy pale, and a little bit mottled like an old snowbank. The eyes were black pits. The face might have been a mask.

She saw, too, that the stranger bore a long staff with a curved, glinting blade on the end of it.

"Oh," she said, barely above a whisper.

"Oh," the other whispered back, mocking her.

"I shouldn't be out like this," she said.

"No, you should not."

"I'll go on home then—"

"I do not have an appointment with you yet," said the other, "for this night or for many, many nights to come. In fact, you are not yet written into my book at all." He got out a notebook and flipped through it with the thumb of one very thin, pale hand. "No, you're not there at all."

At that point she held out either side of her nightgown and curtseyed, which instinct told her was the romantic thing to do, and said, "Then I bid you good night, sir, and will be on my way."

She started to run, but he was waiting for her again at the other side of the empty lot.

And again, as she tried to make for home, he stood up between two parked cars and swept out into the street and blocked her way.

"Nevertheless," said he, "you must come along with me, for none may return from such an encounter. It's the rules."

She twisted away and ran back into the vacant lot, but right where moonlight reflected from a muddy patch, she slipped and fell face down into a puddle. She rose to her knees, sputtering, wiping her hands on what was now the wreck of her nightgown, when she felt an electrifying cold as the stranger took her by both wrists and lifted her to her feet.

"Come," he said.

She tried to scream, but somehow her voice managed no more than a faint rasp. This still seemed to be an exceptionally vivid dream as the stranger led her by one hand, back in the direction of her house, but past it. She turned her head back and saw the porch light and the front door receding behind her, forever out of reach, it seemed.

Even if this was a dream, she was not floating, as one might in dreams. There were no strange transitions. She was walking. She felt the pavement and the grass under her feet. The stranger led her across lawns, behind houses. She recognized the Ryans' house. Margaret Ryan was her best friend from school. The swing-set that creaked softly in the night breeze was for the benefit of Jerry, Margaret's kid brother, who was six.

It became more dream-like when they passed right through the wall of a house and were standing in a dim-lit room where a very old woman lay alone in bed, breathing in her sleep with great difficulty, gasping and wheezing. For just an instant a smoke-like, pale outline of the woman rose above the bed. But the dark stranger made a swishing motion with his scythe—for such it was—and then the smoky outline was gone, and Anna and her companion stood in silence for a moment in that dark room, with the old woman who was not breathing.

That was how Anna became the companion and perhaps assistant to Death. She actually assisted sometimes, at least to the extent of paging through the notebook and reading out those names that glowed in red, burning letters, or sometimes in brilliant, white ones. Yes, she knew who her companion was, having seen such a figure in illustrations in books. The Dark Angel. The Reaper. The End of All Things. There was an old song relevant to her situation, which she'd learned from her mother (who was also of a romantic disposition), and sometimes she sang it softly to herself.

They visited many houses, and open fields, and other places, even a sinking liner at sea, and her companion and master made his harvest.

Despite all this, she found him very dull company. He said little. He muttered softly while writing in his notebook with the tip of a bony finger. (He never used a pen.) When one of the names so inscribed glowed, either bright red or white, there was an appointment and a job to do. So time passed, though it seemed to her that time passed very strangely indeed. She was never quite sure if this wasn't an extension of that first night and that dream-like encounter by moonlight, or if any time had passed at all.

When she asked about these things, she got no answer. When she asked about what became of the souls they took—for she certainly knew what was going on—he only replied, "That is a dark door beyond which I may never go." Did he know anything about the future, the nature of the universe, about God? No, he did not.

For all she had, in a sense, traveled the whole world, she grew uncomfortable, even bored. She began to complain, in a manner that children her age have long since mastered. Are girls better at it than boys? Who knows? There are no statistics on the subject. Suffice it to say that Anna had a full command of the art of getting her way.

She demanded to be allowed to go back and visit her mother. She insisted again and again, cajoled, whined, pouted. Once in a fit of temper she even tore a page out of the notebook and crumpled it up and threw it in a fire. (Whether that made the persons whose names were on that page exceptionally long-lived, or whether they all perished suddenly of a fever, is not recorded.)

So Death relented. She wore him down. It took twenty years, though she did not know that, being in her predicament insensitive to the passage of time.

Nevertheless she found herself one spring morning on the doorstep of her family home, as if only a single night had passed since she'd gone out dancing in the moonlight. The door was unlocked. She turned the knob, creaked the door open, and went into the kitchen and sat down at the table. Her mother, who was there, took one look at her, shrieked, and fell faint to the floor.

Anna sat there, befuddled. But it made perfect sense, of course. Twenty years had passed. From her mother's point of view, if her long-lost daughter were still alive (as she continued to hope against hope, for all the detectives investigating had turned up nothing), she would have to be a grown woman in her early thirties by now; and yet here was Anna, still a girl of twelve or so, barefoot and dirty, her nightgown little more than a rag. She could only be an apparition from beyond the grave. If she had returned with some portentous pronouncement, that would have been bad enough, but when she cheerfully said, "Hi, Mom, what's for breakfast?" it was too much and the poor woman succumbed.

Things did not get any better when her father came running down the stairs, discovered Mother, and tried to revive her. Anna noticed that Father looked different from the last time she had seen him. His hair was white now. Mother's was the same color, but dyed. There were differences in her face and figure, but Anna had not had time to notice them.

Eventually Mother did come around. She gasped. She stuttered. She pointed. But Father could not see Anna. He could not be made to believe that she had returned. He began to fear that his wife had gone insane. Indeed, she seemed quite mad as she talked to the air, as she prepared an extra breakfast of blueberry pancakes (Anna's favorite) and orange juice, and placed it in front of an empty chair. How the plate got emptied, where the pancakes went, he never did figure out, but assumed it was the sleight-of-hand of an obsessively, dangerously deranged woman. In fact, the only other member of the household who could detect Anna was the cat, who looked a bit like Mr. Cuddles, a pet Anna had had when she was genuinely twelve, and perhaps was descended from the same. But it was a different cat, and it hissed at her once, leapt out an open window, and was never seen again.

Weeks went by. The situation grew wretched. Mother wept and shuddered and tried to talk with Anna, asking her about her friends and school as if no time had passed and nothing had happened. Anna tried to comfort her. She didn't know what to say. She slept in her own room each night, which her mother had insisted on preserving exactly as she had left it. She washed and threw out the dirty nightgown and dressed in her regular clothes.

Seeing how much her mother suffered, she thought she should leave. At the same time she still desperately wanted to believe that the two of them could be again as they once were.

Besides which, she had nowhere to go. Her dark companion was nowhere to be seen.

Meanwhile Father brought strange men into the house, doctors, who examined Mother and then conversed with Father in low, grim tones. Another stranger came to the house, a tall, darkly bearded man in his mid-twenties, who, she realized, could only be her own little brother Matthew, who had been the same age as Jerry Ryan and had played with him on that set of swings. Together Matthew and the doctors conferred, and they spoke of sending Mother to some other place. The doctor recommended that they sell the house and move away, "to cut off all ties with her past."

But Mother was a step ahead. One night she poured gasoline all over her bed and herself and struck a match. Father and Matthew tried to rescue her but couldn't, though they managed to save themselves. The firemen could do nothing either; and for just a moment Anna stood before her mother amid the flames and Anna tried to say something, but before she could even manage a lame "Goodbye," the scythe swished and Mother was gone.

Anna was left standing on the lawn in front of the smoldering ruins. There were other people gathered around, and the firemen were still working, but no one seemed to notice her, except her dark-cloaked companion, her master or mentor or whatever, who suddenly rematerialized.

"Well, that is over," was all he said. He checked off something in his notebook.

Anna wept uncontrollably for a long time, as the people wandered away and even the firemen rolled up their hoses and left. She wept for her mother, whom she loved, and for her past life, which was now indeed irretrievably cut off.

If she had not slipped out of her window into the moonlight, things might have gone differently.

If—

But it was over. She understood that.

So she put aside her grief, as suddenly as if she had flipped a page in a notebook of her own, and she resorted to a kind of guile one does not expect in young girls, even a girl who has been twelve years old for the past twenty years.

She said to her companion that he was all she had left now, the closest thing she had to family, so she might as well grow up, focus, and learn the family trade, and be a genuine assistant or even become a partner. She asked to hold the scythe, so she would know how it felt. She hefted it.

Then, as if she had suddenly remembered something, she pointed at the last house at the end of the block, next to the little strip mall where the vacant lot had been twenty years ago, and said, "Didn't we forget somebody back there?"

"What?" said Death.

"Look it up in the book. Look it up."

And while he was turning the pages of the notebook, his back to her, she swung the scythe with all her might and lopped off his head.

The dark figure collapsed with a rattle of bones, into a cloud of dust. For a brief instant a voice seemed to whisper, "At last. I was so tired. Now I am free," but then there wasn't even dust, or bones, just a few bits of the cloak, which blew away like the ashes of burnt leaves.

Anna ceased to be a girl then. She became a great lady, a queen, who wore a gown as dark as the midnight sky, covered with jewels like stars. Her crown was of ice, and it glowed like the risen moon. She bore the scythe, and sometimes, out of deference to tradition, an hourglass, in addition to the notebook she carried in her pocket.

Having seen so much, having traveled through all the lands of Earth, she was beyond sorrow now. Grief and memory passed over her like smoke. She was awesomely beautiful, but dreaded by all. She was alone, utterly alone, in the dark, which was, she realized in a bitter way, very romantic.

Sometimes she danced.

The Festival of the Pallid Mask

I don't know how she got into my rooms.

I was seated motionless at my desk, before the old typewriter on which I banged out my lurid melodramas that no one wanted to stage anymore. Think of it as the Altar of Futility, in its backdrop a large bay window through which one could see only the fog of an autumn evening, set aglow by streetlamps. There, in such a suitably atmospheric and dismal setting, I had been reading *The King in Yellow*. I suppose I needn't have been, for, despite repeated attempts at banning, burning, and condemnation, that beautiful, evil book had already suffused itself through the city like the glowing fog I have just described, so that all were touched by it, its deadly miasma penetrating into heart and brain, draining both of any joy or life or hope.

I hadn't bought the book, I assure you. You didn't see it displayed in shop windows. It just had a way of *being found*, and there it was that evening, atop the papers on my typing desk, a somewhat worn and foxed copy bound in what felt like snakeskin. I cannot say where it came from.

And I read it, right up to the part where Cassilda bids the stranger unmask, when the stranger put her much-bejeweled hand on my shoulder and whispered, "Come, sir. It is time."

I rose and beheld her, in her white, shimmering gown the color of snow in moonlight. Indeed it seemed to give off a faint light of its own, I know not how, as did her mask, which was like a butterfly made of delicate, translucent crystal, or perhaps ice. I could see the eyes behind it, dark abysses into a soul of mystery, and I could only tell that the hair was long and dark and luxuriously draped over the shoulders—all this being as I, a failed writer of trashy, romantic plays inevitably described it twenty years on into the era in which the Yellow King held illimitable dominion over all.

So it was, the city of New York, in the year of 1940.

And my muse, my guide, my cicerone, the intruding phantom took me by the hand and led me to the door. I paused only to grab my hat and coat from the peg. Then I went with her, down the stairs and out of the apartment, into the damp and the fog and the surprisingly silent streets. Her hand was hard and dry and cold, her grasp delicate, but I had a sense of the strength of iron behind it, should I indulge in the unthinkable folly of trying to break away. I, as a melodramatist, even an unsuccessful one, knew better than to attempt to escape such an experience, such a dream, such an exquisite, living nightmare as might now unfold.

Better to embrace it, to let its vapors fill my empty soul like a damp miasma, and draw strength, even unholy inspiration from it.

We came very quickly to the place that had once been called Washington Square, across which now stood another, greater temple than mine, dedicated likewise to Futility, for this was the marble-faced government Lethal Chamber, which had caused such a stir when it was first opened twenty years ago, but was now a familiar part of the landscape, surrounded by beautifully maintained gardens and a forest of stone columns, to which are attached an ever-changing array of metal plaques recording the names of those who have passed through the great, sculpted bronze gates into what I suppose is a better world. I had often sat in those gardens, meditating, as I watched patient queues form before the great gates, or sometimes saw them open and yawning, with no one around, until one frantic soul might come running across the gardens and up the steps and into the Chamber's gaping jaws. Only once in a great while do you see someone, pale, trembling, uncertain, make their way out again. I had always heard there was one last chance to change one's mind in there. Maybe a wise and compassionate counselor interviewed each candidate before he or she passed on into oblivion. Maybe it was just a bored ticket-taker and if you didn't have a ticket, you did not proceed. Maybe there was a small fee required. Two pennies for the eyes? Ha! . . . ha! I make a joke, however inappropriate.

I have never been inside, for all I have spent so many hours in the gardens. I never knew what's in there.

Our business was not within those gates tonight. Quite the contrary. *From out of them* now streamed a veritable procession of gowned, caped, masked figures, most of them glowing, more rising up out of the shrubbery of the surrounding gardens like enormous fireflies, following as my guide led us all away from the gardens, back into the city, into the brilliant light of the risen moon.

Was I still in lower Manhattan? Does that part of the city really have a crystalline staircase that rises, turning and turning again, up among the very stars? Are its buildings all plain white, marble-faced, like the memorial columns in the garden of the Lethal Chamber? Are there thousands of names written on them, the letters illuminated like fire? Is there really a palace there, filled with the enormous light of the risen moon? Do its towers rise still higher, *behind the moon?* I don't think so. I didn't see the ruins of Staten Island beyond. I didn't see the Statue of Liberty with its head blown off in the recent insurrection.

No. We were dancing in a great hall. The music was more something *felt* than heard, something deep inside the skull, almost at the level of pain, a vibration, a desperate transformation of the self, impossible to resist. I cannot say, even I who can heap on words with a trowel. Suffice it to observe that there was no joy in this dancing, no beauty, only a forced adherence to form, out of fear, ultimately driven by mere tropism, the way plants turn toward the light. Do plants dance? Do the shrubberies of gardens of the Lethal Chamber swirl about at night in a stately waltz? Or do they kick up their heels in a can-can. Ha. I make a joke again. Nobody is laughing. They laughed at one of my melodramas once. Laughed it right off the stage. That was the end of my productive career, for all I filled many more pages, whole crates of pages, thereafter, with lines and stage directions and scribbled corrections that no one else would ever read in this life or the next (or in oblivion). At least when the audience was laughing, they were alive.

Now the morbid fancy came to me that as we swirled about like souls imprisoned in Fairyland in some old fable, as we shifted and turned and changed partners again and again in what was definitely not a can-can and wasn't even a waltz and might well have been be a stately pavane—yes, a *pavane*, which I know is stately and dignified and graceful, though I did not know the steps, and could only drift along like winter's last fallen leaf gently floating through a glowing mist—yes, the fancy came to me, it seemed to me that I was dancing among corpses, that most of the revelers had returned from the oblivion of the Lethal Chamber but were *not alive,* only dry, desiccated revenants with nothing in the abysses of their eyes. Yes, that's it. Yes. Every once in a while there was one who *was* alive, who seemed frightened and trapped. These partners I cast from me, bidding them go, escape, drift down into the familiar New York, like falling leaves perhaps. I belonged here. They did not. They might still have some life and color left in them. I, on the other hand, had only one color, the purple gore of my own prose, which would have to suffice for this occasion, as I bled out words, thoughts, my soul, all in a stream of thinning, detestable putrescence.

Once I found myself dancing with her who brought me here, the beautiful lady in the butterfly mask, and I whispered into her ear, asking who she was. She replied, "Don't you know? I am one you once loved."

I once loved someone? I once loved someone other than myself? I once wore something other than the purple cloak of vanity?

But now came the stage directions in someone else's melodrama, not mine.

Music stops, with one last thunderous drumbeat.
CASSILDA: You, Sir, should unmask.
STRANGER: I wear no mask!

All around me, they were unmasking, and I saw that, indeed, most of the company were the dead, their faces little more than bare skulls, and here and there a frightened, pale face that did not belong but which had not managed to escape and would soon be like the rest. She with whom I danced had also removed her mask, and her face too was dead, but perfectly preserved, like a wax effigy, and for all I searched my memory I could not recall her name, but I knew that I had once loved her, in another life that was long over and gone, like a turned page in a manuscript no one is ever going to read again.

I realized how ridiculous I must have looked in that company. Amid the vast garden of fantastic costumes I was wearing ordinary street clothes, a shabby coat and a bowler hat. Not even street clothes. I was wearing pajamas and muddy slippers. I had not thought to change them as I left the apartment.

I reached up and fumbled around the edges of my face, as if I could catch hold of something and lift it off. But there was nothing. I felt only unshaven cheeks.

MYSELF (feebly): It won't come off.
CASSILDA: The Pallid Mask! You wear the Pallid Mask!
ALL (screaming): The Pallid Mask!

Then I committed the unthinkable folly of *breaking away,* of turning from the path of destiny. I forced my way through the crowd and ran down the crystalline stairs, which dissolved beneath my feet like a structure of moonlight, and I was falling. I felt the impact, oblivion followed, but then I awoke, face down in mud, at the edge of the water at the extreme southern tip of Manhattan. It was dawn. I could see, silhouetted in the thinning fog, the headless Statue of Liberty.

But other than the cries of a few gulls, there was silence. No foghorns. No boat whistles. No sounds of the city waking up.

I staggered to my feet, finding myself uninjured. After a few wobbling steps I must have lost my slippers in the mud, and so I looked more absurd than usual, barefoot, hatless, in that old, splattered coat as I made my way north over the cold pavement toward Washington Square.

I saw no one. The streets were empty. I forced open the door of a shop and found only curious heaps of ash on the floor. No one was around. When I got to Washington Square—somehow I must insist on calling it that, even though the name is obsolete—I saw that the great doors of the Lethal Chamber were closed and the gardens were unkempt, as if they had not been cared for in several years. But there was life in them. Squirrels in the trees. Pigeons.

It was like that, indeed, for years, the dead, empty city.

Back in my apartment I discovered the crystalline butterfly mask of the one I had loved on top of my typewriter. When I went to pick it up, ever so gently, it disintegrated into gleaming dust.

I wept then, for I knew I had once loved her, though I could not remember her name. I wept, because I'd once had a life, which was gone.

Now it was my role to wander like Robinson Crusoe in the wilderness. I learned to go armed, first with a club, then with a pistol I had stolen from a deserted police station, because the streets were ruled by packs of feral dogs. I subsisted for as long as I could on canned or dried provisions, but in time I had to teach myself to hunt and butcher the small deer now inhabiting Central Park as the city returned to nature.

What did I do? I tell you that twenty years passed without my laying eyes on a single soul, or even dreaming of one. My dreams were of desolation, while in waking hours I wrote a thousand pages of a self-pitying, melodramatic memoir that no one will ever read, then a five-act farce called *A Comedy of Corpses,* which only a corpse could appreciate. After this, an exhausted pause, and there finally came one exquisite gem, which shines like a brilliant star in the darkness of my soul, a brief *playlet* (not melodramatic at all) in tribute to the one I had loved, whose name and face I could not bring to mind, even as my love for her and my memory of her love for me refused to die.

In this manner I had reached the year 1960. I knew then that I must once more read *The King in Yellow,* but while it is the nature of that seductive tome to appear when it can do the most harm, it also has the perverse ability *not* to be found when you actually seek it. I ransacked bookstores and libraries. In rare-book rooms I pored over many frightful and curious volumes, but never *The King in Yellow.* I resolved, then, to *compose it myself.* I sat for long hours in the ruined gardens of the Lethal Chamber, with a shotgun across my lap to keep off the wild dogs and a notebook, in which I scribbled and crossed out countless lines that tried to be *The King in Yellow,* but were not.

Yet I succeeded. In that year of 1960, fully forty years after its miasma suffused our lives, I reconstructed *The King in Yellow* in my mind. I did not put any of it on paper. It was too delicate, too exquisite for that, but I held it within me. I let it consume my soul, until within me was only its fire. And in such a state I made my way once more to the southern tip of Manhattan, and waited there until the moon rose in all its brilliance and I could see the towers of Carcosa behind it. Then I recited those beautiful and terrible lines, and I burned with them, and in great pain, trembling, I rose up the crystalline staircase into the great hall where I rejoined company I had previously deserted, and once more danced with them the stately dance that was not a waltz or even a pavane, but something I cannot name. My partners came and went, and most of them were corpses. We danced and bowed. I looked for the one in the butterfly mask, she whom I had loved, but I did not find her.

And again the music came to a halt with a thunderous drumbeat, and all unmasked, and they called on me to unmask, I took a sharp knife out of my pocket and with the utmost determination attempted to surgically remove the dreadful Pallid Mask from my face.

> CASSILDA: He cannot remove it! It is his very self!
> ALL (screaming): The Pallid Mask!
> STRANGER: I'm doing my best!
>
> *The* STRANGER *faints. Curtain.*

I feel like Mr. Poe's character who demands to know: *Why will you say that I am mad?*

I am the one who is sane. I am the only one who *knows*.

They tell me that passers-by found me in the mud at the tip of Manhattan, near the old ferry docks. I was fearfully mutilated. Somebody said it looked as if a dog had chewed off my face.

Eventually I was brought to this asylum. It is now the year 1980. I have grown old. The city beyond the bars of my window has slowly returned to life, though since the war there are still many deserted districts. The Lethal Chamber has shut down. It is no longer needed. The gardens have reverted to forest, as there is no one to tend them.

I admit I have made some serious mistakes. It is a mistake to attempt to remove that which cannot be removed. But through suffering I have gained my wisdom.

The miasma? *The King in Yellow?* The doctors say there is no such book. It is an imagined thing. *But I know better.* I have it all, locked inside my mind. I know how it ends, which few who read it—even back in the days of its glory—ever knew, because few ever got that far.

It ends when I gaze out at the night sky and see fleets of airships all emblazoned with the Yellow Sign, for they are sent into the world by the King, who shall rule us all. I hear their engines thundering.

It ends when the moon rises with towers behind it, and I go there, sailing on a golden barge through the mists on the Lake of Hali. I am not a usurper. I am not a threat. I do not aspire to rule in Hastur. Maybe I can be poet laureate. I intend to compose vastly ornate, melodramatic operas to be performed by beautifully costumed corpses.

It ends when she whom I loved and I are reunited, neither in life nor in death.

It ends when the music stops and the time has come to unmask and I do not unmask, because I wear no mask, instead *am* the Pallid Mask, from whom all but the King recoil in terror.

It ends very soon.

A Dark Miracle

The Darkness likewise yieldeth up miracles.—COTTON MATHER

The black thing that came for him wasn't a cat, though it moved like a cat in the night, so fluid that it seemed a living shadow, which detached itself from the greater gloom of the cabin and brushed gently against his face, ever so lightly caressing his chin with tiny, all-too-human hands.

Its whisper was more like something remembered from a dream than actually heard in the present.

"Thou art summoned. Arise."

He knew who had sent it. Therefore Goodman Hawkins arose stealthily and abandoned Rachel, his wife of five years, who had done him no wrong, leaving her asleep beneath the heavy furs and blankets.

The creature rubbed against his bare ankles. He shivered. The floor was as ice, but the touch of the monster was even colder. Yet he made his way over to the hearth, sat down on a crude wooden bench and drew on his trousers, stockings, and boots, then stood and put on coat, cloak, and hat, without having bothered to remove his nightclothes.

All the while the messenger crouched before the faint embers, gazing into them as if into some ineffable mystery, eyes aglow.

It looked more like a rat now, he decided, hideous, yet irresistible as it whispered again, "Now is the time agreed upon. Come." Its face, he saw by firelight, was that of a gnarled old man. Its hands and feet too were bare and pale, the rest of the body coated in sleek black fur.

Goodman Hawkins hesitated, and felt even then as if he were tottering on the edge of some unplumbed abyss. But he knew that he was already falling. Otherwise the thing would not be here.

He slid sword and pistol into his belt. He had some sense of what he had to do this night. He had seen much in visions. Now the messenger, whether a physical creature or a phantasm, seemed to confirm everything he had come to believe.

His rival, Goodman Fletcher, planned to kill him when he could. It was necessary to strike first. There was no other way. Fletcher's wife, Caroline, whom Hawkins so inconveniently loved and who loved him, in violation of all convention and decency, had sent her small colleague to warn him. She was a woman of amazing depths and strange secrets. He feared her too, almost as much as he loved her.

The creature urged him on. He did not look back on his own, unfortunate, blameless wife Rachel, but silently opened the door and followed the thing out into the deep gloom of a Massachusetts winter night.

For just an instant, as he walked between the houses of the village, silent and almost knee-deep in newly fallen snow, the moon broke through the clouds overhead, illuminating everything in a silvery light. He beheld Caroline's messenger, far ahead of him, gliding across the surface of the snow without leaving any trace. He appreciated the irony: even the rumor of such an apparition, even some villager's half-remembered nightmare of it, could have gotten his coveted Caroline and himself hanged at Salem just a few years before, for a crime far more serious than adultery.

But he was resolved to do what had to be done. He had already descended into the darkness of the soul. Now he would be resolute, be bold, and afterwards he and Caroline could escape to Rhode Island together and live happily.

Surely that was what she too wanted. That was why she had sent for him.

The creature and the moon both vanished. There were voices. Hopefully invisible in the renewed darkness, Hawkins listened. He stood still in terror of discovery as a lantern drifted near. But he was not discovered. It was Deacon Sommerfield, a godly, righteous man, performing one more charitable duty by escorting the ancient Goodwife Pike back to her own doorstep.

"... truly Satan is all around us," the deacon was saying. "Our religion is like this single lantern, to push back the darkness, our colony a frail thing on the very edge of a continent otherwise completely ruled by the Evil One, who works his every wile to extinguish the flame of true belief..."

"God protect us then," gasped Goodwife Pike.

"Aye. He alone can," said the deacon, who raised his hand as if to comfort her with a gesture. But of course he did not cross himself in the manner of a papist idolater.

Hawkins watched, while Deacon Sommerfield saw the old lady safely to her door, then turned back toward his own house, his lantern fading in the darkness like that same light of faith which the Devil was so eager to extinguish. And when Hawkins once more stood alone in the darkness, the messenger rejoined him, climbing up his leg, clinging to his boot, and for the first time making faint mewling sounds in mockery of a cat.

He shook his foot in distaste and the creature scampered across the snow, then paused, looking back to see that he was following. Perhaps it was only fancy: the thing's eyes seemed still aglow, though there was no fire here to provide reflected light.

He followed, more often than not completely unable to see or hear his guide. But he knew the way, as he passed unchallenged out of the village and into that same heathen-haunted, demon-ruled forest against which the deacon had inveighed. Now the wind blew, icy branches rattled, and thick clouds covered the moon, and he had to grope his way along, striving to remain on the narrow path, lest those same demons overcome him, whether in the form of painted savages, wild beasts, or the mere cold. On such nights as this, many travelers were lost. None but those of most determined purpose had any business being abroad.

But determined purpose and murder in his heart drove him on, and he arrived before the remote cabin of Esau Fletcher, whose wife he had come to steal away. Fletcher's father, so the story went, had been a regicide, who had fled to New England after the restoration of the monarchy, and had dwelt here apart, in fear all his days, until he finally died and left the cabin to his son.

The creature waited on the doorstep, tittering to itself as if satisfied that its mission had been accomplished.

At once Hawkins knew that something was wrong. There was no smell of smoke in the air. The fire had been out for hours.

The door hung ajar. Snow drifted over the doorstep. The tiny beast looked up once and darted within.

Certain now that some terrible destiny was upon him, Goodman Hawkins hesitated on the threshold. He felt like some doomed king in the poetical dramas he'd read in his youth, back in England before he'd converted to the true religion and come hence. But like such a king, he knew that he was already too far along his shadowed path to turn back. He must see the thing through to the end.

He stepped into the darkened cabin. He sensed, more than saw, that someone sat in a chair by the fireplace, facing him.

Yet no voice challenged him. His boots scuffed on the rough floor.

He heard the messenger whispering, almost in a sing-song, and he drew near, one hand on his pistol.

The messenger seemed to squat in the lap of the person seated in the chair.

"Caroline?"

He reached out and found a hand, and that hand was very cold.

The messenger leapt away into the darkness.

Now Hawkins's mind seemed merely to cease. His hands worked. They knew what to do. He stirred the ashes in the fireplace, blew on the charcoal lumps until he choked, and then at last got a straw alight, from which he lighted a candle, then a lantern.

He placed the candle on the mantelpiece and took the lantern in hand, holding it up to the face of the one who sat in the chair, who was of course the adulterous, infinitely mysterious Caroline whom he loved. Her face as pale as the snow, her eyes rolled up so that only the whites showed, her throat slit from ear to ear, blood splattered and dried down the front of her nightclothes.

Now Goodman Hawkins was like a soldier who receives a fatal wound in battle, but feels only the impact at first, as if he has been hit with a stone, and the pain itself is slow in coming. The soldier is already dead and knows it, but he has a few seconds left. In those few seconds Goodman Hawkins opened the metal door of the lantern wide and flooded the room with light. He saw that the cabin had been ransacked, furniture overturned, trunks broken open, their contents dumped out; and he saw too that there were feathers on the floor, and even a stone hatchet of the sort that savages carried.

In those few seconds he deduced clearly. This was not the work of savages. He noted that Esau Fletcher's cloak, hat, and musket were gone, and of the righteously vengeful husband there was no sign at all.

Then the pain of that fatal wound to his soul closed over Goodman Hawkins like an inexorable tide. He cursed and wept. He knew that he had sinned irretrievably in the harlot's bed; he had borne murder in his heart for all he had not actually killed anyone; he was certainly *not* one of the Elect of whom the Divines spoke, and therefore damned. He had given himself over to the Enemy as surely as if he'd danced naked at the sabbat, rendered the Kiss, and signed his name in the Book.

The black messenger-thing yawned, faintly amused. It laughed at him, and spoke *in his own voice.*

"All this shall be thine, if ye will but fall down and worship me."

Hawkins fired his pistol. The hateful creature yowled and was gone, but of course he had not killed it, nor would he ever be free of it. He was shooting at his own shadow, his accuser, his conscience, his own personal demon, which would be waiting for him at his very grave to convey him into Hell.

Perhaps, for a time, Goodman Hawkins became mad. Certainly he howled. He laughed. He danced a forbidden dance with the corpse of his beloved, covering her icy cheeks with tears and with kisses. He listened to the voice of Satan, which was all around him, in every sound in the night, and especially in the wind, which extinguished the lantern and the candle and covered the coals in the fireplace with cold ashes.

In the darkness, then, the Master and he conversed.

In the darkness, he was bidden to carry his Caroline out into the forest and conceal her in a grave of snow and leaves and branches.

Then he returned to the cabin and waited for the dawn. He thought, once, to put his pistol in his mouth and cock back the flint, but, fool that he was, he had inexplicably forgotten to bring more powder or another ball.

He threw the pistol away.

He saw the messenger one more time, on the mantelpiece, licking its hands, its eyes glinting merrily as it regarded him.

And his reason returned. Everything was clear. He understood the whole nature of the plan by which he had been ensnared, as clearly if it were a map unfolded before him. He marvelled at how cunningly the trap had been laid, years ago, before he even knew her, when Goodwife Fletcher had awakened from a dream and continued to hear a voice that spoke to her out of that dream. She had been no more than a girl at the time. It seemed but a girlish fancy. That voice had spoken, she later recounted to him during one of their own intimate moments, in her dead mother's voice, and her mother was surely in Heaven, so what harm could there be? In hope and innocence she had answered. It told her wonderful things. That had been the beginning. The rest followed logically, inexorably, infernally, a dark and terrible miracle, of which even she was only an instrument, now discarded.

It was part of the continuing miracle that in the morning Goody Pike's granddaughter Sarah came pounding on the door of the cabin, begging to be let in. Hawkins discovered her barefoot and in her nightgown, blue with cold, her feet bloody. He did what he could for her as she gasped out how the village of Deerfield had been overwhelmed by Frenchmen and savages.

Only years later would he see that 1704 marked the beginning of an epoch, the opening move in a great game, as empires clashed for the possession of a whole new world; and that too was only part of some vast and dimly-apparent process.

For now all he knew was that all the inhabitants were slain on that single, terrible night, or carried off to some worse fate in Canada, save for a few, like this girl, so distraught in their own grief that they would never ask questions about the fate of Caroline or how he came to be in this particular cabin.

That was part of the miracle too. It meant there was no Esau Fletcher, no Rachel, no Deacon Sommerfield, no one left to accuse him. He was free as air.

Certainly, reason could have pieced together enough of what had actually happened here: adultery, murder by a jealous husband, an Indian raid, his own coincidental but very guilty escape; the parts sufficient to implicate him in mundane crime and get him mundanely hanged. Possibly the savages *had* come here, beheld the corpse in the chair, and turned away, frightened by unholy dreads of their own.

Or perhaps they too had reasoned, laughed, and gone away, seeing that there was nothing here for them.

Who was left to know, or figure things out? He had been miraculously saved from his own iniquity. An ordinary man in such a circumstance would have breathed a sigh of relief, however much he might have regretted the loss of Caroline.

But Goodman Hawkins came to understand the matter more profoundly. He saw a hand preserving him for some future, unknowable purpose, but that hand, he knew, was not the hand of God. Therefore his days were filled with gloom, his nights with secret horror, as he lived his life out in dread expectation, until, at the lip of the grave, the rat-thing spoke to him one more time, in the calm and measured tones of his own voice.

A Predicament

In the dream I knew that I had done some dreadful thing. Of my guilt, there could be no question. Worse yet, I had been found out. The accusation came in a document, delivered into my hand by a cloaked messenger. I read the paper several times, carefully to the end, futilely turning it over in hope there might be some forgiveness on the back, but there was not. There was no denying its logic.

Even so, I thought I could get away. The first thing I did was burn the paper in a candle flame, tossing away the last bit as the flame touched me.

Then I put on my own dark cloak and a peculiar top hat—not my usual costume, but in the dream what was customarily worn—and stole out, making my way along cobblestoned streets, beneath dripping arches, sometimes groping in utter darkness, sometimes stooping to conceal myself as I passed below candlelit windows.

This was not my native place, or any city I knew, but in my haste to escape I convinced myself that it did not matter where I was, as long as I remained undetected. For that I could still hope.

Even as a wind rose, whistling through empty alleys and moaning over chimney pots, the sound gradually forming itself, in my ears at least, into language, into murmurous words; even as one after another dark shape detached itself from doorways or from out of narrow streets and began to follow me, to swarm around me, until I was an anonymous part of a great throng, with phantoms, with ghosts, with half-glimpsed forms jostling me from every side; even then I could hope to remain unknown, unnoticed.

Wherever I turned, I couldn't see any faces. A hooded cloak obscured my view. A broad-brimmed hat was drawn down in concealment, an almost skeletal wrist and gloved hand holding it in place against the wind. I made my way onward, one more shadow among the shadows.

I did not speak. I wanted to ask where we were going, but I dared not give myself away. I thought only of escape. I still *hoped* to escape.

Was this, then, indescribable folly?

I let myself be carried, a part of the great mass, all of us like ashes on that vigorous wind, out of the narrow streets, into a palatial square, past an empty fountain and some huge statue I couldn't quite make out, but which frightened me. I fancied it the figure of an executioner. But, as I say, I could not see it clearly.

Now a light appeared: an opening vast and curved like the entrance to a cathedral, lit from within, growing steadily brighter, like a mouth, into which every one of us, the great whispering throng along with myself, were drawn, as if some giant were drinking us down.

Yet I could only follow, and a long journey up marble steps ensued, and as we went the appearances of some of my companions became more distinct: here, a tall, majestic man bearing a silver cane, there an old woman, gnarled and bent, leaning on a barefoot, half-naked child that seemed little more than an animate bundle of sticks in its emaciation; here again a soldier in armor, and so forth, but still there were no faces, the tall man's concealed by his hat, the old woman's by her unruly hair, the child's lost in her filthy skirt, the armored soldier's visor down; these followed by great multitudes of anonymous others.

We came at last to what might have been a courtroom, and we all stood trembling before faceless judges seated high above us—faceless because each of the judges wore a featureless mask, a plain covering of what might have been white cardboard. The only light came from little candles placed here and there on a long table.

A herald called us all to order. The court was in session. Clerks read out a list of charges, describing in excruciating detail numberless atrocities. The prosecutors thundered from behind their masks, while the judges sat impassively. If there was any defense, I never heard it. I couldn't think of any basis for one.

But, I told myself, it hardly mattered if I did or didn't, because this wasn't about me. I was just part of the crowd, a witness to these tumultuous events. There were witnesses wailing; others stood still and wordless, yet they were given close attention. So it went on and on, until I almost fell into a kind of swoon. I lost track of what was going on—the motions, the objections, the cries, the gasps from the horrifying testimony. It was so remote, so abstract. It began to fade from my hearing. I hadn't been discovered after all, had I?

From out of darkness and distance there suddenly came in a voice like a thunderclap. I snapped to attention. The verdict was guilty. Guilty of every crime, every impossible evil. The mass of folk around me fell to their knees, some of them fainting, some with their hands clapped desperately to their ears while blood oozed through their fingers. The sentence too was pronounced, too horrible to be repeated in words. It was like a blow.

I felt buffeted about, as if by winds.

But no one laid any hand on me. It was as if I were not there at all. I had been completely overlooked. I wept with enormous relief, in exhaustion at the unexpected mercy of my escape.

They must have convicted *someone else*. It had to be that.

I could barely constrain myself from laughing.

Then the dream shifted, and somehow we all came to be seated at the long table that stretched the length of the room, and by the light of those little candles I saw that a banquet was in progress. There was laughter and music and, I think, even dancing, there in that shadow-filled, high vaulted room. I began to relax. The guests all around me—for surely we were all guests here, myself among them, no different from the rest, entertained by some gracious lord—spoke of pleasant things, such as I could make out any of their words at all. We were at ease. We were merry. All was right with the world. I drank deep of delicious liquor of some kind—how exquisite, how peculiar, that one could *taste* in a dream, and become intoxicated—and pondered how ironic it was that one could lose one's judgment, or common sense, or any and all caution by getting drunk on dream-liquor in a dream— which is exactly what I did when, laughing at last, I nudged the guest next to me, who happened to be the unkempt old woman. Nodding in the general direction of the judges' high bench, I said, "Well, I'm glad *that's* over with!"

And with this, there was absolute silence, every motion ceased, every heartbeat stilled.

The woman next to me shook her head, and I saw her face clearly. I saw the rictus of her terror as she shrieked out in a voice far too loud to have come from a human throat, *"It's him! It's him!"*

In an instant, everyone was screaming, "It's him! It's him!" I saw the crowd melting away in all directions, as there strode toward me a band of tall men in black cloaks and strange, tall hats, members of an ancient ritual order to which I myself belonged and which I had betrayed. How, I didn't know. I was weak on the details. In this dream the most maddening thing was that, for all I understood the irrefutable logic of my guilt and there was clearly no escaping the consequences of my misdeeds, *I did not actually know the nature of my crime.* The testimony I'd heard, I had forgotten. It escaped from my memory like sand from between limp fingers. But everyone else knew. It was taken for granted by the screaming crowds around me, by the tall men in the cloaks and tall hats who laid hands on me and dragged me like a sack of rubbish in front of the chief judge, who leaned down in his high seat above us like a god out of heaven, pointed a great, pale finger at me, and spoke in a voice that made my ears gush with blood, saying only the single word, *"Thou."*

Now as I cringed before him, my hands were burning. There was a flame, and a document, which was *reconstituting itself* out of the fire, as if the whole process of combustion were occurring backwards, and in an instant I could see by its light that what I held was a *confession in my own handwriting*, but I didn't have a chance to read more than the first line or two before it fell from my grasp. Useless. I could only remember how I'd felt alarm, then terror, then false hope and false relief, then terror again—now followed by an angry, petulant sense that *it wasn't fair.*

Did any of that matter?

Will you say, then, that I was suffering only from some fantastic spasm of the brain which had produced this very dream?

I could only wish as much.

And the dream shifted one last time, and those I had wronged, those I betrayed, lifted me up and placed me in a coffin, which had a design in high relief on its lid, part like a deformed vermin, part . . . I don't know. There was an oval opening where my face would show through, to give me the identity of that caricatured monstrosity, whatever it was. I was trapped inside as they screwed the lid into place. I tried to argue, to negotiate, to make excuses. "Can't we talk about this?" and "Hey, everybody has their faults," but grimly they finished their work, the screws screeching through the wood. I was loaded into the back of a hearse, with glass panels. A procession followed, over sere hills and black valleys, beneath a dark sky and pale, unfamiliar stars. The multitude followed, bearing tiny candles flickering in the wind.

Only gradually did I became aware of a light ahead and heat from the same source. I could not see where we were going. I had been placed in the hearse head first, slightly tilted upward, so I could see behind me, the trailing procession, but not ahead. I thought it a sunrise. The sky lightened. The stars faded, as if a huge reddish sun rose over that desolate land.

It was only as they unloaded me and turned me around that I saw that we had not come into a sunrise at all. An immense, fiery furnace gaped, above which my bearers began to swing me from side to side with a heave and a ho—

I tried to reason with them. It was no good. I tried to bargain. Nothing. I pleaded, but they made no answer.

I screamed then, and in my final desperation I cried out, "Stop! Stop! This is a dream! I want to wake up! Please! *I want to wake up!*"

I banged on the inside of the coffin. I clawed at the wood, oblivious of the pain as my fingernails ripped off.

They hurled me through the air.

"I want to wake up! Please, let me wake up!"

But I couldn't wake up, even though all this was truly a dream, *because I was not the dreamer,* and the dream itself was someone else's act of inexorable vengeance.

The Thief of Dreams

The man in the fantastic mask woke me, not out of a dream, but *into* one. He loomed over my bed, in his ragged, dark cloak and his beaked leather mask that gave him the appearance of an enormous raven. His eyes were strange. They might have been glass, mysteriously animated, or real eyes gazing out through the glass of the mask. I cannot say. I felt the power of them, and was both fascinated and afraid.

He drew me out of myself. His hands were long and thin and bony, and terribly pale, like the limbs of some deep sea creature that spent its life in nighted caves. Somehow he took hold of my soul and pulled it out of my body, until I floated beside him in the darkness. I had only a glimpse of myself on the bed, drifting away, and then he opened a door where there had not been a door before, and we two were walking, up damp, stone stairs. The walls were slimy and cold to the touch. We emerged into a moonlit courtyard. Around us rose walls and towers and battlements of some strange, ancient city I had never seen before yet somehow knew.

I too was wearing a black cloak and a mask. Our boots echoed on the paving stones. I began to hear his voice inside my head, reminding me, recalling to memory things I did indeed seem to remember, how we two were members of a secret brotherhood, comrades-in-arms on some indescribable campaign; and so, afraid though I was, I went with him willingly, because I too was devoted to the cause, and he was my commanding officer.

We hurried across an open square. Our long shadows made the two of us look like twin agents of nemesis sent by the gods.

Once more in shadow we confronted something that waited for us, a hunched, squatting, glistening figure that spoke like a man, but not in any language I knew. This thing conversed with my companion for a time, then moved off to one side, out of our way, its motion, I thought, more like a sack being dragged than anything that propelled itself on limbs.

The enemy was very near, I was made to understand.

We drew our swords.

Our task, the man in the raven-mask explained to me, was to apprehend the great criminal, the Thief of Dreams, who moved from world to world and century to century *stealing dreams;* not the petty dreams of longings or anxieties that most people have, but the great dreams, the visions of prophets, of great poets, of human giants of all kinds (including, I suppose, actual giants, who sleep under hills, who have *become* those hills, whose dreams shape the worlds we know when we fancy that we are awake). These the Thief took, and carried with him in a flask of crystal, as if filled with eternal, magical tears.

It does explain why miracles do not happen anymore, the man in the mask said, inside my mind, as if I were forming his words with my own thoughts. It is why the oracles are silent. Very few people are still able to reach deep into the dreamlands, whence miracles come.

"There!" I shouted aloud. The echo was like thunder.

I pointed. Ahead of us, visible for just an instant before it disappeared around a corner, was a speck of light.

We both ran, our footsteps echoing. The streets rose ever more steeply until they broke into stairs, and we scrambled up them. I was straining, gasping for breath, my limbs somehow grown heavy. My companion almost seemed to soar. I was barely able to keep up with him.

From out of half-shuttered windows startled or frightened or perhaps just coolly amused faces peered out at us, some of them human, some of them not.

We saw the light again, gleaming before us, then again gone, and we pursued.

We were climbing a vast tower. Something scaled and winged passed by an open window, eclipsing it, then covered another window, and a third, without uncovering the first.

We were on our enemy's heels. Did he show us the precious vial to taunt us, or was it such that even if he kept it under his clothing, close to his breast, it shone *right through* him?

That did not matter. We had dreamed ourselves very close to him, very close, after (I somehow knew) many centuries of effort, like a pair of arrows that had *almost* found their target.

Now the Thief of Dreams was screaming (or was it laughter?) and the universe filled with sound, so loud it was painful. I felt my ears bleeding.

I struggled upward. My companion soared. Our silver blades gleamed in the moonlight.

We had reached a pinnacle of sorts, where the rising streets ended in space, the top of a tower, the summit of a mountain or of a city carven out of a mountain. Below us, spread out to infinity, were all the stars of cosmic space. Above were faces, floating in the black sky like risen moons, but empty, I felt, the faces of dead gods, for if the dreams of the universe have been stolen the gods cannot live; so there were their corpses, floating above us.

The Thief also wore a mask and a dark cloak. He held the precious vial in his hand. It shone like a brilliant star, almost blinding. He laughed hideously, and just before my companion was able to strike him with his sword, he leapt off the pinnacle, into the starry abyss, and was gone, and once more there was only silence.

My ears hurt. I felt blood on my cheeks.

I looked to my companion, and up to the gods, if gods they were, but as I did the sky began to lighten, and the whole scene faded, and I awoke.

And here was the wonder of it. I sat up in a bed in an unfamiliar room. I pushed the covers aside and slid to the edge. My feet knew how to find slippers. I staggered to the window. My limbs ached inexplicably. I wore only a loose nightgown.

Why didn't I reach for the light switch? I thought to, but at the same time the idea of a light switch seemed somehow absurd. There was a kerosene lamp on a desk. I didn't bother with it. Instead I made my way to the window and raised the blind.

Now the wonders multiplied, almost too swiftly for me to process them.

Someone was knocking on the door, calling out in a loud but strangely muffled voice, in a language I did not know.

I looked out the window and saw, not the New York of 2017, but some European city without skyscrapers or even modern buildings, a lot of slate roofs, the streets filled with pedestrians and carriages, and one almost comically absurd antique motorcar puttering by in a cloud of smoke.

The voice at the door was beginning to make sense, as if now, awakening, I was remembering that language. It was Czech.

Even more surprises: I was and was not myself. I was not Peter Harrow, a tall, long-limbed, blond-haired, smooth-skinned, rather boyish-looking fellow of thirty, who lived in an apartment in the Lower East Side, jogged regularly in Central Park, and worked as a graphic designer in the Flatiron Building. *My* name was Alexander Ivanovic and I was a clerk in a government ministry in the Prague of the Habsburg emperors. I was over fifty, short, stocky, hairy, with a thick beard . . . Peter Harrow, while he yet lingered in my mind, ran his hands through that beard as if it were a great and astonishing wonder. He also touched the top of my head to discover that he was mostly bald, as if that were entirely new to him.

The landlady at the door was reminding me that I would be late for work.

It was good of her to look after me, ever since my wife had died in the epidemic.

I still couldn't make out much of what she was saying. My hearing was impaired. I remembered blood on my cheek. I was entirely deaf in one ear. Possibly I was a military veteran and an artillery shell had blown out one eardrum?

I walked with a limp. No jogging for me.

Ultimately it didn't matter. Whether I was Peter Harrow or Alexander Ivanovic, I wore that identity like a mask, lightly, my waking life no more substantial than a shadow. All I wanted was to find my way back into the dream. I had a mission there, a purpose. But the way was hard.

That was when my apparent madness began. I didn't go to my job that morning, or ever again. I hoarded what money I had (actually I had inherited a sum from my dead wife and was well off, if I remained frugal) and eventually moved to a tiny rooftop garret that I filled with books on strange subjects and spent most of my waking hours in occult researches, searching obsessively for the secrets of worlds beyond our own, which might be revealed in dreams or the exhalations of dead gods. All my efforts remained focused on the single goal of regaining what I had lost.

Then, very suddenly, I discovered an artistic talent I'd never known I had (and quite beyond the mediocre doodles of the scarcely remembered Peter Harrow) and became a painter of fantastic landscapes and obsessive portraits of mysterious figures whose masks and dark cloaks made them look like birds or beasts, and repellent corpse-faces floating in starry skies. (*But sometimes in my dreams those faces opened their eyes, and they spoke to me in a language Alexander Ivanovic didn't know, English.*) As such I enjoyed a certain vogue among the avant-garde and moved among numerous circles where I didn't really belong, among artists and authors. I knew a Jew whose writings were almost as bizarre as my paintings. For a while I thought he understood me, but I was wrong about that, and he went away thinking I was a lunatic. He seemed to view all existence as, ultimately, a big joke, which I tried to convince him it most decidedly was not. His idea was that we are all ultimately vermin, infesting the world like bedbugs in a carpet. Maybe so, but where he laughed at it all, I did not.

Then came the mystics and mediums and charlatans, and a few who actually knew something. There was an American from New England, a very old man who had used numerous names (I called him Simon) in his unnaturally prolonged career, who taught me, too, the technique of extended lifespan, which I mastered imperfectly. He came to a sudden bad end in the 1920s, but it was with his help that I went on to narrowly escape two world wars and occupation and the secret police, until after many changes of identity and a few of nationality, aged, decrepit, limping, and mostly deaf, I became a contemporary of Mr. Peter Harrow of New York. I thought to meet with him, to compare notes, to teach him the secrets I had learned. I was then a hundred and seventy-seven years old, having been born in 1840. My military injuries dated from 1866, the year Bismarck tricked our emperor into a brief spat and handed him a sharp defeat. I had been drafted into the artillery. *Boom.*

But it was not to be. I must have been dying. I had sailed for New York. I was much too old-fashioned to fly, so I had gone by ship. I could afford it. Simon O. had also taught me secrets of finding hidden gold and hoarding it. I remember feeling exceptionally weary on the first night of the voyage. Then my stateroom went dark, as if it filled slowly with black smoke that dimmed, but did not extinguish, the light overhead. I fumbled about for a kerosene lantern, but there wasn't one. I tried to raise the blind over the porthole. A dark angel made to embrace me, black-robed, with black wings spread wide and a pale, so incredibly pale, dead face like a risen moon. This must have been Death, who will have his due in the end despite any number of tricks humans think they have perfected.

But at the last moment someone *else* seized me by the wrist and yanked me away, into the air. We passed through the steel bulkhead as if it were mist. I had only a brief glimpse of the ship, drifting away, and then I was once more in that darkened, antique, otherwordly city with my beak-masked and black-cloaked commander. We were of the brotherhood who sought the Thief of Dreams.

In a tavern, in that place, beneath a low, thick-beamed ceiling, amid the light of smoky lamps, as we sipped a wine that tasted a bit, I thought, like metal mixed with blood but somehow sweet, we conferred with others of our Order. My companion was indeed an officer of some sort, who gave commands, who congratulated others, including myself, for their reconnaissances or other accomplishments. But he was not fully in charge. Others, also hidden behind masks, were his equals, a few his superiors, and I had the impression that they all served some vastly more potent and even terrible personage who was perhaps near at hand, maybe just behind the locked door at the far end of the room.

As a result of my long occult researches and my association with the many-named American I called Simon, I had begun to understand a little. Dreams are more real than "reality." The waking world, the observable universe, is no more than a thin scum on a bottomless, waveless ocean. We were all dreamers, great dreamers, who move through dreams into the minds of any number of persons, sometimes only to take up temporary residence, sometimes to share the mind in the waking world with the original owner, which explains so many reports of demonic possession and quite a lot of madness. Sometimes we displace or merge with the original soul entirely and live out a whole lifetime in a stolen body. We have been doing this for so long that we forget who we originally were. It would have been folly, then, for Alexander Ivanovic to have sought out Peter Harrow. Mr. Harrow wouldn't have known anything. Neither one of them mattered, any more than did the bug-obsessed Jew or the would-be American sorcerer, Simon Orne. We are like a school of fish, swimming in the ocean of dreams. Only rarely do we break the surface and become a waking person anymore.

Our problem was the Thief of Dreams, who had stolen the very essence of our existence, the key to the universe so to speak. He was our enemy, who must be overtaken and destroyed and relieved of his treasure.

"Who *is* he?" I dared to ask.

"One of us," was the answer.

"A fallen, corrupted angel," was added.

"Like Satan?" I asked.

"That may be how you will be able to understand it."

We sailed our ship on the blood-dark sea, the oars breaking the surface, ripping the stars of cosmic space, that lay just below. I pulled at an oar, as did so many others of our masked, black-robed brotherhood. Our captain, the man in the raven-like mask, had climbed the single mast and peered out from the crow's nest.

I heard a drumming from somewhere, perhaps inside my ears. We rowed in time to it.

So we passed through the clashing rocks.

So we battled the sea monsters, striking them with our ram, or beating them away with our oars. Those that clambered aboard, we slew with our swords.

It was the winged, faceless things that were the worst. Those swooped out of the dark sky without warning and carried off much of the crew.

We passed between worlds. The moon grew before us, filling the sky, and we made our way slowly, laboriously through the lunar seas, which were composed of dust rather than water. In the distance, across a gray sea or a gray plain, half hidden by mountains, a black tower rose like a spike, with a single, brilliant light at its top, as if a star were impaled there.

The captain spoke inside our minds. We recalled his words, as if from dreams. *I don't think he's going to retreat this time. I think he will stand and fight.*

That was when something like an enormous hand seized the ship from underneath and cracked its hull like an eggshell. We plunged screaming into the dust.

. . . and awoke from some troubling dream. It was a hot night. Our ship was allowed to drift. The oars were drawn in. I found that I was a broad-shouldered, muscular man, bearded, naked but for a loin cloth. Most of the crew wore nothing at all. The man who lazily climbed up the mast into the crow's nest was entirely naked, which did not seem at all unusual to me. My name—some other self, someone out of a dream, could rattle off lots of names like that, learned from a book, translated through various languages. It did not matter.

That morning, we passed through a narrow strait, but contrary to earlier reports, the rocks did not clash. Once we emerged into the sea beyond, we saw no monsters, only seagulls and dolphins. The diviner among us said that was a good sign. We had made sufficient sacrifices to the gods at the outset of our voyage of trading-and-occasional-piracy that our luck should hold out.

We had painted eyes on either side of the prow of our ship when we dedicated it. They guided us well.

The next evening, we spied a tiny village on the shore. We put on armor, gathered our weapons, and waited, concealed behind a small headland. About the second hour of the night, we struck with great success. We killed the men and took some of the women captive, either for the crew to enjoy, or to sell later on when we came upon a town too large for us to take.

Later, shortly before dawn, we were at sea again. I watched the moon setting. I fell asleep and dreamed a strange and terrifying dream in which our ship had been crushed, most of my companions slain, and I was swallowed up in dust.

I tried to discard my cloak, but could not. It clung to me. No more can a raven discard its wings. Somehow I knew it was essential to retain the mask. The integrity of the dream required it. We dreamers must remain anonymous. The raven-masked man burst to the gray surface nearby, scattering dust. He caught hold of me. His superior strength saved me. I don't think I could have made it by myself. When at last we made it to the barren shore, and stood gazing across the lunar plain to the spiked tower with the glowing tip, I saw that we two were the only survivors. We had both managed to retain our swords. I wasn't sure they would do us much good.

Together we marched toward our goal.

My companions and I drifted lazily on the water. But our luck did not hold out. The following evening most of the captive women seemed resigned to their fate and became compliant. We were all drunk with stolen wine. One of the women even grabbed me by my manhood and said, "Come here, lover boy," before, in the midst of frenzied and unfeigned lust, she produced a small knife from somewhere and tried to slit my throat with it. I broke away. I got a deep gash across my chest. I killed her with a blow to the face so hard it smashed her skull. But her compatriots had been more successful, and most of the crew was dead.

The rest were struggling with captives who fought like harpies or Amazons, some of them having snatched swords from the crew. They knew how to use them. In the course of all this the ship crashed onto some rocks. By the time I made it to shore the situation was entirely reversed and the gods had clearly forsaken us. Only the captain and I survived. We found ourselves surrounded by armed survivors from the town and three or four very angry, very bedraggled women, who screamed for vengeance, and got it. The captain's heart they cut out as some kind of divination. Me they crucified.

This is how the dream ended.

But the dream cannot end, because it is the sea on which the universe floats like so much scum.

Nevertheless—

My raven-masked companion and I were closing in on the Thief of Dreams. The Enemy was fighting us with everything he had.

I cannot tell it all. It is a whirlwind, a tempest, a storm of memory.

There were dragons. We slew them.

We struggled for days or weeks or months across that desolate plain, suffering terrible thirst, but we did not die, for our dream selves are not like our physical selves and can endure far more.

More than once I fell into a delirium and it seemed I was dying on a beach, nailed to a cross.

The winged, faceless monstrosities attacked again and again, but we were blessed by some extra sense, something gained through our long ordeal and many lifetimes, and we could not be taken by surprise. They could not carry us off. We left the dust splattered with their remains.

More than once I seemed to awaken, into some pleasant memory, the perfect moment in someone's life, though he might not have known it at the time. There was the strongest temptation to just remain there, forever, like an insect in amber, in perfect happiness. For Peter Harrow of New York it was simply a scene on a Christmas morning when he was eight years old (actually his family lived in Woodbury, New Jersey then), sitting on the living room floor playing with an electric train while the house was filled with the smell of turkey cooking and Christmas music playing on the phonograph. But then the black-cloaked raven-man lifted up the phonograph arm gently and the music stopped, and before Peter could even call out, the raven-man had grabbed him roughly by the hair and leapt upward, through the ceiling, lifting him into starry darkness.

There was something similar, involving a naked Greek boy playing with shells by the seashore. Then a dark figure loomed over him.

"Are you a god?" he managed to ask.

Alexander Ivanovic, aged twenty, in love for the first and only time in his life, sat alone in a room holding a little box in his lap. In the box was an engagement ring. When his beloved came in through the door, he was going to fall on his knees and propose to her. But it wasn't she who came through the door.

So many others, more than I can count or recite to you. Distractions. We overcame them all. We reached the base of the dark tower in the midst of the barren, lunar plain. The tower was made of rough, irregular stone.

It was possible to find handholds and footholds, and we climbed.

It was possible to climb while yet more winged ones attacked. It was possible to climb while burning oil poured down over us. We shielded ourselves with our cloaks and continued on our way.

The tower writhed like a living thing.

But we made it to the top and confronted the Thief of Dreams on a narrow platform. He wore the vial of precious dreams on a chain around his neck. It gleamed like a captive star. His drawn sword gleamed too, but like polished white bone.

We fought. It was one of those prolonged, epic battles of which the poets sing, the kind that goes on for what might be hours or days, physically impossible in the waking world. But here in the world of dreams, as the climax of so many lifetimes of striving, so many visions, so much pain, as a secret ritual drawn from such long researches into the occult secrets of the universe, why, yes, of course, it went on. Sparks flew. I, having been trained and shaped and molded for this very moment by my raven-masked captain, to whom I owed loyalty for so long that I had forgotten who I originally was—or as my spirit swam beneath the surface of the sea of dreams for centuries upon centuries, only occasionally finding respite in the shallows and awakening into some lifetime or another—I did most of the fighting. I struck the countless blows. I suffered the many wounds. But my ardor did not fail. I would have fought into eternity if necessary, had not my master, the raven-masked one, slipped behind my opponent and slyly run his sword through his heart, in through his back so the blade protruded out of his chest (and so giving me a deep gash). Then he cut out that heart and examined it, reading it for divination, after which he removed the dead man's mask and gazed into his face. It was not any face I recognized, and it faded into another unfamiliar face, and another, and another, hundreds perhaps, all blended together until there was no face there at all.

Only then did he remove the precious vial from around the slain enemy's neck. He held it up for me to see. I was nearly blinded. I had to look away. I *felt* its immense power, drawing to itself all the great dreams of the universe. I too was a dream or a thing of dream. I knew that if he were to remove the stopper, I would be sucked into the vial and be lost utterly, like a drop of rain returning to the ocean. At the same time I wanted the vial, to hold it, to keep it as my own, more than I can possibly explain.

He stood there, holding it.

"What now?" I asked. "Our mission is done. Aren't you supposed to return it to the one we all serve?"

I looked up into the sky. I saw the enormous dead faces of the gods, gazing upon us like corpses floating face down in water.

And among them, descending toward us with hands outstretched, was the pale-faced, black-garbed, and black-winged angel.

Was that it, then, that the purpose of the dream was to end the dream forever?

My raven-masked companion placed the chain and the vial around his own neck.

"I am afraid I can't give it up," he said. "I want it too much."

Then he pushed me off the tower, before leaping off himself in the opposite direction.

The universe was screaming.

*   *   *

If you die in a dream, do you truly die, or do you just awaken into another life? I don't know. It will take me a while to sort this all out. *Did* I die in the dream, or did the raven-masked man, the traitor, actually spare me, out of some kind of mercy, or just to appreciate the irony?

I tumbled through space for a long time. I dreamed and died many times, on a cross, from the guillotine, in battle, as an old, tired man in a bed in an unfamiliar room. Each time my body came to die, I was able to leap free, into dream, swimming, to surface again somewhere else. Each time I was able to evade the grasp of the black-winged, pale-faced angel.

Think of a billiard ball that hits another, so that the force is entirely displaced into the second one. So I hit, transferred into the other, bounced, rolled, awoke . . . in a gutter in New York City, in some year that Peter Harrow might have found familiar. There were huge, roaring things all around me, and somebody yelled, "Hey, kid, get out of the street!" and I was yanked up onto the sidewalk. I tried to take stock of myself. I was a child, maybe ten or twelve, very skinny, clad in ragged trousers that only came down a little past the knee and were held up with a piece of rope. My shirt was very loose and might have had once buttons, but was held shut, such as it was, with string. I wore a ragged jacket. No buttons. String. My hair was very long and tangled. I was barefoot and very dirty and very lost.

Maybe Franz, the Czech Jew I had met, was right and it's all a joke. How else to explain that I awoke not only as someone else, but toppled a couple centuries out of that someone's native time?

The boy's name was Tommy. He spoke English, more or less, but he could not explain to the authorities who he was or where he came from. He was completely unfamiliar with the features of modern life: light switches, automobiles, television. His teeth were already bad. When they took him to the dentist he was absolutely terrified and had to be sedated. The cream of the jest: a street urchin from London, circa 1700—Tommy couldn't read but he'd heard of a Queen Anne—an untraceable orphan, is very likely going to be institutionalized after he is diagnosed as completely insane, and is consequently unlikely to master the mystical arts or learn the secrets necessary to find his way into the Dreamlands and continue the pursuit. At the very least, his quarry intended to have a considerable head start.

Tommy can remember Peter Harrow and Alexander Ivanovic and the ancient Greek pirate and all the rest, but not clearly. It will take time. But I am he and he is I and we are all determined to hunt down and slay the Thief of Dreams.

Killing the Pale Man

It was a night for telling stories, inevitably, if only because we two were the only guests at the inn, the TV in the lounge wasn't working, and it was the kind of place where as likely as not your phone wouldn't get any signal. North-central Pennsylvania, the flyover part of the state, as some had unkindly put it: the blank part of the map that you reach if you go up through the Poconos and turn left, into rolling hills, dark woods, and a great deal of nothing occasionally dotted with little towns with biblical names, like Chorazin and Bethsaida and Emmaus. You can hear odd stories in these parts, about the *Waldgänger* in the woods, and witches who can swim through the earth; but it fell upon my colleague and myself to tell our own stories.

The theme was to be coincidence. It was a coincidence that I had not been in this region in many years. In fact, I had never expected to come here again, since at my age I could have retired, as I am in that interval in life where you're definitely a senior and people start opening doors for you, but you're still fit and able to do what you want, even if you know you may not have a lot of time left. So when the high-end booksellers I consulted for asked me to go and evaluate the library of the estate of Marcus Rottenberg, noted author, occultist, and eccentric millionaire, it sounded interesting enough that I overcame any reservations I might have had, and I went.

The house stuck out in the brown, wintry landscape like a Gothic castle, though I suppose it was more a Victorian pile, like something out of a Charles Addams cartoon; in any case totally incongruous after you'd driven past those little towns and Amish farms and long stretches of forests. Mr. Rottenberg had been very rich—how he got that way was the subject of much mystery and speculation—and he was a man with decidedly individualistic ideas. Very likely he had had the place built (or at least altered) to his specifications. But he'd also managed to alienate such family as he had and die an embittered recluse, alone and without servants, because, so it was said, no one would work for him regardless of how much he offered to pay them. The house was shut up after his death.

That was why when the other estate evaluator and I got there, the electricity was off and we had to make do with kerosene lanterns, and there was no question of staying in that place overnight. We were met at the door that morning by a lawyer, who had a key, and who came by early in the evening to see us out.

The book collection was indeed fabulous, not merely expensive, but astonishing and even, by its implications, terrifying. A real treasure-trove for collectors and scholars and perhaps even the occasional madman like Mr. Rottenberg. I took a lot of photos with my camera phone just in case my employers did not believe me.

But the books are not really central to the stories Jeremy Hodder and I told, so I will not go into detail. He was a younger man, in the employ of an auction house, who was there to catalogue the antique furniture, the paintings, crockery, and the like. I gather that he too was impressed by what he found.

As I drove back to the inn, a few miles distant, I noticed a band of children, maybe five or six of them, in flowing white sheets and masks of some sort, out in the middle of a field, amid the dead cornstalks.

Later, at the inn, as we settled down in the lounge by the fire, Hodder remarked on them. He'd come in his own car, but he'd seen them too.

"It's too late for Halloween," he said.

"Yes, it is," I said. "But it's an old custom."

"Some of the customs around here are pretty strange."

"Stranger than you think," I said.

Outside it had begun to storm. Sleet rattled against the windows. I hoped those children had gotten home safely.

The landlord had provided us with a bottle of wine. I poured both of us drinks and began my story, as if I were unburdening myself of a secret I had been carrying all my life. It was just the right time for it to come out. I can't explain more than that.

You see [I began], I *know* what those kids are up to, because once upon a time I was one of them. It was, obviously, very long ago, well before you were born, I should imagine. My parents collected antiques. Also, my mother was a painter of the would-be Brandywine school—the Wyeth tradition and all that—so she loved these landscapes with their subtle shadings of browns and grays and the occasional deep blues of winter evenings. Whereas the Wyeths had done much of their painting in southern Pennsylvania, she hoped to find fresh inspiration in the north. Between these two interests, we were out in this region quite often. No, we didn't know Mr. Rottenberg, though I suppose we heard a few things people said about him. My parents had made friends with another couple, antique dealers and farmers, and we stayed on their farm sometimes, usually over weekends or on school holidays. They had two children, with whom I became quite friendly. Adam, the boy, was a couple years older than me. His sister Judith was three years younger. So when I was twelve that made Adam fourteen and Judith nine. There were only a few other children around, from neighboring farms, so age differences between us did not matter for much, and when we got together we formed our own little gang, of which I became an honorary member of sorts. Adam, who was the oldest of them all, was the natural leader.

    I will skip the unimportant details. We played games. I helped Adam and Judith with chores, which, to a city kid, were curiously fascinating. I had never been around a cow before, much less helped herd one into a barn. The barn was filled with cats, which were semi-feral, though people who knew them could treat them as pets.

    Never mind that. What matters is that on a night rather like this one, cold and windy, though it wasn't rainy, Adam told me to put on my coat and come with him. Our parents were elsewhere in the house. We didn't tell them we were going out. I wasn't sure why we were going, but Judith knew to be quiet and Adam's manner made it clear that

I should be quiet also, so we slipped away. He was carrying a large satchel, like an army duffel bag.

We hurried off into the empty fields. It was indeed late in the year, well past harvest, too late for Halloween, just mud and dead cornstalks beneath a darkening sky. Too late for Halloween, but when we met up with the other children—there were seven of us in all—Adam set down his satchel and got out costumes for everybody, white sheets, which each of the others put on without being told what to do, though someone had to show me how to adjust it over my head so I could see through the eyeholes. We were all garbed as ghosts, only we wore little metal crowns with horns on them, made of tin, I think.

By this point I was quite puzzled and maybe a little frightened. I wasn't sure if this was a game. Adam merely said to me, "It's what we do. You have to do it too."

"Do what?"

There was no answer. We trooped across the fields, and gradually the others began to sing. I couldn't make out most of the words. Some of them were just gibberish. Some of them were in another language. It might have been Latin or something that once was Latin. *Peetra partra perry dicentem.*

Then, as we approached a barren hilltop, the lyrics switched to English, a low chant, something like:

> *Comes the pale man,*
> *comes the moon,*
> *comes the pale man,*
> *very soon.*

It was all very much like a dream to me. I was swept along in something I didn't understand. But these were my friends. They wouldn't hurt me. It couldn't be bad. It had to be some kind of secret they were letting me in on.

I tried to convince myself of that as we filed up to the summit of the hill, chanting. I didn't like this place. I felt an impulse to run. I saw stones arranged in a circle. No, not like Stonehenge, and no sacrificial altar, just round boulders the size of mailboxes, half sunk into the ground and covered with moss, as if this place had been prepared very long ago.

For what? I wanted to ask, but didn't, as Adam reached into his bag again and started handing out clubs, some of them sticks, a couple pieces of metal pipe, and, for me, a baseball bat.

Now the others were singing:

> *Kill the pale man,*
> *kill him dead,*
> *break his bones*
> *and smash his head!*

We danced around and around, inside the circle of stones, singing more of the gibberish, more of the Latin scraps, and quite a bit of *Rise up moon* and *coming soon*. We whooped and did what I could only think of as a war dance, waving our clubs, closing in on a bare spot at the center of the stone circle.

Meanwhile the moon, a little past full, had risen over the fields.

And the Pale Man came to us. At first I thought there was a scrap of cloth on the ground, in the middle of the circle, but no, the earth was heaving up and something of a dirty white color was climbing out, something very thin and shriveled, more than a skeleton though less than a man. Its eyes were terrible, burning. They transfixed me. I faltered. I stopped singing and staggered back, and I would have turned and run if Adam hadn't caught me by the arm and hauled me back into my place. He and the other children sang all the louder, the Latin scraps, the gibberish that I was sure none of them understood but knew they had to repeat just then, just right. Even so, another of our number faltered, one of the youngest ones, a girl, and the pale man caught hold of her in his talon-claws and his teeth chattered, and he was hissing, and the little girl was screaming, while all the rest of us chanted very loud and did what we had come to do.

I hit the Pale Man on the shoulder with my baseball bat, and his arm snapped off and he let go of the little girl. Adam sank his pipe through the skull. We all did our bit, striking again and again until the Pale Man, who had not even fully emerged from the ground, was broken into bits. We had snapped him off a little below the knees. Just to be sure, Adam reached into the hole from which the Pale Man had emerged and yanked out the remains of two stick-like legs and two bony feet, and methodically beat them into powder. Then we scooped up the powder and the bits of bone and dropped them back into the hole and covered it over with dirt.

By now the moon was high overhead. We were out late. We had done what we had come to do.

The little girl whimpered. Adam and I and the rest of us looked at her and saw she was cut pretty badly. Adam tore some strips from one of the sheets and bandaged her legs as best he could. He lifted her into his arms, so her head rested on his shoulder, and he whispered to her, "Next year you will do better."

He glanced at me, as if to say the same thing. I had nearly fumbled. Next year I would do better.

And so we returned home. I never told my parents what had happened. I don't know what Adam and Judith told theirs. The girl who was hurt was carried home by her siblings. There were no repercussions. Nobody said anything. A few days later I was back in the Philadelphia suburbs and it all seemed remote and far away, like this story as I am telling it to you now.

It sounds crazy, doesn't it?

So I stopped telling my story.

Jeremy Hodder had lit a cigarette. "You don't mind . . . ?"

"Oh, no," I said.

He flicked some ashes into the fireplace.

The storm outside had become quite violent, the wind howling. I very much hoped those children had gotten back safely.

"Did you ever ask yourself why there had to be a next year?" he said.

"No," I said. "I suppose I could have made a fuss and demanded that we not come here anymore, but I would have been lying and, worse than that, I would be betraying my friends, who had let me in on their secret, as if I'd joined a secret society and now was fully initiated, and there was an inevitability to it. Every year, for five years, we smashed the Pale Man."

"And then what happened?"

"We grew up. For some reason this has to be done by children, and we weren't children anymore. Adam got drafted and went to Vietnam and got killed. I went to college."

"Oh," Hodder said, and we were both quiet for a while. The fire burned low. The storm outside raged.

"It surprises me, I must admit, that you seem to believe every word," I said. "I could be insane, you know, or pulling your leg just to give you the creeps on a night like this."

"But you're not," he said firmly. "I know you're not. Because I went through the same thing you did, only my experience was considerably worse."

Now *that* was astonishing. Talk about coincidences. Here was a stranger, at least twenty years my junior, met under circumstances which had nothing to do with the subject of our concern, and *he too* had been one of those children, years ago, but not as many years ago.

He told me his story.

This will surprise you [Jeremy Hodder said], because I'm the kind of guy who will wear a three-piece suit to a rummage sale, but I actually grew up in this county. My parents owned one of these farms. I was a farm boy. I did all the usual farm boy things, and like other children in the area, I learned from other children those odd songs that none of us understood but which we recited in secret among ourselves.

Those who lived within a certain short distance of that hill with the stones upon it knew all about the Pale Man.

In time I was taken there when I was ten, but we screwed it up. Our leader was a thirteen-year-old named Tommy. He wasn't a farm boy at all. His father owned the garage in the village. He was a bright kid. He was interested in a lot of things, not all of them helpful at this point. Ideas travel slowly in this part of the world, so for all that things like that were long since passé where you come from, Tommy had just discovered hippies, New Age stuff, Oriental mysticism, and all that. He was into psychedelic music and posters and what he thought was philosophy and flying saucers and Atlantis and reincarnation. He called himself a guru. He said he would lead us to enlightenment. Part of enlightenment, he told us, was disbelieving everything we'd been told about the world. Everything was "bourgeois," he would say. That was his favorite word. That meant something was to be dismissed from all consideration. Only he wasn't bourgeois.

Since the rest of us younger than him and he was amazingly persuasive for a thirteen-year-old—he could have grown up to be a politician or the world's greatest car salesman or maybe Charles Manson—the rest of us did what he told us to. It so happened when that night came around, when you go out and smash the Pale Man, Tommy had other ideas. We put on our ghost-sheets all right, and he carried our clubs, and we sang our gibberish songs, but Tommy led us up quite another hill, where there was an old abandoned shed. On that hilltop we sang very different songs that he taught us, and did different dances, and made strange motions that he called "rites."

Then we all crowded into the shed by the light of a flashlight Tommy had, and he revealed what else he'd brought along for the occasion. He called them "sacraments," but they were really a more familiar and illegal form of enlightenment. He had coffee tin of marijuana, several pipes, and even some magic mushrooms.

So we performed esoteric rituals that night, but they weren't the "bourgeois" ones. Tommy said this was a better way to banish evil from the world. A couple of the smaller kids got scared and one of them threw up, but Tommy wouldn't let any of them leave; and as for me, I can only tell you that, subjectively, the evening was . . . interesting. I might have seen a couple flying saucers. At one point I was absolutely convinced that Tommy was the Maitreya, the Buddha to come, and the world was ending because "everything is relative," and for a while I felt really good about that, but then I had a sense of utter emptiness as if the world *had* ended and I had been left behind. Once the shed filled with light and Tommy's face was burning with soft white fire, and then it wasn't there at all, just a black void where his face had been, which detail was terrifyingly prophetic, considering what happened afterwards.

I don't know how many hours passed, but ultimately the lot of us got up and staggered into out the night, coughing and reeking. It was very late. The moon was almost down. Without any ceremony our little company parted and made for home. I had my little brother, Charlie, with me. He was seven that year. He never got to be any older.

It was only after a while, as I led Charlie by the hand across one of the endless, empty fields, that my mind cleared to the extent that I could begin to realize the enormity of what we had all done—or failed to do. I was afraid then. I nearly yanked Charlie's arm out of its socket as I turned and ran and dragged a wailing, sobbing kid brother after me. We arrived breathless at *the hill,* the correct hill, the one with the circle of stones, and without any chant or songs or other ceremony we went straight to the middle of the circle and saw what was there.

"He got away," Charlie said.

There was just a hole in the ground, with dirt heaped around it, as if, indeed, something had unburied itself.

The Pale Man was loose.

Charlie and I could only go home, still wearing our sheets and our crowns and dragging our useless clubs. Our parents had discreetly left the back door unhooked, so the two of us could quietly make our way up the back to the bedroom we shared.

Charlie just flopped down on his bed the way he was, but I went into the bathroom, did my best to wash the pot odor off myself, changed into pajamas, and then just sat on the edge of my bed thinking about how things had turned out. There were no stories about what happens when the Pale Man gets loose, because no one would ever allow that. That was impossible. It couldn't be.

I was still trying to convince myself when I thought I saw the moon rising outside my window. But my window looked west, and I would see the moon setting that way, and the moon should have been nearly down by now anyway. Yet something softly glowing *rose,* and no, it wasn't the moon, but the face of the Pale Man, who shattered the glass and lunged into the room.

Charlie let out no more than a gasp or a grunt, and then the Pale Man was coming for me, and I stood up, backing away from him, into the adjoining bathroom, all the while sobbing softly and trying to form the words to the magic songs—they had to be magic, they had to mean something—but I only managed a few syllables until I was backed up against the bathroom mirror and the Pale Man reached out with his terrible, stick-like claw and ripped the front of my pajama top right off. He carved an X in blood right in the middle of my chest, and about the time I whispered, "I'm sorry, please don't hurt me," he hooked one taloned finger into my armpit and with a savage yank damn near tore me in half, which left me screaming and huddled on the tiled floor clutching my belly, desperately afraid that my guts were going to come out like steaming sausages.

At that instant my parents burst in. They only saw a faint flicker, apparently, and then they turned on the electric light and they found me in the bathroom, bleeding and badly hurt, though my guts hadn't fallen out. I suppose my ribcage had saved me. But Charlie was worse. He was dead. His head was missing.

When he had finished Jeremy Hodder said, "If this were a chess game I'd say check and checkmate. I win. Mine tops yours."

"Yes, it does," I said grimly.

"There's more too. Tommy, our would-be guru, never even made it home. He was discovered later the next afternoon, face down in a field, well away from the road, and he was only found because the buzzards had started to settle. There wasn't much left of him. It was a terrible winter. Most of the other children died, either bloodily or from some kind of disease that was going around. Animals died too, lots of them. Farmers were ruined. Billy Sanders, who had been with us that night, said he had seen the Pale Man dancing in the moonlight in the pasture behind his house, and then Billy disappeared. It went on and on until spring, when the Pale Man finally crawled back into his grave. But both of my parents were dead by then and I went to New York to live with relatives, and I did everything I could for the rest of my life to distance myself from the farm boy I had once been, to become sophisticated, a city-slicker, the kind of guy who wears three-piece suits to rummage sales and antique shows. But I've still got an impressive scar. No, I won't show it to you."

"You don't have to."

"I couldn't very well use all this as an excuse not to come out here, could I? So when my firm ordered me, I had to come. Who would believe me?"

Coincidentally, I would.

I merely nodded.

I should add that I actually had an excuse. As soon as I turned in my preliminary report I would say that I wasn't feeling well and was retiring, and someone else would have to come out and oversee the removal and sale of the late Mr. Rottenberg's library.

Neither my companion nor I went to bed at all that night. We just sat there till dawn, until the storm died down and the sleet stopped rattling against the windows.

My God, I desperately hoped those children we had seen had gotten back safely, and that they had fulfilled their role in immemorial tradition.

How can I explain any of it? I can't. The coincidence of my meeting a total stranger who happened to have a story that topped even mine? Was that the synchronicity of fate or the Pale Man's last revenge? Certainly my dreams have been uneasy of late. I cannot rest. I see the pale face rising outside my window. Sometimes I hear scratching on the glass. Sometimes I am not sure I am dreaming.

I don't know how Mr. Hodder is doing. I haven't heard from him. I hope he is well.

Is it possible that we two violated some ancient, terrible compact by confiding our stories, even to each other?

I hope for those children.

Why children? Was it because only children could actually *see* the Pale Man for some reason, and all adults could see was maybe a flicker of light before they found the bodies? Maybe children knew the answer, if no one else did, and they shared the secret with other children, as they first taught the younger ones the strange lyrics—*peetra partra perry dicentem* and all that—and then initiated them fully into the mystery. As they became adults, they might forget some of it or convince themselves it was all a dream, though they might still bear scars. Who could possibly confess such a thing and not be thought mad, except, coincidentally, to someone who had shared the same experience?

I don't think it had anything to do with the sinister Marcus Rottenberg, reputed wizard, who was said to call monsters out of the sky at night and converse with invisible presences in broad daylight in front of witnesses, and to play cards with the Devil on his front porch. Maybe Rottenberg was attracted to this place because it was already contaminated with evil; but I think the evil is much, much older, something the Indians had to deal with thousands of years before any white people ever arrived. It was they, after all, who set those stones in a circle. I could well imagine their young people smashing the Pale Man with tomahawks, once a year, as it had to be done.

I think the Pale Man was some kind of god of cold earth and the moon and winter, and he has been around forever, dead, resurrected, dying again.

I can assure you that neither Hodder nor I had any intention of hiking up there to make sure there wasn't an empty hole amid the stones.

We could only hope that the children we'd seen had gotten home all right.

I'm retired. I'm not going back.

Everything depends on the children.

Appeasing the Darkness

Think of these as pictures in an exhibition:

1

With reluctance deepening into dread, perhaps, Jeffrey Quilt recognizes the town from his dreams. In the evening twilight, it seems a picture-postcard image of a New England resort in late summer, forested cliffs overlooking an enclosed harbor, the windows of the houses agleam with the orange of the setting sun, the white steeple of the old Congregationalist church above the common like a brilliant beacon. Several levels of streets and terraces down, tourists gather like moths in the gathering darkness, drawn to the soft glare of storefronts and restaurants. Boats bob gently at anchor.

But Jeffrey Quilt, who is after all an acknowledged master of such things, has also somehow captured a sense of lurking menace just below the too-perfect scene. He is not given to quaint New England landscapes of the sort you can find in any sidewalk art show.

No, as *he* saw it, in his dream, and as, indefinably the painting suggests, the pleasant sunset, the church, the cheery windows, the tourists gathered like moths are all just a façade, a mask, inadequately concealing a howling labyrinth of empty streets, windswept, artificially lit, along which *just recently passed* a long, black automobile that carried the artist's death. He knew it as certainly as if he were wide awake and staring down the barrel of a gun. There. The end. The pain from which there is no hope of healing. Some kind of dream-knowledge allows him to know that the car *had been* through a specific intersection just moments before the instant captured on canvas, that it had parked *here*, then moved on, leaving what can only be described as a faint miasma in the air, which you can almost make out if you stare long enough.

The sounds of the tourists and buoys ringing in the rocking tide, the seagull cries, all that fades away. You hear the whisper of tires, as if on a wet pavement at midnight.

Jeffrey is not so melodramatic as to show the pavement wet with blood, but he implies it.

The colors, the textures, the hidden little images peeking out from painted doorways and sketched windows let us know that the black car is parked just beyond the edge of the frame, and footsteps move, behind the painting, through a back street, drawing nearer.

And more, completely incongruous but for the Quilt genius: animal paws, padding, the stealthiest sound of all.

I think that if I look long enough, I can just begin to make out three men in black tights, slightly silly in their bowler hats, but almost graceful in their silver masks, the tattoos on the backs of their hands faintly luminous in delicate, swirling traceries.

They crouch down before a prone figure of the Dreamer, of Quilt himself. Their knives rasp. The dream leopard crouches beside them. (I can see it now, yes, quite clearly, like something rendered as an illusion by M. C. Escher.) It moves to raise the sleeper's face gently off like a mask, hooking its claws under his chin until the blood starts to flow.

There were a few brownish stains on the original sketch, I remember, when I saw it.

But by the time I reach that particular town along the Maine coast, Jeffrey Quilt has painted his picture and moved on. The image, a slide mailed to his publisher, is as much a taunt as a finished work. Shake your head, turn away, then look back, and it's just a seacoast town.

But there has been a death there. I saw, at least, the chalk-marks where the body was found, on the sidewalk by the common, beneath the steeple of the Congregationalist church.

I am told there was a lot of blood.

But not Jeffrey's. I know him better than that.

2

When Jeffrey was sixteen and I was thirteen, back when dinosaurs ruled the earth, the Beatles were still together, and there were no cell phones, Jeffrey Quilt (he was *never* "Jeff") took me out at night onto the old golf course in St. David's PA—the one that's no longer there, any more than herds of stegosauruses still graze in the bushes or we are still young. I remember the night more vividly than just about any in my life, the moonlight on the newly cut grass, Jeffrey's long hair flowing in the faint breeze like spider-silk. He was in his short-lived hippie phase, with flowers in his headband and wearing bellbottoms and some sort of weird African shirt that flapped and fluttered and left his whole, pale chest exposed. I shivered in the night air. I was just some dorky kid in blue jeans and a plain T-shirt and Keds whom he'd allowed to tag along. He was barefoot and moved silently on beanpole legs, like a scarecrow come alive, silent as a ghost, a magic person in my imagination, some kind of prophet.

I'm sure he thought of himself the same way.

He actually *took me by the hand,* which under other circumstances I might have thought queer, but if Jeffrey did it, no, that was different. He led me, out over the golf course, into the moonlight, and we paused atop a little rise, and he pointed and said, "Look there. I want you to see this. There's magic."

I didn't see anything but the moonlight on the grass and the lights of houses in the distance, and I didn't know what he was talking about.

"I *know*," he said, as if confiding some great secret.

For a moment I wondered if he was going to offer me drugs.

Then I saw it: almost as if a mist had risen out of the ground and taken shape, points of light, drifting about like fireflies, settling, darker shapes solidifying. I saw tents, pennons flapping on poles, a huge wheel turning in the sky—

"What's a *circus* doing here?"

It was an absurd question. I knew perfectly well circuses were put on in big sports arenas, not in tents anymore. This was like something out of *Toby Tyler* or a Ray Bradbury story. It couldn't be real, not now—

"Quiet!" Jeffrey put his hand over my mouth, and I didn't resist, but stared, wide-eyed, at that wheel, the huge Ferris wheel turning as silently as a cloud rolling in the wind.

He took his hand away. He raised both arms into the air, like some fantastic conductor of an impossible orchestra.

"I *made* this all," he whispered. "I called it up out of my dreams. And here it *is*."

In that moment I certainly believed him, and Jeffrey Quilt became more than just somebody I wanted to be when I grew up. He was God.

We walked closer, among the tents, my sneakers squishing in mud. It was after hours. The circus was closed. Once I saw a face peer out at us from behind the fold of a tent, then vanish back inside. There was something wrong with that face. It was more like an enormous black cat than anything human.

And the wheel turned, noiselessly, but somehow I heard its music well beyond the range of actual hearing. It was something I felt, something that came into my mind of its own accord; and there were voices, a faint and faraway babble like the wind, but filled with fear and pain, it seemed, but I couldn't be sure, I couldn't make out anything; they were calling to us. I distinctly heard them say, "You are welcome, Jeffrey Quilt," but in a tone that didn't imply welcome at all.

"Let's get out of here," I said, as softly as I could.

"No. This is the Dream—"

"Yeah, right. We're dreaming."

"Not dreaming. *The Dream. That's different.*"

We were so close to the wheel now. I could see it almost clearly, though by some trick of the mist and the moonlight I *couldn't* see it clearly, and there was only a hint of a vast structure, not of metal, but of bones, it seemed, no, *alive,* like some immense and prehistoric animal, twisted upon itself, turning, turning; and there, among the spokes of the wheel, turning, swinging, rising, falling, were *others*—I won't say they were people, just *others*—and I could barely see into the swinging seats, see who was riding on that enormous wheel, up into the night: a skeleton like a dancer decked with flowers, a fat lady who didn't seem alive at all although her eyes burned, something with the face of a frog, and more. They kept changing, shifting. There were two children, a boy and a girl, who seemed trapped there, who wanted to get off; but they didn't say anything and swung by us and were gone.

"The Dream," said Jeffrey Quilt. "Embrace the dream. *Carpe noctem*. Let the darkness flow inside of you and set you free."

He reached out to catch hold of the wheel, but either he missed or his hand passed right through it, as if through smoke, and he caught nothing.

And then it was gone, and Quilt was gone, and I was all alone in the middle of the St. David's golf course, hours after I had set out. The moon was setting. By the time I got home, cold and covered with mud, it was almost four in the morning, and my father was waiting up with belt in hand. That was the last time I saw Jeffrey Quilt for many years. I was told his family had moved away. The reader will recall that he achieved fame as quite a young man for his series of Ecstatic paintings, many of which were sold as psychedelic posters, even though their creator soon reinvented himself in black leather, studs, and very closely cropped hair, particularly after his hairline began to recede prematurely, the totality giving him a look one newspaper writer once described as being halfway between that of an emaciated motorcycle hoodlum and a priest. Before long, his imagery was far, far grimmer, and he entered his celebrated Charnel Period, from which, in truth, he has never quite emerged.

One of the first jobs he ever got was doing a poster for the movie *Circus of Terrors*. The poster was *much* better than the film, although it was not, I think, taken from the Dream. No, it was just something Jeffrey knocked off for the money.

In those days, he could still play jokes like that.

3

The sinister stories about Jeffrey Quilt began to circulate very quickly. I think he encouraged them. I think they amused him. "I will tell you about my life," he once told an interviewer, "only on the condition that you believe nothing I say."

4

The *Dream,* he later told us, over and over again, is like an endless, lightless ocean, an infinity pressing in on us from all sides. We float on it like chips of cork, and most of us forget that it's there, that we *are* floating, but every once in a while one of us learns to lean over and touch the ocean, to take the water into his hands, and that person is a great poet, a painter, a genius, a criminal, a madman—all one and the same in the context of the Dream.

We *don't* create it, he said, contradicting his teenaged self. It is merely *there.* Perhaps it creates *us.*

5

Again, Jeffrey Quilt sitting on a bench, in that town, in New England, in the darkness below the Congregationalist steeple. It is almost dawn, well after the police have gone away, well after *I* have gone away, I who pursue him by chasing after the hints of the *real* and enigmatic Jeffrey Quilt left behind in his paintings. He is rumored to be a hoax, a madman, the actual Howard Hughes or JFK, who didn't die but found the fountain of youth, drank from it, and was irreparably and grotesquely *changed.*

A tabloid once suggested that he is a vampire. No, nothing so trite. Believe me.

Jeffrey Quilt, sitting there. A brief sketch then, his self-portrait. You can see it in his *Nightmares of Damnation* series, out from Serpentine Books. He sits, sketching, charcoal on a pad in his lap, while the denizens of his other paintings cluster around and gaze upon him admiringly: cobras with the faces of dark pharaohs, toad-women with breasts like pendulous, rotting sacks; hunched, hairy troglodytes; a stick figure with the face of a bird, like something decapitated and stuck on a pole, but alive.

Beyond these, he has rendered the background as an interlocking pattern of dark and light, shadow and moon, so that the real is a reflection of the unreal and vice versa, while in the distance the three men in black tights and bowlers and the cat the color of midnight with eyes burning out of Hell draw ever nearer.

He has to hurry.

Someone else will die tonight.

Jeffrey, I must find you soon.

6

It's called *Let's Have a Party!* A fire on the pavement in front of a gift shop, cavorting demons roasting spitted tourists. But this is no mere satirical cartoon. It's so real you can smell the flesh burning. You can hear the screams. Eyeballs sizzle like ice cubes on a grill, a detail left over from Jeffrey's EC Comics–influenced phase.

Jeffrey, closing his sketchpad, racing away in his rented car. Somewhere behind him, a glow of light. Sirens.

7

"Embrace the Dream," he'd told me. That was what I tried to do. I don't know if the dreaming ever stopped. Am I still thirteen years old and muddy, standing in that moonlit field, never having awakened?

Dream. I think it is because he took me with him that night. Something happened, we are linked, you and I; Jeffrey, I dream your dreams and I can see your paintings in my mind before you paint them, and I know why you *must* paint them. This makes me more than your leading advocate in the critical community, more than your unofficial biographer and author of *Jeffrey Quilt: Master of the Macabre*, a cliché title, I assure you, which was not my own.

Every time I see one of your paintings for the first time, in a gallery show or published in a book, I have an overwhelming sense of *recognition.* Yes, I know what you went through, each time.

It's more than telepathy. We have the same mind, Jeffrey, you and I. Increasingly, we are the same, two dreamers, one Dream.

Dream. You're right, Jeffrey. You found out at a very early age, that we stand on a placid island of ignorance while the tides of *Dream* erode our crumbly shores from all sides. We are not the Dreamer, who lies in the depths, and is unknowable, neither God nor the Devil, though you have sold your soul to him nonetheless. The *Dream* flows over us, obliterates us. You'd lectured me on at some length in an adolescent barrage of Gnosticism and occult psychobabble that I didn't understand at the time and I don't think you did either. But the gist of it is this: You reached out. You touched the Dream. It responded. The deal is roughly this: your amazing inspiration comes directly from the Dream. You have insights, visions, like nothing of this earth, because, indeed, they are not. I don't deny your technical skill, but your *genius,* if I may call it that, is borrowed from the Beyond, if you will pardon the phrase.

But there is a drawback. The men in black with the knives, and the leopard, they too arise from the Dream, summoned by your conscience, perhaps, or else just demanding payment for your Faustian bargain. They will destroy you, slowly, painfully, and your soul will not be set free when you die. The only way to keep them at bay is to paint your nightmares, to make them real.

And when you make them real, someone else dies instead.

Convenient, huh?

Jeffrey, we are brothers.

8

Jeffrey, in flight, in his rented car. His latest masterpiece, and it *is* a masterpiece, something that takes the breath away and leaves the viewer shuddering: a dark sky in oils, suggestive of the stormy paintings of Winslow Homer, but in the foreground three old, ragged women have discovered a child's headless corpse in the ebb-tide on an otherwise empty beach, two of them beside themselves with grief, the third, standing a little apart, smirking toward the onlooker, holding something large and round in her soiled apron.

A real child will have to die tonight, somewhere.

9

He has returned to the sinister circus, to that Ferris wheel of the dead and the never-alive and the denizens of Dream. I lie on the bench in front of the Congregationalist church, which Jeffrey has so recently been, and I sleep there, and I share the dream he has left behind like a glamour in the air. I see the people, and things, riding that wheel, and I know them all, from Jeffrey Quilt paintings, past, present, and to come; and I can see adolescent Jeffrey, barefoot, with his long hair trailing in the wind, trying to climb up the middle of the wheel, to grasp onto the enormous bones that are the structure; but he cannot; they are like shapes of cloud to him, passing by him, through him.

Then I awaken, or seem to awaken, within the larger Dream, there on the bench in front of the church. The moon has almost set. By the faint light I can see that something has tracked dew from the grass out onto the pavement in front of me.

The paw-prints of an enormous cat.

10

Now, dreaming still, I rise up and get into my own car. Once I pass something long and black on the road, a limousine perhaps, with all the windows darkened, its metal agleam, its tires like whispers. I pass it and speed up ahead, so that the roar of my engine shouts through the night.

No more delays now. No more fooling around. It is as if I am rejoining myself, I the astral body hurtling back from a jaunt to where my physical self lies waiting. Can't miss.

He and I are one. *In the dream of the man who is dreaming, the dreamt man awakes.*

In his motel room, Jeffrey Quilt sits up with a start, terribly afraid when he hears car tires crunching in the driveway, but then realizing that the sound he fears would be heavy, steady, slow, and this is fast and sloppy, like a speeding Volkswagen skidding to a stop. He is irritated, almost angry, when he gets up, irritated again, then amazed, and, in some terrible way he cannot define, *glad* when he opens the motel room door.

"Hello, Jeffrey," I say. "Long time, no see, huh?"

"Yeah, long time, Kev." He called me Kev when we were kids, not Kevin.

"Hi. Going to let me in?" *You'd better,* I don't have to say. *You don't have much time. I passed Nemesis on the way here, doing sixty.*

I step inside. He locks the door.

"So what can I do for you, Kev? You want an interview for your next book? You wanna see my latest work, *Portrait of the Artist Devoured by Ghouls*?"

"No, Jeffrey," I say. "I have to talk to you."

"Not about art criticism?"

"No, about murder."

11

When I knew him as a kid, Jeffrey Quilt lived with relatives, but he had a real family once, a mother, a father, and a little brother he didn't like very much, and I happen to know, because I saw it in a dream, that Jeffrey murdered the lot of them. Oh, it was bad between them before that, because of the kid brother, whose name was Stevie, and one day Stevie managed to fake some photographs that made it look very much as if sibling rivalry had segued imperceptibly into bondage, torture, and sodomy. It was very convincing. Stevie could have been a special-effects maestro if he'd lived, but if he'd lived Jeffrey's life was over, and he knew it: a long, grinding hell of psychiatrists and institutions and people whispering and pointing, of his parents' terror and loathing and pity. No, the only solution was to make a clean break with that past, so that was when he'd walked out into the darkness that is more than a mere absence of light, when he'd found his way into the *Dream* that lies beyond life, when he spoke to something he called The Outside Man, which might have risen out of his own mind; and he painted his first painting, a bit crude but curiously powerful, showing a boy's hand crushing what looked like a glowing red Christmas ornament—only inside were screaming faces, Mom, Dad, Stevie—and there was way too much blood on the hand, as if it had been dipped into a bucket of gore, and the broken glass fragments clung in the moonlight like gleaming scales.

Only I knew that. Now, looking at me, there in the hotel room, he knew I knew, if he hadn't before.

He offered me a chair.

"So what have you done?"

"You cut to the quick, Jeffrey."

"We don't have much time."

"Indeed we do not."

I cannot weep. I am beyond all that, because of what I have done. That's why I needed to seek out my brother, Jeffrey Quilt, because of what I have done.

Because I stayed behind when we were teenagers, and I didn't even try to catch hold of the magical wheel and ride up into the sky with the dead and the never born; because of that I got to grow up, to be "normal," to have a career in journalism, get married, have two-point-five kids, a dog, a house in the suburbs, while all the while, inexplicably, like sand leaking out of a broken hourglass, my soul died; and it is trite and useless now to go over the petty quarrels, the indignities, the endless humiliations—and why *will* you say that I am mad? Hearken! and observe how healthily, how calmly I tell you the whole story—until I was like a single pebble falling in an avalanche into the darkness, and in that darkness I discovered myself with a pistol in my hand, and I—or that other, the one I saw in the dream—shot my wife right between the eyes and waited for my two-point-five kids and shot them too when they came home from school, and shot the dog, and the goldfish, and then left, saving the last bullet for myself, but I was already dead by then, and I could only think back to when I was still alive, that night when I was thirteen on the golf course, and I knew I had to find Jeffrey Quilt and explain it all to him, because he would understand, and when I had, he sat back silently in his own chair and rubbed his eyes and spoke at last.

"My God. You're a monster."

"No. The pain was my pain. Now all my rage is spent. There's nothing inside me now. I don't feel anything. You know that."

"Yes," he said. "I know it."

And he showed me a series of paintings, of my own house, which he had never seen, my wife dead in the bedroom, the children, whom I still loved, dead at the base of the front stairs.

The darkness had already swallowed me up.

Jeffrey shook his head slowly.

Outside, something heavy, slow, and steady crunched on the gravel driveway.

"Another masterpiece," he said.

"Who's the monster?"

"We don't have much time," he said.

"Who are they coming for, you or me?"

12

He begins to sketch. There is no sound from outside now. The night is absolutely still, but for the scratch, scratch of his pencil.

An indoor, domestic scene again: TV set flickering, tea kettle at boil, ironing board set up. But the window over the kitchen sink has exploded inward, glass littering the floor, curtains billowing in the breeze. The central figure, on the floor, resembles nothing more than Mary Kelly in the Jack the Ripper photo, carved leftovers after the party's over and all the revelers have gone home, exquisitely detailed, of course, worlds-within-worlds of ingenious gore . . . and for an instant his artistry seems to fail.

Remorse, conscience, or dread of what is to come?

Hasn't it always been thus?

Didn't he draw a similar picture of his old friend Kev with a gun in his hand?

Now something, an animal, is scratching at the door. Quilt barely looks up. I am dead. I feel nothing.

Jeffrey made me do it, I want to explain, feebly. Not the Devil. It's his fault.

But no one is there to listen.

My mind can't quite follow what happens next, the sequence of events, flashback, memory, or real-time, cause and effect all jumbled together and stirred with a stick.

The phone rings.

Quilt stops sketching and answers it. There are footsteps outside. The scratching at the door is louder.

I can hear both sides of the conversation, as if Jeffrey and I are one and the same:

"Jeffrey?"

"Ah, Freddy. Not now."

"It is never *now*, Jeffrey."

"Was it ever, Fredericka?"

"When you loved me."

He sighs. "Yes, there was a time when I, perhaps, actually loved you, impossible as that may seem."

I wrote about his tormented, on-again, off-again romance with Fredericka Barnes in *Jeffrey Quilt, Master of the Macabre*, but little information was actually available. What a scoop. Secrets revealed. I could do a sequel.

Useless.

"I'd like to chat with you, Freddy, but—"

"—not now. Let me guess—"

"I'm with an old and dear friend, and we are somewhat preoccupied."

"I'll bet."

"What exactly do you want, Fredericka?"

"I'm pregnant."

"How very . . . awkward."

I lean over and glance at the sketch. Bending his head to hold the phone against his shoulder and thus free his hands, he starts sketching again. I realize that what he is executing is a portrait of this Fredericka, whoever she is, some long-lost love, some one-night stand, some woman he has betrayed. Somehow, in the picture, her remains are not the biological scraps you'd expect, but a swirling vortex of fire, broken glass, brilliant light, and deepest darkness, like something torn out of the fabric of the universe to reveal the unguessable awfulness beyond. This is going to be Jeffrey's finest work, I am sure.

Fredericka is sobbing.

"I wish, Jeffrey, that we could be together again. Somehow."

"You wouldn't want that. You don't know what you're asking."
"Yes, I *fucking* do."
"Okay then."
"Okay?"
"May I ask you a seemingly irrelevant question, my dear?"
"Yes . . . what?"
"What were you doing just now, before you called? And where were you?"
"Ironing. In the kitchen. Why?"
"I'm weird. I ask odd questions. Remember?"

Then I can hear glass breaking and she's screaming over the phone. He hangs up and blasphemously entitles his drawing, with characteristically enigmatic Quiltian humor, *The Flagellation of the Virgin.*

He hands it to me, as if to say, *See, I am a monster too. We have both been morally and emotionally bankrupt for a long time. The only difference is that I make art out of what I do.*

To think I admired you, Jeffrey. I wanted to become just like you.

And so you have. It was so easy.

13

"You want to know," says Jeffrey Quilt, "what hope there is for us, what redemption. I say to you that there is no redemption, for we have lived out our own damnation, you and I, who are as one, you and I, damned together, dying together, art and artist confused and conflated. You are a multiple murderer of all your loved ones; your soul is dead; I am the artist, you the subject; which is cause and which is effect? I speak to you of the inner *gnosis,* which is light, encrusted by the foulness that is our life here on Earth, which may only be set free in the Dream, if only we can return to the Dream, which I have learned to touch, to embrace. Therefore I call on you to put aside these trifles and these toys, these memories—look! I cast aside my pens, my brushes, my sketchpad!—and rise up. We open the door. Yes, there are three men in black with sharp knives waiting, and a leopard, which now has an almost human face, a woman's face. Yes. I see it. You see it. But we sally forth bravely, and, behold, they stand aside and let us pass, and we walk across the gravel driveway, into a field, not toward U.S. Route 1 and the ocean beyond it, but into an archetypal field, which partakes of that old St. David's golf course, which was but a shadow of the true field, cast upon a cave wall, which is the waking world. And we shall walk into the field again as we were when we were young and relatively innocent—remember?—I in my bare feet and you in your Keds, squishing in the mud as we make our way through the tall grass—it's tall now, like wheat, rippling in the wind under the bright moon. It's an adventure now, the mystery and wonder all before us. Look, we creep among the tents, in the darkness. The circus is closed, its delights shut away, but *we* will find them, because *we* know that after the hours of life and death when all crimes are forgotten and all passion and rage are spent, *they* appear on the Ferris wheel, they who are lost and damned as we, they who are dead or never born, they who will comfort us and keep us company, for we are of their kind, not of the human kind, not anymore. And we climb up, up, into the turning, turning structure, among the great bones that stretch inside the wheel; we climb there, and we hide there, unable, unworthy to come out into the seats, to ride properly and look out into the Dream. We are not ready yet, because we cannot weep, and we must hide in the darkness until we can rediscover our tears inside ourselves and weep for our many sins."

14

But it's not as simple as all that. There, you can see him, Jeffrey Quilt, clinging to the bone spokes, among the faces and hanged figures and ghosts; there he goes, and there—

He is changing again, as he did for just an instant that first time we came here. Then, it was a kind of future echo, a glimpse of what he might become. Now it is. He is not the slightly scruffy, slightly innocent hippie boy. He is the Ringmaster in his top hat and costume, who is filled to overflowing with guilt and with memory, the dreamer who is himself dreamt, as damned and trapped as any, but also our leader. It is he who orchestrates these events, even as he has damned and trapped himself.

I want to follow him.

But I cannot climb. I reach out. It is as if I am touching smoke.

I hear footsteps sucking in the mud.

The three men in black surround me now, and their leopard, which glares at me with burning eyes and speaks with my own wife's voice and with Fredericka's.

I think to die here, as I merely deserve, to protect Jeffrey, whom I somehow still admire, even love.

But no. One of the men hands me a knife. He indicates that I should hold it in my teeth.

And we begin to climb, up into the turning wheel, among the dead and the never born. In the fullness of time we will catch him. We are very patient. In the fullness of time it is our fate to cut out his heart and pour fire into his pale chest, not to kill him, but so he may live forever, as part of the Dream and as the Dreamer, filled to overflowing with pain and with wisdom, for he is the Ringmaster, whom we all follow upon the turning wheel.

The Bear Went Over the Mountain

Yes, I think I know what happened to Professor Richard Spencer. We had a long talk before the end, and he told me a great deal, and at the end itself I witnessed something more.

It began, I am certain, with him sitting at his desk in that farmhouse on a winter afternoon, staring out the window and coming to the conclusion that he was neither a good father nor a good person. I was not convinced, but to him it seemed irrefutable.

"I have two daughters I am supposed to love, a dead wife I am supposed to be grieving for, and I don't feel anything," he told me, later, when we talked. "I'm hollow behind, like one of those ghosts or spirits that's open in the back, and just a shape filled with wind, nothing there, really, nothing inside."

"That's an odd metaphor coming from a mathematician rather than a folklorist," I said, "besides being utter nonsense."

"Don't try to comfort me, Henry. It's useless."

"If you really were a sociopath or whatever, you wouldn't feel that there's anything wrong. It is impossible to feel guilty about being incapable of guilt."

"Don't try to trap me with logic, either, because it *fucking* won't do."

That set me aback. I had known him for twenty years now, and I had never heard him raise his voice, much less use such language.

So he told me about it, how on a winter's evening quite like this one, he had sat at this very desk and stared out that very window at the black, leafless trees silhouetted against the red sunset—just like that one we saw now. They still have Daylight Saving Time here, and if you're in a place that still follows Daylight Saving Time the shadows deepen and the darkness comes on *very early*, so it was indeed almost dark—just a trace of red gleaming along the rim of the hill—and his two girls were playing outside, rustling the dead leaves as they sang or chanted something that sounded like "For He's a Jolly Good Fellow" but wasn't.

He had come to this very remote place, in what we used to call the flyover parts of Pennsylvania, after the disturbances in Philadelphia—such as were happening in most cities in what people were beginning to call the Former United States by then—had left most of the area around the university burned and the city schools shut down. So it seemed the sensible thing just to leave a note on his desk declaring himself on sabbatical and hightail it up here in a leased car he would probably never have to pay for, just himself and the girls and some luggage, computers, and a few books. Hours of driving through long, dark valleys and dark woods, made all that much darker by Daylight Saving Time and what other fragments of the old order of things still drifted over the landscape like ashes from some distant fire.

Here, at least, in the summer cabin that had belonged to his late wife's parents, he could continue his work, and he was a workaholic, he knew perfectly well, even an obsessed workaholic on the verge of a breakthrough that would completely rewrite our understanding of space and the sequences of history and the need for Daylight Saving Time.

He had neglected his late wife, Allyson. He saw that now, too.

"Cancer can catch you by surprise," I said. "At least you had time to say goodbye."

"But I didn't," he said, leaving me to ponder precisely what he meant by that.

It had been at that specific moment some nights before, as he sat at his desk staring out the window, half listening to his daughters in the back yard, that it came to him: his wife's death had not pained him as it should, it actually meant nothing to him, his daughters were total strangers to him—he had, after all, married late to a much younger woman and had never expected to be a father at all—*ergo* he was not a good person, because he had not been able to go through the prescribed Five Stages of Grief as if completing a mathematical proof.

I didn't dispute him on that, didn't interrupt at all as he told me, even though it was abundantly clear that he was in fact grieving. He just wasn't finished yet. He was in the Anger stage.

N-dimensional spaces and transfinite numbers aside, the strangeness had been right here, in this room, in his heart, and just outside that window. Felicity, aged ten, and Charity, aged seven, could have as well been squirrels chattering on the branches that scratched against the panes.

Finally he had rapped on the glass to get their attention, but they went on with their game or whatever it was. He got up and went to the door and opened it. He could not see them. They were back in the bushes somewhere, in the dark, skittering around in the leaves. Now he could make out the words to the song. He knew it from his own childhood, but he was certain he had never taught it to them.

> *The bear went over the mountain.*
> *The bear went over the mountain.*
> *The bear went over the mountain,*
> *To see what he could see.*

He clapped his hands and tried to summon them in for dinner. But they didn't seem to hear him, so he had to wade out into the yard, the darkness, and the underbrush, something he did with considerable reluctance, because he had been a city kid and had barely ever stepped off the sidewalk in his life, even if, somehow—they didn't get it from him, surely—the girls took to the woods as if they belonged there.

And that was when, he told me later as we two sat together in his study and had our conversation, what you might call the fraying thread that kept him attached to conventional reality snapped, and he went plunging into some incomprehensible abyss. Yes, it had been then, though he'd only realized it retrospect. It hadn't seemed all that dramatic. He was standing ankle deep in leaves, pushing aside thorny branches because he was too large to crawl under them into secret places the way a child could, and he heard more words of the familiar song:

> *And what do you think he saw, saw?*
> *And what do you think he saw, saw?*

What was disquieting was that he had the distinct impression that there were more than two children out there, that he was surrounded by them, all hiding and laughing in muted voices, and one of them—definitely not Felicity or Charity—singing on in a very strange voice that almost sounded like barking or grunting, barely able to carry the tune, going on with words that were definitely *not* part of the song as he'd ever learned it. Something about a dead town and a red town and a man made all of bones.

Angry or afraid or certainly displeased with all this, he clapped his hands again, as loud as he could, and shouted, "Hey, you two! Come in! Time for supper!"

The singing stopped. The rustling of leaves stopped, and after a moment the bushes disgorged two regulation, dirty children, whom he, as a regulation parent, shooed into the bathroom to clean themselves up as best they could. When his wife was alive, she'd always gone in with them and done a better job of it, but he left them to their own devices and when they emerged again Charity still had a streak of mud on her forehead and both of them had bits of leaves in their hair.

Over microwaved dinners he ventured to ask, "So who are your friends?"

"What friends?" said Felicity.

"I heard them before I called you in. Did they go home?"

"It was just us," said Felicity.

"Just us," said Charity, "not counting—"

Her older sister gave her the look that every child knows and every parent recognizes, the one that means *Shut up. You're not supposed to tell. That's a secret.*

"Not counting the bear, Dad," said Felicity. "It's part of a game."

There might have been a time when Richard could have made a joke out of this, and they'd all have gotten a good laugh out of it as he warned them not to let the bear eat them, but now he, a hollow shape with nothing inside, was merely going through motions. Another possibility might have been the recognition that the girls were obviously lying and hiding something from him. It was like a form to be filled out, only he hadn't checked either option off.

Somehow, for all he allegedly didn't feel anything inside, the whole matter became an obsession with him. What precisely *were* the girls hiding? What *was* over the mountain? It was like an equation he couldn't quite solve, left hanging in the air.

In the spirit of scientific inquiry he began his investigations. You know how the rest of the song goes, *And what do you think he saw, saw? Why! The other side of the mountain, the other side of the mountain,* and so on, it being one of those mindless songs that loops around and goes on forever, like "Ninety-Nine Bottles of Beer on the Wall" only without the intellectual challenge of counting.

Only Richard didn't think it was as simple as all that. He made inquiries. The nearest town he was familiar with was about twenty miles away, a place called Bethsaida.

"*That* way," he said to me, pointing in the direction away from the window and the hill.

In Bethsaida, where he bought his groceries, people told him, somewhat reluctantly and evasively, that there was another town in the opposite direction from where he was staying, a few miles over the mountain but actually much closer than Bethsaida, a place called Chorazin, which had a very bad reputation. Something about the people there, or what they did, or maybe their religion. Nobody really knew. Nobody went there.

"Lots of Bible names in this part of the state," Richard said. "I looked it up. Chorazin is one of the 'impenitent towns' cursed by Jesus. See Matthew 11:21. The story goes, the Antichrist will be born there. But guess what? Jesus cursed Bethsaida in the same verse, so where the fuck do they get off criticizing their neighbors? Of course *that* Chorazin and *that* Bethsaida are in the Middle East somewhere, but who except lunatics or people given over to witchcraft or whatever would name their towns after places the Lord Himself cursed? Is that why neither one of them is on the map?"

So were kids from this other Chorazin sneaking over the mountain to play secretive games with his daughters, somehow never introducing themselves to him or allowing themselves to be seen by anyone other than Felicity and Charity?

That was seriously crazy? It was like believing in fairies.
And what about the bear?

"My girls have insipid names," he said. "I mean, who the fuck names their kids Felicity and Charity in this day and age? It's not like we're fucking Victorians or Puritans or something."

The answer was, of course, that his late wife Allyson had done it. Some while ago he had told me, quite content with the idea then, how they'd agreed that if they had girls she would name them, if boys, he would. At the time he'd said the names were just fine. He'd called them "Steampunk names."

Less and less did Richard Spencer sound like himself.

He tried spying on his daughters. He listened at the door of their bedroom at night, sometimes with a wine glass to his ear as if that would increase his sound pickup. But little girls, like cats, seem to have better senses than grownups do, so they always seemed to know when he was there, and when he was they were always silent, even though, time and time again, when they were out in the yard, he heard them singing.

He struggled with his work for hours every day, but much of the time he could not concentrate. The problem gnawed at him. His mind turned down channels very uncharacteristic for the professor I had known all these years: alchemical symbolism, allegory. What did the alleged bear stand for? Was the red town red with paint or fire or metaphysical enlightenment? Was it just possible that his own work, his mathematics, his own mental concentration had opened some sort of door through which the Apocalypse or the Antichrist or the end of the world would arrive? After all, cities were burning, the world was ending, or might as well be, so why not?

Was it even possible that his two daughters, without any complicated formulae, had achieved the same effect with a mere song?

The bear came from the red town.
The bear came from the dead town.
The bear came from the burning town.
With the man made all of bones.

* * *

What followed, I am certain, was not entirely a dream, though it came to Richard in a dream.

He had been spying on the girls again, ridiculously listening at their bedroom door with the wine glass. Maybe he'd drunk a bit of the wine beforehand, maybe too much—he rambled and never got to that point—but in any case he fell asleep there, in the hall, lying against their door. Somehow, while he was asleep, part of his rational mind was working, and he realized how awkward this would be if one of them had to go to the bathroom in the middle of the night and found him there. How would he explain himself? Then there was a transition and the door *was* open, and both of his daughters were standing there in their pajamas and bathrobes and slippers, but with winter coats on over that, as if they intended to go outside.

And he said to them, "I want to join your game. Let me come too."

But Felicity, the elder, said very solemnly, "You can't, Daddy."

"And why not?"

"Because you didn't begin at the beginning, Daddy."

They both went out the back door into the yard.

Only after a moment could he react, sluggishly, clumsily. He lurched to his feet and said, "I'm coming too."

He ran after them. He saw them disappearing into the woods, climbing up the hill behind the house. He began to shout rather than sing, *"The bear went over the mountain! The bear went over the mountain! The bear went over the fucking mountain! And whaddaya think he saw?"*

He caught up with Charity, the younger, and took her by the hand, but they were still running forward. He felt the compulsion too, in his dream. The girls had shed their winter coats and lost their slippers and were running barefoot through the cold mud and the leaves, and the rational part of his mind, very remote from the action now, worried that they were going to catch pneumonia that way. But they ran, and the hillside was filled with light, as if a mysterious, unscheduled sunrise were taking place from the wrong direction. The sky streamed with burning red light. He thought the forest was on fire. He thought he saw shapes in the light, or fire, or whatever it was.

The rational part of his mind managed to converse with Charity, who explained to him, in a vocabulary and with concepts that did not sound very much like a seven-year-old talking, that it was indeed because he had neglected them, because he had treated his two daughters as mere duties, as *things* to be managed, that their lives had drifted far, far away from his.

Because he was a bad person, a bad parent, hollow inside with nothing there?
She told him that did not matter.

They drifted into another reality? The rational part of his mind struggled with the concept. Maybe out here in the wilderness the curtain of "reality" was so much thinner, and you could do that, just press through into somewhere, some*thing* else.

That did not matter, either. She told him not to try to understand. What mattered was that the two of them, Felicity and Charity, had made a game of sitting out in the woods at night and listening to the sounds they heard there, at first just animals and birds. But then words, and finally songs. They sang to the voices in the sky. Were they afraid? No, they were not, because the Burning Lady would protect them. She was covered in fire, but she did not burn. She came to them from tomorrow and from yesterday and was there always, because even though she was dead she would never die. Her friend was the Bone Man, who came up out of the ground. He rode on the Bear, which came over the mountain when the stars were in the right places in the sky, and took them to the Burning Town, which did not burn but was filled with light, and there were songs coming out of the air, and they heard wings flapping behind the clouds.

That was as much as he got out of her before the climax of the dream occurred, at the point where the Burning Lady picked up Felicity, shrouding her in flames for an instant, then handing her unharmed to the Bone Man, who sat astride the Bear. The Bear itself was huge, itself like a mountain that crawled. The living mountain had come over the stone mountain, so to speak, smashing trees like matchsticks as it moved.

"Me too! Me too!" Charity shouted.

"Come, Charity," said the Burning Woman.

But Richard still had his younger daughter by the hand. He yanked her away so hard he might have dislocated her arm. She screamed as he picked her up, heaved her up onto his shoulder, and ran with her down the hillside, crashing through bushes and thorns.

He "awoke" by the bedroom door. He had Charity in his arms. Her pajamas were stained with mud and she was badly scratched from the thorns. But he knew that he could deal with that later. What he had to do first was make sure the Bear and the rest didn't come back for her. So he carried her into her bedroom and tied her into a chair, using a couple of her T-shirts out of a dresser drawer as ropes. She had stopped screaming by then and just whimpered.

"And so we take leave of this cozy domestic scene, Henry, and consider the real reason you have entered the narrative at this point. I summoned you, yes, but it may or may not have to do with a breakthrough . . . on the generalized Riemann conjecture perhaps . . . that I wanted to share with my former favorite graduate student and now esteemed colleague."

The house was silent. I wondered where the girls were.

Richard, I should mention, looked more than disheveled. He was a mess. I noted that there were scratches on his hands and face, just as if he'd been running through underbrush in the dark.

He started to show me some notebooks filled with calculations. It was maddening. I really wanted to look. But I couldn't. I pushed them away.

"I'm calling the police," I said.

"And why would you do that?"

"Because you're insane, and you'd pretty much admitted injuring at least one of your daughters and losing the other. That's a good enough reason."

"Go ahead and try. The phone service is down again. Oh, and just before you arrived I had the news on. Somebody nuked New York. They think it was domestic terrorists. The world's coming to an end. I am sure if we went out and looked, the sky would be filled with signs and wonders. The gateway is open, and what rough beast, his hour come at last and all that. Nothing matters."

"Your children matter."

"But didn't I tell you? I don't have them. They're *both* gone now."

I felt only cold terror in my gut. Maybe it was true about New York and millions were dead, but more immediately I needed to know if the madman had killed his own little girls.

He got up from his chair. "Oh, I have been very rude," he said. "I haven't given you a tour of the house. Come this way."

I followed him, past a kitchen with the sink filled with dirty dishes and trash on the floor. Then we came to what was obviously the girls' bedroom. A stuffed toy, a couple socks, and a pair of pink leggings on the floor in the hallway. The door was painted white. There were stains on it.

He paused with his hand on the doorknob.

"I don't have the younger one because I dozed off for a while, from exhaustion I guess, and in my dreams I thought I heard her singing that song, with more and more new verses, and then I heard the older one singing back to her, from out of the woods, somewhere behind the house."

We went inside. I felt a cold blast of air as if we'd stepped outside, because, in effect we had. The whole wall of the room was ripped out, as if someone had come through the window with a back hoe.

"They came and got her, you see."

The two of us returned to his study. I went through his mathematical notebooks and examined his conclusions. I'd need time to study this. It would take hours or days of study, but at a glance it seemed that he had indeed made the breakthrough he'd promised—an indirect connection between Riemann's music of the primes and the theory of discrete random walks . . . and what was this? Wanderings into unrelated areas: Kepler's spheres, Gerard 't Hooft's spaces, even daring to attack Ramanujan's conjecture? Was he trying to tease an answer from his subconscious?

The implications were huge.

And they didn't matter one bit. Not anymore.

The Internet was down. The radio wasn't working. There was no phone service. We couldn't find out if New York had been nuked or not. I can't tell you if some sort of gateway had opened and the apocalypse was at hand.

I can only tell you how Richard Spencer's personal story ended.

He got up again and went outside, not through the door, but through the back of his daughters' bedroom, where the wall used to be. I followed him at a little distance and saw and heard everything.

He began to recite *that song*, not really singing, more chanting. There were a lot of verses I'd never heard before.

Trees snapped off like matchsticks. The Burning Lady was there. So was the Bone Man, though he wasn't really a man, more of a skeletal spider with at least eight or nine legs. The thing they rode on was not ursine at all, but it is hard to describe, so the word is convenient.

He did not resist. He was going where his daughters had gone. The Bear came over the mountain and took him far away.

The Interrogator

My badge, from one of those agencies most people barely know exist, got me past the guards without difficulty. I was ushered into the bare, underground room, where he sat at the table. I sat down at the other side, opened my briefcase, and reviewed the files I had with me.

Sunlight filtered in fitfully from a slit of a window. From overhead you could hear fair sounds of traffic. We were supposedly under New York, near Central Park.

"Doctor Leonard Tremblay—"

He looked at me sharply and said, "You can't kill me! I am too valuable. I know too much about *them!* I will never be executed, regardless of what you think I have done."

One hell of a way to start an interview, as anyone might have said.

"You *need* what I know," he continued.

"I am not an executioner," I said.

I shuffled through the files, pulled out a couple of exceptionally gruesome photographs, and showed them to him. He had no reaction at all, no apparent empathy.

"Doctor Tremblay, you are accused of some very serious crimes."

At that he sat up straight, folded his hands on the table top, and said almost cheerfully, "Guilty as charged. What are you going to do about it?"

I sighed. "As I said, I am not your executioner. I am not here to *do* anything about it, because of course once an action has been committed in the past, there is nothing to be *done* about it. It is only possible to do something about the present or the future. I am here to understand."

"That is very logical, but we humans sometimes go on more than just logic—"

I continued, controlling my impatience. I did not *like* this smug bastard, as the common idiom would describe him. I made a note of that.

"Doctor Tremblay, you were a member of the Secondary Magnetic Expedition to the Antarctic, were you not?"

"Not mentioned in the published account. One of the also-was-there-in-the-crowd types. Third lieutenant sub-deputy aide."

"This is not a matter to joke about."

"Assistant biologist."

I made a note. "You were Doctor Blair's colleague," I said.

"I had been his graduate student. He'd kept in touch after I got my degree. I was honored that he asked for me to come with him."

"I didn't ask you, 'How did you feel about Doctor Blair?' yet."

"Sorry. You must understand that we humans sometimes get ahead of ourselves."

"Is that an attempt at humor?"

"No, just bad taste."

I made a note.

"So how did you feel about Doctor Blair?"

"I won't say I loved him, but I had deep respect for him. He was smart. He had the right instincts, even when that instinct was to trust no one, even me. In the end, as you doubtless know, he trusted no one and went off by himself and locked himself in the shed."

"I have read the report," I said. "I know that by the time they got back to the shed, Dr. Blair was no longer Dr. Blair."

"And you believe that?"

"I do not think the report is a work of fiction."

"Wasn't it just too convenient the way the alien tissue samples melted down into their component molecules and the strange gizmos they found in the shed turned back into junk—like fairy gold it was, you know, the gold that seems to be a great treasure, but the next time you look at them, they're just dead leaves? Like that. In the fairy tales. But you don't read fairy tales, do you? Just reports."

"I have not had the time to read fairy tales."

"But *we* do. We find the time, at least when we're kids, when we are growing up. There's a time in our development when we are open to anything imaginative, when the boundaries between what is possible and what is not do not seem at all firm. Some of us even carry that into adulthood. It's called imagination. Creative people have it. But you, Mr.—you never did introduce yourself, did you? Make a note of that. It's what humans do. It sets the subject at ease—"

I detected that his heartbeat had increased, that he had begun to sweat. He was fidgeting. He pounded his fist on the table top. I assessed the threat level and determined that there was none. This was merely an emotional reaction.

"My name is Joseph Norton, Doctor Tremblay. Did that set you at ease?"

"Not particularly."

"Were you lying then, Doctor Tremblay?"

"Not particularly."

For a moment he said nothing, just staring at me.

"I put forward to you, Joseph Norton, if that really is your name, if you even *have* a name, that what was in that report, what I've told the others before you, very much resembles the delusions of a madman, not a word of it true, not even this what I tell you now. A liar paradox, in other words."

"I am aware of the liar paradox, Doctor Tremblay. 'All Cretans are liars. I am a Cretan. Therefore I am lying about everything, even that Cretans are liars and I am one of them.'"

"Maybe that should be 'cretins.'"

"Please clarify."

"Attempt at humor. Failed. Make a note of it."

I made a note of it.

Then I pushed one of the particularly gory photographs across the table to him. He picked it up and studied it for a while, then put it down again. "That was McReady," he said. "Only it wasn't. Liar paradox again."

"You hunted down and killed five members of the expedition. In each instance you tried to destroy their bodies with fire, acid, or both."

He tapped the photo with his finger. "Hell on the plumbing, to do that in a bathtub."

"You committed murder."

"Let us say that McReady and the rest were not themselves. I destroyed what they had become. It wasn't murder."

"I don't see the importance of this distinction."

"You wouldn't."

"Doctor Tremblay, I am going to be candid with you. Put my cards on the table, as the saying goes—"

"You're learning our idiom fast—"

"What I wish to learn from you is *how* you were supposedly able to recognize that your colleagues had changed. I have read the report. You have too, I am sure. It says that the extraterrestrial creature, if that is what it truly was, had been completely destroyed before any of you left the Antarctic. All the dogs that were no longer dogs, the cows that were not cows, and the men who were not men, up to and including the late lamented Dr. Blair. So I ask you to consider: Is it possible that everything you thought you perceived afterwards *was* a delusion, the actions of a man in shock after the horrific deaths of his companions?"

"You're asking *me* if I'm a raving paranoiac?"

"Consider the possibility."

"Liar paradox. That is all I have to say about that. You figure it out. Take as long as you need."

He sat with his head in his hands. It took several minutes for me to get him to talk again. Then it was a long monologue. A tirade.

"I don't think any of *them* came with us onto the steamer going home," he said, beginning slowly. "What walked up the gangplank were humans. I am sure of that. We had all been tested. We had destroyed the last fully developed monster in Doctor Blair's shack. Everybody had been tested one more time. Yes, we were mourning our lost comrades, but we also felt like men coming back from a war. *We had survived.* We were going home. We would see our loved ones again and get on with our lives.

"On the voyage back there was almost a party atmosphere, but with a tinge of desperation to it, as if everybody still had to prove he was human. Barclay on the banjo and singing dirty songs at all hours. Men playing cards and drinking beer and watching movies and doing all those stereotypical things rough, tough explorer types do in their leisure time to distract themselves from really thinking about what had happened.

"I stood on the deck as we headed north, watching the Antarctic continent receding behind the ship, thinking that we would never know all its secrets, that we shouldn't have ever gone there, that some things are better left the hell alone. Which is not the correct attitude of an inquiring scientific mind, I will admit, but that was how I felt.

"The auroras looked odd, somehow threatening. I was afraid again. For the next few days and nights I kept mostly to myself. If anybody asked, I said I was working on my data. A lot of guys were like that, actually. Real scientists. Maybe we had beaten a hasty retreat from Big Magnet, but we brought our papers, our data, which is what any scientist would rescue from a burning house.

"It was a week later, or more—the air had grown warm by then; we were somewhere in the Southern Temperate Zone—that Henry Gould knocked on my door, came into my cabin, and confided in me. You don't know Gould. Another one of those also-in-the-crowd types, an aviation mechanic's mate. But he came to me, and he was worried, and the next night Gould brought Doctor Copper—the physician— along, and we three confided in one another, compared notes, and concluded that all this enforced jollity, or even resumed diligence with scientific work, just wasn't natural. It was *too normal.* You know the joke about how you don't want to be too normal because that's not normal and then people will *know.* Well, we knew. We hadn't figured it all out yet, but we knew that the real Barclay never played the banjo so obsessively or that Norris and Benning were not that good at cards. Somehow monsters had gotten onto the ship with us, and very likely mankind and the whole Earth was doomed.

"So the following evening, after most people had gone to bed, we invited Barclay down to my cabin with the promise of some very special booze, and Gould put a sack over his head and I smashed his skull with a crowbar. Then Doctor Copper served as lookout while we bundled Barclay up onto the deck and over the side.

"Well, that, I assure you, put an end to far more than the banjo-playing. The party atmosphere was gone. The only conclusion had to be that Barclay had snapped from the strain after the fact—think of it as something like battle fatigue—and jumped to his death.

"The rest of the voyage was quiet. Everybody was trying to be watchful and compassionate and looking out for the first signs that his buddy might be about to crack. A lot of us did our scientific work, as best we could, usually not in our cabins, alone, but in the common mess room. The place had the atmosphere of a very grim school right before final exams.

"Acting Commander McReady wrote most of his report then, the one you have seen. He passed it around to the rest of us for comments and additions. I contributed a paragraph or two myself. All the while I could not get it out of my head that this was a report by a Thing for Things, in a world of Things.

"Then Doctor Copper really did commit suicide. He called me into his cabin. He explained what a *goddamned stupid* thing we had done disposing of Barclay like that, how, if the world of men ever had a chance to survive, we had just decreased it by several orders of magnitude. Why? Remember how all the dogs had become infected—taken over—because they had tasted Thing blood? Well, if Barclay had been a monster, and we'd just tossed him over the side, alive or dead, when the crabs and fishes or even oceanic bacteria had gotten finished with him, they too would be infected—would become Things, large or small, swimming, flying, or just drifting until they had reached every corner of the Earth and every level of the biosphere. If Things are to be destroyed, it must be with fire or with acid. They have to be *wiped out*, every cell of them, or it does no good.

"Doc Copper sobbed as he told me this. He was shaking. I actually held him in my arms as if he were a child. He said it was his fault, inasmuch as he had gone along with our plan or even originated it. I actually wasn't sure whose idea it had been.

"Then he told me that he had already taken poison, and before I could do anything for him he dropped to the floor in convulsions and died, frothing at the mouth. But he did not melt or turn into anything else. He died human.

"Well, *that* put an even greater damper on the rest of the voyage, you may be certain. The rest was positively funereal. No celebrations as we crossed the Equator. *Some* of what happened got into the report. But not what he had said to me, of course, or what we had done. No, that was a secret. I don't suppose there is any point in keeping it now.

"I think I spent the rest of the trip home in my bunk. The report says 'nervous breakdown,' doesn't it? Not quite the case. I spent that time dreaming. The dreams came from outside my head, I am certain, as if I were a radio antenna picking up faint signals that were getting stronger and stronger. I dreamed of the white wastes of Antarctica, and what it was like to lie beneath its ice there for millennia waiting, vaguely sensing—as if in a dream—the evolution of the world outside. I dreamed too, from the perspective of Things, as they infiltrated themselves into every human society on the planet and gradually took over. I saw their black metal cities rise above the ruins of ours, like Mountains of Madness. I saw them soaring in metal ships like swarms of enormous bees, spreading out to the stars. I saw them touch our sun and make it bluer and hotter, burning off most native life from the Earth except for what they chose to keep in reserve—for study perhaps, or as food.

"And when we got to New York, I was examined first by psychiatrists, but I kept my secrets from them. I was brought in, like the rest of the survivors—if that is what they still were—to testify before some very, very secret committees.

"I kept on dreaming. It was as if my mind were no longer my own, as if I were becoming part of something larger, more grand than an individual human being. But at the same time I hated that and feared and fought it.

"But how can a man fight his own dreams? And for how long?

"I think you know the rest. I knew I had little time left. Once I was able to work my way free, I sought out Henry Gould—who had retired from exploring and was hiding in an apartment upstate—explained to him the conclusions I had reached through impeccable logic and what I had to do as a result of them, compared notes with him on our dreams, and then killed him and dissolved his body in acid in his bathtub. It had to be done, you see. That is all I can say about any of my actions. They had to be done. I had figured it all out, you see."

After Dr. Tremblay had stopped speaking, there were a few minutes of strained silence. I shuffled papers. I took the gory photo back from him and put it in my briefcase. I made some more notes. He just sat there, motionless, like a machine that had been turned off.

"The most obvious conclusion I can come to," I said, "is that you, and some of your colleagues on the expedition, succumbed to a mysterious group psychosis. To any objective, rational person, your entire testimony does sound, you must admit, completely insane."

"But as you well know," he said, "in science the obvious answer is not always the right one. We have long since discarded Occam's Razor for Occam's Swiss Army Knife. There are multiple possibilities."

"You claims are also illogical. There are numerous gaps in your reasoning. You have not reached your conclusions through valid means."

"Call that an intuitive leap. And there were the dreams. I would not expect your kind to understand."

"Why did you kill Henry Gould? To silence him about the murder of Barclay?"

"No. I killed him because he sneezed."

I took more notes, then said softly, "I do not see where you are going with this."

"You don't? I had figured it all out, you see. You are trying to trick me, or torment me, or maybe both, by the question you *did not ask*. I think you don't want to ask it because you already know the answer and you know I know, and I know you know I know, and so everybody knows and it would be redundant to explain away the eight-hundred-pound gorilla in the room, which is, if all those expedition members were human when they boarded the ship, how did the alien creature, or some element of it, *get off Antarctica?* We thought we really had extinguished the last of the Things when we cornered what had been Blair and then cremated all those bodies, but we overlooked *one detail,* didn't we? It was right in front of us. It was explained when

McReady and the others did their clever thing with the electric wire that made a drop of Thing blood behave like an individual being and leap out of a test tube. If each *cell* of the Thing can function as an individual creature, and slowly absorb other organic material to gain size and strength, how could we *ever* hope to stop it? It didn't have to devour men or dogs or cows to take us over. All it had to do was scratch its dandruff or fart or sneeze. Particularly *sneeze*. That's the perfect way, the innocuous way that nobody thought of, to get a few cells airborne, after which they were just lying in wait patiently in our lungs or on our skin and clothing until we let our guard down, and then, slowly, stealthily, those cells call out to other cells—in dreams, perhaps—and come together, and *whammo!* They take over the planet. That is what I figured out. I should have noticed it earlier.

"About the time we put Barclay over the side, Gould was sneezing a lot. I should have noticed. It's well known that after about a month in the Antarctic nobody sneezes, because everybody at the base has already caught everybody else's colds and developed immunity to those particular strains. On the ship, on the way back, we had not yet been exposed to anyone but our own colleagues. There were no stops in South American ports. No fooling around with beautiful Latin women. But there was Gould, sneezing away. After a while I noticed that the others were sneezing a lot too. Particularly Substitute-Commander McReady, who had taken over after Commander Garry had proven to be one of *them*. Aa—choo! It aroused my suspicions, I tell you, but I was too distracted. My head was filled with dreams. I couldn't concentrate well enough. It took me a while to work out the implications. By then we were in New York, sneezing away. Gould was sneezing too damn much. Even when I killed him, he was still sneezing. Aa—choo!"

I closed my briefcase, placed it on the floor, and folded my hands on the table. I leaned forward.

"And tell me, Doctor Tremblay, when you killed Gould, did he melt into a shapeless blob?"

"By the time I had him the bathtub and was pouring acid on him, he certainly did. Hell on the plumbing."

"But not before then. Not when he was merely dead."

"How could I be sure he was dead, and not filled with alien monster cells that he had been sneezing all over the place?"

"Either you are telling the truth, Doctor Tremblay, and the Earth faces an extraordinary peril, or else you are completely insane and *you* are a danger to your fellow men unless you are locked up forever."

"You want to keep some of us around, as breeding stock, for food, or for study, don't you? Start with me. I am a particularly interesting specimen. I know you are fascinated. Aa—choo!"

At this point I deemed it a strategic necessity to provoke him deliberately. An emotional response can be like the light from a stellar explosion. You can read much data in the spectral lines.

I got up as if to leave. "My God," I said. "I don't believe a damned thing you have told me. You have no secrets, Tremblay. You haven't figured anything out. You are merely a sniveling, pathetic psychopath. You have murdered several men quite uselessly. None of this happened. There was no monster in Antarctica. You somehow spread the contagion of your madness there too, murdered several more of your colleagues, and deluded the rest. This is useless!"

"That's not a very professional attitude, if you want to cure me, Doctor," he said. He sneezed at me.

"I never said I was a doctor. I am not here to cure you," I said.

Tremblay sneezed again, deliberately, as if to ridicule me, then laughed. He pointed his finger at me. "Of course you're not, because you can't. *You're one of them.* You're an imitation, not a human being. I could see through you all along. Maybe you've already taken over the planet and are just keeping a few of us humans around for study. You're trying to figure out what makes us human. Is that it? Your individual cells make up a kind of collective, but you can't comprehend what it is to be an individual, not in the human sense, not a complete being rather than a mass of protoplasm pretending to be a complete being. You still want what we have that you haven't got. Is that it? *Is that it?*"

I turned to him sharply and pointed back.

"I posit, Doctor Leonard Tremblay, celebrated individual that you claim to be, a completely different hypothesis. What if *you're* the liar?

What if *you're* the extraterrestrial monster pretending to be a man? Huh? What about that?"

He screamed at me, with a howl you wouldn't think a human throat could make, and his face began to shift, but only within the range of what his facial muscles allowed. It was a vivid emotional display, eyes wide, frothing at the mouth, as he screamed and screamed. For a brief while he became articulate again and said, "Then I'll have to reveal my *true form* and sprout a few tentacles and claws, and hypnotize you with my three burning, red eyes while I break this table into bits and club you to death with it before I rip your head off and dissolve the rest of you in my drool." And he screamed some more, rising to his feet, attempting to lift the table, to tip it over, straining with all his strength in a white hot fury of indescribable rage.

But he could not lift the table because it was affixed to the floor. He could not tear my head off because he had no tentacles or claws, and in the end he just dropped to the floor, helpless and sobbing, as I pressed the buzzer and two guards came and took him away.

I must report that this session has been a failure. The experiment has yielded no results. The conclusion before us is that humans possess some quality that we, for all that we perfectly mimic their physical forms and replicate their thought processes, cannot share. It is as if there is another sense, beyond sight, hearing, taste, touch, smell, or even dreaming which somehow enables them to detect its absence in ourselves. I do not think they fully understand it themselves. They refer to it disparagingly as "madness" or "paranoia." It is a powerful weapon that we must add to our arsenal. Until then, we are not complete. Recommend further study.

In the meantime we dream of black cities rising, of the planet's sun changing color, and of our race, no longer the last survivors fleeing some unimaginable conflict deep in the universe twenty million years ago, but reinvigorated and renewed, soaring once more to the stars to conquer them.

The White Face

Many times in my dreams I saw the Great White Face, like a vast mountain beyond the world's edge, a piece of the universe left unfinished, a blank place which all but filled the sky. By daylight it gleamed, almost too bright to look upon, and beneath the moon it shone like a cascade of luminous snow; always featureless, always out of reach, an ineffable, inexpressible mystery. Even in my dreams I could not go there, but only gaze on it from afar, no more than could the men of any of the countries of which I dreamed. Whether I soared or walked through the streets of fabulous cities, still the White Face was ever distant, like a sunrise or moonrise, touching the uttermost rim of a desert no one had ever crossed, whether awake or asleep, in flesh or in spirit.

It was something of an affront to my pride that I, who was a god in my own dreams, should encounter such a limitation.

I resolved to do something about it.

Therefore and in secret I acquired from a chemist a special drug, which increased the power of my dreaming a thousandfold; and I dreamed a most powerful dream, and came to where the Merimnian Empire stretched to the edge of the world and the capital city of Zadrakhan was builded at the periphery so that the puissant and terrible emperor, Kavadh Vladic, could show that he alone dared venture that far, to the most remote extent of created things; so that he who was feared as the thunder is feared could gaze out from his throne room atop his highest tower and look upon the White Face as not even the gods dared look upon it.

My intention was to confront even this Kavadh Vladic, to awe him with my own power as dreamer of dreams, and learn from him the secret of the White Face or even compel him to discover it for me.

It was in my dream, then, as I was newly arrived in those lands, that an *imperfection* was first sighted, moving across the White Face: a black speck, drifting from side to side, and slowly descending, like an insect on a windowpane.

I cannot say if Kavadh Vladic was the first to see it. I do not know. But I, soaring like a bird over cities and fields, saw it.

Drawing on the strength of my dream-drug, I alighted and walked the streets, and so came to the central forum of Zadrakhan. There statues lined the roofs of the buildings on either side, representing, on the right, the emperor's ancestors, each of them larger and mightier than the last, until the greatest of them all represented Kavadh Vladic himself, a giant in golden armor so lifelike that you would think him able to leap down onto the pavement with the force of an earthquake. On the left, circling the forum in the opposite direction, were representations of all the gods and goddesses of the lands of dream, those that looked like men and women, those that looked like beasts, and those that were winged, each more magnificent than the one preceding, until the greatest of them, who was both man and beast and something more than either, seemed to be holding the very White Face itself in outstretched hands as an offering to Kavadh Vladic.

So were the statues cunningly positioned, to give this effect to one who viewed them from below, but now with the dark imperfection moving across the pure whiteness, the result was more disconcerting.

Certainly by the time I reached that place, the phenomenon was visible to all, and crowds of the citizenry gathered to point and stare and wonder. I saw a mother cover her children's eyes with her hands and lead them away, that they might not see it any longer. I saw philosophers in deep, troubled discussion, one of them holding up a kind of glass, so he could get a better look. By now trumpets blasted from atop the city walls. Alarm bells rang among the battlements, and you could see the armored soldiers racing this way and that, to take up their stations.

It was clear that someone, or something, was descending from that whiteness beyond the edge of the world, coming into the lands of men, into the Empire, into the city.

This was impossible, men said. It was something they most greatly feared. Here came an intrusion from *beyond the end of the universe,* from out of the *abyss of uncreation,* and it could only be coming as a challenge to Kavadh Vladic, whose wrath would be terrible to see.

When I remarked casually that I would go ask Kavadh Vladic about it, one of the philosophers made a sign with his hand to ward off evil, while another looked on me with pity, as if I were both mad and doomed.

Yet I, the dreamer, went on. I didn't bother to explain. I passed through a gate beneath the two greatest statues. There were sentries, but none challenged me. I climbed a long, marble staircase in semi-darkness, the way lit here and there by flickering lamps held aloft in the hands of more statues, more half-men, half-beasts, which looked alive, and might well have been, although frozen in place forever by some magic or command of Kavadh Vladic.

After a very long time I came to the top of the stairs, again encountering sentries, but I went unchallenged.

Beyond stretched a vast audience chamber with a floor as bright and as polished as a perfectly motionless sea. Enormous stone pillars rose to impossible heights, and live dragons, curled around the capitals, from time to time took flight among the groinings of the ceiling, like bats in a cathedral.

On the walls, mosaics told the histories and accomplishments and downfalls of all the kingdoms Kavadh Vladic had overthrown, and there were endless figures of the kings and princes of those lands, now kneeling in supplication. There were, too, at the far end of the hall, great numbers of people, gorgeously robed and jeweled, likewise kneeling, the ministers and great people of the city, all awaiting audience, when Kavadh Vladic himself would descend among them and speak.

So they gathered, and waited in silence.

In this time of crisis, that was all they could hope for. But I, who was like a god, could hope for more.

Beyond them was another door, which was guarded by a single giant, clad, it seemed, in living flame.

I walked past this one too, feeling, I confess, more than a little smug, for I was not afraid while all the others trembled in terror, because I was the dreamer and this was my dream.

A further stair, which twisted around and around in the darkness. The walls were covered with representations of stars and swirling clouds and comets. At times I seemed to be traveling through space itself, though still I clung to an iron railing.

And again, a door, this time very plain, with no sentry, and only the monogram of Kavadh Vladic marked on it in gold, which, in the lands of dreams, was the most powerful and dreadful of all symbols.

I pushed the door open, and my footsteps echoed inside a darkened chamber as I approached a large, vaulted window.

It was dark. So long had passed during my ascent—or perhaps time flowed differently in my dream—that while it had been daylight when I crossed the forum, it was now night. I made my way to a large, vaulted window and looked out into moonlight, for indeed the moon had risen and illuminated the White Face. I felt the night breeze on my own face, the cool air blowing out of that desert which stretched to the world's uttermost rim. There was a slightly sulphurous smell to it, which was the smell of the void beyond the boundary of created things.

I watched for a time, as the black speck zigzagged across the face, like a man on a horse descending a mountain, I thought, or maybe not a man on a horse, but a fabulous beast, like a centaur perhaps, drawing ever nearer.

"You, have you any purpose here?"

I turned. The reflected moonlight had illuminated some of the floor just inside the window. The speaker sat on a throne, in darkness. Gradually the light shifted as the moon rose further, and I could see the one seated there. Kavadh Vladic was as I had always known he would be, though I had never before seen him, even in dreams: a long, pale face with dark beard elaborately curled, the crown on his head like an inverted bowl, with a golden dragon on the top and strings of pearls dangling from either side; his brow heavy, his hair dark, his eyes darker still and piercing. He wore a midnight-colored robe, embroidered with tiny jewels like stars, and there was a sword at his side. The intensity of his gaze, its power, not even I, who had dreamed him, could look on directly for very long.

"I am the dreamer," I said, and I began to explain how I had dreamed of this place, of Zadrakhan and the Merimnian Empire and of all the lands around, and of the White Face too, but never of anything beyond it.

The reason there was nothing beyond it, I said, was that I had not yet dreamed it.

I was, in effect, the creator god of the universe, for I had dreamed all there is.

"Is that so?" said Kavadh Vladic.

I did not like the look on his face or the tone in his voice.

"It is," I said, and I went on to speak of my own country, and of the things of my waking life, describing cities of steel and concrete, highways filled with automobiles, the sky filled with airplanes; but he just made a dismissive gesture and said, "That is absurd." He seemed particularly unwilling to believe that I came from an Earth that was a sphere, without a rim, to which notion he actually laughed aloud and said, "Why don't you fall off?"

How *dare* he laugh at me?

I tried to explain, but he broke in and said, "You have wasted my time long enough," and he pointed, and I turned to see what he was pointing at, and I saw that the White Face was once again pure and spotless, for whatever had moved across it had now reached the bottom, and was in the desert, approaching the city, and for a time invisible.

Kavadh Vladic rose, his robe rustling as it swept along the floor.

I could only follow him across the floor, to the top of the spiral stairs, like a child following a parent.

This was the first moment in which I was certain my dream was not working out the way it should.

Down we went, among the stars and planets and comets and clouds, and I felt myself drifting in space, as if indeed we were moving between worlds, even though I could still feel the railing once more.

In the room below, the courtiers and ministers all fell to their knees as the emperor came among them, and the flaming sentry stood aside; but there was only a sigh and a whisper as he passed through the crowd, parting them like a sea. Above, the dragons drew away, wriggling up further into the vaulted groining. Now a great procession followed. I walked at the emperor's side, struggling to keep up. The courtiers paraded according to their ranks, and soldiers, and heralds blowing on trumpets, and the mass of the common people behind.

Outside, in bright daylight, the pure White Face dazzled. Then it was night again, and the Face shone in the moonlight; and the emperor and all his subjects gathered on the wall and rooftops of Zadrakhan and gazed out into the desert, whence would come, in due time—whatever would come. The power of Kavadh Vladic was fully manifested then, like a cloak outspread, his countless soldiers in position with their spears and their bows, heavy cannon as massive as trees wheeled to the edge of the battlements, and even bronze, dragon-mouthed siphons protruding above the city gates, ready to spit fire.

All was in readiness, and they waited for the one who had descended the White Face to cross the desert.

Day followed night and night followed day. It seemed a long time and none at all. I felt no sense of weariness or hunger, and I do not think that, waiting, I ever slept and dreamed a dream within my dream; or if I did, I quite forgot afterwards any vision of my own country or my round Earth, as if they were, indeed, quite trivial and absurd, as Kavadh Vladic had proclaimed them.

In the darkness of night, something moved toward us across the pale sand. The soldiers on the wall strained to see. They made ready their weapons. All stood tense, for whatever had come to them from beyond the world had now arrived.

We waited. I could make out footsteps, steady, but strange, irregular ones, so that I could not tell if I heard a man walking, or a man on a horse, or some impossible beast drawing near.

We all turned to Kavadh Vladic, drawing strength from his own lack of fear.

"I will go down," he said at last. "I will speak with this newcomer and demand his secret."

Then I will demand it of you, I wanted to say. But I kept silent, afraid, not of his wrath, but his ridicule.

I was a god, was I not? Sort of a god? By the standards of my own dream, a god, surely.

So Kavadh Vladic went down. He commanded his soldiers to put up their weapons, and the boiling oil inside the fire-siphons hissed, and there was no other sound until metal bolts were slammed back, and hinges creaked, and a sally-port was opened, and the emperor stepped out into the desert.

I could not be sure what I saw, even though I was the dreamer and this my dream. I think there was a wind that blew around us as the emperor stepped through the sally port. His robe rippled. The sand stirred. I think I saw something floating in the air, like the face of a skull, like a mask made of delicate ashes, carried aloft on the night breeze, but in the blinking of an eye it was gone, and the emperor was just standing there, a little ways off.

For a moment even Kavadh Vladic looked a little bit foolish. I was at a loss to explain. So was he.

He came back inside.

Then the screaming started.

It was a plague, more terrible than any ever before seen in those lands. Its entire progression, from infection to demise, took at most minutes, or even just a few seconds, as the victims hands or face would seem to shrivel away, and then the whole body would be consumed like a paper cut-out tossed into a fire. Not even bones remained.

I saw the soldiers again raise their weapons. A moment later the weapons and the soldiers' empty armor fell to the ground with a clatter. The people turned and fled away in all directions. Bells rang the alarm. Trumpets blasted. Very briefly, fire spewed out of the bronze siphons, into the desert, to no effect. One of the cannons boomed. Annihilation washed over the city like a tide, overtaking fugitives in the streets and squares, or in towers, or locked in vaults.

Kavadh Vladic drew his sword, which gleamed brilliantly against the night sky, and he called out for the enemy to come and fight him.

But no one fought him.

All around him, the city died. The empire died. All the lands of dream died.

I tried to stop it. I said to myself, no, I am the dreamer, and this is not what I intended to dream at all. I would not allow it.

But still the destruction went on, as if the whole of the dream universe were drawn on a paper map and it had been cast into fire.

For a time messengers came to him from outlying regions, to report new terrors, doom and desolation spreading farther and farther, each messenger crumbling to dust at the emperor's feet as soon as he was done speaking. Then the messengers stopped coming.

I raised my hand. I tried to cast a spell, as a god or magician might, to reverse everything, but it was useless and no one was paying attention.

Kavadh Vladic retreated to his throne room and sat before the window, his drawn sword across his knees, gazing out at the pure White Face, weeping in rage.

He looked up at me. His face was more terrible than any I had ever seen in all the lands of dream and nightmare.

"I would cut off your head," he said, "if I believed in you. But I do not."

"I am the dreamer," I said one more time, feebly.

"You say so and this is your dream. That all this is your doing. What evil thing are you?"

Absurdly, I fell to my knees before him. I *knew* it was absurd. This was a *dream*. I was cringing before one I had dreamed into existence. How could that be? I babbled. I tried to explain. But somehow I just couldn't wrap my mind around any explanation. I began to laugh like a lunatic. If this was all a dream, I wanted to wake up now. It had been glorious for a time, or at least amusing, but I had had enough and it was time to wake up to the sound of an alarm clock in some fabulous, distant, impossible city with a name like New York or London, but I wasn't sure I believed in any of those myself. If not, then I was stuck here, in the dead city of Zadrakhan, in the soon to be extinct empire of Merimna.

Somehow my limbs had become distorted. I was nearly naked. The emperor held me on a leash, attached to a collar. I was not a god, not a spirit or apparition that might command any respect, but his freak, his hop-frog, his jester of sorts to whom he would address questions when he desired only the most ridiculous answers.

Such was the transition of the dream that it seemed it had always been so, and that my memory of the waking world, of tall cities where I might wake up to the sound of an alarm clock began to fade away. It was like grasping at a shape made of floating ash. The very act of reaching out for it destroyed it.

My master rose from his throne and paced about the room, and I followed on my leash, *hop, hop, hop.*

The thought came to me that perhaps the drug I had taken to give myself this dream was either wearing off or was impure, and, indeed, the very impurity of it was that black speck which came down across the White Face to devour the universe that I, as a god, had created.

It was a plausible explanation, finally, and I, as a philosopher, now attempted the implications.

Hop, hop, hop, hop.

I wasn't very good at plausible explanations, or at philosophy.

My master paused. Now occurred the final cataclysmic confrontation, the ultimate revelation of nothing.

At the top of the spiral stair, the air had darkened more than the surrounding shadows. There was an ashen mask floating there, like the face of a skull.

Kavadh Vladic stood calmly before the other, with great dignity, resolute, and he said, "Now that you have come for me at last, speak. Tell me your secret."

But the apparition merely spread its arms—if it had arms; I cannot be sure—and the darkness and filled the whole room, and only the dead face was floating there, and it said, "I did not come for you."

Then, madman that I was, I tried to leap to my feet and grab hold of the apparition with one hand, and I shouted, "What about me? I am the dreamer!"

The other replied, "I did not come for you either."

Then the darkness passed out of the room, and Kavadh Vladic and

I both gazed out the window at the White Face. I had to cling to the window ledge to haul myself up to see. I had only my left hand now. My right, with which I had tried to grasp the apparition, was gone, and my right arm was crumbling into ash.

After a time we saw the black speck, climbing up the featureless slope of the White Face, crossing from one side to the next, ascending, like an insect crawling up a window pane. Then it was gone.

I, who was the dreamer, was the one who wept, who gibbered, who huddled in a misshapen heap at the feet of the one I had created in my dream; but Kavadh Vladic, I must admit, was made of sterner stuff. He looked boldly out at the White Face, which was blinding now. Day followed night like the alternating dark and light pages of a book blowing in a desert wind.

Dark, light, dark light.

In the daylight he gazed. In the moonlight he formed his resolution. In daylight again he went down into the city, and through the sally port, and out into the desert. By moonlight I saw him, like an insect on a window pane, ascending the White Face, *criss, cross, criss-cross,* and then gone.

I could only cling to the window ledge and hope. My right arm was gone entirely now. The disease was spreading. My whole body was disintegrating. I wanted to wake up so badly, to hear an alarm clock and traffic noises and the sound of a television left on in the next room. But it was not to be. I was the maimed hop-frog thing, naked and misshapen. I still wore a collar and chain, like a dog. The chain rattled a little as I fell back from the window and lay on my back on the floor, hoping against hope that Kavadh Vladic would return for me in time and redeem me, with whatever secret he had learned amid the unknowable mystery beyond the White Face.

Acknowledgments

"All Kings and Princes Bow Down unto Me" was first published in Penumbra #2 (2021).

"Appeasing the Darkness" was first published in Strange Attraction, ed. Edward Kramer (Shadowlands Press, 2000).

"The Bear Went Over the Mountain" was previously unpublished.

"Boxes of Dead Children" was first published in Weirdbook #31 (2015).

"Come, Follow Me" was first published in That Is Not Dead, ed. Darrell Schweitzer (PS Publishing, 2015).

"A Dark Miracle" was first published in Black Gate 1, No. 3 (Winter 2002).

"Down to a Sunless Sea" was first published in The Mountains of Madness Revealed, ed. Darrell Schweitzer (PS Publishing, 2019).

"The Festival of the Pallid Mask" was first published in Under Twin Suns, ed. James Chambers (Hippocampus Press, 2021).

"The Girl in the Attic" was first published in Black Wings VI, ed. S. T. Joshi (PS Publishing 2017).

"Going to Ground" was first published in Searchers After Horror, ed. S. T. Joshi (Fedogan & Bremer, 2014).

"The Hutchison Boy" was first published in a slightly different form in The Dragons of the Night (Postscripts 36/37, 2016), ed. Nick Gevers.

"The Interrogator" appeared in Short Things ed. John Betancourt. Wildside Press, 2019.

"Killing the Pale Man" appeared in Penumbra #3 (2022).

"Madness on the Black Planet" was first published in Tomorrow's Cthulhu, ed. Scott Gable and C. Dombrowski (Broken Eye Books, 2016).

"The Martian Bell" was first published in Nameless (2021).

"No Signal" was first published in The Grimscribe's Puppets, ed. Joseph S. Pulver, Sr. (Miskatonic River Press, 2013).

"Not in the Card Catalog" was first published in Tales from the Miskatonic University Library, ed. Darrell Schweitzer and John Ashmead (PS Publishing, 2017).

"Odd Man Out" was first published in Cemetery Dance #71 (2014).

"A Predicament" was first published in Nightmare's Realm: New Tales of the Weird and Fantastic, ed. S. T. Joshi (Dark Regions Press, 2017).

"A Prism of Darkness" was first published in Black Wings IV, ed. S. T. Joshi (PS Publishing, 2015).

"The Red Witch of Chorazin" was first published in Black Wings V, ed. S. T. Joshi (PS Publishing, 2016).

"The Return of the Night-Gaunts" was first published in His Own Most Fantastic Creation, ed. S. T. Joshi (PS Publishing, 2020).

"The Thief of Dreams" was first published in Apostles of the Weird, ed. S. T. Joshi (PS Publishing, 2020).

"Uncle's in the Treetops" was first published in What October Brings, ed. Douglas Draa (Celeano Press, 2018).

"Were—?" was first published in Flesh Like Smoke, ed. Brian M. Sammons (April Moon Books, 2015).

"The White Face" is previously unpublished.